BORN IN A TREACHEROUS TIME

Book 1 of the Dawn of Humanity trilogy

By Jacqui Murray

Born in a Treacherous Time by Jacqui Murray

Other books by Jacqui Murray

Crossroads Trilogy
Survival of the Fittest (Book 1)
Quest for Home (Book 2--coming Fall 2019)
In the Footsteps of Giants (Book 3—coming Fall 2020)

Dawn of Humanity Trilogy
Born in a Treacherous Time (Book 1)
Law of Nature (Book 2—coming Spring 2022)

To Hunt a Sub

Twenty-four Days

Non-fiction
Building a Midshipman: How to Crack the USNA Application

Over 100 books, ebooks, and other non-fiction
resources on integrating tech into education available from
the publisher, Structured Learning LLC

Praise for Jacqui Murray

A blistering pace is set from the beginning: dates open each new chapter/section, generating a countdown that intensifies the title's time limit. Murray skillfully bounces from scene to scene, handling numerous characters, from hijackers to MI6 Special Agent Haster. ... A steady tempo and indelible menace form a stirring nautical tale. – Kirkus Reviews, about Twenty-four Days

***

... a satisfying read from a fresh voice in the genre, and well worth the wait. The time devoted to research paid off, providing a much appreciated authenticity to the sciency aspects of the plot. The author also departs from the formulaic pacing and heroics of contemporary commercialized thrillers. Instead, the moderately paced narrative is a seduction, rather than a sledgehammer. The author takes time rendering relatable characters with imaginatively cool names like Zeke Rowe, and Kalian Delamagente. The scenes are vividly depicted, and the plot not only contains exquisitely treacherous twists and turns, but incorporates the fascinating study of early hominids and one ancestral female in particular who becomes an essential character. – Goodreads reader about To Hunt a Sub

***

A fusion of technology, academics, and archaeology make "To Hunt a Sub" a thrilling ride. The stakes are high as a PhD student and an ex-Seal risk all to stop terrorists from stealing American submarines carrying nuclear weapons. The writing is clipped and crisp, fitting well with the genre—there's little fluff. The author's expertise in technology shines through. A quick read I finished in just a few days. Solid debut novel. – Amazon reader

***

Born in a Treacherous Time by Jacqui Murray

So last night I couldn't sleep and finally got up about 3 o'clock in the morning and thought I would just read for a while and maybe I would get to sleep. Unfortunately, I read your book. Needless to say I was only halfway done when I started at 3 a.m. and by 6 a.m. I had finished the book! Too good to go to sleep. Excellent book. Can't wait for the next one. WOW – Amazon reader

***

This is a complex layered story that successfully blends well researched archaeology and cutting edge technology, with a high stakes terrorist plot to steal nuclear submarines. It's got characters to root for, and villains to loathe. –Amazon reader

***

I loved the way the author combined vulnerability and strength in her main characters. I loved where the macho character 'Rowe' takes Kali's hand even though she pulls away. And there is this beautiful raw, insight into what it can cost you to be a mother. Otto is very cool too. – Amazon reader

Born in a Treacherous Time by Jacqui Murray

Published by Structured Learning LLC
Laguna Hills, Ca 92653

This is a work of fiction. Names, characters, places, and incidents, are the product of the author's imagination. Any resemblance to actual persons, living or dead, events, or locales, is entirely coincidental. The publisher does not have any control over and does not assume any responsibility for author or third-party websites or their content.

Printed in the United States of America

ISBN 978-1-942101-45-1

Table of Contents

CHARACTERS

RAZA'S GROUP

Ahnda
Baad
Brum
Ch-hee
Dar
Falda
Gleb
Grg
Hku
Kaavrm
Kelda
Ma-g'n
Mir:
Raza
Sahn
Sweena
Voi
Voivoi
Vorak
Yoo

GARV'S ADOPTED GROUP

Klvda
Pan
Small
Qweg

TREE-MAN

Ba
Boah
Hee
Shee

MAN-WHO-MAKES-TOOLS GROUPS (HOMO HABILIS)

Garv's adopted Group
Lucy's old Group
Raza's Group

Author's Note—Non-fiction
Introduction

Like a favonian breeze, life burst forth on Planet Earth about 3.5 billion years ago. Our story begins much later, a brief two million years before present, during the waning days of the Pliocene Epoch, itself part of the 65-million-year-long Cenozoic Era. The primordial continent of Gondwana splintered into chunks and warm-blooded, furry mammals have replaced the dinosaurs. The climate is cooling and the growing glaciers have locked billions of gallons of Earth's water into icy prisons. South America has moved to its present position contiguous to North America and the land bridge connecting Asia with Alaska still exists.

If you telescope in, you see we are in Africa. The capacious tropical jungles created during hotter Miocene times are giving way to dry savannas surrounding the Great Rift Valley. Peer closely and you see a band of hominids hunting, playing, eating, and sleeping, oblivious to their destiny as the Father of Man. One female stands out, more inquisitive, always peering outside the confines of the tightly-knit group. Her name is Lucy which is the sound she hears when her band calls her.

For reasons scientists will never agree on, Lucy prospered in this cobbled confluence of climate and geography. When we study the clues she left, we can find few reasons why out of all animal species, this bipedal primate and her successors survived Nature's challenges. Why did she, with paper-thin skin, nails instead of claws, and flat teeth rather than sharp tearing incisors, metastasize throughout the world? What crude traits made Lucy a survivor?

To understand her story, scientists decoded the clues

encased in the rocks, soil, and the few artifacts that remained of her kind. We might be shocked by Lucy's resemblance to us. She walks upright. Her face is well on the way to Thinking Man's (that's us—*Homo sapiens*) forward-facing eyes, receding forehead, and understated nose. Her skin is lightly furred and dimpled with millions of sweat glands. Her gluteus maximus has enlarged to facilitate running and her thorax has raised so she can draw the full breaths required to fuel her cells for extended jogging. The encephalization of her brain represents a milestone in primates: She is the first species to on average surpass the cerebral rubicon described by the British anthropologist Sir Arthur Keith requiring 750 cubic centimeters to delineate the genus *Homo* from other species.

But physical appearance tells only part of her story. How did Lucy conduct her everyday life? How did she handle illness? How did she hunt for food while stalked by predators bigger and meaner than she? How did she solve problems? For these answers, I read a multidisciplinary assortment of scientists. Paleobotanists study plant seeds buried with her bones. Paleoanthropologists examine the condition of her teeth and calcification of her skeleton. Paleontologists study the tools she created to infer their use. Paleogeologists dig through the horizons in the land, the geologic content of rocks and soil, the detritus surrounding the ossified skeleton. Paleoclimatologists recreate ancient atmospheres.

By melding their collective research, Lucy's life comes into focus, as though a mist has lifted, revealing her existence on the savannas of Plio-Pleistocene Africa.

Yet, even this fails to convey the compelling provenance of her world. Where are the inevitable life and death struggles accompanying days and nights ruled by Nature? Where is the stress that travels hand in hand with her ability to make decisions? Where is the drama integral to existence as a thinking man? Terry Pratchett says, "...there's nothing like millions of years of really frustrating trial and error to give a species moral fiber..." For with Lucy's reasoning skill comes the need to take responsibility for her deeds.

When I first met Lucy, I saw only an animal—more great ape than human—but as I peeled away her life, I found a person with dreams, passion, the will to live, and a daunting need to thrive.

Pretty much like all of us.

Lucy was a scientist, seeking new approaches to problems. She became one of the first primates to use tools to make tools, to control her environment and make choices rather than submit to instinct. Thanks to her capacious brain, she thrived in the most dangerous habitat known to mammals, evolving from a plant-eating herbivore to a decidedly-unchoosey omnivore. Because she was so much more efficient at these jobs than any other primate, she possessed surplus time and used it to invent tools to enhance her quality of life.

It's important to note that this is a fictional story. I present no new evidence or research, rather extrapolate from the work of others. Lucy's manner of speaking, grammar, and sentence structure has been lost so I studied Dr. Lev Vygotsky's research on primitive societies. He found primitive man to be *a thorough communicator, his conversations rich with detail about his surroundings and even of places he only once visited.* Lucy's communication includes a smorgasbord of devices to convey her message—vocalizations, body movements, hand gestures, intonations, facial expressions—skills we vaguely understand and often discredit. I have translated her words and those of her band into a *Homo sapiens sapiens*-friendly language.

Additionally, Lucy had no concept of numbers so based it on the research of Dr. Lev Vygotsky—again—and Dr. Levi Leonard Conant from his 1931 book, *The Number Concept*. For example, Lucy will never say her band consisted of fifteen individuals, rather she will describe a band with "enough females to gather fruit and nuts and care for the children, and enough males to hunt and protect the Group".

I hope you enjoy Lucy's story.

Prologue

Billions of years whooshed by in a rush that made sentient beings dizzy. Planetary systems formed and life evolved. On Earth, vast landmasses collided with such brutality that the ground buckled into crenulated piles of lofty peaks and yawning valleys, or splintered into ragged continents that floated away on infinite oceans. Molten hotspots blew liquid rock through the fragile crust and splattered volcanic archipelagos like asteroids bobbing in the darkness of the Universe. The erratic climate melted glaciers and rainforests with equal ease.

Nature's life forms were no better. They came and went, crushed by Earth's ever-changing habitats. The survivors, like the desultory horsetail fern and the chirruping insects, were boring. The first had no flexibility and the second, no mental strength. Then, a muscular slope-shouldered hominid named *Orrorin* appeared. Though his head was no larger than a fist, he fingered his food as though wondering at its texture. Hostility intrigued rather than frightened him.

One day, *Orrorin* disappeared, replaced by the apeman *Ardipithecus*. His clear eyes roved his world with calculated interest. He rubbed callused fingers over the plants and sniffed, even tasted the seeds and dirt around them—and then he too vanished, replaced by a revolving door of species, each more cerebral than the prior.

When Lucy, the first species in the genus *Homo*, arrived, mankind took a huge leap forward.

Chapter One

The scene replayed in Lucy's mind, an endless loop haunting her days and nights. The clear sun-soaked field, the dying Mammoth, the hunters waiting hungrily for its last breath before scavenging the meat, tendons, internal organs, fat, and anything else consumable—food that would nourish the Group for a long time.

But something went horribly wrong. Krp blamed Lucy and soon, so too did Feq.

Why did Ghael stand up? He had to know it would mean his death.

Lucy wanted to escape, go where no one knew what she'd done, but Feq would starve without her. He didn't know how to hunt, couldn't even tolerate the sight of blood. For him, she stayed, hunting, scavenging, and outwitting predators, exhausting herself in a hopeless effort to feed the remaining Group members. But one after another, they fell to Snarling-dog, Panther, Long-tooth Cat, Megantereon, and a litany of other predators. When the strangers arrived, Feq let them take her.

By this time, Lucy felt numb, as much from the death of her Group as the loss of Garv. Garv, her forever pairmate, was as much a part of her as the lush forests, Sun's warmth, and Snarling-dog's guidance. Now, with all the other deaths, she could leave his memory behind.

Forests gave way to bushlands. The prickly stalks scratched her skin right through the thick fur that layered her arms and legs. The glare of Sun, stark and white without the jungle to soften it, blinded her. One step forward became another and another, into a timeless void where nothing mattered but the swish of feet, the hot breeze on her face, and her own musty scent.

Neither male—not the one who called himself Raza nor the one called Baad—had spoken to her since leaving. They didn't tell her their destination and she didn't ask, not that she could decipher their intricate hand gestures and odd body movements. She studied them as they talked to each other, slowly piecing together what the twist of a hand and the twitch of a head meant. She would understand it all by the time they reached wherever they headed.

It was clear they expected her to follow. No one traveled this wild land alone but her reasons for joining them, submissively, had nothing to do with fear. Wherever the strangers took her would be better than where she'd been.

Lucy usually loved running through the mosaic of grass and forest that bled one into another. Today, instead of joy, she felt worry for her future and relief that her past was past. She effortlessly matched Raza's tread, running in his steps at his pace. Baad did the same but not without a struggle. His sweat, an equal mix of old and stale from the long trip to find her and fresh from trying to keep up, blossomed into a ripe bouquet that wafted over her. She found comfort in knowing this strong, tough male traveled with her.

Vulture cawed overhead, eagerly anticipating a meal. From the size of his flock, the scavenge must be an adult Okapi or Giraffe. Even after the predator who claimed the kill—Lucy guessed it to be Megantereon or Snarling-dog— took what it needed, there would be plenty left. She often hunted with Vulture. It might find carrion first but she could drive it away by brandishing a branch and howling. While it circled overhead, awaiting a return to his meal, she grabbed what she wanted and escaped.

Feq must smell the blood but he had never been brave enough to chase Vulture away. He would wait until the raptor finished, as well as Snarling-dog and whoever else showed up at the banquet, and then take what remained which wouldn't be enough to live on.

Sun descended toward the horizon as they entered a dense thicket. They stuck to a narrow lightly-used animal trail bordered by heavy-trunked trees. Cousin Chimp scuffled as he brachiated through the understory, no doubt upset by the intruders. Only once, when a brightly-colored snake slithered across her path, did Lucy hesitate. The vibrant colors always meant deadly venom and she didn't carry the right herbs to counter the poison. Baad grumbled when her thud reverberated out of sync with Raza's, and Cousin Chimp cried a warning.

Finally, they broke free of the shadows and flew through waist-high grass, past trees laden with fruit, and around the termite mound where Cousin Chimp would gorge on white grubs—if Cheetah wasn't sleeping on top of it.

I haven't been back here since that day...

She flicked her eyes to the spot where her life had changed. Everything looked so calm, painted in vibrant colors scented with a heady mix of grass, water, and carrion. A family of Hipparion raised their heads but found nothing menacing so turned back to their banquet of new buds.

As though nothing happened...

Lucy sprinted. Her vision blurred and her head throbbed as she raced flat out, desperate to outdistance the memories. Her legs churned, arms pumped, and her feet sprang off the hard earth. Each step propelled her farther away. Her breathing heaved in rhythm with her steps. The sack around her neck smacked comfortingly against her body. Her sweat left a potent scent trail any predator could follow but Lucy didn't care.

"Lucy!"

Someone far behind shouted her call sign but she only slowed when the thump in her chest outstripped her ability to breathe. She fell forward, arms outstretched, and gasped the damp air into her tortured lungs. Steps thumped louder, approaching, but she kept her eyes closed. A hand yanked her head back, forcing her to look up.

Despite the strangeness of Raza's language, this she did understand: *Never do that again.*

Feq followed until Lucy had reached the edge of her—Feq's—territory. Here, he must let her go. Without Feq, the Group's few children and remaining female would die. She threw a last look at her brother's forlorn face, drawn and tired, shoulders slumped, eyes tight with resolution. Lucy dipped her head and turned from her beleaguered past.

Maybe the language difference made Raza ignore Lucy's every question though she tried an endless variety of vocalizations, gestures, and grunts. Something made him jumpy, constantly, but Lucy sniffed nothing other than the fragrant scrub, a family of chimps, and the ever-present Fire

Mountain. Nor did she see any shift in the distant shadows to signal danger.

Still, his edginess made her anxious.

What is he hiding? Why does he never relax?

She turned toward the horizon hoping whatever connected sky to earth held firm, preventing danger from escaping and finding her. Garv credited Spider's web with that task, said if it could capture Fly, it could connect those forces. Why it didn't always work, Garv couldn't explain. Herds and dust, sometimes fire, leaked through, as did Sun at the end of every day. Lucy tried to reach that place from many different directions but it moved away faster than she could run.

Another truth Lucy knew: Only in Sun's absence did the clouds crack and send bolts of fire to burn the ground and flash floods to storm through the canyons. Sun's caring presence kept these at bay.

A grunt startled her back to the monotony of the grassland. At the rear of their column, Baad rubbed his wrists, already swollen to the thickness of his arm. When she dropped back to ask if she could help, his face hardened but not before she saw the anguish in the set of his mouth and the squint of his eyes. The elders of her Group suffered too from gnarled hands. A common root, found everywhere, dulled the ache.

Why bring a male as old and worn as Baad without that root?

Lucy guessed he had been handsome in his youth with his commanding size, densely-haired body, and brawny chest. Now, the hair hung gray and ragged and a white line as thick as Lucy's finger cut his face from temple to ear. In his eyes smoldered lingering anger, maybe from the shattered tooth that peeked through his parted lips.

Was that why he didn't try to rut with her? Or did he consider her pairmated to Raza?

"Baad," she bleated, mimicking the call sign Raza used. "This will help your wrist," and handed him a root bundle from her neck sack. "Crack it open and swallow the juice."

Baad sniffed the bulb, bit it, and slurped up the liquid. His jaw relaxed and the tension drained from his face, completely gone by the time they passed the hillock that had been on the horizon when Lucy first gave him the root.

"How did you know this would work?" Baad motioned as he watched her face.

Why didn't *he* know was a better question. Lucy observed animals as they cared for their injuries. If Gazelle had a scrape on her flank, she bumped against a tree that wept sap so why shouldn't Lucy rub the thick mucus on her own cut to heal it? If swallowing certain leaves rid Cousin Chimp of the white worms, why wouldn't it do the same for Lucy? Over time, she'd collected the roots, blades, stems, bark, flowers, and other plant parts she and her Group came to rely on when sick.

But she didn't know enough of Baad's words to explain this so she shrugged. "I just knew."

Baad remained at her side as though he wanted to talk more.

Lucy took the opportunity. "Baad. Why did you and Raza come for me?"

He made her repeat the question as he watched her hands, body movements, and face, and then answered, "Sahn sent us."

His movement for 'sent' was odd. One finger grazed the side of his palm and pointed toward his body—the backtrail, the opposite direction of the forward trail.

"Sent you?"

"Because of the deaths."

Memories washed across his face like molten lava down the slopes of Fire Mountain. His hand motions shouted a rage she never associated with death. Predators killed to feed their families or protect their territory, as they must. Why did that anger Baad?

"Can you repeat that? The deaths?"

This time, the closest she could interpret was 'deaths without reason' which made no sense. Death was never without reason. Though he must have noticed she didn't understand, he moved on to a portrayal of the world she would soon live within. His location descriptions were clear. In fact, her Group also labeled places by their surroundings and what happened there—stream-where-hunters-drink, mountains-that-burn-at-night, and mound-with-trees. Locations were meaningless without those identifications. Who could find them if not for their surroundings?

His next question surprised her.

"Why did you come?"

Bile welled in Lucy's throat. She couldn't tell him how she failed everyone in her Group or explain that she wanted a better life for the child she carried. Instead, she grunted and pretended she misunderstood.

That night, Lucy slept fitfully, curled under a shallow overhang without the usual protection of a bramble bush barrier or a tree nest. Every time she awoke, Raza and Baad were staring into the dark night, faces tight and anxious, muscles primed.

When Sun reappeared to begin its journey across the sky, the group set out, Lucy again between Raza and Baad. She shadowed the monotonous bounce of Raza's head, comforted by the muted slap of her feet, the thump in her chest, and the stench of her own unwashed body. As they trotted ever onward, she became increasingly nervous. Though everything from the berries to the vegetation, animals, and baobab trees reminded her of home, this territory belonged to another group of Man-who-makes-tools. Before today, she would no sooner enter or cross it as they would hers. But Raza neither slowed nor changed direction so all she could do to respect this land-not-hers was to move through without picking a stalk of grass, eating a single berry, or swallowing any of the many grubs and insects available. Here and there, Lucy caught glimpses of the Group that called this territory theirs as they floated in the periphery of her sight. She smelled their anger and fear, heard them rustling as they watched her pass, reminding her she had no right to be here. Raza and Baad didn't seem to care or notice. Did they not control territories where they lived?

Before she could ponder this any further, she snorted in a fragrance that made her gasp and turn. There on the crest of a berm across the savanna, outlined against the blue of the sky, stood a lone figure, hair puffed out by the hot breeze, gaze on her.

"Garv!" Lucy mouthed before she could stop herself. *He's dead. I saw it.*

No arm waved and no voice howled the agony of separation.

"Raza!" Baad jerked his head toward the berm.

"Man-who-preys?" Raza asked with a rigid parallel gesture.

Lucy's throat tightened at the hand movement for *danger.*

"Who is Man-who-preys?" Lucy labored with the call sign. "We don't prey. We are prey." Why did this confuse Raza?

Raza dropped back and motioned, "I refer to the one

called Man-who-preys—upright like us but tall and skinny."
He described the creature's footprints with the distinctive
rounded top connected to the bottom by a narrow bridge.
She knew every print of every animal in her homeland. These
didn't exist.

"No. I've never seen those prints."

He paused and watched her face. "You're sure
Mammoth slaughtered your males? Could it have been this
animal?"

"No. I was there. I would have seen this stranger."

Raza dropped back to talk to Baad. She tried to hear
their conversation but they must have used hand motions.
Who was this Man-who-preys and why did Raza think they
caused the death of her Group's males? Worse, if they
followed Raza from his homeland, did that bring trouble to
Feq?

Lucy easily kept up with Raza, her hand tight around an
obsidian scraper as sharp and sturdy as the one the males
gripped. Her wrist cords bulged like the roots of an old
baobab, familiar with and accustomed to heavy loads and
strenuous work. Both males remained edgy and tense, often
running beside each other and sharing urgent hand motions.
After one such exchange, Raza diverted from the route they
had been following since morning to one less trodden. It's
what Lucy would do if worried about being tracked by a
predator or to avoid a group of Man-who-makes-tools. They
maintained a quicker-than-normal pace well past the edge of
her world. That suited her fine though she doubted that Man-
who-preys could be more perilous than what preyed in her
mind.

Chapter Two

They never asked if she was tired. Why would they? If she needed rest, she would stop, and they would stop.

Lucy didn't worry about the young one, Raza, but the longer they traveled, the more Baad strained to keep up. She heard his labored breathing, his heavy steps behind her. A few times, she glanced back, sure he had collapsed, but he never did and never lagged. When he scooted forward to talk with Raza, his fatigue washed over her but he never asked the younger male to slow down.

They had gone too long without water when Raza finally stopped at a pond. She drank eagerly next to an Hipparion mare and her colt. Their elegant heads high, chests heaving, lustrous tawny coats glistening, they unknowingly provided a buffer between Lucy and a pack of snarling-dogs, also drinking at the water's edge.

This pond was more crowded than most. There must not be many options in the area. Horse-that-walks-upright hefted its stocky body against a tree trunk and with its clawed toes, tore vegetation from the upper limbs and squeezed it into its undersized mouth. The sweetest, youngest leaves were near the top and it seemed determined to reach them. After devouring everything within range, it dropped to the ground and ripped away mouthfuls of closer but more bitter stems, grunting at their dusty, rough taste. A few steps away, a short-necked Wild-beast, its horns more like Gazelle than Giraffe, splayed its squatty legs and dipped its muzzle into the coolness. Behind it, in the reeds that flanked the pond, Mammoth yanked up chunks of grass while a brother pulled leaves from a neighboring tree and dropped them by her squealing calf.

"Crocodylus." Lucy indicated the distinctive claw marks and sweeping tail marking the reptile's entry into the water. It took only a moment to find the bulging eyes that interrupted the smoothness of the water's surface. When Lucy was a child, Crocodylus snatched a youngster, thrashed his hapless body through the water, and then rolled with it into the murky black depths. All that remained were pink and white bubbles.

They raced on in the windless air and the baking Sun, past sag ponds plopped amidst crinkled plateaus and through scree beds at the base of volcanic hills. The further they traveled from her memories, the better Lucy felt. They skirted boulders and bounded over outthrow scattered haphazardly over the flatlands. The tough soles of her feet protected her from the grit and detritus and insulated her from the hot ground. Dense hair shielded her shoulders and skin from Sun and her protruding brow shaded her eyes. As they ran, she snagged handfuls of succulents and packed them into her neck sack.

Without warning, a bank of dark clouds formed overhead and a gale blew out of nowhere, bringing with it a monstrous wall of dust and dirt that stampeded toward them.

She glanced around for shelter but found none. The storm already stretched higher than the loftiest trees of her homeland and extended as far as she could see in both directions. It roared like a charging Mammoth and billowed like Fire Mountain when it spit smoke. One moment, it licked at Sun's base; the next it enveloped the brilliant orb in a gloomy forbidding maelstrom that blotted out everything.

"Raza!" She called but got no answer.

She bulled her way forward but could no longer tell if she headed toward Raza or away. A hare smacked into her as it tumbled ears over tail, knocking her face first to the jagged ground. When she couldn't push back to her feet, she started to crawl. Pain shot through her knees and her palms shredded but she kept going.

There! A bush! She grabbed it and clung, head tucked against her chest, eyes closed against the grit, mouth filled with flying insects and the acrid flavor of fear, relentlessly surrounded by the cacophonous beat of the wind, sure at any moment the flimsy plant would be uprooted but it gamely hung on to the dry cracked earth. The air was thick with so much silt, she held her breath until she couldn't anymore and then cupped a hand over her mouth. She panted shallowly and listened for some sign of Raza or Baad but heard nothing other than the howling storm.

"Raza!" The wind blew her voice back at her. Sand and pebbles stung her cheeks leaving a stench in her nostrils. Something slashed by within a hand's width of her head and she screamed, becoming more frantic the longer she didn't see Raza or Baad.

Out of nowhere, Raza snatched her hand and dragged her forward. All she could see was fingers around her wrist, the rest of Raza lost in the thick shroud of swirling dust. After what seemed like forever, he placed her hand on a

rough surface and she wrapped her arms around the tree
trunk. The ground shook and dirt spiraled into tiny twisters
that slapped her arms and legs. There she huddled, face
buried in her chest, fighting to find something to breathe
other than dust. Her ears rang from the storm's constant roar,
much like the time she stood under a waterfall.

As quickly as it began, the rumbling faded, the air
cleared, and the wall of dirt roared over the edge of the earth.
Baad clutched the opposite side of the same tree while Raza
trotted to the bluff of a nearby berm. There he stood,
motionless, staring over the crest while she and Baad brushed
grime and muck from their fur and reveled in the joy of clean
air.

To her surprise, Night Sun was already a hand's width
into the dark sky. Quickly, she collected what thistle bushes
she could find and surrounded the tree with a barrier the
thickness of an adult's height. Baad crawled inside and fell
asleep immediately but Raza stayed on the crest of the berm,
his dark grey form limned against the sky.

Baad snored serenely but Lucy couldn't sleep. Night Sun
curved overhead as though an edge had been sliced away with
a stone chopper. Each day it lost some of its size. Soon, it
would vanish, preparing to rebuild itself slowly, a piece at a
time. Why did it hide like that and how did it always reappear,
full and round? Garv said Night Sun protected them—which
made sense. When Night Sun smiled, most predators slept.

She hoped Night Sun would visit her new home.

She remembered the day Garv taught her about the
lights that traveled with Night Sun. She needed honey to heal
cuts. Garv found a hive and beat on it until the bees burst out
and then he fled, the bees after him. With the hive empty,
Lucy scooped out handfuls of honey. Some she set aside but

the rest, she and Garv devoured when he returned, stuffing themselves until they couldn't lick another finger.

Then they sat, sated, enclosed in the forest's verdure, gazing up at the rich green above them. Each layer of leaves obscured the next darker one which in turn hid those above until the canopy blurred into a black-green haziness so dense only the rare shaft of light penetrated—except one spot where Night Sun and its twinkling lights managed to shine through. She thought they were wildfires that had scorched the black night but why then did they never grow or burn themselves out like every other fire? When she asked Garv, he fell silent for a moment as he often did when thinking, and then told her the holes were entry points to an unknown world but didn't know if it would be better or worse than where they were now. What he did know was that the lights moved around in Night Sun's sky and that movement told when the rain would come, the animals leave, and the fruit blossom.

He had just begun to teach her how to read them when he died.

The next day, Raza, Baad, and Lucy set out as soon as Sun awoke and kept going until Sun reached the opposite side of the sky.

"We rest now. Tomorrow, we cross Impassable-rift," Raza motioned.

Again, Baad fell asleep immediately but Lucy joined Raza on a hill that overlooked the Rift. They sat in silence, listening to the chorus of night sounds.

Finally, when it became clear he would neither welcome her nor push her away, she motioned, "Why do you call it Impassable-rift?"

"We easily traversed it long ago but over time, the

canyon walls steepened, became more jagged, and the floor deepened. Some from our Group crossed it but didn't return. I have never even attempted it but Baad has and unlike others, always returned."

Ah. That explains why Baad joined this trip, Lucy thought to herself.

"After Baad's last trip, he swore to never again cross what he came to call the Impassable-rift—and he didn't until Sahn insisted the benefit outweighed the risk. No one argues with the Primary-mother." He shrugged as though this was obvious even to a stranger.

"Once we're across, I will show you quarry-where-stones-grow-for-tools and lake-where-children-play. You will meet Dik-dik and its cousin Gazelle, Long-tooth Cat and its shorter-toothed cousin, Mammoth, and Oryx. You already know Snarling-dog who stalks by day and Hyaena-cat who hunts at night."

Raza's gestures were eloquent, his face expressive as he described the world he clearly respected and one she would soon face. Lucy understood 'quarry', 'lake', and 'stone'—these defined her environment, too—and actions such as 'stalks by day' and 'forage for roots', but not those that dealt with his unique environ like 'lake-seen-by-Sahn' though she hid her confusion behind a passive, intent expression.

Raza paused, as though to collect his thoughts. She liked how he often stopped to think before talking, just as Garv had done. It made her want to trust him.

Finally, he simply concluded, "You will like it."

"How do you know?" she motioned with awkward, rigid gestures.

"Sahn-that-sees-all tells me." A kindness and affection imbued Raza's motions for the female he called Sahn.

"You often mention this Sahn. Tell me about her."

Although Lucy flawlessly reproduced his hand movement for the call sign 'Sahn', Raza responded with a quizzical tilt of his head.

"They say she has been to your land. Do you not know her?"

Stories swirled through her Group of those who crossed the Rift and never came back. Could Sahn be one of those?

When Lucy didn't answer, Raza left and she massaged her breasts with the juice from the same root bundle she gave Baad for his wrists. To her side, Spider worked on an intricate web.

"Go, Spider! Spin your web where sky meets earth. Let nothing slip through that will threaten us," Lucy whispered.

All of a sudden, Baad yipped and Night-dog howled. Lucy jumped up, wound her abundant hair into a rough knot at the base of her skull, and prepared to join Baad.

"Stay!" Raza commanded with a downward chop of his hand and then he and Baad were gone, swallowed by the darkness. Lucy drooped her head. He thought she would be afraid but she hadn't felt fear in as long as she could remember.

In his absence, she would construct a neck sack for him to carry his cutters and choppers. She preferred the stomach or bladder of Gazelle slathered in mud to tamp down the odor but that would have to wait until they found carrion. For now, a large leaf would do.

She smoothed the blade and perforated the top with her cutter to create evenly-spaced openings. Then she selected a Giraffe tendon from her collection, long enough to encircle Raza's wide neck. Fibrous stems would also work or the inner bark of some trees, or even certain flexible grass stalks. With deft fingers, she separated a shred as she would section a stringy shoot, ran it expertly from hand to hand to make it pliable, and strung it through the holes in the blade.

Much later, Raza and Baad returned. Baad went back to sleep but Raza squatted by Lucy, surprised to see her still awake. Despite finding no danger, the moisture over his upper lip and the tension in his eyes told her he worried.

"I am used to not getting much sleep, Raza. Like you. I will be fine tomorrow."

She hung the new neck sack around his neck and then rolled back on her haunches as he tipped his head trying to see it, between the nipples of his chest.

"Put your cutter in it. Your hands will be free, like mine," Lucy motioned.

He nodded and said nothing. Lucy curled up, surprised how much better she felt with Raza's safe return, and fell asleep. In her dream, she strode forward, confident, a chopper in one hand and Gazelle's haunch over her shoulder. A twig snapped and she turned...

Chapter Three

When they set out that morning, Baad scowled at the leaf sack hanging from Raza's neck and then ignored it. Before the dew dried on the grass, they had reached Raza's Impassable-rift. Craggy walls plummeted to a distant basin, colored in layers, brown-red becoming obsidian-black in the width of a finger. Here and there, scorched rubble stood out like scars, the healed remains of some violent battle.

There, tucked into a shady nook, Eagle nested with its chicks. The colors of their feathers, beaks, and even claws blended into the background. A smudge of movement signaled a rodent family as it scampered to shelter. Warm air, perfumed with juniper and sage enveloped Lucy. Insects hummed and one lazy raptor circled above. The Rift in Lucy's homeland, the one she deftly crossed as a child, was but a scratch in Earth's skin compared to this boundless chasm.

Lucy raised her eyes to the flat land that spread on the opposite side. In place of verdant rainforests flowed an endless field of golden forbs sprinkled with massive boulders, and spotted with intermittent gentle berms. Even from this distance, the grass rippled where Long-tooth Cat passed. Mounds of talus encircled Fire Mountain. Its cousins lined the horizon, some so tall their peaks penetrated the swirling whiteness of the clouds, others just a glow of red with fiery rivers that slithered down their distant slopes. When Lucy traveled in her old territory, these behemoths, visible from anywhere, always guided her home.

She tried to swallow but her throat wouldn't let anything down. She wanted to tell Raza she'd changed her mind, that she feared for the safety of the child she carried, but she knew, whatever bad decisions she'd made in the past, leaving with Raza was the right one. To keep her hands from shaking, she dug her nails into the skin of her arm until the shock of what she saw paled against the misery of what she felt.

After a sniff she hoped Raza didn't hear, she caught site of a plant she hadn't found in a long time and grinned.

"Bitter-leaf!" Old One used Lucy's last on an injured child. Its uses were varied and the results always effective so everywhere she went, she searched but hadn't found any since leaving her homeland. Until now. Glad for the distraction, she stuffed as much as she could into her neck sack, already bulging with herbs for her new life. The aromatic Cat-ear, chewed to a sticky pulp would reduce swelling; Blood-weed's absorbent blades for her bleeding time; and the Maniese blooms for vomiting.

Satisfied, she sat under a leafy acacia to wait on Raza.

"Are you ready?" Baad leaned over her. Startled, Lucy shook herself awake. Baad continued, "We leave."

One after another, they walked, step-by-step, a hand's breadth from Impassable-rift's edge. Raza stopped occasionally to study it but never seemed satisfied. He must have left cairns on the trip over but why make them so difficult to find unless he was hiding from someone.

Who did Raza hide from? She clenched her cutter and ground her teeth to bite back the anger that threatened her good intentions. Why fail to warn her if she and her child were at risk?

Sun's rays shone directly in her face by the time Raza found his markers and they began the descent. Raza took the lead followed by Lucy and then Baad. The damp hot air reflected off the rock wall, almost suffocating Lucy. Sweat poured from her body making her handholds squishy and loose and causing her feet to slip. Something slithered over her back and ants crawled into her mouth. Her breaths were labored as though saturated with Fire Mountain's ash-heavy air.

A caw shattered Lucy's lethargy. There, Eagle floated overhead in lazy circles, calling to his family.

He was hunting.

To Eagle, they would appear to be tasty morsels, defenseless as they clung precariously to the almost-vertical face. Any moment, the powerful raptor could knock them to the valley floor and tear their flesh from bone, and take the meat to its hungry eaglets.

"Raza, we must hurry!" She shouted but that only made him huff in irritation. Lucy bit back her own annoyance. Surely, he had climbed worse. She had. Did his damaged hand and knee make him slow? Another caw and still Raza maintained the same sluggish pace.

"Raza!" She shouted his call sign just as Eagle screeched a harsh *kloo-ee kloo-ee*, tightened its ellipse, and dove. As it hurtled past the rim of the Rift, Lucy tore a rock loose and flung it with all her strength. It hit the raptor's chest with an audible thump at the same moment that Baad shrieked. Eagle squalled and withdrew to assess the damage.

Lucy twisted toward Baad who hung one-handed, feet

flailing as he bounced off the jagged cliff. Lucy slipped sideways, trying to position herself underneath his body.

"Baad! Step on my shoulder!"

Before he could, he lost his tentative hold. He tumbled past her, eyes bulging, fear gushing from his body. Lucy wrapped her fingers around a chunky bridge and snatched his wrist as he flew by, then leaned into the wall and crooked her elbow to absorb his fall.

"Raza!" She screamed as her hold loosened. "Move over!" Meaning, slip beneath Baad to provide him a foothold.

She panted, willing her body to hang on even as numbness washed up her arm and into her shoulder. Then came the pain, as though the arm clinging to Baad was being torn from her body. Baad flailed, unable to find anything to grip. Just when she thought she could take no more, the strain eased. Raza, face a taut mask, muscles roped, hands grappling unsteadily at rocky outcrops, somehow managed to position himself beneath his partner and then force his shoulder below Baad's foot.

"Baad," and Raza signaled with his chin at a ledge to Lucy's side. Baad swung his foot, snagged the projection with a toe, and pulled himself over. As his weight shifted, Eagle dove again. Raza flung a melon-sized rock that struck its wing and sent it spiraling away in search of easier prey. The Group rested, fingers and toes gripping, sweaty bodies flattened against the hot cliff wall, too tired to speak, and then continued downward.

The lower they moved, the faster Sun fell. By the time Lucy's feet hit the valley floor, Sun was hidden behind the steep walls where only dull grey light could reach them. Baad collapsed next to Lucy, chest heaving, breath coming in ragged gasps, and muzzle dripping.

"You are strong."

Lucy shrugged. With no males left in her Group, she had carried many carcasses. Baad weighed no more than Oryx.

Baad motioned haltingly, "I would be dead… if not … for you," and left, shoulders hunched.

Raza tapped her shoulder. "Rest before we continue," he motioned with a smile, and trudged to the meager but satisfactory streamlet that flowed through the center of the valley. He buried his face in the water and inhaled long contented slurps.

Lucy closed her eyes as a scent wafted past her. Snarling-dog. She stiffened and scanned the distant ledges and brush-dense slopes, finally finding his scat, tucked under a bush but old and with no trace of pups. Relieved, she trotted over to the stream, drank her fill, and waited for Raza to speak.

In a mixture of hand and fascial gestures, he motioned, "The Group adopted Baad and his sister Sahn—my Mother and the Group's Primary-mother—when wild-beasts trampled Baad's Mother and Father. Baad taught me to track and knap cutters. If not for him, Fire Mountain would have taken more than part of my finger."

Raza massaged the smooth stump. Lucy still found it difficult to understand his gestures but each time they talked, it got easier.

"The Group would suffer without him." He scuffed at a pebble. "Sahn was right to send me for you."

Saying nothing more, he pointed to the sky, indicating they would leave when Sun reached that point in the sky—about a hand and another past Sun's current spot—and then he and Baad left to explore the valley. Lucy went the opposite direction in search of travel food and healing plants.

The bed of Impassable-rift had looked deceptively flat from above but proved to be crisscrossed by huge cracks, some so deep and broad she had to detour rather than risk jumping. A small patch of a plant that cooled fevers became her first find. With her chert digger, she chipped away until the roots released and then loaded them in her neck sack. Next, she found some good-sized leaves, soaked them in the stream, folded them over, and tucked them into her sack next to her herbs. She would chew these when she could find no water.

Raza sounded her call sign. He wanted to leave.

They jogged through debris collected at the base of the Rift's walls ranging in size from massive upright chunks taller than Lucy to tiny gravelly pieces that rolled underfoot making running difficult. They continued until Raza found a sleeping area with a cliff to their back and far enough from the stream to avoid thirsty animals—if there were any down here.

The night air was warm and comforting. Without the distraction of vision, she sensed everything around her—boulders that blocked the breeze; the gentle pulsating chorus of ticking, zizzing, and humming, the pitch telling her the location of each creature; the lack of any aroma attached to animal dens or homes; and the swish of Snake finding a sleeping hole for the night. The air moving off the Rift carried strong, dusty scents she couldn't identify but she breathed a quiet sigh of happiness to still see Night Sun and its sprinkled lights. Feq would be watching the same sky. Did he wonder about her?

She shook off the memories and left in search of herbs to heal her sore body. Raza made no move to stop her. As she walked, hot plumes of steam like that from Fire Mountain's anger shot into the air. Strange colored stones speckled the ground. One tasted like ash, another salty. The abundance of boulders and fissures forced her to weave through the terrain.

What caused these?

Even Fire Mountain at its angriest didn't birth such boulders—and why fracture the ground so brutally?

She kept to the edge of the streamlet, sure it would lead to edible vegetation—which it did, a rich patch of berries bursting from an outcrop of rocks hidden behind a copse of trees. After gulping down a handful, she set about gathering more for Raza and Baad when a noise stopped her. It took only a moment to identify it as an animal in distress. That usually meant a predator which meant food.

The sound came from the other side of a boulder. She quietly approached and then flattened herself against the rough side of the massive stone. Chest-high grass separated her from a clearing where she heard another groan, this one accompanied by the unmistakable whiff of blood. When she parted the grass, a pig lay in a puddle of red midway across the clearing. One dull eye found Lucy and then moved to a long narrow stick protruding from its chest. Every time it drew a breath, bright red blood pumped from the wound. Frothy pink bubbles billowed from its snout and its hind leg shook. Lucy shuddered at the agony Pig must be in but could do nothing until she confirmed that the hunter who brought it down wasn't around.

Moving only her slitted eyes, she scrutinized the basin, the scrubby bush, and the tiny stream bed. Nothing concerned her but the hair on her neck bristled.

One final breath rattled in and out of Pig's destroyed lungs. Lucy flared her nostrils and listened for the one who would claim this kill but still smelled nothing that shouldn't be there.

Why did the hunter leave the pig?

Was he frightened away or did he have another bigger kill and couldn't take both?

Finally comfortable she was alone, Lucy shucked the animal over her shoulder using the stick in Pig's chest for leverage and moved under an overhang as she scanned the chasm one last time. When she glanced up the chasm's wall, she gulped. A figure stood silhouetted, tall and erect with wide muscular shoulders and sturdy legs. He grasped a long stick in one hand, like the one through Pig's chest, as his head swiveled back and forth across the valley floor. His musky odor, a mixture of scat and carrion, made her rub her nose and step deep into the shade of a tree.

"Why do you hide?"

Lucy jerked. "Raza," she whispered.

The snap of Raza's head told Lucy she spoke his call sign properly.

She motioned, "At the top of the precipice. Do you see it?" But the creature had vanished. "It was a male with a vaulted head and long neck searching for something down here," she motioned, hoping Raza could interpret her hand motions.

Raza swept back and forth over the bluff as tension rippled through his face and chest. "Next time, come get me," he ordered, and then noticed the animal she carried. He jerked back as though stuck by porcupine's quill. "You—you use this stick?"

Lucy shook her head. *No.* "Someone else. Maybe the male up there," and she jutted her chin toward the top of the cliff.

Raza paled. They hurried back to camp. Without taking time to eat, he left with Baad, following the blood trail back to where Pig died. Lucy was too hungry to wait for their return and tore chunks of meat from the carcass. Finished eating, she hung the remainder of Pig in a nearby tree where Raza and Baad would easily find it upon their return and then blocked off her sleeping area with thorn bushes. Inside the barrier, she added a pile of hand-sized rocks. Predators would start with the carcass. If they wanted live meat, the thorns would deter them long enough she could frighten them off with rocks.

She woke once when Hyaena-dog called his brothers and a final time when Raza and Baad yelped as they stumbled over the barrier and stabbed themselves with the thistles.

Sun awoke, spreading its light over the graben valley. The strip of sky between the steep walls blossomed with fluffy clouds in a field of iridescent blue. The Group ate as much of Pig as possible knowing they couldn't carry it up the cliff wall.

She motioned to Raza, "Did you find the predator?"

"I think it was the creature you saw atop the chasm. He probably couldn't find a route down."

Lucy thought about that for a moment and then motioned, "Is the path we will take up the only way?"

"Yes, but it's far from here and well hidden. No one can see it who doesn't know where to look. Don't worry. He won't be a problem."

Lucy wasn't worried. Male-with-stick couldn't hide if she wanted to find him. Her tracking skills exceeded most males.

Out of nowhere, a breeze that smelled like water blew across her muzzle. Her body tensed at the dark, heavy clouds that had appeared out of nowhere. Where had they come from?

"Raza!" She hitched her chin at a high water mark on the cliff wall, well-above her head. "Rain! It will turn this chasm into a river. If we don't get out, we will die!"

Her arms felt stiff at her sides as images washed through her of another flash flood that roared through a valley such as this. Raza left the camp at a distance-eating stride. Baad at his side, Lucy behind, she caught snippets of guarded motions— *"Man-who-preys"*, *"stalks"*—but the males didn't include her in their conversation.

Long after Lucy accepted they would die in the coming flash flood, Raza stopped in front of a craggy portion of the wall. At first, it resembled the rest of the cliff, but then Lucy noticed gouges leading up, smoothed by an endless line of feet. She gathered her hair into a knot, tied it with one of the tendons she kept around her neck, and followed Raza, Baad behind her. Again, Raza ascended slowly, placing first a hand and then a foot, wiggling both to be sure they were firm before moving on. Lucy forced her mouth into a tight line and was glad Raza couldn't read her thoughts. To her, climbing felt like flying. Often, her hands and feet didn't even touch the rock wall but they instinctively knew where to find their next hold.

As the first fat drops of rain fell, the group pulled themselves up over the lip. Lucy collapsed on the damp ground, letting the refreshing water cool her body. Breathing slowed, she bid farewell to her past, and opened her eyes.

Flat savannas dominated the landscape dotted with scraggly bushes, enormous boulders, and the infrequent copse of trees. Graben valleys nestled between soaring peaks, all stained a patchwork of earthen colors. The aroma of brush, soil, and dry wind assaulted her accompanied by bird songs and buzzard cries.

For a long time, she crouched, frozen, taking in her future.

Until the gentle rain turned into biting squalls that blew as fast as Cheetah chasing prey. Baad took the lead, motioning ahead toward a cliff. Lucy flew after him, running flat out despite the slick wet ground. She slipped once, caught herself hard on her hand, and felt a sharp pain shoot through her wrist but kept going.

The dense sheets of rain hid everything so it didn't surprise her when she slammed head first into the low lip of a cave. Her feet flew out from under her, her head snapped back and she landed with a thud on her bottom, hands buried in the damp detritus. Dirt and old scat flew up in a whirlwind as she sputtered and coughed.

When she could again breathe, she muttered, "You could have warned me," but Baad paid no attention. He must have used this cave before because no one who didn't know of its existence would find it in this storm. She sniffed for predators but found only mold, old urine, and decayed tissue.

Several blinks and her eyes adjusted to the darkness.

"I see tracks but they are covered by bone shards and molted fur and those by dust," Raza motioned.

Lucy was unconvinced. "The animals who live here may be hiding. I will look."

The cave reached not even as tall as Lucy so she stooped as she stole down the narrow tunnel at the back of the cave, prepared for the glow of eyes or a shift in the shadows. Fortunately, she found neither. Even in the cave's depths, insect markings overlaid everything else. Finally, the exit she knew must exist appeared, a dim winking light that would guide them out if they must flee.

Satisfied, she returned to the front and watched as the valley turned into a roaring river. The torrent pounded the ground like hands against a hollow trunk. A crack startled her and a chunk of the cliff wall crumbled. Fiery flashes fractured the sky accompanied by a rumble that drowned out even the rain's voice.

They nibbled food from her neck sack, drank from the curtain of water that fell like a waterfall over the cave opening, and waited for the deluge to end. Only once did Lucy venture out, to relieve her overfull bladder. A row of birds crowded wing-to-sodden-wing on a tree limb. A mammoth family huddled, heads drooped together as water poured over their bodies. A canis trotted along the edge of the plateau, tail tucked between its legs, a bedraggled rat in its mouth.

As Lucy completed her business, a baby squirrel fought to right itself in a puddle too deep for its young body, paddling bravely with limbs not meant to swim.

"Squirrel, does your mother miss you?"

Lucy laid it a safe distance from the puddle and then dashed back to her shelter.

At long last, Sun beat back the dark clouds and pulsed yellow in a sky the color of water, although within a hand of the horizon. The Group decided to sleep in the cave and continue in the morning.

Chapter Four

A rumble shook Lucy awake. Through the mouth of the cave, Sun's faint light drove away Night Sun's shadows. Raza passed her without a word and stepped outside just as a high-pitched snort vibrated through the thin air.

"Argh!" He yelped and dove backward as wave after wave of frenzied hooves pounded past. Sharp neighed commands from the lead stallion split the air and dust choked the enclosed cavern. Lucy covered her ears and scrunched her eyes shut until the cacophony receded to a dull roar.

When she peeked out through her fingers, in front of her stood a spindly-legged, knock-kneed brindle-colored Hipparion foal. Its elegant head canted and the glossy mane shimmered in the early light. Its liquid brown eyes were fringed by dark lashes, its mouth open, its aroma equal parts sweat and curiosity.

As Lucy gaped, stunned, the cave's entrance darkened with the feral presence of an enormous ebony stallion. Work-toughened muscles rippled under a lustrous pelt, hooves wide under well-developed shoulders, breath a wet mist in the dust-laden air. He whinnied and shook his head as though to warn Lucy she wanted no part of him. The colt snorted, turned with a flip of its mane, and dissolved into the herd.

Lucy ventured out of the cave but all that lingered of Hipparion and his foal was the insidious memory of wanton wildness. Her hands trembled so she took a calming breath before calling out to Raza but he and Baad were already gone, chasing Hipparion. Lucy started after them but paused at the crumpled body of a squirrel. She drooped, recognizing the animal she saved not long ago, but then stuffed the mangled flesh into her sack and hurried after the males. It would be a tasty snack later.

By the time she caught up, Raza and Baad had joined Snarling-dog to chase an injured Hipparion. No Snarling-dog pack could consume an entire Hipparion so if Raza could keep up with the pack and remain patient, his Group would eat. Lucy often hunted with Snarling-dog. It pleased her Raza did too. Pace steady, ears tweaked, eyes scanning back and forth and back again, they traveled single file across the sweltering terrain under a blazing sun.

Sun crested above and Raza veered away from Hipparion, leaving Snarling-dog to hunt alone. They would have to find other food.

By now, Raza's shadow stretched longer than his height. They soon must find a place to sleep. As though he read her thoughts, Raza headed toward a nice outcropping of rocks sitting where the land crested and dropped down. Lucy curled next to Raza and Baad, sharing their warmth, using the boulders as protection.

They left the next day as Sun's first brilliant shafts lit the boulders.

The closer they got to their destination, the more stories Raza shared of life within his Group, as though to prepare her. Hearing about Sahn, Ma-g'n, and the youngsters Yoo and

Gleb and Ahnda made Lucy like this small but sturdy group. The only worry that concerned her came when she asked Raza how often new members joined and he answered with a shrug, *Never*.

Would this group, together since Raza's birth, accept a new female?

To assist the process of blending in, she memorized the facial expressions, hand gestures, and body movements that Raza and Baad used. Some matched those of her Group but many she just had to remember. For example, Raza often supplemented what his mouth spoke with hand and facial gestures. She appreciated the clarity provided by the mixed signals but wondered why he vocalized so much when quiet hands communicated more safely. Did they have fewer predators in his home?

What matched perfectly with her old life were his vocalized cries and grunts. In fact, these were often the same. Whenever possible, she talked to Raza and Baad using their movements and gestures. Sometimes, they looked at her quizzically but more often, they responded.

In the end, making a good impression on Raza's Group mattered only because she wanted a home for her child.

"Lucy. Tell me about the plants you collect."

Raza plopped down at Lucy's side as she gulped water from the pond. This was the first stop of the day and her throat felt so parched she had difficulty swallowing. She finished drinking and even wiped a hand across her mouth before answering.

"Smell this," and she handed him a hairy root bundle from her neck sack. He rolled it between his fingers and puckered his nose. She smiled.

"It stinks, but will quickly cure cramps."

One by one, she pulled plant parts from her neck sack and described their healing properties. He listened intently, never relaxing, eyes roving over their surroundings. She couldn't shake the feeling that he asked for a specific reason, or knew of a problem, but he didn't tell her what that might be.

She finished one particular description and then instead of going on to the next plant, asked, "Are we in danger?"

Raza blended the gesture for 'predator danger' with the vocal 'food for scavenge'.

Lucy shook her head. "I don't understand. Will I be safe with you?"

"The Group's Primary-male—my Father—always protects us."

While Raza voiced the sounds for 'Father', his hand rotated open-palmed over his chest, an indication of that rare friend who required both hands to describe, like what she had felt for Garv.

"You will be pleased with him. And Sahn. They are the reason I came to your land in search of a pairmate," but his body told a different story. When she prodded, he explained Sahn chose him for this dangerous journey not so much to find a pairmate but to find Lucy.

Chapter Five

Twelve months ago

When Raza first encountered Man-who-preys, he and everyone else in his Man-who-makes-tools Group accepted them as friendly cousins, like the chimps. He found comfort in their silhouettes limned against the night's blackness knowing predators like Hyaena-dog must pass them to attack the Group.

Then, with the males far away at the quarry excavating stones for cutters and choppers, the creatures attacked the homebase and kidnapped the children. Even the Group's best hunters couldn't track them. The loss devastated the survivors. They couldn't persist without children. It became the responsibility of each male to mate with every female old enough to carry a baby. Soon, gurgling voices and the scent of breast milk filled the air and life crept back to normal.

Not for Raza though. His child, Dok, had been all that remained of his pairmate. His hunt partner Vorak didn't understand his distress.

"Children can be replaced but I will never let anyone steal you."

Vorak, with his lean sinewy build, strong prognathic snout and happy attitude, made it sound simple. Raza offered a hesitant smile. Everyone would be alright. As Vorak suggested, he took a new pairmate.

Food always became scarce when the rain ended. On the most recent hunt, Raza and Vorak found the fresh dung of Gazelle and tracked it, hoping to find a sick or weak animal struggling to keep up with the herd, one a predator would take down and they would share. Instead, after tracking Gazelle for much of Sun's journey through the sky, they reached an entire herd of sickly creatures, smaller than usual and so thin their ribs stuck through their skin. Raza spotted one old adult that limped along behind even the slowest of his herd. Normally, the hunters would leave such a scrawny animal but times weren't normal. The males spent the next day following the wounded animal until Snarling-dog brought it down and the Group scavenged its share of the meat. It didn't even provide enough for a meal.

Raza rubbed the stubby end of his damaged finger against the smooth white welt on his scarred knee, injured long ago by molten lava. The mindless process helped him think. The inferiority of the herds was only one problem with this area. The other continued to be Man-who-preys. Though they left the Group alone, these predators took more than their share of food, didn't leave sufficient berry bushes or nut trees to regrow, and scavenged the Group's territory rather than stay in his own. Every animal, even the meat-eater Snarling dog and the grass-eating Mammoth, lived companionably with Man-who-makes-tools by keeping to themselves.

Man-who-preys shattered those rules. The question

became what to do about it.

The sweltering heat and endless sun continued to slowly drain the life from the grasses and trees. Raza watched daily for the dust cloud that would signal the return of the herds. When it didn't arrive, Hku determined the Group must leave. This was common. When food became sparse in one area, they moved to a new one, cycling through a series of locations and ultimately returning to the first. This gave fruit trees time to regenerate, berry bushes to replenish, rodents and reptiles to replace their populations, and the herds to regrow their numbers. Everyone agreed if they found any trace of Man-who-preys in a new location, they would skip it. Surely, one of their homebases would be safe from the predator.

Night Sun disappeared and reappeared once and again before the Group finally settled on a new home. By now, the rain had arrived and with it, the herds. Raza and Vorak marked the territory with their urine and feces to warn other Man-who-makes-tools' Groups to stay away. All seemed safe until the night Man-who-preys reappeared. As before, they hovered just outside the homebase's boundaries, watching, never so close to be considered a risk and never responding to Hku's hails.

This time, though, their focus seemed to be the females.

Raza rose with Sun's first light, coating his body with mud and dung to defend against the blistering heat, stinging mosquitos, and biting fleas. The instinct to stay in a Group be it to work, hunt, or sleep was as embedded in Raza as the urge to breathe. Today, though, after greeting his father Hku, he set out alone, heading the direction Man-who-preys always went when leaving the Group's homebase. He couldn't shake the feeling that soon, again, Man-who-preys would decimate his Group. Once Raza uncovered where they lived, he'd get help.

The day couldn't have been more perfect. Scattered clouds shaded the parched ground in cool splotches. Fire Mountain slept after days of ground-shaking growls that spit smoke and ash over the land. Raza had no trouble following Man-who-preys because his tracks were unique—bulbous at the bottom with splayed nubs on top. The depth of these prints said they weighed less than Raza.

He stooped down and sniffed, then jerked back and shook his head to clear his nostrils. They stunk like spoiled meat. How could these creatures stand being close to each other? As if these smelly traces weren't enough to ensure he could follow them, they always carried a long skinny pole that left a round hole next to the footprints.

Raza followed the odd prints through the talus field that bordered homebase and across the savanna. His face dampened with heat and a ripe cloud floated from his dung coat. Sun seared his back and then his neck, but he didn't slow. Nor did he feel the scorching earth or the prickly detritus through the hard soles of his feet.

The scent of water tickled his nose. He lowered to a crouch, listening for what his eyes couldn't see. Behind decayed vegetation crushed by numerous and relentless hooves, Raza found their stench. He slid forward like Snake until he entered the dense thicket of reeds that edged a pond. The surface shimmered like a watery flame. Waves rippled gently from the edge as prey and predator alike lapped up the fragrant water. At one end, a long-eared dik-dik and a lone Hyaena-cat drank. A pack of Snarling-dogs feasted on a bloated Mammoth calf while a motley horde of flop-winged vultures squawked their impatience. A female Mammoth, the calf's mother, flared her ears and swayed her giant forefoot at Snarling-dog. With a last trumpet, she trundled off which left Raza an unobstructed view across the pond.

At Man-who-preys.

Raza slit his eyes and hunkered into the reeds, concentrating on the beings that should be asleep. Yet, there they stood, gaunt and thin, legs long like Ostrich, sparse fur a poor barrier against Sun's sizzling rays or the droves of biting fleas and mosquitos. Their bodies were grotesque—heads too bulky for the skinny necks, faces flat and narrow with tiny mouths. Dirty clumps of hair hung to bony shoulders. Weak-looking chests tapered to pinched hips. Their legs were too long, arms too short. Their vaulted foreheads rounded high above unobtrusive brows and broad muzzles—like Raza's but crushed almost flat. If he hadn't seen the damage they wrought, he'd think them weak.

Sometimes, looks deceived.

Unlike the soundless creatures who stood outside Raza's homebase, these yipped, barked, and hissed. At first, Raza thought they were call signs but no one turned to the sound or responded with hand motions so that couldn't be the goal. The next probable reason was they were talking—as his Group did occasionally—but why with predators around?

His plan to follow their footprints to their homebase had just fallen apart. He doubted they lived here at a waterhole. No animal did. More importantly, why were they awake? In the past, Man-who-preys hunted with Night Sun as did Owl and Hyaena-dog. Did they hunt also during the day like Cat's cousins Panther and Long-tooth? To answer this, he must follow Man-who-preys when they left the pond and hope they returned to their homebase.

That, he couldn't do alone.

The heat pressed down on him as he waited for them to

leave. The air grew thick and hot but Raza remained still and quiet, just another part of his surroundings. A slight breeze touched his skin, perfumed with the scent of dying plants, dung, and sweat. His breath came in shallow pants as moisture dripped from his brow and chin. He rubbed his knee but made no sound even as a cloud of mosquitos bored through his mud-and-dung coat and gorged on his blood. Silence was his most potent defense.

By the time Man-who-preys left, Raza had been away from homebase much longer than he planned. Hku would understand once Raza explained and then together, they would find this creature's homebase. Raza slithered back past the reeds and cattails, through the bunchgrass that scratched his skin, and over the slight rise that concealed the pond. Snake taught him to move without noise or tracks. Once he became invisible to Man-who-preys, Raza sprinted homeward.

Hku was waiting when he arrived at homebase. Raza almost collapsed, barely catching himself, his body slick with sweat and chest heaving, but Hku didn't seem to notice. He stepped forward, mouth a tight line, anger billowing like smoke from Fire Mountain. Raza didn't have to guess why. As a new adult, he represented an important piece of the Group's security. He must always be with his partner Vorak, never alone.

"Man-who-preys is at the waterhole," he motioned before Hku could say anything. "He's awake and headed to his homebase."

Hku stiffened, eyes darting behind Raza. "Show me."

Though exhausted and ravenous, Raza pivoted and led Hku back across the savanna. Instead of Snake, he moved like Snarling-dog—bold, quiet but quick.

When they reached the waterhole, Hku sniffed and motioned, "Get Baad and Vorak."

Raza ignored the ache in his throat and the pounding in his chest, didn't bother to ask if he had time to eat, and again sped homeward.

Baad watched him approach, eyes dark pools of fury. A handsome male in his prime, he stood a head above any other male. His work-hardened muscles corded the length of his legs and bulged beneath the dense fur of his chest. Raza didn't know if the frown that greeted him was in response to his solo travel or Baad's usual unrelenting fury. Since the last raid when Baad lost his only child, rage bled into his every movement, terrorizing the children and subadults who had never known the kind even-tempered male Raza knew, who helped the females forage and taught the children new games.

As Raza explained, Vorak appeared. If his partner was once angry that Raza left without him, he'd forgiven him. Vorak didn't carry a grudge, ever.

"Hku needs us," Raza motioned, and they left.

By the time they reached the elder, he'd crossed the pond and tracked Man-who-preys' far enough to know where he headed.

"They either return to their homebase, there," and he pointed at the massive blackened flank of Fire Mountain, "or they make no effort to hide their trail so we will follow."

Raza rubbed his sore knee as he tried to think this through. Man-who-preys could have hidden his tracks, easily. This must be what Hku meant.

Raza wanted to ask about that but Hku had already left so he turned to Baad. "Why would they want us to follow?"

Baad grunted and jogged after Hku, Raza and Vorak behind him, keeping Fire Mountain to one side and the rolling berms to the other. Raza chirped the signal that told the females to return to the homebase. In the flat empty vastness, it could be heard as far as anyone could travel in a day.

Hku's long fluid strides ate up the endless expanse of waste scrub. The rhythmic thump of feet gave Raza time to think more about what Hku had said. No matter how he mulled it over, he couldn't come up with a reason why Man-who-preys would use a waterhole so far from their homebase or why they'd purposely leave tracks. No one wanted that. Everyone wanted stealth, invisibility.

Since Baad hadn't answered this question, he'd ask something else that made no sense.

"Baad." The call sign sounded like Raza clearing his throat. The elder slowed to let Raza catch up. "Why would their homebase be by Fire Mountain?"

Baad shook his head and motioned, "It wouldn't be. No one is brave enough to live there."

Baad was right. Fire Mountain could explode in anger and flames without warning. He and the other hunters traveled there only to mine the hard rocks needed for choppers and cutters, the ones that must not crack when they bit into bone. Surely Man-who-preys shared that fear.

When they'd traveled long enough that Sun moved a hand overhead, Hku stopped and stepped into Man-who-preys' print. Raza and Baad gulped air but Vorak didn't even breathe deeply. Little tired Vorak.

Hku flattened a finger in one of Man-who-preys' prints and then measured the space between the steps against his own stride.

"They run hard as though chased, but they aren't." Hku frowned and Raza shrugged. There must be a reason. No animal moved without purpose.

The males jogged along the well-defined trail, across a shallow washout and around wild brambles. The first night bird warbled its call and Hku slowed to a stop, eyes focused on the ground a distance to the side.

"Man-who-preys camped here. There are many more than were at the waterhole, more than our entire Group." Hku crouched. "The trace is old, probably this morning. Some went that direction, to the waterhole, and others that way."

Raza's stomach tightened into a knot as he identified the end of Man-who-preys' forward trail.

His homebase.

For the first time, he wondered how much trouble they were in. Hku bared his teeth as he punched his splayed fingers, a blend of 'danger' and 'predator'.

The Group sprinted homeward, taking the most direct route. Every so often, they stopped so Hku could examine the prints. Raza panted, happy for the break. Vorak barely showed a sheen of sweat. Baad, though, wheezed, fighting to catch each breath. How much longer could the older male continue at this pace? Hku didn't notice. Fear had turned his face white.

He motioned, "Man-who-preys' has not slowed at all."

Shadows were slipping up the rocks by the time they rounded the boulder that marked homebase. Raza barked his entry call and heard only silence. Ma-g'n should have been there to greet them but his usual seat was empty. The normal end-of-day sounds—females pounding, children rough-and-tumbling, and Sahn contentedly humming by her shadow stick—were absent also. Raza inhaled, finding the scent of some Groupmembers but not all. How could that be? Did they not hear his warning to return to homebase? He rushed into the clearing where the Group gathered to eat, groom, and sleep. There, finally, he found Ma-g'n, face pale, mouth open, eyes on Hku. Around Ma-g'n milled some of the males, most of the subadults but few children and females. To the side sat Sahn.

Hku eased down next to Sahn with a crackle of joints but she refused to look at him. After a breath, he gently lifted her chin, forcing her eyes to meet his. "Where are the others?"

Her hands gripped the shadow stick until it broke; then she stretched her fingers out, flattening them to the ground and finally placing them in her lap.

"They are gone," she motioned and then pulled away, terror in her eyes. Hku patted her shoulder and motioned Raza and Vorak to search the fields where the females and children foraged.

As Sun's last rays faded and Night Sun began its travels across the dark sky, everyone returned, discouraged and disheartened.

Raza shook his head as he met Hku's tense gaze. "We found choppers and diggers beside piles of freshly-dug tubers and roots. Around them were the bodies of the males responsible for guarding."

Fury and fear clouded Hku's face but for just an instant. Then, he stepped in front of the subadults, palms down and parallel to the ground. "Do not worry. We will figure this out." He scratched his upper arm. "When Sun awakes, we track them."

Raza relaxed. He never doubted Hku would know what to do. Man-who-preys had tricked them. The pride of his discovery earlier in the day soured like meat rotting in the sun. What was his purpose other than to defend his Group?

"Why our females? Long-tooth never breeds with

Leopard nor Hyaena-dog with Snarling-dog."

Hku had no answer and Raza didn't expect one. Tears spilled down Ma-g'n's face as he groomed his son Ch-hee. The child tipped his head up and offered his father a radiant smile. The children might recover but would the adults?

The next day, as Sun pushed aside Night Sun, the males left, panic on their faces. Ma-g'n stayed behind. If everyone died, Ma-g'n must lead the remaining Groupmembers to a new homebase. They followed the tracks until they disappeared into a stream bed. After a futile search in all directions, they returned to the homebase, dispirited and dejected. The day's meal consisted of nuts, wild onions, ants, tubers, a few snails and fewer slugs. This depleted the last of the forage. No one slept well that night.

When Sun rose the next day, the Group gathered whatever they could carry and left to find a new homebase far from Man-who-preys. They traveled each day until Night Sun shrouded the land in darkness then curled behind a barrier of thorns, beginning again when Sun returned to light their path.

After another sizzling day of endless walking and a night that was more about passing out than falling sleep, Raza awoke to the gray sky that marked a new day. His body ached, the bottom of one foot bled from a sharp stone he'd stepped on, and his damaged knee throbbed relentlessly. He felt beaten down, his energy used up, but he rolled his shoulders back, pushed his head up, and forced himself to walk without trudging, willingly preparing for another day of grassland, bugs, and heat. He stopped midstride, almost through a morning stretch. Sahn sat cross-legged and unmoving. Her eyes were closed, head tipped up, toes touching a shallow trench that encircled a smooth slender twig embedded into the ground and aimed at the sky. A pebble the size of a thumbnail rested where the stick's shadow cut the circle. There were several more at points along the trench.

Beside her stood Hku, relief etched across his face. "Sahn has found our new homebase."

"Raza. Take another pairmate. Baad took Falda. I have one." Vorak grinned as he knapped a chert stone into a cutter. "Why do females matter except for children?"

The rains had come and gone since the kidnapping and life had returned to normal. Orphaned children were adopted; males found new pairmates; and all considered this homebase better than the old one. To Raza's surprise, Vorak pairmated with Kelda, an abrasive whiny female who survived the attack only because she'd hidden while the other females were herded away. When Raza asked why he picked one so different from his first, Vorak said that was why.

Raza, though, couldn't move on. An eviscerating fury bled the joy from his life. It waned when he hunted with Vorak or played with the children but always, like Fire Mountain's wrath, returned with a vengeance. He growled at his Groupmates, even the children, and refused to mate with the available females though duty required it.

Finally, Hku ordered Raza to pick a pairmate. This shocked Raza. The Group had no official leader, though everyone turned to Hku for guidance, and no one could force others to do or not do anything—like choose a pairmate. Raza exploded. Despite the younger male's quickness and strength, Hku did not back down. Baad stepped to Hku's side and Vorak to Raza's. The other males backed away, stunned into silence.

"I will—"

"Yes, you will." Sahn inserted her fragile body between the raging tempers. Her voice remained quiet, eyes locked on Raza. "She is our future. You must bring her to us. Go now."

After a pause, Sahn added gently, "Through her, we will defeat Man-who-preys."

With that, she turned back to her shadow stick, eyes on the ground, muttering about males and their stubbornness, but stopped for a final proclamation. "Baad will join you."

Gray drizzle filtered down from the cloud-choked sky the day Raza and Baad left. They followed the forest as long as they could, keeping the trees close so they could leap into them if chased. When they thinned to nonexistence, the males veered into the middle of the savanna's copper-colored fields. At least from there, they would see the attacker.

Every time Raza turned to find a landmark to guide the backtrail, there stood Hku. The old male moved from hillock to berm to highland until his image faded into the colors and textures of the surroundings.

Chapter Six

Present

Sun had just slipped behind a cliff when Raza cupped his hand around his mouth and chirped his distinctive trill. Lucy had grown increasingly anxious about this moment and now shook openly with unaccustomed fear. Raza told her not to worry, that everyone supported her arrival, but that wasn't Lucy's experience. In fact, in her life, it always came down to who you knew and she barely knew Raza.

As they passed a tall boulder, so many smells assaulted her, she couldn't help but gasp. How could one Group have this many members? More than one had rotting teeth. Several had festering wounds that must hurt. Another's illness would soon end in death. Lucy took a shallow breath and unconsciously clutched her neck sack. Her new pairmate never slowed. Stride long, muscles relaxed, a slight smile shaped his lips.

"Home," Baad motioned as he hurried by.

In a blink, everyone she smelled blocked her way, huffing and grinning greetings to the males. Their fur, thinly layered over dusty-black skin, made them invisible against the brown of the rocks and dried scrub but their scent saturated the air, dry and dead like the land with none of the sweet fragrances and thick lichens she left behind. Judging by the babble of hand gestures and the huffs of call-signs shouted too loud, the group missed Raza and Baad.

As they entered the barren expanse of what must be the Group's homebase, Lucy edged closer to Raza until she walked well within his shadow. His Groupmates sniffed her like Cat would a herd, searching for weakness. Lucy gulped, trying to not retch from their stink. Children ducked across her path and laughter bubbled out as they nearly ran her down, casting sly glances her way before resuming a game Lucy recognized. Sounds assaulted her senses, everything from the shuffle of feet to the uneven gate of someone limping and the ping of rock against rock. The boney remnants of scavenge littered one side of the clearing and tool making the other. Beyond, the horizon shimmered with Sun's last warm rays.

As Raza described.

Mechanically, she panted, her stomach twisting and knotting as her gaze ricocheted through the crowd. She forced one foot in front of the other, determined to smile— or at least not frown—as she clenched and unclenched her fists. Someone thrust stalks into her hand which she greedily chewed, feeling the welcome juices flow down her parched throat.

Somewhat better, she took a closer look at her new Groupmates and froze, arms rigid at her sides, mouth an O, shoulders so tight they almost touched her ears. The males had broad shoulders atop squashed trunks, eyes the same dark color as their skin, their heads shrouded in kinky black fur. The females were smaller, their small dark eyes bouncing between Lucy and Raza and Baad. Why didn't Raza tell her?

With her huge light-colored eyes and skin the shade of Dik-dik's fawn, as smooth as theirs was wrinkled by Sun's rays, they must think her a freak. Her straight black hair glistened and swayed, slapping against her back with every step. She must look as peculiar to them as Tree-man to her.

They would never welcome her.

She wanted to flee but where would she go? In her anguish, she barreled into an old female, head reaching just below Lucy's chin. Her thin hair billowed around a kind face lined by age. Her eyes crinkled with pleasure as she leaned forward.

"He found you!" She folded Lucy into a warm embrace and touched gnarled fingers to Lucy's soft visage. "You are different. In a good way."

Lucy struggled with the hand movement for 'different'. Like Chimp? Or Cat?

"'Different'?"

The elder didn't explain. Instead, she motioned, "The figure on the berm—it was not Garv."

Lucy gasped. "How did you know?"

Sahn blinked in Sun's unfiltered glare. Sadness flitted across her face and settled into the fine wrinkles around her mouth and eyes. In place of an answer, she showed Lucy how to rub the gooey interior of a thick-stemmed plant over her burned hands and face. Lucy smiled, the relief instant, wondering how long it would take to adjust to such a malicious Sun.

"You are accustomed to forests. Here, we spend much time in Sun's radiance," she added as a lean male approached.

Hair-fur the reddish color of one of Cousin Chimp's cousins, long curled fingers and arms that dangled down to knobby knees, he met her worried gaze with a warm smile.

"Sahn is the Group's Primary-female and Raza's

Mother."

His hand motions for that label were similar to Raza and Baad's but they had never explained what it meant.

"Primary-female?"

"The mother to all children of the Group." He cocked his head as his full lips spread into a smile. "You must have such a person?"

Lucy shook her head. "But Raza talked often of Sahn. I feel like I know her."

"Ma-g'n," a grunt from a male who seemed familiar. She studied him for a moment and gave up. Raza must have discussed him in the stories. "Come here."

"I must go."

Lucy tried not to wince when Ma-g'n smiled. No one else seemed to notice but Lucy couldn't miss it. The pinched mouth, the frown, the pallid color of his face—he suffered a chronic pain she knew too well. Lucy motioned, "I can help you, Ma-g'n."

Confusion clouded his face for a moment and then he offered the same practiced smile Raza used. "I welcome you to our Group."

He squeezed her arm with a callused hand and headed toward the young male who perfectly fit Raza's descriptions of his partner, Vorak. Muscles burst from his chest and back. Dark hair sprouted thickly a hand above a shelf-like brow. Raza talked of him as a trusted friend and one Lucy would come to rely on.

When Ma-g'n reached Vorak's side, the din of conversation hushed. Vorak turned to his partner.

"Raza, your Father…" Vorak's youthful hands faltered.

Raza's skin paled and he flinched. Misery wiped away the joy of his homecoming. Vorak patted his shoulder. Raza shuddered and then his face hardened as he greeted the rest of the Group.

Lucy tensed and motioned to Sahn, "Should I go to him?"

Sahn shook her head. "His Father, my pairmate Hku, died peacefully. Many don't. Come." Sahn guided Lucy to a small group of females, not even enough to forage food and watch the children. "We have work."

Lucy straightened her back, tipped her head up a notch, and smiled stiffly at each female. Though she mated only once, experience made her much older than most of them. Who had watched their Group destroyed? Who lost so much that they preferred life with strangers to life with family?

Who swore to never again fail, no matter the cost?

Lucy shook herself and motioned, "Sahn. I need to release my water."

Raza's Mother beckoned a sour-faced female. When she turned her back, a younger one took Lucy's hand.

"I'll show you," she motioned. "I'm Falda," and she guided Lucy around the lone baobab, beyond a sandstone bluff, to a waste trench downwind of the camp. Here, Lucy took care of her business and joined Falda to prepare the food.

Chapter Seven

Night Sun disappeared and reappeared while Lucy acclimated to the rhythm of her new Group. Soon, she recognized each Groupmember's scent and could tell from a distance who was in the camp, if they were injured, and what poultices would mend the wound. If no one needed healing, they wanted nothing to do with Lucy. She didn't care. She came here for her child, not friendship.

Only Sahn, Raza's Mother and the Group's Primary-female, continued to welcome her: In this staunch elder, Lucy found a friend as dear as any she'd ever had, like a warm rock slab on a cold day or the bright light in Night Sun's sky. At the day's end, when small groups groomed each other, Sahn always beckoned Lucy over. After grooming, they reveled in the lights floating overhead. Sahn would point out those that had brightened since the prior night or reappeared after winking out at some earlier time. Sahn explained how these changes predicted the movement of the herds, when berries bloomed, and trees fruited. Lucy spent many evenings sitting quietly with Sahn, watching the lights, blissfully content, believing life could get no better.

If she had another friend, it would be Falda, though the

relationship always felt strained. When they worked together, Falda babbled incessantly as though silence was the enemy, gaze bouncing between her work, Lucy, and Kelda who always stared at her. Falda never asked about Lucy's homeland or why she left. She either didn't care or didn't think about it. Either reason worked for Lucy because she didn't want to talk about her past. If Falda ran out of topics, the silence became brooding and awkward. When Lucy asked questions, Falda answered with noncommittal grunts and huffs.

Lucy believed Falda befriended her either because they were the only females carrying babies or because of Sahn's position as Primary-female. She found out the truth one evening as the Group curled together, sharing body heat behind the thistle barrier. Lucy overheard Falda and Baad arguing, about her, though it seemed to be more Baad ordering and Falda shaking. The next time Lucy wrapped Baad's wrists in poultices, she told him that fighting off Eagle didn't mean Falda must be her friend but he gave her a funny look like he'd tasted something he wished he hadn't, and left.

While spending time with Falda left Lucy nervous and wishing she could be alone, with Sahn, Lucy always felt like smiling. They talked about everything. Silence, when it arrived, was comforting.

One day, the females gathered in the meager shade of an acacia, waiting for Sun to leave so they could groom each other in the relative cool of Night Sun. A light breeze rippled the air with the sweetness of the nearby river where Kelda played with the babies, far enough way she wouldn't hear the chatter. Not that she wouldn't try. She prided herself on knowing everything about the Group whether the members wanted her to or not. Lucy took the opportunity to ask Falda about Kelda.

"From the day I arrived, Kelda has gone out of her way to snipe and harangue me every chance she gets. At first, I took it personally but I now realize she attacks everyone, including Vorak."

Falda didn't answer. The silence grew though that no longer bothered Lucy. Falda did things at her own pace and wouldn't be rushed. Finally, after the young female finished digging under a rock for grubs, chewed a desiccated root, and scratched an angry red welt on her arm until it bled—one that never healed and she refused to let Lucy cover with sap—she answered.

"Children are our future, Lucy." Falda patted first her belly and then Lucy's expanding girth as she drew a line of blood down her arm and licked it. "Kelda is... short-tempered... with everyone except the children and subadults but especially with females who are growing babies. Until you joined us, she picked on me viciously."

Lucy expected Falda would return to her usual prattle but she surprised Lucy and asked, "How did you save Baad? I mean, you're a female."

Her hands moved low, where Kelda couldn't see the question. Lucy debated explaining how she got strong, why she reacted so quickly, and why nothing frightened her, but decided it would only set her apart more from these females who never considered aggressive or defensive actions their responsibility. Besides, Falda would tell Kelda and that couldn't be good.

She rolled back onto her haunches and settled on, "Who wouldn't save a Groupmate, given the opportunity?"

Falda snapped, "What does that mean?"

"Well, I had a chance to save him. Why wouldn't I at least try?"

"Because if you die, the baby you carry dies with you. No Lucy, we forage. If daylight remains, we knap, rest, and groom. The males risk their lives."

Lucy didn't respond. What was there to say?

Hunger gripped Lucy like Cat's jaws. There weren't enough tubers and roots and grasshoppers around to dull the ache inside her belly. Only meat did that and the males couldn't find enough. She shadowed them one day as they hunted a Wild-beast and was appalled. When they found fresh carrion, they didn't try to push ahead of other scavengers and if they were there before Snarling-dog or Vulture, they fled rather than defend the food.

Lucy hunted as Garv taught her.

One day, she finished foraging plants and went in search of healing herbs. Instead, she found a dead gazelle. Though gnawed by Hyaena, its meat hadn't yet been stripped by raptors and the bones were uncracked. The marrow would provide rich food for the Group, especially the pregnant females. After devouring what she wanted, she muscled the carcass back to homebase and dumped it into the communal pile. As she turned to leave, Kelda blocked her way. Face twitching, spittle spewing from her mouth, she bobbed from one foot to another and jabbed Lucy's belly, crowding forward with each frantic bounce.

"Males hunt. You are here to breed! Why does Raza keep you?" Scowling, Kelda brandished a hefty root the length of her lower arm and about the same size. If she hit Lucy with it, it could break her arm, at the least knock her out.

Sahn barked and inserted herself between the females, arms taut, legs spread. Kelda harrumphed and with a final slash—through the air—clomped off.

Lucy was too shocked to react and then the moment passed. Still shaking, she left the clearing and set to work scratching the earth for the root she knew hid below. No one spoke to her, not even Sahn. Unexpectedly, Ma-g'n squatted by her side and joined the digging, saying nothing but cheering her with the warmth of his presence. Sun had reached its downward path and she had still not reached the root so she rolled back to her heels and flattened her hands to the ground. She felt the herds, close enough to reach before Sun went to sleep if she left at first light. She had felt them there the day before and the one before that.

"Ma-g'n. The animals are close. I could reach them before Sun disappears. One animal limps. It will not keep up. We haven't had meat since Night Sun was full. If I follow Snarling-dog and Vulture, they will find the injured animal but if I don't go soon, there will be nothing left."

Ma-g'n leaned forward and placed his hands on Lucy's. "Shall I tell Raza?" *Or do you want to?*

Without looking at Ma-g'n, she nodded. He left, returning as Raza and Vorak sprinted from homebase.

Together, she and Ma-g'n returned to the effort of digging out the well-buried root but Lucy's thoughts were elsewhere. Finally, she asked, "Did Raza bring me here to gather berries and bear children? I can track, hunt, and scavenge better than any male here. Why am I wasting my time foraging?"

She stopped as understanding dawned. "Raza told everyone why I left my old Group and they don't trust me."

Ma-g'n touched her arm. "No, Lucy, and I don't know what you're talking about. Sahn sent Raza to find you because we have too few females, not enough children, and the males can't provide enough meat. Somehow Sahn knew that you can do all that. But more importantly, you are a survivor. Our

Group needs that above all else. Ignore Kelda. You are cherished."

Tears welled in Lucy's eyes and she kept her gaze downward, hoping he wouldn't notice. She ached deep inside in a place she couldn't reach. She didn't trust herself to answer.

"If you want to tell me what happened, I'm a good listener." There was something hopeful in his gestures that she hadn't seen in a long time.

A chorus of birds and the hum of insects laced the air. A snake slithered past her feet, its scales an iridescent green in the sunlight as it whisked itself to shelter. A dragonfly slapped into Ma-g'n's shoulder and dodged the spinning spirals of flesh that dangled from his ear.

Something ruptured inside of her and she started to talk.

Chapter Eight

6 Months ago

The day dawned hot and cloudless under Sun's opalescent glow. The night rain left the air sweet and loamy. A mammoth bellowed while Cousin Chimp chattered. Lucy scattered her nest and left with the rest of the Group.

She and everyone in her Group were desperate for food. They had consumed all the corms, tubers, bulbs, roots, eggs, berries, and nuts they kept for starving times and the areas scorpions, lizards, and snakes were smart enough to hide as soon as footsteps approached. If they didn't find food soon, they would all die.

Lucy checked daily for signs that the herds were returning. The tangy aroma of sweat and dung would announce them long before she saw them, telling her the herd's size and how many babies traveled with them. Quickly after that, the fragrance of flowers would saturate the air, springs long dry would refill, glistening pools would nourish the desiccated land, and the hollow tree trunks would fill with water.

An internal sense told her the herds and water should

have arrived by now but she had no choice but to wait even as hunger gnawed at her insides and the baby kicked weakly as though it too was famished. She had resorted to stealing seeds from Shrew's burrow. Even these were insufficient and she began to fear she would die.

Today, she and the Group traveled outside of their territory to an unclaimed area that abutted Fire Mountain. It was bountiful but menacing. Without any warning, Fire Mountain could disgorge rivers of molten fire, break the ground apart, and swallow whatever it touched.

But it was their last chance

Sun's warmth had moved from their faces to overhead by the time the Group reached the meadow, surrounded by rocky crevices and a meager copse of trees and embellished with arid scrub, patches of brittle grass, thirsty vegetation—and the berries Old One remembered from an earlier visit. After filling herself on the sweet fruit, Lucy crouched, back hunched, and hacked at the hard soil, intermittently eating grubs and the occasional slow lizard as she worked. The air shimmered with heat. Even breathing hurt.

She rolled back on her heels to listen to Mammoth grazing, ignoring the insignificant hominids. The sociable Great-dog or maybe Giant-great-dog—Lucy couldn't tell which from this far away—loped across the plateau. Its enormous bushy tail swept the air. Garv respected these amiable canines who lived in Groups so Lucy did, too.

Despite the joy of food, Lucy wanted to cry. Tonight when the Group gathered for their meal, the new pairmates would go first. A female mated freely until she bled and then accepted a pairmate to feed her while she cared for a new child. Lucy and Garv should have been pairmates. Now, she would have Ghael.

Lucy wrestled the scrubby stalks from their earthy coffin

and duck-walked over to Old One to offer her a bite. The elder's thin gray hair ballooned around her face and her hunched back forced her eyes forever down, locked on the hard brown earth. She had located a sprig of green on the surface that should indicate an underground root. During the rains, she would ignore it because the root would be shriveled and bitter but when the rain stopped, the root filled with nutrients and water to feed the plant during the dry time.

If it was even there.

Lucy with a chopper and Old One with the horn of a dead warthog dug first to the depth of a hand and then a wrist where they found a buried vine that would lead to the root. Old One rolled back on her heels and rubbed her shoulder but then resumed digging until she uncovered the root, as deep as the length of her forearm, and pulled. When it finally popped out of its earthy coffin, it was as big as her arm and as heavy as a ground-nesting bird. One root usually meant more. That would take the rest of the day to dig out but feed the Group for a long time.

Ticks bit Lucy's skin as her fingers teased the earth to loosen it. A scorpion darted forward and paused, pincers extended. Lucy snatched it, chopped off the poisonous stinger with her digger, popped the creature into her mouth, and went back to work.

Old One grunted as she eased the pressure from her ancient ankles. When they got back to homebase, Lucy would apply a salve she created from a flower found in the shadows of a crevice. She liked working beside Old One. Her wrinkled skin, gray hair, clear eyes—all told of wisdom learned through a life well-lived. Calluses, stiff and yellowed with age, protected her fingertips and feet. As she worked, she patted the ground as she might a youngster, and asked it for help. Today, she seemed satisfied.

"At least today, the predator within Fire Mountain sleeps."

That's when the earth shuddered. Lucy pressed an ear to the ground and went back to digging.

"Mammoth," and then she paused again, this time as a scent drifted across her muzzle.

"Old One. Do you smell that?"

The Elder tilted her head up as a carrion bird wheeled lazy circles, the beat of its wings a sign of food.

"I'll see to it," Lucy motioned.

She wrapped her waist-length hair around her hand and tied it off with a Hipparion tendon. Keeping her mane long shielded her neck and shoulders from the hordes of insects in the forests and provided warmth during the rains, but this sticky cloying heat made her want to chop it off.

Sun had moved a hand's width by the time Lucy found an injured mammoth lying on its side at the base of a hillock. These slow-stepping, swaying behemoths roamed unchallenged from Fire Mountain to the Great Rift. The rumble of the earth and the crack of branches shredded by their passage made them easy to avoid, but this matron would rule no more. A ragged white bone poked through a tattered laceration. Thick crimson liquid poured down her wrinkled forefoot. To her side rested her weathered tusk, shattered in the fall.

Lucy reconstructed what must have happened. Mammoth stood on that overlook across the gully, head high, engulfed in a wealth of her favorite leafy food. When she stepped too near to the edge, the ground collapsed under her weight and she tumbled into the gorge. Her effort to rise popped the ruined bone through her skin.

The cow snorted hot air and mucous as her head bounced in the mud. Ants poured from a dead stump over her lower body in an endless mass of legs and thoraxes. Her stubby tail couldn't swat them and their tiny mandibles couldn't pierce her thick epidermis.

She bellowed and, from the overlook where the cow had been before she fell, her calf trumpeted back. He begged Mother to stand and lead him back to the herd. Along with his mother's calm low came Snarling-dog's growl. The calf bleated, his skin too thin and stature too short to ward off Snarling-dog's attacks for long.

Lucy called to Ghael and he sidled up beside her.

"There, the cow," Lucy motioned, her disgust for this male thinly disguised.

Where most males' hair grew thick and long on their heads, patchy on their backs, Ghael's clumped in wiry tufts, even in his ears and on the underside of his hands. His facial hair held rotted morsels of blood and tissue. The stink announced him long before he came into sight and so disgusted every female, none would groom him.

That would become Lucy's job with Garv gone; no other unpairmated male remained.

"And there to the side, is the baby."

Ghael dismissed her with an abrupt wave, barked the call that would summon the hunters, and scuttled toward the dying mammoth. In his hand, he clutched Lucy's cutter, flaked from obsidian and tough enough to slice meat from bone quickly, in the moments between the cow's death and the arrival of Snarling-dog. The hunters hunkered down to wait, some by the matron and others by her calf.

As Sun crossed the sky, mother's calls grew feebler. She could no longer lift her head but continued the lethal thrusts, giving her herd precious extra time to rescue her calf. The baby stood stiff-legged. Lucy circled back to the cow but Ghael waved her to the meadow's edge toward his sister Krp.

Lucy obeyed, slipping in beside the female. She glanced away but not fast enough to hide her gaping mouth and shaking body.

"You have never hunted?" Lucy motioned.

Krp shook her head. "I f-forage. F-females don't h-hunt."

Lucy bit back her disgust that Ghael allowed Krp to be so fragile. Every child of the Group should know survival skills like butchering the herd animals and stalking prey. Still, Lucy's brother—skinny gawky Feq who threw up at the sight of blood—picked Krp as his pairmate and begged Lucy to guard her.

Lucy would do anything for Feq.

Anxiety wafted from Krp and made Lucy feel faint, though that might have been something else. She leaned into the sticky gooiness of the bark. Horse-that-walks-upright had sharpened its claws here and made the tree bleed. She broke off a piece of the sap and popped it into her mouth, offering another to Krp. The sweetness would stifle her hunger but the fragile female was too busy nervously picking a scab on her arm to even look at Lucy. When it bled, she switched to another. Lucy would cover them with honey and a leaf when they got back to homebase.

The trumpet of the female mammoth yanked Lucy back. Snarling-dog nipped at the cow and suffered her bruising kicks with a stoic acceptance while others in its pack charged the calf. Though young, power exuded from the baby's sturdy frame. A wave of his trunk sent one canine airborne, warning that many would die before this battle ended.

As Sun's light faded, a wall of mammoth bulls answered the mother's baleful bawl. Their ears blew out as they pulverized everything in their way. Their trunks lashed the air, daring any to approach. Ignoring the hazard, Snarling-dog charged. The bulls reared up, slammed their forelimbs to the ground, and rammed through the canines, yelping bodies thrown aside like wilted reeds. The stench of blood and feces permeated everything.

At some point during the battle, the cow died, her work protecting the calf completed. Her sorrow would soon be forgotten, replaced by other calves and other battles. The lead mammoth slapped his trunk to call the calf and turned to leave.

The males of Lucy's group squatted silent and still while the calf rejoined his herd. Just a few more breaths and no one would go home hungry.

Then Krp started to shake.

Lucy hissed, "Stop! They will see you!"

Krp didn't seem to hear. "Ghael will die! I have no one else!"

"Shush!" Lucy hissed again, but someone—Ghael?— heard Krp's plea and called to her. Lucy gasped. Why would anyone do that? The voice rang out again. This time, the Mammoth herd bawled, flailing their trunks and searching for the threat.

Ghael picked that moment to stand. "Krp?"

"Ghael!" Lucy screamed. "Get down!"

His mouth gaped, body stiff. The lead bull found his fear, carried heavily in the hot air. Ghael shrieked as a line of massive heads turned toward him. Their ears flared and the meadow echoed with their trumpets. Every other male exploded from hiding like a covey of quails and sprinted for the trees but Ghael froze, arms rigid and mouth open in a silent scream.

"Ghael! Run!"

His head snapped toward Lucy. When she screamed again, he blinked awake and fled, running smooth and long-strided. Until he tripped. In slow motion, he shook, crawled forward, and stood. The onslaught split to either side of him. If he had remained still, he might have survived but he wobbled, which put his body too close to one substantial trunk. Lucy heard a smack followed by an *oomph* as Ghael flew through the air and dropped with a thud amidst the stampede.

Lucy could no longer watch and turned toward the other males, hoping against everything she knew they would be faster than the lumbering Mammoth. It was not to be. With a mighty bray, the lead bull swung a tusk through the fragile hominid line and flung them aside like straw. They were crushed before they uttered a sound, lifeless eyes staring at the receding pachyderms.

Foe defeated once more, the Mammoth wandered without purpose. The matron rocked her forefoot like a seedpod on its stalk, toenails raking the hard ground. She poked the cow's motionless body with her tusks, caressed her with her trunk, and then trumpeted *'Follow me!'* as she left.

Krp refused to raise her head as Lucy searched for any indication of life in the bloody carnage. A shadow scurried across the edges of the devastated field and disappeared from sight. The hackles on Lucy's neck rose and an inner strength blossomed. There would be no more deaths today. Somehow, she would get her brother's pairmate home.

"Krp. We must go."

Lucy brandished a limb with one hand, to keep Snarling-dog at bay, while checking each eviscerated heap. She hoped for life but found only desolation. Tears flooded her eyes when she came to Old One, root clutched in her hand, face peaceful.

What were you doing here?

Snarling-dogs rumbled from the edges. Their bared

canines sparkled with saliva as they closed in on Krp and Lucy. With her own vicious snarls, Lucy backed away, leaving the massacre to the scavenger and dragging Krp toward the cow. They had only a brief time to harvest the meat before Vulture arrived. Lucy thrust a cutter into Krp's trembling hand. "Like this!" Lucy hacked at a haunch until the tough hide cracked open. Hot stinking fumes washed over her but Lucy slashed again and again until the leg snapped loose. Krp whimpered but did the same until they both shouldered bloody haunches and fled.

Shadows darkened to purple by the time they reached homebase. Feq greeted them, face tight, eyes wide and tinged red. She didn't need to explain; the carrion feast drenched the air.

Feq, one old male, and a few females and their children were the only survivors of the slaughter. There were other Man-who-makes-tools' Groups around but no one considered joining them. Grief consumed Lucy but instead of mourning, she drove herself from dawn to dusk hunting as Garv taught her. If she didn't succeed, her Group would starve.

But the biggest reason for her frenzy grew from the desperate need to exhaust herself in an effort to exorcize the horrid images of blood and death that visited her each night. It didn't.

When Lucy found Krp's body over a tree limb, one arm chewed off, eyes picked out by Vulture, she gave up. She wasn't angry at Leopard. He preyed on the frail as any predator would. Lucy sat on a vacant termite mound, face turned up at Sun, a light breeze cooling her fevered skin. This silent orb never judged her. As her ordered world crumbled beneath her feet, she asked for help and heard Sun's answer.

When just child, she watched a lone water-mammoth limp into the river, its passage marked by the blood that poured from a yawning gash on its hind-quarter. The dying animal knew its weakness imperiled the herd so its last gift to its brethren was to lead danger away from the calves who couldn't defend themselves.

Lucy must do no less.

***

She started stalking the young male with the missing finger and his old companion with the battered face when they crawled over the bluff of the Rift. She followed them up and down hillocks, over the narrow streams, and around ponds. They never noticed her. No one would if Lucy didn't want them to. The young one never tired, his head always erect, scanning the surroundings, strides long and carefree. He slowed only when his older partner fell behind. They signed to each other. Some of their motions, Lucy understood; most made no sense.

When Feq stepped in front of the strangers, he didn't know Lucy squatted above, hidden in the leafy boughs of the tree.

"I seek a female for my pairmate," the youth motioned.

Lucy found his face with its thin lips and fire-black skin intelligent and kind. His short, dark, kinked hair exposed pointed ears that twitched at every sound. His powerful back tapered to a narrow waist. But Feq, whose diminutive body would easily fit in the young male's shadow, distrusted him and did something Lucy had seen him do only once before: He lied.

"We have no spare females, stranger-with-the-odd-looks."

Feq shifted uncomfortably when Lucy dropped nimbly

from overhead. The stranger turned as though expecting her. Feq didn't try to change her mind.

Chapter Nine

<u>Present</u>

Life's predictability here in Raza's territory comforted Lucy. The savanna fed the herbivores who fed Cat and her cousins who in turn nourished Lucy and the Group. Night Sun arrived every night except when it didn't but always came back. Most days, when the work of scavenging and child tending ended, plenty of time remained to join Groupmates as they groomed and talked. For reasons unknown to Lucy, "talking" was important among Raza's Group.

The colors of Lucy's new world life her breath away—flowers as dark as storm clouds or as red as wounded flesh and snakes as yellow as a bird's plumage. Mammoth lowed its pleasure at the world. Lucy memorized every tree and talus field, every cave and nest and burrow where forage could be found and how long she must wait to re-harvest. She shared her discoveries when they gathered at the end of the day, as did all Groupmates, and asked questions. If she could make sense of this environ, she would be safe.

In return, the females snubbed her and the males frowned. Only Sahn understood and invited Lucy nightly to contemplate the shadow-stick with her. Over time, talking with Sahn, Lucy realized that Sun appeared on the same side of the blue and white landscape each morning, moved always at a walking pace, and disappeared on the other side.

When Sahn was busy, Ma-g'n took time to answer her questions and muse with her over curious events.

"Why does one boulder become warmer than another when Sun shines as brightly on both?"

"Why does Sun change colors—pale like thirsty grass some days and the bright orange of fruit on others."

"Why does bark grow thicker on one side? My hair grows the same all over my head."

With the passage of time, Lucy's memories of her Group muddled like the ripples in a pond far from the center. Soon, only faint threads persisted of what life used to be.

The air here never cooled but today was hotter than usual. Though the forest lay just a short jog away, the Group spent most of their time in the open, the only shade provided by the rare baobab or the shadow side of a baked boulder. Sand and dust hid everything. The sizzling air sucked the moisture out of every bush, cracked the earth, and wilted every bit of life.

Lucy dumped water over her head and shook from toes to prognathic snout, fluffing her fur, hoping it would cool her. Kelda carped nonstop about Lucy's weakness, always blaming the female's slender build, unsuited to the demands of the scorching savanna. It took all of Lucy's strength to remember she chose this.

Chores completed, Lucy left quickly before anyone could call her back. If she didn't find replacements for her herbs, Ma-g'n would be in agony, Baad's wrists would ache, and the females would have no salves for the cuts received foraging.

When she could no longer hear the Group, she turned her attention to the ground and immediately found a plant. As she tugged at a stem, carefully protecting the roots, she froze. There, close enough to be dangerous, rose a massive termite mound well above the tips of the grass. It wasn't the mound that alarmed her; it was that Cheetah often rested here, where she could see everything and catch whatever breeze fluttered by. This one showed Cheetah's prints padding down and into the surrounding area.

Cheetah was hunting.

A bird cawed to a mate, and Cousin Chimp chattered. Lucy followed Cheetah's track, noticing they became deeper in the front than back with more space between them the further the Cat went. She was gaining on the fleet Gazelle and would soon bring it down, take what she wanted and leave the rest for scavengers.

Like Lucy.

Cheetah's kill would feed the entire Group, which would make even Kelda forget that Lucy provided it.

But Cheetah's strides slowed and she staggered. White foam dripped from her mouth. Lucy imagined the big cat watching Gazelle escape, massive chest heaving, toothy maw dripping saliva.

What happened? Why did an animal as quick as Cheetah tire?

Lucy experienced no fatigue, no shortness of breath from the chase. When she retraced her path, she almost ran into Raza. He crushed her body to his, his face ashen.

"Lucy!" His agitated hands added, "You are in danger!"

She raised her hands above the ground, palms down and shook her head. "Cheetah-that-is-tired left. Feel the scat," and she pushed Raza's finger into a cool pile, far from the steamy softness of fresh dung. "Gazelle escaped," and she told the story of Gazelle's stamina and Cheetah's failure.

The next day, Lucy went hunting with Raza.

Chapter Ten

A hunt succeeds or fails at pivotal moments. The first is stalking the prey, the next is slaughtering it, and the last is passing the leftovers on to scavengers. The predator controls each of these steps—finding the weak or old animal in the herd, deciding whether to attack or break away, and determining when scavengers can take over the feast.

Those who survive off the work of a predator have no say in how any of this happens. They wait patiently as the predator attacks, kills, eats, and finally signals his finish. If Raza missed that signal, be it a huff of pleasure or a yawn of contentment or even the simple flick of an eye that transferred ownership of the carcass from predator to scavenger, Snarling-dog and Vulture would beat him to the food. Raza would then have to wait until they finished and what they left wouldn't be enough to feed the Group.

But Raza never missed.

Today, he crouched, patient and still, awaiting the signal, impervious to the world, his thoughts focused on one goal: Survival, of himself and the Group who relied on him for leadership.

Lucy wasn't patient but she read trace like no one Raza had ever known. She understood the animals as though she were one, connecting signs and unraveling clues as though they spoke to her. When Raza hunted with her, they always returned with meat—which made the females treat her worse. *Do you not trust the men to hunt? I did your work while you were gone!* Like every herd, the Group honored rigid cultural norms and Lucy failed. Pairmating with her served the Group in the short term but would ultimately fail. When, Raza didn't know but until then, he would learn everything he could from her.

The Sun seared Raza's arms and chest as Long-tooth lazed on a bed of crushed grass, head between her paws and snout buried in the bloody remains of Oryx. How did Long-tooth tolerate scorching days like today with such a thick pelt?

Raza carefully adjusted his position, moving one hand to the hardscrabble ground, the other to his damaged knee. Long-tooth's shadow had almost doubled in the time Raza had been waiting for her to leave.

That predators hunted and Raza scavenged what they killed had never bothered Raza before Lucy joined the Group. It didn't matter to him that the cat couldn't knap cutters, throw a rock to scare off an attacker, or even come up with a new plan if the first one failed. When the big cat got too old to chase down prey, another—probably one from her pride—would drive her away and she would starve. That wasn't how Raza's Group worked. Baad couldn't keep up with the younger males and his strength failed him at times, but the older male made up for it with his knowledge of the hunt. His value to the Group meant they'd never allow him to starve.

Still, Long-tooth Cat, be it this one or another, hunted live meat and Man-who-makes-tools scavenged the carcass.

Raza mentally shrugged. That's how it had always been done though he suspected Man-who-preys had their own rules, as they did for everything else. For example, he had no doubt they killed the pig Lucy found abandoned in the Impassable-rift. What he didn't understand was why kill a dangerous animal when they could have scavenged fresh meat with less risk.

A mosquito bit his arm and sucked out blood. If it annoyed him at all, it was because he hadn't made his dung coat thick enough to survive Sun's melting heat. His thoughts returned to the hunt and Long-tooth and the meat his Group desperately needed.

To Raza's side squatted Lucy, her expanded girth hidden by waist-high reeds, motionless in spite of the tickle of sand fleas scurrying over her skin. Her nose quivered from the whiff of blood as Long-tooth tore another gory hunk from Oryx's carcass. She bit back a grunt when Mouse scampered over her foot, nipping a toe as it passed. Raza calmed her with a hand on her knee, twitched his eyes up to Vulture and over to Snarling-dog, both focused on Long-tooth and not the scrawny hominids, and she settled in to do more of what she hated: waiting.

Long-tooth stretched her huge jaws in a feline yawn wide enough to swallow the head of many prey. She weighed as much as Great-chimp and won most fights she picked. Blood stained her tawny pelt and darker ripples accented the undulation of her muscles, ears flattened against her head as she concentrated. Her yellow eyes drooped as she lingered over each bite, certain that Snarling-dog and the hominids would wait until she consumed her fill.

Long-tooth prevailed over all other animals in no small

part because Nature endowed her with one of the finest defensive designs. Her sharp claws immobilized prey while her spiked canines pierced the brain-stem and turned the living animal into dinner. No other predator possessed these weapons. The claws of the skinny, big-headed, hairless creatures too stupid to hide from their enemies were thin and weak, their incisors dull. They frightened no one.

Though one of Long-tooth's canines had been shattered in battle, she remained a deadly foe. She feared no animal, especially not the upright mammals. Like Rodent, they scavenged her kills. Once, after a long period without a kill, hunger drove her to taste the grass they ate only to spit it out in disgust. 'Revolting' seemed no criteria for the upright creatures' food selection.

Long-tooth sorted through the olfactory clues, her stumpy tail moving side-to-side slowly as saliva dripped from her muzzle. The herbal aroma of red oats hit her first but she learned as a cub to go beyond the early scents. There, she found raptor and Snarling-dog and the stink of the upright creatures—one close and one further away. She sniffed again—a whiff of days-old scat, maybe from this same oryx. Underneath that, Hipparion, moist green plants, humus-rich soil, and even more subtle, the omnipresent tang of the volcano.

Her whiskers twitched as she sought danger attached to the fragrance.

None. Satisfied, she turned back to the tasty oryx.

Downwind of Lucy and Raza, not at all interested in Long-tooth Cat's leftovers, Xha of the band Man-who-preys flinched. He was slender with a muscle-bound body accustomed to hard work, skin the color and feel of Pig's hide. One look told his enemies that the slightest mistake would unleash a maelstrom of retribution.

Why did he smell Mammoth but didn't see the behemoth? He flicked through his memories and got it.

"Man-who-makes-tools." They were smart enough to hide behind Long-tooth Cat's enemy's odor but too stupid to notice the herd had left.

Xha talked to himself because he traveled alone, his preferred approach when scouting a new area. His wrist cords bulged as one hand clasped an obsidian cutter, knapped on both sides to a deadly edge, and the other held a long spear. These evened the odds with any prey. His spear killed and his cutter opened. No Long-tooth canines, no Eagle claws, no Cheetah speed ended life with more accuracy.

He could see Long-tooth Cat devouring Oryx while Snarling-dog waited far enough away to be safe but he didn't see the Man-who-makes-tools' hunters. It didn't matter. Today, Xha hunted Hipparion. He soundlessly padded along the perimeter of the thicket until close enough to kill his prey. He raised the spear to his shoulder, sighted in on the animal's neck, but was distracted by a slight out-of-sync movement.

He turned just his eyes to where he thought the sound came from—there. He'd moved far enough around the clearing to expose the Man-who-makes-tools' hunters. Xha scoffed at the scrawny creatures with too many bones and too little meat. They hunkered behind a dwarf scrubtree, awaiting Long-tooth Cat's left-overs, no idea there were easier ways to hunt. Something about the female made him shiver. Could it be her hair, straight and shiny, though she'd rubbed mud through it to dull the glow? Why did he recall her?

Xha mentally shook. It didn't matter. He was hungry. These creatures tasted like old Gazelle but were easier food than chasing down the fleet Hipparion by himself. He pivoted his spear from Hipparion to the indent beside the backbone and under the shoulder of the male. Xha's muscle-bound arm drew back and his stance stiffened. All else faded from his sight as he bored into his prey.

A nicker. The panicked Hipparion pawed the ground. She smelled danger. Xha's head canted back, even as the point of his spear maintained its target. The horse would be tastier. As if he felt Xha's eyes, Hipparion took off, limping.

Xha sprinted after it. He would let the dull-witted hominids live. Today.

Chapter Eleven

Vulture shrieked, voice echoing off the cliff walls, beckoning its many cousins. With strong wings that spanned wider than Lucy's arms, it floated on the thermals, preparing for the death dive it would begin when Long-tooth left.

"Vulture claims this carcass."

The tips of Lucy's ears burned, followed by her back. So much sweat dripped down her legs, off her nose, and over her abdomen that a puddle formed under her body. Ants tickled as they crawled over her feet and ticks burrowed through her fur to the tasty skin. Mice scurried past, sometimes over her. A cool breeze floated above the grassline but she crouched below it, ignoring the overwhelming urge to scratch at the tiny creatures who considered this their home. Snarling-dog showed no sign that he suffered. All he did was swat the incessant flies with his tail and pant.

Raza adjusted his position, adapting the hold on his cutter to the missing fingertip. Snarling-dog yipped a throaty bark which made Lucy smile. She understood Snarling-dog's huff of contentment and celebratory yelps, the long hollow bay when he laid claim to a territory and the short yap when he found food. This particular yip meant the attack was about to begin.

Vulture angled its wings, preparing for Long-tooth's departure. Lucy tensed, arms planted on the ground so she could quickly push forward.

Then everything changed.

Long-tooth perked to a sound and her snout wriggled. Lucy heard it too, a whinny directly behind Lucy's position though she didn't dare look. Long-tooth moved her head side to side, searching, and finally fixed on Lucy's hide-and-wait spot. She purred her displeasure and ambled forward. Lucy had coated her body in Mammoth dung to confuse Long-tooth but the determined twitch of the delicate snout worried her. Did she recognize there were no mammoth sounds attached to the aroma?

A noisy crunch saved Lucy. Long-tooth snapped her head toward the sound. Another crunch and Lucy watched Shrew as it darted toward Long-tooth. Shrew reeked of fear as the big cat's chest rumbled a throaty purr that drowned out everything else. Undeterred, Shrew diverted around a swiping paw, barely avoiding the snapping jaws, and bolted with a single-minded focus. A small part of these remains was all Shrew needed.

Long-tooth pounced, missing the agile animal as it pivoted to the side, seizing a sliver of the meat, and made a run for it. Cat gave chase.

Raza, Snarling-dog, and Vulture all leaped at once toward the carrion. One hand readied his cutter, the other prepared to wrench loose the foreleg after he loosened the underlying tissue. Lucy must slow the raptor's approach to give Raza the time he needed. Vulture began the death dive. Snarling-dog decided he could beat Vulture and charged forward. Long-tooth, caring nothing for the melee she caused, never wavered from her goal of stopping Shrew.

Raza was already chopping away at a haunch by the time Vulture emitted its distinctive *kree-kree*. Its talons would eviscerate Raza but must first get past Lucy. At the edge of the meadow, a squeal went up as a swipe of Cat's sharp claws sent Shrew airborne. It let loose of the morsel, doubtless to deter Long-tooth's interest, and scuttled under a log. Raza slashed at the bloody body again as Lucy loosed a missile at Vulture. The baby she carried did nothing to diminish her power. A strangled caw and the raptor backed off, trying to unravel what happened.

Lucy launched another rock, this one at Snarling-dog. With a squeal, he stalled and Lucy flung her final rock at the perfect target framed by his motionless figure. A crack loud enough to break a bone boomed and Snarling-dog re-evaluated. Raza tossed a gristly haunch toward Lucy and started on a shank.

"Arghhh!" He roared as another Snarling-dog tried to sneak up.

The canine paused and decided to await reinforcements. In smooth practiced motions, Raza slashed through the hide and muscle of the untouched shank, shouldered it, and fled, Lucy already away. Vulture made one last swipe but missed Raza and settled atop the bloody corpse. More raptors landed, prepared to pick Oryx clean until nothing remained but hard bones and teeth.

Long-tooth shook his head at their furious activity.

Chapter Twelve

Lucy could only sprint for a short while before her lungs and legs gave out but all she needed was to put sufficient distance between herself and the carcass. While Snarling-dog could easily sniff out the blood trail, he would only abandon the remains if she was close enough he thought he could catch her instead.

A howl reached her, further away than the last one. "We are safe, Raza. Snarling-dog claims Okapi. He won't chase us."

Raza lurched to a halt, chest heaving, hands on his thighs, and caught Lucy's eye as though to say, *You did well.*

Lucy collapsed beside him. Arms like wilted reeds, she dropped the heavy haunch, barely able to hold herself up. Dirty sweat pooled in her shadow as she pulled air into her starved lungs. She pushed up to her feet and took a wobbly step but shook so from exhaustion, she had to stop.

Raza jerked his head toward the backtrail. "We aren't safe yet. When he finishes, if he smells our scavenge, he will come after us."

Lucy wheezed. She disagreed but nodded anyway and smiled to herself. It had been yesterday's yesterday since the

Group ate and that only nuts and old roots. They needed this meat. Without another sound, Raza took off. Lucy secured the ripening haunch to her shoulder with mammoth tendons, dropped the chert cutter into her neck sack, and chased after Raza.

The rhythm of her feet marked the passage of time. *Thump-thump-breath out. Thump-thump-breath in.*

Lucy lost herself in the cadence, Sun's methodical movement, and the gentle bounce of Raza's shape in front of her. They ran over brindle-colored plains, past highlands to one side, hills to the other, and through a stretch of woodland that thickened as it neared the hazy mist of the Great Waterhole. She never let her guard down, scrutinizing the shadows, scanning for colors out of sync. Many predators slept in the midday heat which made it the safest time to travel. The air was damp and wet. Mosquitos stuck to her skin and sucked the moisture from her eyes and nose. Cousin Chimp chattered in the trees as did the many birds that called this area home. Though all around her seemed normal, she stayed alert. If this area's inhabitants sensed a threat, they would squawk or fall silent.

Raza thundered past yet another pond without stopping so Lucy handed him a water-soaked stem. She understood why he hurried—the hunt had taken longer than expected. Sun already sat too close to the horizon. When Sun left, Hyaena-dog and Panther arrived as did Man-who-preys. All of them had better night vision than Man-who-makes-tools. She and Raza must be home before then.

Her stomach tightened as Raza dropped back to her side. "The little one doesn't slow you."

She smiled at his gesture for 'little one'–fingers splayed

as he rolled a hand over his belly. He didn't wait for a response before he sped forward again. The Group always moved in a column, one behind the other, stepping in each other's prints.

Raza shunned both the well-worn animal routes and their own backtrail, careful to leave as few traces of their passage as possible, even burying their scat as Cat did. The riparian woodland gave way to arid savanna studded with thick-trunked baobab and desperate acacia. Far away loomed Fire Mountain, the master of this land. Most days, Fire Mountain spilled thin airy clouds of soot into the blue sky but when angered, it spewed fire and lava over the land and sent all life fleeing to the protection of the river.

Raza never moved faster or slower as they traveled through scrub brush and prickled thorns, over the hillocks and berms that dotted the topography, or around spotty collections of trees. The scavenge weighed heavily on Lucy's gracile body but she didn't ask for help. Her strength exceeded most males. She'd needed it to keep her old Group alive.

Only the few times Lucy hunted with Raza had she traveled outside the homebase and its foraging fields so she soaked in the richness of this world. Where she was born, she could see no further than the next tree and from canopy to forest floor. Here, her vision swept outward farther than she could run in a day and upward as high as Eagle soared. It tingled with life and promise.

Raza finally veered toward a pond, dragging her from her thoughts. Together, they eagerly drank beside Horse-that-walks-upright, Snarling-dog, and a lone gazelle. On their opposite side, a Wild-beast dipped its mouth into the cool liquid. The enormous long-haired beast never started a battle nor did it lose one once begun. It slapped at the droves of flies that rode its hide, shook its hairy head spraying water over its neighbors, and ambled off. No one cared about preying on anyone else. Right now, water was more important than food.

Lucy dumped handfuls of water over her body as a Mammoth bellowed its presence and plodded into the mud. Like Long-tooth Cat, Mammoth didn't knap tools or dig termites from a mound, or attack other animals. Lucy considered that. They had trampled the males in her former Group because they felt threatened, not for food. In fact, Mammoth ignored their carcasses. Why? Lucy couldn't think of a time she had ever seen them consume anything other than vegetation. She tried Mammoth's grass diet once but no matter how much she ate, hunger persisted. No wonder Mammoth browsed all day.

The matriarch picked up a trunkful of water and hurled it over her back. Next, she sprayed behind her ears and under her belly, and repeated the process on her calves.

Horse-that-walks-upright abandoned the waterhole for a nearby tree, heaved its rhinoceros-like body up and dug its claws into the bark for balance. Settled, it devoured the delicate new growth with noisy chomps and crunches. Finished, it plopped to the ground where it stood motionless, dull eyes fixed on Raza and Lucy. After a breath, its diminutive ears twitched and it galumphed away.

Raza glanced at Snarling-dog who was eyeing Okapi's carcass.

"We go."

Ma-g'n coiled and recoiled the tattered strips of his earlobe. He needed to release his water but remained frozen by the memory of what he'd seen. He had returned from hunting early, just as Sun peaked overhead, the carcass of a monkey over each shoulder. Sahn met him by Tallest-boulder, away from the females watching the children and subadults knapping. Her face was grim, arms folded over her chest, as though she knew.

When he moved to avoid her, she blocked his way. "Their stench sticks to you."

"I remained hidden."

"They left these monkeys so they could follow you."

"I watched my backtrail. I would have seen them."

"We aren't safe here."

"We'll never be safe from Man-who-preys." He patted her bony arm. "I'll talk to Raza."

He deposited the carcasses in the communal pile and climbed up to the top of Tallest-boulder to await the rest of the hunters, Raza in particular.

Sun hovered barely a hand above the horizon. Every group had returned except Raza's. Ma-g'n had been tracking a shape too big to be Raza and Lucy for a hand of Sun's voyage overhead. It appeared to be either an unexpected band of Man-who-makes-tools or an uninvited group of Man-who-preys. Both meant trouble. He squinted into the glare of Sun's failing light, trying to get a better idea whether he should warn the Group or wait a bit longer. It could be Raza carrying something bulky and heavy but that was unlikely. Most of the scavenge found during the hot times might be awkward to lug around but didn't have enough meat to be heavy.

He sighed. In another hand of Sun's movement, if Raza and Lucy didn't appear, he would have to send Vorak to look for them. Not only would that be dangerous but, without Sun's light, he couldn't search for long.

Finally, the blurry figure crested the hillock at the edge

of the plateau that bordered homebase. Now he could differentiate more than one individual, maybe Raza and Lucy but that was doubtful. Though Lucy had brought meat back from every hunt so far, this carrion weighed the hunter down, bent his head forward and kept his feet close to the ground, almost a fast shuffle. No one expected her to be strong enough to carry a carcass as heavy and bulky as what Ma-g'n saw. It must be someone else.

A breeze wafted the dusty scent of death across Ma-g'n's nostrils. Whoever these figures, they came from the direction Raza should be returning from and headed directly toward Cliff-that-can't-be-climbed and the switchback along the river that marked the edge of the Group's territory. They couldn't do that if they didn't know the location.

When grasshopper finally chirped, Ma-g'n answered with the call of Cousin Chimp. He hadn't realized he'd been holding his breath.

"Greetings, Ma-g'n!"

Raza and Lucy rounded Tallest-boulder, glistening with sweat, panting as they labored under the weight of the meat, happy with their success. Lucy's neck sack bounced between her breasts. Relief at their safe arrival washed through Ma-g'n. The Group had just enough members to hunt and protect each other. Without every male, the Group would perish. In their absence hunting or collecting stones, the Group couldn't defend themselves from Man-who-preys.

That was the first reason Ma-g'n exulted at their safe return, not the least of it that they carried an enormous carcass, big enough the feed the Group. Still, Raza's excitement would dampen when he saw the monkey carcasses with the holes in their chests.

The last reason Ma-g'n desperately awaited Lucy's return was personal. She had assured him that the trees that grew the Pain-bark were along the path she and Raza would take. If she hadn't found it, Ma-g'n didn't know how he'd survive.

Lucy inhaled deeply, almost shaking with hunger. She smelled the tang of cracked bones, the unusual aroma of monkey, melons—what a treat!—and a variety of roots and tubers.

She and Raza shrugged Okapi's carcass onto the communal pile, resting it on a generous layer of poacea to absorb the blood and juices. That would be consumed by the elders and children whose teeth couldn't tear skin. The Group wasted no food. She was conflicted, knowing that her hunting skills made her child less safe and better fed, but she couldn't help but respond to the pleasure that showed around Raza's eyes and mouth. His happiness, her pairmate, became her happiness.

Chapter Thirteen

While Lucy greeted Groupmembers and salved Baad's wrists, Ma-g'n headed for the pond. His skull might as well have been stuffed with burning cinders. He staggered but fell, unable to keep his balance. Sounds muted and his vision faded to grey as his head split open and drool dripped from his mouth. Eyes tight, he beat his head against the ground. It did no good.

When the firestorm receded, he pushed to his feet, legs shaking, and stumbled across the camp, desperately hoping Lucy found what he needed. How did he stand this before her arrival?

Kaavrm whined from across the clearing. "Ma-g'n sent me back here for help."

Ma-g'n strained to think beyond the battering waves of pain but didn't remember sending Kaavrm away. Why would he? That left him hunting alone and no one did that. As usual, Kaavrm stood by himself. Talking to him meant hearing a litany of complaints and whines and everyone avoided that. His red mouth gaped open and his beady eyes skittered from one Groupmember to another in search of an ally but found none. Even his sibling Falda turned away, head dipping as she chopped corms. A guffaw from Baad drowned out whatever Kaavrm said next.

Ma-g'n braced himself as the next searing wave roared through his head.

Lucy laughed as Ahnda wriggled past her to Raza's side, eyes glittering with excitement. He tilted his head up to the male he considered perfect, the one he desperately wanted to grow up to be. The youngster's face was smooth though darkening around his mouth and nose, a signal that he approached maturity. A hint of muscle in his shoulders and a slight thickening of his chest defined who he would become as an adult. Soon, he would join the hunt as a scout. When he proved himself, he would go out with a partner, probably Gleb.

Ahnda skittered to a stop in front of Raza and tugged his arm. "How did you get Oryx from Snarling-dog?" The child never tired of hearing Raza's hunting strategies.

Though exhausted, Raza managed a smile and chuffed the youth's head. "First food then stories, Ahnda."

"Ahnda-without-Yoo!" Lucy motioned, distracting the child so Raza could relax. "Where is he?"

Ahnda jerked side-to-side as worry flitted across his smooth face and then he brightened. "There!"

Yoo, a denuded twig over his shoulder, imitated Raza's march with the oryx haunch. Lucy laughed that Yoo—who hated the taste of blood—imitated the hunters. Had he grown up since she left this morning?

"Do we have a new adult?"

Lucy smiled at Kelda's children Dar and Sweena as they popped up and down like grasshoppers and trotted after Yoo, Brum's son Gleb close behind, eyes never leaving the children. Though still a youth, Gleb had always been more serious than his Groupmates. If Lucy didn't know how young he was, his height and size would make her think he was a subadult, ready to hunt with the males. Someday, maybe soon, he would.

"Sweena! Dar! Come!"

Lucy flinched at Kelda's churlishness but ignored her and approached Baad. His wrists were as bad as she'd ever seen. She chewed a leaf from her neck sack and layered the pulp around the swollen, red joints. Then, she coated it with leaves and secured the poultice with tendons. Lucy left when Baad's face relaxed. Now, to find Ma-g'n.

Ma-g'n picked his way past the trough of food hidden under a layer of noxious shrubs—a trick learned from Snarling-dog—and gagged. Something had spoiled; he would clean it out tomorrow. He hurried onward, ignoring the pile of discarded shards, a testament to the toolmaking that took much of a male's time. Here, they forged the cutters and choppers necessary for hunting and foraging. Other than during meals, someone always worked here.

The comforting twitter of lake birds called him as did the muffled snuffling of a pig and the swish of Cousin Chimp watching the excitement brought by the hunters' return. The tussock grass that edged the water hole swayed as Ma-g'n stepped into the water. It bubbled over the black pebbles and disturbed the silt at the bottom. This small pond supported all life from butterfly to beetle, serpent to lizard. Here the Group drank, splashed water on their steaming heads and backs, and gathered reeds and sedge stalks for food.

Behind him, Brum called out to Raza. A short male with stumpy legs and fur so thick you couldn't see his skin, he talked to no one except Raza, and that only because the younger male saved the life of Brum's son, Gleb. Ma-g'n had seen Raza's bravery first-hand.

"The heat had been stifling since the rain left. Every animal that could migrated, leaving the Group desperate for food. That day, male and female alike foraged for tubers, roots, worms, insects, even scorpions. The herds wouldn't return until Night Sun regained its full size once and again and the starvation food—what little the Group possessed—had long since been eaten. Brum's baby, Gleb, quietly watched the adults, blissfully bouncing on his bottom. Eagle squalled but no one considered Gleb in danger.

Except for Raza. When the bird dove, he was ready. He crashed chest-first into the raptor, blocking the deadly claws with his own body. Gleb remained oblivious to his close brush with death. When Brum grabbed his only child to his chest, the youngster gurgled at the excited faces around him. Brum never forgot. From then on, Brum and everyone else called Raza an adult. Saving a life ranked as high as a first kill."

Lucy tapped Ma-g'n's shoulder and he startled, calmed, and then offered her a water-laden leaf. She readily accepted. Her throat was parched from the long hot day and Ma-g'n, of course, would think of her needs first. She studied his face. She'd never seen him so tormented.

"Here." She pulled a stiff bundle from her neck sack before beginning to suck on the leaf. "I found it less than a day's walk from here. We can get as much as you need."

The sticky bark, wrapped in on itself, stunk like dung but Ma-g'n didn't care. He stripped pulp from the underside, stuffed it into his mouth, and chewed. The rest, he stored in the neck sack Lucy had made for him from Long-tooth's bladder, which the cat no longer needed.

Then he sat, feeling the numbness move up his neck into his temples.

"You and I are the only new members of this Group, Ma-g'n. How did you come to live here?"

Ma-g'n twisted a finger through his shredded ear and told a story only a few of his Groupmates knew.

"I couldn't even crawl when Man-who-preys attacked the homebase of my Group. My mother stuffed me in a hollow tree just before they slaughtered her and everyone else. Cousin Chimp found me the next day, wailing from hunger and thirst, and adopted me. I rode on the back of an older female without babies until I could walk and then I joined the other youngsters as they chased through trees, leaped limb to limb, and scampered from forest floor to canopy.

"Soon, I forgot about my birth Group. No one cared that my arms and legs didn't wrap around tree trunks like the others. They liked that I could coax termites from mounds and bees from their hives. Though I couldn't travel as quickly or agilely through the trees as they, I could run further and faster across the savanna. What they liked best was I could create tools and plan attacks in ways they never thought of so they always included me in hunts.

"When my playmates grew as tall as adults, they began rutting with females. I tried, chasing down one female with a prominent red rump who seemed willing, but my body showed no reaction. My chimp mother explained that some youngsters start later and I accepted that as the reason.

"One day, I was flying, swinging from tree to tree, filled with the joy of life in the canopy, when I missed a handhold my playmate easily reached. I remember gut-wrenching panic as I fell, grasping frantically at branches, bouncing off everything in my way, speeding downward through layer after layer of leaves. I recall the confused look on my playmate's face as he watched me thud to the ground, surely wondering how I had missed the tree limb he grabbed so easily. After that, I heard only my breath rasping in and out.

"My playmate howled at me to get up but my legs wouldn't move. A noise--something coming along the path--made him flee. I couldn't turn my head but recognized the stench of Man-who-makes-tools and it terrified me as much as the fall. They must have heard my cries and came to investigate. They poked and prodded me and then grumbled something I didn't understand. One slung me over his shoulder and I blacked out. Sometime later, I awoke in a strange place with odd faces peering at me. I didn't realize for a long time that they accepted me only because they considered me one of their own.

"I adjusted well, learning to appreciate what I'd always called imperfections—straight legs that ran more efficiently than curved and a well-placed thumb that made grasping cutters and choppers much easier. But then, before Night Sun had come and gone, the pain set in, hot and unrelenting, searing through my head. I awoke nauseous every morning, fell asleep blinded by it. I couldn't hunt, scavenge, or even watch the children because at any moment, I might collapse. Passing out was as much as I could hope for but usually I remained conscious, curled into myself, waiting for the fire to quit. I began traveling alone, hoping a predator would end my agony but Hku always sent hunters after me. I stopped doing that when one of the hunters injured himself trying to save me. In desperation one day, I gouged my head, intent on releasing whatever hurt so inside. Blood poured from the gashes but I kept at it until I fainted. When I jerked awake, Rat was chewing on my blood-stained ear. He would have eaten the whole thing and started on my lips if not for Raza."

Ma-g'n twirled his tattered ear.

"Then, Lucy, you showed up with your bark." He stared

off into the distance, eyes moist. "For the first time in as long as I can remember, the fires dimmed, replaced by a blissful peace."

Lucy remembered that day, too. After chewing the bark's pulp for no longer than it took to place the leftovers back in her neck sack. Ma-g'n's demeanor changed from stiff and tight to relaxed. And happy. Before he could do more than smile, Kelda started screaming at Lucy for wasting time searching out healing herbs for Ma-g'n that would never work. Falda hid and Sahn lost herself in her shadow stick. Lucy closed her eyes, waiting for the screeching to end when, mid-shriek, it did. Astounded, she popped her eyes open to see Ma-g'n, back to her, gaze on Kelda, head cocked, hands smiling.

"Thank you, Lucy," was all he said without taking his eyes from Kelda.

After a moment, Kelda shuffled away, grousing under her breath and Ma-g'n guided Lucy to where he'd been foraging. What happened next was the biggest surprise of all: He asked her questions. And listened to her answers. As they dug roots from the ground, they found a shared love of the forests, guilt over the death of beloved Groupmembers, the need to right those wrongs, and a fierce determination to never again destroy what could be saved.

"Vorak. I miss hunting with you."

Vorak grinned at Raza, eyes sparkling, his even white teeth glistening. "I found bones. You and Lucy found oryx. I don't mind loaning out my partner if it means so much meat for the Group."

Raza smiled back. The Group thrived in large part because Vorak exuded strength and confidence; everyone felt better around him—with the exception of his pairmate,

Kelda. She complained to anyone who would listen that
Vorak picked her to provide children, nothing else. Vorak
never disagreed.

"It looks like we succeeded today," and Raza motioned
to the wealth of food overflowing the poacea bed but froze
when his gaze reached the carcasses of the dead but pristine
monkeys with the ragged hole in their chests.

"Who brought these?" He asked as he turned toward
Vorak. Instead of his hunting partner, he almost bumped into
Ma-g'n.

"Yours?"

Ma-g'n grunted. He should have shown pride in this
carrion, thick with unchewed meat and bursting with the
nourishing internal tissues which were always consumed by
the predator who made the kill before the Group got their
turn at the body. He should have grinned with excitement at
such a successful hunt but instead, Raza tasted abject fear.

Chapter Fourteen

Sahn hunched forward, oblivious to the excitement bubbling around her. When the Group first arrived at this homebase, she'd cleared a space as large as a thornbush, stripped and scraped a stick until the shaft was smooth, and then embedded it deep into the earth as far away as she could reach from where she now sat. Around it, she etched a circle. Daily she watched the stick's shadow steadily move around the circle like the petals of a flower surround the center, placing pebbles on the pathway at places no one understood.

But she did. When the shadow reached the pebbles she'd placed on earlier days, they could predict when the hot days would arrive and the fruit would ripen, when the air would become cold, Night Sun would be full and bright enough for tracking, where new shoots and berries would pop, and whether the next day would bring rain. Everyone shook their heads in confusion when her advice always came true.

Today, she hadn't moved from this spot since talking with Ma-g'n. Diaphanous threads wound around Sun's face like a spider's web. Sahn quivered, knowing what that meant but afraid she couldn't do anything to stop it.

"Sahn…"

Sahn inhaled Lucy's aroma but couldn't waste a moment answering. She kept her face turned upward, to the sky, her mind trying to work out a way to save her Group.

Kelda once admired Raza, hoped he would pick her as his pairmate, but now he snorted approval at Lucy with her eyes like dik-dik and ears like the small-headed rat. If Raza's first pairmate, Kelda's sister, had lived, she would never have allowed Lucy to join the Group.

Kelda smashed the hammerstone against a fibrous corm, splitting it open, preparing it for the meal. Lone-baobab, located at the edge of homebase, provided enough shade for all the females if they squeezed together but Kelda spread her elbows which forced Falda into the failing but still-hot Sun, knowing the younger female wouldn't argue, and scratched her back against baobab's crusty trunk.

As she worked, she muttered to herself, "Why does Lucy hunt? Does she think the males fail? She is the failure!"

But that wasn't true. The baby Lucy carried proved that. The Group only persisted because of new children and this time, Kelda remained barren while Lucy grew fat. Each time of births, when flowers washed the meadows and the herds migrated, Kelda fattened with a child but not this time though she mated relentlessly with Vorak and then the other males. She refused to consider that she had reached the status of elder, responsible for overseeing the children of ripe females like Lucy.

Kelda slammed a cleaver into a rounded hipbone Vorak had brought from his hunt. It cracked but held its shape. She pummeled the joint, pretending it was Lucy, until it finally splintered and exposed the marrow which she set aside. Next, she swapped the cleaver for a cutter and chopped a celery-like stem as bitterness welled in her chest. All her children—Mir,

Sweena, and Dar—now belonged to the Group. She wished she could develop a vibrant red rump like a female chimp to show her readiness to mate but instead she bloated like a dead fish and bled.

Lucy cringed and edged closer to Sahn but the elder didn't notice. In fact, she seemed unusually distracted.

"Rain is coming, Lucy. And trouble."

Lucy tipped her head up. Sun floated in a cloudless sky, as it had the day before and the day before that. She turned to Sahn, not caring about the rain.

"Sahn..." Lucy's voice dwindled. "Tell me about the child."

Children in Lucy's experience clung to Mother's chest like Cousin Chimp's babies. This left the female's hands free to carry, work, or simply navigate the jungle. Here, Mother secured the child on her hip with one arm while the other tried to perform the labor of both. This, like so many practices in Raza's Group, puzzled Lucy.

Sahn didn't respond.

"I'm worried, Sahn, that I will make mistakes."

Ma-g'n approached. "Lucy. Can you help me?"

Lucy motioned a farewell which h Sahn didn't notice and followed Ma-g'n to a spot far enough away that they were alone. He didn't need help, that became clear; he wanted to help her. She squatted on her heels and stared into the distance. Ma-g'n said nothing, giving her time. Finally, she motioned.

"Being able to feed the Group calms me as the Pain-bark does you, Ma-g'n. As having children does for Kelda. Why does no one understand that except you?"

Ma-g'n's finger twitched through the shreds of his ear. "My life with Cousin Chimp was easy because the rules always applied to survival. The most important task we had was to save lives. If a rule didn't, it was changed. Life here is like crossing a lava flow on a narrow log. One misstep can destroy you. Every moment, Lucy, be prepared for that log to roll. Learn to walk carefully and depend only on yourself."

Somehow, Lucy knew Ma-g'n no longer talked about her. She flashed back to the look that had passed between Ma-g'n and Sahn earlier, before she'd given him the Pain-bark. He told Sahn something and whatever it was, she didn't like. Since then, she'd been sitting at her shadow stick, staring.

"I made promises to my child which I must keep, Ma-g'n. What haven't you told me?"

His face clouded and tension gripped his face. "We are in trouble, Lucy. They are back."

Chapter Fifteen

Raza crouched to one side of the food, balancing over his feet, tucked between Lucy and Ma-g'n on one side and Vorak and Kelda on the other. Baad, Falda, and Sahn hunched across from him and Brum to the side where his odd-handed eating didn't interfere with others. Kaavrm pushed in between Vorak and Kelda. The rest of the adults filled out the circle. The subadults and children huddled behind the adults, awaiting their turn.

As the ones who contributed the most meat to the meal, Raza and Lucy went first. With chert flakes, they started on the flesh, separating muscle and tissue from bone, and then selecting what they wanted from the grubs, roots, sprouts, bulbs, slugs, and melons in front of them. Then everyone else dug in with gusto. No one knew when the next meat would arrive.

Raza motioned as he bit into a juicy monkey thigh, "Give Yoo some of the melons, Ahnda." Yoo wouldn't eat meat that bled wetly.

Ahnda thwacked one and it burst open. He molded a leaf around his fingers and swiped out the flesh and seeds, handing these as well as the rind to Yoo. He used a similar scoop on the brains in monkey's cranium for himself. When done, he and Yoo swallowed the leaf scoopers, slurping and hiccupping as they sucked fluids from their fingers, reveling in the tantalizing collection of flavors.

"Today has treated us well," Raza motioned to Lucy.

Warmth rippled through his body as he gazed at the satisfied faces of the Group he would live with forever, give his life for, at the children who expected he would protect them. He wondered if his Father, as Primary-male, felt this after a good hunt.

Night Sun rested, the pond's blue-black water bathed in dark heat. An owl hooted, fair warning that she hunted. At the edge of the forest, a canis bounded off to rejoin her pups. Appetites sated, story time arrived. The adults moved aside and the children scooted up for a better view of the storyteller.

"Vorak. You start," Raza motioned.

Vorak smiled at Raza and frowned at some of the children until they stilled their nervous jiggling and turned their faces up to him, eyes gawking, mouths open. To them, the stories were as exciting as the food. When only the click of grasshoppers in the dry night broke the silence, Vorak began.

"Brum and I crossed the flatland heading for the clearing-where-herds-browse when Vulture flew past. We followed him beyond lake-by-home-base, down river-where-tree-shades until he disappeared over berm-with-termite-mound."

Everyone huffed. Some landmarks were familiar; others new and the Group would store them in memory. Vorak's body movements and expressions conveyed as much as his grunts.

"We chased. Before Sun moved a hand across the sky,

we caught up to the dust trail of an Okapi herd, pursued by lone-Megantereon." His hands swayed gracefully across his torso, fingers poking down for Megantereon's long canines and up for Okapi's horns. Man-who-makes-tools often hunted with this lithe cousin of Long-tooth Cat. As tall as Vorak's chest and more muscular, Megantereon was both aggressive and deadly. The advantage of hunting with this dangerous predator was it didn't eat as much as others, leaving more to scavenge.

"As we approached the herd, Megantereon fell back to track a struggling female with a ragged gash across her hind leg. White froth coated her pelt and she spewed fear dung as she ran. We could hear her blowing breath."

Yoo motioned, "I wish—"

"Shshi!" Raza scolded. Children never intrude on a storyteller.

"Megantereon waited for the injured female to fall behind its herd and then they attacked."

Vorak's palms became jaws and he clamped them shut on Yoo's neck, as Megantereon's serrated canines did to Okapi. The children squealed with joy.

"Megantereon finished, Snarling-dog ate, and then our turn arrived."

"Why did Snarling-dog go first?" Yoo chirped, and then slapped his hand over his mouth. Raza smiled. Yoo had been listening to Lucy.

Vorak shrugged. "Bravery is often patience. We eat after Snarling-dog," though he paused to give Raza a meaningful glare. "After us come Vulture and the flies. Each consumes only what they need so there is enough for all."

Vorak sat back as the children roared. Many hunts ended with long bones and scraps of meat. When everyone quieted, Baad told how he and his partner chased a dik-dik fawn over a high bluff and harvested the haunches ahead of all other scavengers. Why dik-dik ran over the edge, Baad couldn't explain.

A stillness enveloped the audience as Raza began his story. "It was Sahn who led us to Vulture who found the meat."

Everyone turned to the Elder as she sat, callused palms resting on the ground, bent fingers splayed and rigid, old eyes closed, a deep frown on her worn face. "Plants grow with a quiet scratch. Animals migrate with a rhythmic thump. But a chase, it rumbles beneath my fingers…"

Raza puffed approval. "We followed the raptor who followed Long-tooth who chased Oryx." Raza's fingertips dimpled like claws and slowed to a stealthy creep. Then, they spiked up like horns and his eyes burst open so wide that white surrounded them as he mimed Oryx finding Long-tooth.

"Oryx escaped but after a while, stopped to rest. White foam dripped from her mouth and her sides heaved. When Long-tooth caught up, Oryx was too exhausted to go any further and he killed her."

A collective sigh arose. Everyone shared the joy of Long-tooth's hard-fought victory.

Yoo's high voice interjected, "But why is there so much from your hunt and so little from Vorak's?" Yoo had interrupted again but this time no one chastised him. They wanted to hear the answer.

Lucy tensed as Raza seemed to weigh his reply. If the Group knew the danger she and Raza—and her unborn child—had been in, she might not be allowed to hunt again. She waited, trying not to fidget, wondering how he would respond.

"We were able to take it before Snarling-dog arrived."

Lucy relaxed. He told the truth though skipping some—many—of the details. He must agree with her: All anyone needed to know was that she and Raza brought meat for the Group.

Raza continued, "All hunts are different, young-one. You will see when you grow up."

A murmur filled the air followed by a hoot of congratulations.

When the noise quieted, Raza turned to Ma-g'n. "It is time for your story."

A muscle in Ma-g'n's temple throbbed. His eyes darted between Raza and Lucy and then he began.

"At the edge of forest-that-spreads-darkness…" His arm waved over his head to describe a particular stand of trees so dense Sun's light shone through as dimly as Night Sun. "…monkeys—many of them—flew through the understory."

Ma-g'n brushed his fingers over his chest. "They moved with ease, playing a game I recognized." One arm pointed forward while the other swayed in a wide gesture in front of his face. "All of a sudden, one of them screamed a warning and they all flew upward through the trees to a point high in the canopy. There they would wait until the danger passed." Ma-g'n called so authentically, Cousin Chimp shrieked in response.

"I hid in the trees too, far enough from the monkeys they didn't smell me but close enough I could see the threat when it arrived. It didn't take long to hear the shuffle of feet and crunch of twigs as someone moved through the debris on the forest floor—"

"I went for help rather than hide—as I should!" Kaavrm interrupted, but everyone knew he'd abandoned Ma-g'n.

Ma-g'n nodded absently. "I expected it to be a group of

Man-who-makes-tools—maybe I'd accidentally wandered into their territory—but when the creatures finally entered the clearing, it was much worse."

His hands described the creatures—taller than Man-who-makes-tools with swollen heads on tiny necks like fat melons grow on skinny vines, carrying sticks in one hand and cutters in the other.

Lucy gasped. "Man-who-preys? The ones Raza thinks shadowed us from my homeland?"

Kelda spit out, "You are the reason we are in such danger?" Her hooded eyes narrowed in disgust.

Surprised eyes turned toward Lucy followed by angry muttering, "They are here because of her?"

Is that true? Did I lead them here? Lucy started to shake but Ma-g'n patted the air with his hands as though to tamp down the growing unrest. "No. These predators have been here before Lucy arrived. Everyone knows that."

That's right. Raza said Man-who-preys kidnapped the Group's females and children.

Fear thickened until it vibrated through the adults. Someone wailed, "You told us we left them behind, Raza. Why are they here?" Many took up the whine with several keening in misery.

If they are here, my child—and Falda's—are in danger. This made Lucy shake even harder but she said nothing.

Raza stood, joined by Vorak and Baad. "Let us listen to Ma-g'n. He is the first to observe these creatures up close since we, with Hsu, followed them from the waterhole."

Kelda stood also. She edged closer to Raza and shouted over the anxious voices. "Yes, Raza is right. We must be calm. There is much to learn from Ma-g'n's story."

Falda chimed in, "Our males will keep us safe." Her voice was serene, even happy, leaving no doubt she believed what she said.

Finally, the adults calmed which quieted the children and Ma-g'n continued.

"Monkeys-that-fly screamed and showered Man-who-preys with twigs and nuts, even feces. None of this affected the intruders. They lifted their long straight sticks to the height of their necks, tilted their bodies, and thrust upward with such force, many of them dropped over backward."

Ma-g'n imitated Man-who-preys, aimed stick-that-kills at the sky and then fell onto his bottom. The children giggled and many adults smiled. Ma-g'n didn't.

The laughter changed to gasps when Ma-g'n continued, "Many Monkeys-that-fly plunged through the tree limbs and landed squirming at their feet. They pulled stick-that-kills from their bodies and kicked them aside. Blood gushed from deep chest wounds and then stopped as they died."

A hush rippled through the Group. No one could kill an animal hiding high in the canopy. How did Man-who-preys do that?

"Man-who-preys threw stick-that-kills again and again, hitting many more Monkeys-that-fly. Only those that fled survived."

Ma-g'n's face paled. "Th-they huffed in pleasure and then trotted away, leaving the bodies."

Lucy sat silently, stunned. No Man-who-makes-tools killed animals. They scavenged carcasses brought down by apex predators like Long-tooth Cat and Panther, and none enjoyed watching the end of another's life. It was acceptable only because it provided food.

Until now.

She thought back to the dead Gazelle abandoned at the bottom of the Rift. Raza believed a hunter killed it from the crest of the Rift and couldn't descend to retrieve it. Maybe;

maybe not.

With that, the Group separated to begin their end-of-day chores, subdued by Ma-g'n's story. No one chattered while moving the left-over food to the cache where it would be secure from scavengers. The children didn't giggle as they placed thistle bushes around the sleeping area. The males spent more time than usual checking the boundaries of the homebase.

Falda touched Lucy's arm. "The monkey meat tasted delicious. We are lucky Ma-g'n found it!"

Lucy gulped, dipping her head to hide her amazement, understanding now why Falda allowed herself to be pushed around by Kelda. She responded simply, "Yes, you're right," but what Lucy really wanted to do was shake the young female until it rattled enough sense into her that she might live to be an elder. Had Falda heard only about the food and missed the danger that stalked just outside their territory? If she thought Baad would be able to save her when Man-who-preys attacked, she hadn't been listening.

Lucy had learned the hard way that one misstep changed life irretrievably and forever. She didn't wish this on anyone, especially someone as gentle as Falda, but by blundering so drastically, Lucy had gained a healthy respect for the responsibility she bore for her own safety.

"Falda," Lucy croaked but she turned away, shoulders so tense they hurt, hands so shaky she wasn't sure she could talk. Falda stood for a moment and then hurried away.

Lucy breathed deeply in and out, blowing away her frustration, finally able to look at the fragile female, now skipping to the opposite side of the clearing. She giggled to herself, hands moving as she collected and stored the left-over food. The other females glanced at her awkwardly, not offering to help, which bothered her not in the least. When she finished her work, after assuring herself Baad didn't need anything, she casually plopped to the ground with several of the children and joined their game of rock-and-toss.

Lucy shook her head and muttered to herself, "You, Falda, may be the only one tonight who is actually happy," but Lucy surprised herself by admitting that she shared Falda's fantasy. They both yearned for a world where the Man-who-preys they'd met represented an aberration, that those vicious predators didn't always kidnap children and kill animals with glee. In a future as bright as the one Falda envisioned, the child who kicked inside Lucy's stomach would be safe. She patted what must be its head and tickled what was probably a foot.

It didn't calm her so instead, she tried to understand why Falda had such a different reaction to the same story that created such a visceral dread deep inside Lucy's insides. Why did this female ignore everything frightening or threatening, living instead in a past that slipped away day by day? Lucy couldn't; didn't even want to.

"Maybe I'm mixing up my worries from the past with this new life."

One look at Raza and Ma-g'n shook her back to reality.

"Maybe Fire Mountain will never again erupt."

Before Lucy could stomp over to Falda and say something she'd be sorry about, Kelda approached her.

"Lucy, do you have anything for these welts? They itch!"

She stuck her hands forward. Angry red swellings like spider bites covered both of her hands, some weeping, others already festered into pus-filled nodes. Even worse, her face was pale and her skin sweaty.

"Kelda—what happened?"

"They're from a berry bush. I haven't had berries since the herds migrated so when I found a patch, I should have

covered my hands with leaves but I didn't, and then I ate too
many."

Her honesty surprised Lucy. She must feel even worse
than she looked. Blue juice stained the fur on Kelda's chest
and chin but Lucy couldn't place blue berries in her mental
map of their territory.

"Where did you find the bushes, Kelda, so we can all
stay away?"

Kelda licked the sores, trying to tamp down the
irritation. "I followed Cousin Chimp." Rather than bending
forward to indicate a short trip, she gazed off into the
distance. "We went past lake-where-herds-drink, through the
jungle-with-stream-running, to a meadow filled with bushes
that brimmed with ripe berries. Thistles surrounded them but
I didn't care!"

As she talked, she tore at her skin until it bled, licked the
blood away, and then again scratched the tender skin. "Lucy?
What will stop this itch?"

Lucy almost asked why Kelda would pick fruit without
padding her hands with leaves but stopped. It wouldn't have
mattered. The thistles didn't cause these welts. Kelda's body
itself was fighting against the berries.

"Have you ever eaten these before?"

Kelda shook her head. Lucy had seen Groupmembers
get sick from blue berries, like Kelda, while others ate them
with no problem. She almost chastised Kelda for eating so
much of an unfamiliar food but again bit back the words. In
her old Group, everyone learned this lesson either by
suffering themselves or seeing what happened to others but
when she thought back, she'd seen no one in this Group
react against any food. No wonder Kelda didn't know.

Only one thing mattered now: She must end the awful
reaction or it could kill Kelda.

"I can stop the itching and inflammation but don't eat these anymore. Some can eat them but others, like you, can't."

Lucy knew she sounded abrupt but couldn't take the time to explain. Kelda's brow was damp with prickled sweat and her breathing had become shallow.

"OK. Thank you for helping me, Lucy." Kelda's face filled with hope and trust, traits foreign to the bitter female Lucy knew. Could she grow into a wise elder? She *had* tried to help Raza calm everyone earlier. Ma-g'n told Lucy that Kelda's sister had been Raza's first pairmate and Man-who-preys had kidnapped her. Who wouldn't hate the next pairmate?

Lucy softened. "Come. Let's get started."

First, she hurried Kelda over to a cache where she kept the remedies that wouldn't fit in her neck sack. She pawed through until she found a stem blackened from a grass fire. She broke off a chunk and handed it to Kelda.

"Eat this. It will neutralize the berries you ate and stop the welts from getting worse. Now, follow me."

With a wave of her hand, she motioned Kelda past where lake-by-home-base merged with river-where-children-fall-in, to tree-that-shades-from-sun, the only tree that kept enough foliage to cool them when the rain stopped.

"Dig up this plant's root bundle," and Lucy pointed out a flower with serrated leaves. While Kelda dug, pausing often to pick at her sores, Lucy found a flat stone and a round hammerstone. She then pounded the root into a viscous paste and spread it over Kelda's hands.

Kelda brightened immediately. "I feel better already, Lucy. How do you know these things?"

"I listened to Old One, an elder I... used to know," but Kelda didn't understand either the call sign for Old One or the motions Lucy added to indicate the wisdom of an elder. Lucy shrugged. "Tomorrow you must show me this field."

Abruptly, Kelda pulled her hands away. "One full with baby cannot go there. You could get sick like I did and injure the child."

With that, she grabbed the rest of the paste, turned her back on Lucy, and joined a group of females. She whispered something and the group smirked. Lucy huffed, turning away, refusing to react to Kelda's unpredictable attitude.

The children rough-and-tumbled along the lake as the last of Sun's stifling heat drained into the muggy night. Once darkness fell, Falda began a canorous rumble. The purity of her voice relaxed everyone. Lucy added her higher pitch and soon, others joined. Contentment replaced fear. Everyone agreed Forest-that-spreads-darkness where Monkey-that-flies lived must be located in Man-who-preys' territory. Ma-g'n missed their sign and entered when he shouldn't have. The Group would be safe if they avoided that area. Ma-g'n didn't contradict them.

Groupmembers lazed under Night Sun and slapped the ground as though to mimic the contented beat of their hearts. Lucy's head bobbed in rhythm with the *pat-pat-pat* of many hands. Outside the Group, Owl hooted. Hyaena-dog wailed in the distance and a hare—or Shrew—pitter-pattered around the edges of the homebase.

Somewhere, thunder rumbled, the sound like a throaty laugh.

Chapter Sixteen

They squatted, Hee, Shee, Ba, and Boah, camouflaged by the russet shades of their fur. The stout bough on which they stood was higher than the stubby-legged pig could leap. Outside on the plateau, puddles were so deep that if Boah fell into them, he would drown. Boah didn't know how to swim—couldn't understand how anyone did—but here under the canopy, the driving rain felt like just a heavy mist. In this thicket with layer upon layer of abundantly-leaved boughs, Boah felt at home. Even on sunny days, only slender rays of light penetrated. Shee insisted they shelter here and Hee agreed to whatever she wanted.

Boah stomped his foot. A small patch of fruit had just ripened at the edge of his hunting territory. If he didn't get there soon, someone else would eat them. He shook a leafy twig at Pig but the pudgy horned creature ignored him. Boah remembered a time when he burst from hiding, saved from the snap of the Giant-pig's jaws when Hee snatched him away by the scruff of his neck. Hee told his sole male child that life revolved around waiting. Since then, Giant-pig's piglet birthed its own family and Boah adopted much of what Hee and Shee taught him.

Today, here, he waited.

Boah cocked an ear toward a surfeit of unnatural noises from the tall, skinny hominids.

Why are the big-headed creatures so noisy!

The wind, the patter of rain, the drone of insects—none of these stood out because they were always there. Others— the crunch of dead grass, the scrape of stone against stone, the guffaws and chortles made by these beings—attracted hunters like this pig. Boah felt exasperation, maybe anger, though he possessed no understanding of these emotions, nor could he communicate them.

Do they have no elders to teach them how to avoid danger as Hee taught me?

Every time one of them yowled—'*wooseeh*' it sounded like—the female with the big belly turned. He liked the way she ran with her long steps and odd thrusting arms. Boah tried to mimic her once, moved his arms forward and back as he ran, but it tangled him up so he had to stop and shake his body until he rid himself of the peculiar movements.

In the tree next to Boah perched a chimp family. The smallest, still with light-colored facial skin, shrieked as he swayed back and forth on his perch. Mother should secure him but she'd wrapped one arm around the trunk and the other around a small, lifeless chimp with vacant, fly-infested eyes. Its arms dangled and head lolled like limp fronds on a hot day. No matter how often the female gave it her breast, its flaccid mouth wouldn't suck, and it refused to hold Mother's chest hairs. Even the youngest in Boah's troop did that.

Boah scrunched his nose. The baby stunk like carrion rotting in the sun.

How can they ignore that vile stench?

The mother seemed too distraught to notice either the

squalid stink or her other child's danger, too intent on cuddling the slack infant to her chest, ignoring both the older child and the pig.

Boah motioned, "Too noisy!" *Pig is waiting for baby Chimp to fall. If we are quiet, it will leave.*

Boah learned long ago, if he stood motionless on a limb above the pig, it would forget him and wander away. Why didn't the young chimp know that? Boah scratched his armpit in confusion.

Why don't these cousins understand me?

Boah understood their exchanges. Every member of his troop used grunts similar to these chimps, as well as facial and hand gestures, to share important information.

The pig by this time was in a frenzy. It marched anxiously back and forth beneath the tree, shaking its pointed curved tusks and scratching at the trunk as it snorted a terrible 'Oy!' sound. It didn't frighten Boah but the baby chimp kept up his caterwauling, accompanied now by risky leaps in the air. Boah jostled the branch to silence him but it caught the youngster off balance. He emitted a horrified cry and floundered for a handhold, his mother— anything—to no avail.

The female must drop the putrid bundle she cuddled in her arms or lose her youngster. Boah screeched to alert her but too late. The child thudded to the ground with a wail and the hunger-crazed pig snapped him up, shook him until he stilled, and then scurried off.

The pig gone, the mother descended. She sniveled, shuffled for a moment, and then glanced upward at Boah. Her baleful eyes held no anger as she clung to her flaccid infant. The jungle delivered life and death in equal parts.

My Mother too would be upset.

Boah wanted to comfort her but he took so long arriving

at that conclusion, she had left, probably to return to her troop, the rotted infant still clutched in her arm. The only sounds she made were to mew and cry as she wandered uselessly.

With the circle of life complete for the moment, Boah smacked his lips in anticipation of his favorite food. He motioned his intentions to Shee and Hee and swung through the canopy, hoping he wasn't too late.

Once he exhausted the fruit, he descended to the forest floor and hurried to a more abundant and just-as-tasty food source: termites. When he reached the substantial mound, a mother chimp and her baby were already there. The mother cleaned all the bumps and growths from a twig as her youngster watched and then inserted it into the mound's entry tunnel. After a breath, she withdrew a mass of wriggling termites, slurped, and repeated the process under the intense scrutiny of her child. Only once did she share. It seemed the youngster must replicate mother's actions or starve.

Boah watched, too. The procedure appeared simple and the tool not unlike one he'd used in the past but not for eating from a termite mound. After both mother and child left, Boah retrieved the discarded stick, placed it in the hill, and twirled. His offset thumb made the motion simpler for him than the chimp but he removed it too quickly and knocked the termites off.

I see.

He tried again and again and discovered that if he pulled slower, fewer termites fell off.

That worked better.

After several more attempts, he executed a passable imitation of the mother chimp and was rewarded with one stickful after another of tasty food until the shadows shrouded him and he knew he must leave or Hee would worry. With a loud hoot, he alerted Hee to his return.

Hee cocked his head. Though muffled by a berm and scattered stands of acacia, Boah's call told Hee his only child headed home. Another call echoed—Cat reminding all of her dominance. This one hunted far away but Hee survived by knowing where Cat stalked.

Hee journeyed far in search of food every day and it took most of the light hours. More and more, he left the safety of the trees for the wealth of food in the grasslands. There, he collected wild oats, eggs, ground-nesting birds, wheats, melons, and fibrous shoots, filling his hands and sometimes the inverted end of a rhino horn. On good days, he gorged on berries, nuts, and squash.

Today was good. He even found a rotting carcass that he scavenged for marrow. His heart burst with joy for the wealth of his life.

Today, at least today, he lived well.

Chapter Seventeen

"Ahnda. Hand me that one." Raza indicated a craggy gray fist-sized rock.

With the basalt and chert exhausted, the selection of cores that would become flakes, choppers, and anvils when knapped with skilled and patient hands was poor. To create tools capable of separating tissue from a carcass, cleaving bone to find marrow, and penetrating the parched soil required hard rocks like those around Fire Mountain. Tomorrow, the males would go there, as well as subadults who made their first kill. They would learn how to select the best stones and then help carry them back to homebase. The trip would take days and imperil both those going and staying, but it must be done.

Ahnda worried he wouldn't be included even though everyone admitted his eyes were sharper and reflexes faster than most adults. Of course, Gleb would go. As he knapped, he thought back to how Gleb achieved his first kill.

He and Gleb were supposed to teach the youngsters how to look for the signs that food was hidden underground. Gleb would say he sensed it and they should too. Most of them didn't but Ma-g'n understood what Gleb meant because the Mother Chimp who raised him insisted he trust his instincts. But, even Ma-g'n admitted, few of the children had a clear understanding at their young age what 'instinct' meant. As a result, Ahnda always ended up the one to teach the children while Gleb watched.

That bored Gleb so he left. His plan, as far as it went, was to collect so much food that everyone would forget he went hunting alone.

It worked, they forgot, and that's how Gleb became an adult.

Gleb admired Ahnda. His friend always noticed much more than footprints, everything from the wrecked stems that marked an animal's passage to the scratches nails made on flat surfaces, the condition of the scat, uneaten food, claw marks in tree bark, and lingering olfactory clues.

The last time they hunted together, Ahnda showed Gleb how to find tree frogs so when he drifted away from Ahnda and the group of wide-eyed children, that's where Gleb started. Their bumpy skin blended into the knotty trunks but if you stayed still long enough, they always moved. Then, it was a simple matter of grabbing them before they leaped to a new location. Gleb would find one for himself and one for Ahnda.

He crept to the first tree but found nothing other than a quick movement within the roots. He prodded the ground and out popped an angry rat, long teeth bared. Gleb seized it, snapped its neck and downed it fur and all, followed by the white, juicy grubs the rat had been feasting on. Hunger sated, he gave up his search for tree frogs and went to find food for the Group. After a short walk, he found prints overlaid with black and white feathers.

Ostrich! Based on the print depth, this bird weighed at least as much as he did. That meant an adult, which could mean eggs—and not the tiny ones of most nesting birds. Ostrich's eggs were so huge, they required both hands to carry and would feed the entire Group.

He couldn't believe his luck.

Without hesitation, he followed the trail until it vanished on the parched ground. Gleb asked himself, "What would Ahnda do?" And knew the answer: Follow Ostrich's scent trail.

Gleb sniffed but found nothing more interesting than Snarling-dog's dung. It must be stalking Ostrich. Hunting with Snarling-dog should be done in a group but its trace was easy to follow so Gleb decided to try it alone. It took until Sun had moved past overhead for Snarling-dog's prints to intersect with Ostrich and that in the form of dried saliva.

"Ostrich is so exhausted, it's drooling!"

It must be hurrying back to the nest, worried about leaving it unprotected for so long. Now he could follow the trails for both Snarling-dog and Ostrich. Where one disappeared, the other remained. They led him through the savanna grasses, over a rock bed, and into a patch of thistles. If he'd had the bird's long skinny legs, he could easily have cleared most of the thorns but he didn't so when he exited the thistle bed, he had to stop to extract them. How did Snarling-dog survive this?

Finally barb-free, skin pocked with red welts, Gleb followed Ostrich into a talus field along a well-traveled path. As Gleb neared the top of the hill, a horrific caterwaul rolled over the rise. He flattened himself to the ground and peeked through the stalks of grass. Below, a flock of Ostrich squawked their dissonant calls and galloped across the savanna. Their flightless wings fluttered and their lanky necks stretched forward as they hurtled onward, pink beaks wide and gigantic eyes bulging.

Behind but keeping up he could see Snarling-dog.

Gleb thought about giving chase but quickly decided they were too fast for him, a lone hunter. No wonder hunting with Snarling-dog was done in groups. "At least Snarling-dog will feed his family."

But there was a straggler, so far from the flock that Snarling-dog missed it. The distraught bird cried as it fell even further behind. It tried to leap over a pile of deadbrush but tripped and plunged forward, its bulbous head falling into the yawning V created by the intersection of limbs. It shrieked in terror but its flock continued onward, as did

Snarling-dog.

When it didn't get up, Gleb selected a heavy palm-sized stone and crept down the hill toward the stricken bird. Maybe he could pummel it to death. Before he got there, Lone-ostrich emitted a final gargled shriek and then silence. Gleb sighed. Another predator claimed it. He sniffed to identify who that would be but found only Lone-ostrich's dung. He could leave but decided instead to find out what happened. Maybe the predator would leave meat for him.

He crouched forward, keeping his shadow from crossing in front of the bird. He passed first Lone-ostrich's long still legs, then its disheveled wings and finally the reason for its silence.

In its horror, Lone-ostrich yanked so hard, it decapitated itself!

Gleb tucked a wing under each arm, forsaking the gourd-shaped cranium, and began the slow process of dragging Ostrich back to homebase. The bird stretched longer than Gleb was tall and much wider and heavier but he never considered abandoning it. By the time he reached homebase, Sun had dipped below the horizon leaving only a dusky orange glow.

After slapping him for going out alone, Brum called him a hunter. Ahnda congratulated his companion and meant it.

Ahnda handed a gray rock to Raza. He ran his fingers over it and grumbled, putting Ahnda's finger on an invisible fissure.

"It will crack," and he discarded it.

The Group had used up the best stones and must resort to the less-desirable ones found in streams and at the edge of ponds. These were dark and shiny with few of the edges that promised strength. Ahnda discovered a hand-sized chunk of chalcedony with smooth even surfaces. It would require more time but that was plentiful.

Raza whacked one side with a hammerstone to chip away the earthy crust, hoping it would reveal a strong interior, sufficient at least to create a digger that could extract food from loose soil. His deft hand gestures, steady gaze, and impassive face explained everything the eager children needed to know about knapping: Exercise control, stay calm, and never hurry.

Raza wrapped his fist around the stone until it barely peeked from between his fingers.

"Is it the right size?"

He didn't expect an answer, just wanted the children to think. Ahnda adopted this method when showing the youngest how to gather food. Ahnda sighed, shook his head, and fumbled through the ever-smaller pile.

Day after day, he sat with Raza and learned the secrets of knapping. When Sun's unrelenting heat pushed every other child into the shade or the cool water, Ahnda knapped with the males, adopting their emotionless expressions and detached grunts. He never giggled or romped anymore because adults didn't. His every action prepared him for the day Lucy and Falda would no longer contribute food.

Raza held the core in his weaker palm above a base. "Hand me my hammerstone, Ahnda."

Raza had a favorite hammerstone, chipped away on both ends. He would use it until it fractured. Ahnda handed it to Raza and the male slammed it against the core, chipping off an edge that exploded upward, narrowly missing his face. Raza didn't seem to notice.

"Ahnda. Test this flake."

Ahnda slashed his fingertip and the blood beaded in a bright red line. Raza grunted approval, rotated the core clockwise, and knapped a steady stream of cutters. Each was different as each oryx in a herd differs, but nothing this sharp existed in Nature.

"You try, Ahnda." Raza handed the core and

hammerstone to Ahnda. "Show the youngsters," and he leaned back on his haunches to watch.

Never had Raza asked Ahnda to demonstrate flaking. Raza was testing him. Somehow he knew that his actions here would decide whether he went to the quarry tomorrow.

The youngster flattened his lips into a tight line as his mentor did. He checked the height of his uplifted hand, the position of the hammerstone in his fingers, and the core in front of him. The angle and its point of collision must be perfect. With the confidence of youth, he raised the hammerstone, steadied the cobble, let power flow through his arms, and struck.

He emitted a satisfied grunt and turned to Raza, prepared for congratulations but found disappointment.

"How long does a flake last?"

Ahnda frowned at Raza's question. Of course. Raza never created just one. The youngster's mouth clamped shut and he started over, trying to model the rhythm so natural for Raza.

Deft actions, sure and fast. Why is it so difficult to do?

When the core had been whittled down to a piece too small to be used, he selected another at random and tried again and again with an inborn patience. Ahnda matched the coordination of his hand to the focus of his eye as he smashed hammerstone into cobble.

That flake is too dull.

He checked Raza's reaction and turned back to his work.

He sends talon-sharp flakes, one after the other, that scatter to the ground. I can do that, too.

Laboring.

Raza makes it appear easy.

He tried again, without complaint, for why would he complain?

Around him scattered the debris of the many flakes Raza rejected. Lucy scowled but Ahnda nodded. Males worked with patience. Males turned weathered rocks into tools. He would learn. Ahnda held the cutter against the tip of a twig and shook his head.

First, I learn to knap. Next, I learn to make stick-that-kills.

To his surprise, when he paused to take a break, he was alone.

"Who goes tomorrow?"

Lucy wriggled into a more comfortable position for her expanding girth and continued scraping hairy roots from tubers. She smiled as Ahnda perked at her question. Raza massaged his truncated finger as his attention moved from Lucy to Ahnda.

"We need Ahnda, Raza. I will guide him."

Raza looked surprised she chose to go but said nothing as he left to check the perimeter. By the time he finished, the sky had turned as black as Leopard, the darkness violated only by the limned outline of the baobab and a smear of grey as a pack of Hyaena padded slowly around homebase's invisible barrier. Heads low, tails partly raised, they radiated hostility, calling to each other in short low-pitched whoops. Finally, they disappeared as quietly as they arrived, realizing there would be no food here tonight.

Hyaena didn't worry Lucy. Man-who-preys, again hunting within the Group's area, did. The creatures stalked her thoughts like hungry wolves. They wouldn't bother her Group with the Hyaena pack around but still, Lucy checked the escalating darkness around Cliff-that-can't-be-climbed and Tallest-boulder. As far as she knew, they never slept and she had never seen one dead, didn't know if they could be killed.

But every animal had a weakness. Once she found theirs, she would defeat them.

Ahnda and Gleb stacked small boulders and bramble bushes around the Group's ground nest while Sahn groomed Lucy and Lucy groomed Falda. With long fluid strokes, Lucy removed the ticks from Falda's fur, examined each and tossed it aside or consumed it. Sahn began a low hum, as soothing as water over rocks. Kelda joined in, her voice a step higher but harmonious, like the scrape of the cutter complements the thwack of the chopper. The babies Sweena and Dar curled into Kelda's lap as Raza plopped to the ground.

"Sahn," Raza shaped a subtle hand movement toward the elder. "Should we go tomorrow?"

Sahn said nothing, grooming Lucy, fully engrossed in the next buried bug. That was his answer.

Later, fur glistening and clean, Lucy leaned up against her pairmate's chest and closed her eyes. Somewhere, far off, beyond where sky met earth, Hyaena howled to his kind.

Chapter Eighteen

"Stop her!" Kelda blustered as Lucy prepared to leave. When no one listened, Kelda grabbed Vorak's arm.

"She carries a child of the Group—she cannot go!"

He shoved her away so fiercely, she almost tripped over one of the children. Without apology, the big male went back to organizing the subadults. For many, this would be their first trip to the quarry.

Lucy ignored Kelda as she distributed the neck sacks to each male, made from animal stomachs. For those who didn't understand, she looped it over their shoulders and demonstrated how it held tools and food which left their hands free to carry other items. Only when she pointed to the one around Raza's neck did they acquiesce. That done, she packed hers with scrapers, flakes, and tubers as well as a collection of medicinal herbs.

Chronic unrelenting worry dampened the excitement of every long trip. Would they find enough rocks? Would those who stayed behind be safe? Would anyone be injured? Every adult remembered the raids that stole the Group's children and females—both while the males were absent. Before leaving, Lucy searched the perimeter one last time for sign of

Man-who-preys. If she found any, they would abandon the trip but all she uncovered was Hyaena-dog, Panther, and Shrew, and those outside of the urine barrier.

The last of Sun's morning dew dried on the grass as the Group set out. Raza and Vorak led, Ma-g'n at the rear, Lucy in between with Ahnda and Gleb far to the front. The hunters wouldn't see them unless they found danger or it was time to sleep. When Lucy glanced back at the homebase, Sahn's eyes were on her. Kelda stood to the elder's side, legs spread, mouth open, and eyes squinted. Her arms motioned something Lucy didn't understand and Sahn didn't acknowledge.

Then they were gone, hidden by the towering Tallest-boulder, and the hunters headed toward Fire Mountain's glistening black dome, flanks bathed in the light of Sun, hazy with heat and resplendent with thorny scrub, acacia, and blocks of overturned earth-laden slabs. Using a mental map created on the last trip to the quarry, the males followed a path parallel to river-around-mountains, curving between the ponds that studded the terrain. Raza established a strong ground-covering pace but one everyone could maintain most of the day. The sky was cloudless, the air oppressive but no one noticed. They were always hot and sweaty, even during the rainy times.

As Sun peaked overhead, the Group veered to a less-used route that hugged the edge of Lake-where-herds-drink. Lucy and the others splashed through thickets of reeds and cattails and tall sedge beds where they plucked water-filled stems. They trotted across monotonous grassy mounds and depressions that tripped them if they didn't pay attention. Swarms of sandgrouse and ants hurtled through the dense stalks. Hooves clattered over the ridges of a distant cliff and a black-bellied Vulture searched for food from high above. A striped cousin of Snarling-dog rose from a bed of boulders, considered the Group too large to bother with and withdrew into the shadows. Old carrion and new blood wafted on the moist breeze.

The Group spread apart to widen their footprint but stayed in a column, one after the other. They moved deliberately and carefully among the brittle stalks and dead weeds that peppered their path. Sage and thorns dotted the landscape, in some places thick and tall and in others sparse. The distant ridges were rocky with the same spare growth. Since this was Lucy's first trip to the quarry, she built an internal map of their backtrail, memorizing the trees, valleys, rocky outcroppings, the occasional thicket, and other landmarks that would guide her home and out again when needed.

Sun peaked in the sky and began its downward path as the Group entered terrain riddled with cavernous fractures. Lucy had never seen anything like it. She slowed until Ma-g'n caught up.

"What is this place?" She signaled.

Ma-g'n scooped earth from one crevice. "See the moist sides? These cracks are recent. The newly-exposed earth hasn't dried yet." He winced, paled, and fumbled a piece of bark into his mouth. It worked quickly but each time, she noticed he took more. Soon, she must find something stronger.

As Lucy prepared to ask a question, Ahnda appeared and motioned her ahead. When she caught up with him, he pointed to fresh tracks. The leading edge pressed into the hard ground and the front and back hooves overlapped.

She punched her chest with her fist. "Cheetah killed Okapi not far from here."

Ahnda grinned. "When Cheetah finishes, we will have

meat."

They split up, Lucy to share the news with Raza and Ahnda to rejoin Gleb on a high bluff where they hoped to find the kill. Soon, he returned.

Raza and Lucy listened as Ahnda explained, "Cheetah and her cubs are eating. Already Snarling-dog has joined them." He paused, thinking, and then motioned, "Sun will have to move that far," and he pointed to a spot in Sun's downward path to the horizon, "before we get our turn."

Waiting would delay the trip to Fire Mountain. Being away from homebase that much longer than planned would put those-who-stayed-behind in greater danger.

Lucy didn't wait for Raza's answer. "We are finding plenty of food on the way. We don't need the meat."

That was all Raza needed to hear and he motioned the Group to continue. Lucy reverted to the work of memorizing every hill, boulder, bush, river, ravine, and valley they encountered. What she remembered might make the difference between life and death on a future trip.

A herd of Mammoth plodded serenely toward whatever their destination. What would it be like, she wondered, to be safe within an impenetrable Mammoth family? They consumed what they wanted, when they wanted, and no animal dared stop them.

Sun had moved one hand and another overhead when Lucy picked up a reverberation under her feet. She stooped and pressed her ear to the ground. There, a *thump-thump-thump*, too muted for the many hooves of gazelle's herd or the weight of Mammoth. That meant either Man-who-preys or Man-who-makes-tools.

Lucy motioned to Raza and silently crawled up a steep hillock, Ma-g'n and Vorak behind her. Once she reached the crest, she peeked between sedge bushes at a group of Man-who-makes-tools. They moved so slowly, if attacked they couldn't escape. Their mouths hung open and chests heaved. Desperation leeched from their bodies like smoke from a fire. Their hair was matted with sweat and eyes dull as though they already knew they'd fail even as they followed Gazelle across the open meadow.

Raza motioned for all to freeze. Even the slight sway they might make in the reeds would reveal their presence.

A pack of Snarling-dogs joined the hunt. They circled Gazelle, forcing her to slow down, and nipped at her legs. One canine snagged the thin skin of her hind leg. She tripped and like that, furry snapping jaws buried her. They bit and tore and feasted while several of their clan stood apart to warn Man-who-makes-tools that this belonged to Snarling-dog. Hunters-without-food wandered purposelessly, dejected, and then faded away into the bordering forest.

All except Adag. He remained. He didn't have a particular plan, simply lacked the energy to continue. His hand gripped and regripped his cutter and his muscles etched sinewy ropes on his gaunt body. Hunger consumed him and desperation washed over his face.

Only one Snarling-dog-that-protects-kill stood between Adag and the scavenge. The canine snarled savagely to give his brothers time to finish. Sun came and went many times since Adag's last meal, and that was just a bite before Man-who-preys stole the pregnant hare from him. More than Adag suffered. The hare would have provided a mouthful of meat for each individual in the Group. Now, thanks to the odd-looking stick-holding savages, they all went hungry. The creatures took the Group's children, their women, and now their food. The males agreed to find a new homebase away from this predator but must wait until they grew stronger. As Adag rested one night with his female and child, a leopard dragged the screaming child away. By the time he chased them down, his son hung dead over a tree limb awaiting the feline's return.

Adag snarled back. "Not again. This time, I eat."

He brandished his cutter at the solitary sentry. Other canis glanced up from the feast, noticed this weak, small, and frightened upright creature remained. One Snarling-dog left Gazelle's half-eaten carcass to join the sentry who still growled his dominance. Another sauntered over, panting.

"They leave. I will get food for my Group!"

If he were stronger, he would recognize not the departure of a competitor but the start of a hunt. Snarling-dog now stalked the weak member of a herd. Adag stepped forward, flourished his chopper and howled in his most fulsome voice. One Snarling-dog backed up to draw Adag into their field. The others moved to the side, as though to depart, but circled around to the back. As Adag advanced, the pungent aroma of meat assaulted him. His stomach boiled and churned.

"They are full. My turn has come."

Before he formed his next thought, they attacked. His howl rang out, but no one heard. By the time Snarling-dog and Vulture stripped the bones and the smallest scavengers devoured everything else, no memory lingered of his bravery. The circle of life claimed another casualty; for Snarling-dog, it was a good day.

Chapter Nineteen

The Group fled, accompanied by the noise of Snarling-dog's yips and howls, calling his brethren to a successful hunt. The pack was already huge, much bigger than what Lucy usually competed against for scavenge. No fulsome barks and blandishing of twigs would frighten them off and when they finished, there'd be nothing left. No wonder the Group of Man-who-makes-tools who lived in this area starved. Still, their desperation wrenched at Lucy. What got them to this point?

A tantalizing aroma wafted past Lucy, of shade trees and cool water, but Raza didn't stop. Lucy pulled wet reeds from her neck sack, passed some back to Ma-g'n and some forward to Raza and then returned to thoughts of predators and prey and how they kept each other from starving. She was so distracted, she almost missed the signs.

"Raza!" she barked and faltered beside the familiar long-toed footprints. They were deep—Man-who-preys ran hard—and so recent, no debris overlaid them. Ahnda and Gleb should have seen the hominids from their oversight position.

Raza chirruped Cheetah's danger call and everyone

dropped to a crouch. Lucy pricked her ears but heard only the hum of flies, the muted swish of Eagle's broad wings, and the harsh rasp of a bird's wistful refrain.

After a breath and another, Raza motioned them onward but instead of memorizing landmarks, Lucy scanned the horizon and the tree line, senses on alert for Man-who-preys' rounded heads, telltale out of sync movements, or clumps of hair fluttering in the breeze.

She found nothing.

The Group halted for a long-awaited rest and Lucy squatted on her heels, nibbling a corm from her neck sack while her gaze moved forward and back over the surroundings. There, in the far distance, stood Fire Mountain, its flanks dark and crusty. A whiff of smoke glided up into the blue sky from its peak. Beyond it loomed a herd of distant harsh peaks, tips white and sides stony. A smile tugged at her lips as Canis bounced across the edge of the clearing. If this sociable animal didn't worry, Lucy wouldn't either.

A shadow flitted through the darkness at the base of the forest beyond Canis, followed by the rustle of leaves.

It could be Ahnda and Gleb. Or someone else?

Ahnda took his scouting assignment seriously though it was one usually assigned to youngers. As much as possible, he brachiated high above the forest where he could see everything, descending to the ground only when necessary. Gleb happily followed Ahnda's lead.

They were traveling through a particularly dense section of the forest and Ahnda couldn't see much beyond the next tree, so he listened, intently, trying to pick out anything that didn't fit the norm. There! A rumble filled the air, like thunder but below them, not in the sky. He climbed upward, muscular arms swinging branch to branch, nimble legs pushing him ever higher until he reached a spot above every surrounding tree. It took only a breath to find the rumble's source.

Hipparion!

The herd filled the entire valley. Ahnda couldn't see where it started or ended. It shook the ground like the earth quaking and filled the air with choking dust as the whinnies and snorts of the equine leader steered its charges across the grassland. By the time Gleb caught up, Ahnda was on his way down.

Gleb motioned, "Should we tell Raza?"

Ahnda shook his head. Even if Raza missed the herd—which he doubted—Lucy wouldn't. If the Group planned to stalk an old or ill member, they were already on it. Ahnda dropped to the jungle floor, leaving Gleb to catch up, and found a narrow path that led the direction they needed to go.

The local animals cast curious glances at the upright beasts, accompanied by an ear-twitch or a snort. They watched the hominids hurry, baffled. Predators hunted; prey hid so why did these lightly-furred creatures do neither?

Ahnda had been following fresh footprints shaped somewhat like his hand for a while. They could be a cousin of Cousin Chimp whose feet were much like extra hands but these were too large and heavy.

Gleb dropped to his partner's side. "Giant-ape. Recent."

Of course. He should have seen that. "But they come and go. How could a creature as immense as Giant-ape simply vanish and then re-appear out of nowhere?"

Both subadults shrugged and continued. As they passed under the next tree, a shell bounced off Ahnda's arm. When he tipped his head up, he stared directly into the beady brown eyes of Giant-ape. Horror washed through his body. It was all he could do not to scream and run but showing fear could be a deadly mistake. Giant-ape was huge, twice the size of Cousin Chimp, strong of body with bulky arms and a muscle-bound chest. Its face jutted out, blunt and chiselled, mouth open as it chewed, exposing chipped yellow teeth. A white puckered scar extended from the corner of its cracked lips to the bushy fur of its neck. It scrubbed at its broad flat nose and sneezed, blowing mucous on their faces. Other than that, it barely moved, sitting tranquilly on the tree limb, enjoying a life without the worry of finding food or avoiding Man-who-preys.

Ahnda took several shallow breaths and adopted the veneer of calm Raza did when faced with a threat. "It might think we're prey, Gleb."

"We're not plants."

That didn't put Ahnda at ease. Cousin Chimp mostly ate plants but enjoyed meat when available.

A rustle followed by the crunch of underbrush sent a sudden chill through Ahnda, like diving into a pond on a hot day. Something other than Giant-ape headed toward them.

"Gleb." Ahnda tipped his head to movement a stone's throw away and approaching fast.

Giant-wild-beast, like Wild-beast but with longer horns, a stockier body, and shorter legs, galumphed through the vegetation following a scent trail Ahnda was sure would lead to them.

"He's not the only intruder," and Gleb pointed the opposite direction. A warthog, alarmed by either Giant-ape or Giant-wild-beast, bulleted toward them, skidded to a stop, reversed, and managed to forge a retreat by bounding between two trees, banging its horns without even slowing. The subadults leaped out of the way of both animals, to a branch adjacent to Giant-ape. Its eyes twitched toward them once, registered disinterest, and flicked away. No other part of his formidable body moved.

Giant-wild-beast rooted around at the base of the tree, finally tilting its head up to follow the delightful aroma of the scrawny upright creatures. Instead, it discovered the gaze of Giant-ape. Giant-wild-beast snorted, squealed, and fled, apparently deciding the warthog would be an easier meal. The subadults waited until it was far enough away to be no danger and then they dropped to the trail and sprinted. They didn't feel safe until they reached a brush-choked pile of boulders at the base of a ridge, far enough they could no longer see Giant-ape or even the tree he sat in.

"Let's rest up there," Ahnda gasped, his chest aching. He pointed to a hill. "It's high enough."

They scrambled up the rocky slope, slipping on losing pebbles as often as not, finally collapsing on the bluff where they had a view of the vast grassland where the Group travelled, though they weren't yet in sight.

"We'll wait for them to arrive and then continue scouting the forward trail."

Ahnda's stomach growled. He'd already eaten all of the travel food he carried in his neck sack as had Gleb. Just back of the bluff, to the side of where they rested, he'd seen a termite mound. Ahnda denuded a stick, poked it into one of the vents, and extracted his meal while Gleb harvested finger-sized grubs from under a rock.

They had been eating for about a hand of Sun's passage overhead when a group of hunters appeared at the distant edge of the clearing below. Both of them scooted behind a thistle bush, comfortable they couldn't be seen, and watched.

Gleb motioned, "I can't see clearly but they're upright. It's either Man-who-makes-tools or Man-who-preys."

Ahnda munched on a termite. "Their heads are big. Bigger than mine." He fingered from his brow to his hairline. That space was much wider on them too. They must get cold at night.

Gleb motioned, "What are they carrying?"

Ahnda leaned forward and studied the sturdy straight branch clutched in each creature's hand. It was long but powerful and the creatures wielded it as though it weighed nothing.

"That must be the stick that killed Monkey, the one Ma-g'n described."

Together, they motioned, "It's Man-who-preys."

The skinny hunters with long legs and big heads broke into a fast trot and lifted their sticks.

***

Raza had called a halt, to rest, just as Ahnda appeared. His chest heaved and sweat prickled his forehead and shoulders.

"I have something to show you," he motioned.

Lucy followed Raza who followed Ahnda through a boulder bed to the crest of a hill.

"Down, so you won't be seen." Ahnda pointed below as the hunters hid behind scrubbrush.

A vast swath of Hipparion galloped across the plain, turning it into a black flowing river. This must be the herd Lucy had felt earlier. Its very size guaranteed it would be tracked by all the local predators.

In this case, that included Man-who-preys.

A lone colt struggled to keep up. White froth speckled her mouth and her chest heaved with exhaustion. She nickered, tried once and again to push her way to mother's side but was shunted aside. Man-who-preys moved forward, expertly cutting her away from the herd's protection until they could surround her. The foal shook her elegant head in confusion, whinnied an urgent call for help but it went unheeded.

Man-who-preys closed in. The foal stomped, charged first one direction, then the next, unable to find a route around this enemy. Man-who-preys crept toward her and then leaped screaming to their feet. The colt reared and pawed with her hooves. She neighed to scare her enemies as her mother taught her but they stabbed her back and head. One brawny male bashed the filly's legs with his stick and knocked her to the ground.

That ended it.

Lucy had never seen anything like this. Her Group didn't kill live prey. They always took dead scavenge from predators. Where did Man-who-preys get those magic sticks that beat the life out of the Hipparion foal? Were these the same hunters who slaughtered so many of the monkeys? A glance at Raza told her he too was stunned.

A group of females emerged from the shadows and joined the hunters tearing meat from the carcass, devouring the internal organs, and consuming almost all the tissue and muscle. When they left, they made no effort to carry the marrow-rich long bones back to their homebase.

Lucy's stomach clenched and fright gripped her chest at the thought of getting so close to Man-who-preys but she prepared to scavenge what remained before Snarling-dog or Vulture arrived. Raza stopped her.

"We go."

She huffed agreement, relieved, and backed away carefully, rolling toe to heel, moving nothing around her, until she reached the bottom of the hill. Instead of returning to their forward trail, Raza veered away, following one that led the opposite direction of this ruthless group. They'd still get to the quarry; it would just take a little longer.

It would also be safer.

Long after Sun settled over the horizon, the Group stopped for the night. Lucy held the leafy boughs with her feet and wove them into a springy platform. That completed, she braided thinner foliage into a bed and cushioned it with vegetation. Her tree nest was ready. In their hurry to put space between themselves and Man-who-preys, everyone had abandoned the meat they carried so the day's meal consisted of a hairy tarantula divested of its poison sack, a small snake, and a handful of grubs found under the bark of a dead tree. Once they ate, they crawled into their nests to sleep.

Nocturnal life buzzed around them as columns of red ants marched, grasshoppers clicked, and scorpions ventured out of their burrows. Lucy placed her hand on her belly, comforted by the quiver of new life.

What makes me jeopardize this child? What if I am hurt?

She had tried many times to stop, to no avail. Again, she resolved to quit at least until her child arrived. That decision allowed her to sleep, though restlessly.

Lucy tracked a wounded Mammoth when the tall dark-skinned male with the glistening forehead and narrow chest emerged from the treeline. Disdain radiated from his hair-free face. His thin-lipped mouth curled upward and his dead eyes bored into hers. He kicked stick-that-kills toward her and hefted one of his own. She picked it up, matched his waist-high hold, crooked elbow, his power-handed grip, and sprinted after him.

"Wait," she huffed.

"You must keep up."

The sounds came from his mouth without hand movements or facial expressions. The words made no sense but the tension in his muscles, the tilt of his head, the fire leaping from his eyes told her everything she needed to know.

She ran faster.

After enough time for Sun to move far overhead, they finally met up with more Man-who-preys' males. Each held stick-that-kills.

"Why am I here?" she motioned. Surprise blossomed in their faces as they coughed what sounded like 'Xha'.

"Food. Our food," and he pointed ahead to a mammoth herd.

"They are Cat's food, and Panther's," Lucy motioned, but Xha had vanished.

She started to follow but to her side, the pitiful low of a mammoth calf called her. She made a decision. A foreign cry escaped her lips. Her arm extended back as power surged through it. Her grip tightened and her fingers adjusted the aim. Then, she thrust forward and released.

Chapter Twenty

"What..." Gleb croaked as he spit out a mouthful of dirt. He remembered crawling into his nest last night but not how he ended up on the ground.

"You fell," Ahnda motioned and tossed him a water-soaked leaf.

Gleb stuffed it into his mouth and shook himself awake. That brought an agonizing spasm to his shoulder which he massaged while kicking the rock that must have caused it. Pain shot through his foot and now his toe throbbed along with his shoulder. He limped in a circle to walk it off.

Lucy soaked leaves in a tiny waterhole off to the side of where they'd nested and gave them to Ahnda to distribute. Gleb hobbled over, favoring his throbbing foot.

"Over there are roots. Dig them up." She handed him a digger and turned back to her work. Gleb rubbed the last of the sleep from his eyes and bent to his task.

The Group set out as Sun spread its bright presence over their world.

Sun trailed toward the horizon, preparing to yield the sky to Night Sun. It had been a long day and the Group made good progress. Ahnda and Gleb hadn't been seen since morning which worried no one except Lucy. Last night's dream bothered her. How did she know how Man-who-preys hunted? And why had she joined them in taking Mammoth's life?

Her eyes swept back and forth as she walked, hand gripped tightly around her cutter, steps light to avoid the noisy crunch of debris underfoot. Just as she decided to hunt for them, Cousin Chimp cried from a nearby hill.

Ahnda.

Raza acknowledged the call and motioned everyone to follow. Lucy hugged the edge of the meadow, hiding among the edging trees, and then noiselessly climbed the hill that led to Ahnda. Small boulders peppered it. A soft groove about the width of a finger marked Snake's passage. It would make a good meal and her stomach rumbled. She tracked its graceful curves across the path but lost it in the shady recesses of a rock bed. Snake would live another day.

When Lucy crested the hill, she crouched. The damp air pressed in on her body, alive with the buzz of the biting fleas in the grass. She separated the stalks to reveal a pond surrounded by tall trees. Horse-that-walks-upright chewed the last mouthful of low-growing leaves on the nearest tree and then stretched her long neck up to the tender young shoots closer to the top. She ate some and dropped others down to her calf. Mammoth trumpeted as she led her charges to the water. Chevrons rippled across the surface—Crocodylus infested the lake.

No Man-who-preys. What had the youngsters seen?

As though he read her thoughts, Ahnda materialized, a cluster of figs in each hand. He passed one to the Group.

"Man-who-preys' tracks are everywhere," he motioned. "He moves without stealth and without marking his territory," which meant he didn't claim this area; he like the Group was traveling through, not staying.

Raza grunted. "Drink. Silently. We leave quickly."

That changed when Gleb arrived, before Lucy even swallowed one mouthful of the tepid water. One hand clenched the long thin stick of Man-who-preys. A chill ran through Lucy.

"I found this in the back of a dead female—from a Man-who-makes-tools' Group."

Lucy went numb. "They hunted her but didn't eat her? Like the monkeys." It made no sense. Why kill if not for food?

Raza took stick-that-kills from Gleb and moved his hands along the smooth shaft with no leaf buds or growth nodes, the end tapered to a point tipped with a dry tacky crimson fluid. It was taller than any in the Group with the thickness of Lucy's wrist—and strong; it wouldn't bend even when Raza jammed it into the ground.

Lucy cringed. *The fluid on the tip is blood.*

Raza started to toss it aside but Lucy motioned, "I will carry it."

Her eyes hardened as she gripped the shaft, balancing it front to back. It felt natural, like the one in her dream, almost comfortable.

I will use it to find food, as Man-who-preys does, and to defend the Group.

Ahnda offered Lucy the last fig but she shook her head. She could only eat between the bouts of nausea.

Ahnda shrugged, downed the fig, and joined Gleb in a tree nest for the night.

They left when Sun awoke, licking dew from the leaves and eating roots from their neck sacks instead of visiting the waterhole. They traveled uneventfully, arriving at the quarry as Sun peaked.

Ma-g'n motioned to a shiny black ledge that jutted out of the talus field. "There!"

His excitement made Lucy forget the tightness she'd felt in her chest all day. Vorak lifted the enormous slab over his head and slammed it to the ground. It fractured into smaller chunks that everyone loaded into their arms. When everyone was fully burdened, after only a hand and another of Sun's passage, they set off on the return journey.

The return trip always went faster. No one wanted to stop for any reason, worried about their safety but more so for those left at homebase. When they arrived home, happily, all was well. Lucy leaned Stick-that-kills against the cliff wall. Her arm ached from carrying the heavy limb but her nausea had dulled, giving the baby time to remind her it needed food. The communal pile held the remnants of the dik-dik scavenged before they left for the quarry, a few mushy roots, and the body of a shrew filled with rotting tissue and white worms that should have been thrown away. Lucy pulled away at the smell, rubbing her fist under her nose. She gingerly picked around the flesh, looking for edible pieces. Some sections were an abnormal grey and others green. She finally found a mouthful she could choke down without vomiting, doused it with cool pond water, and then fell asleep behind the prickle-bush barrier.

No one mentioned Man-who-preys.

Chapter Twenty-one

Lucy awoke to pain. It twisted her insides as though tearing the baby apart. She panted shallow breaths, held her distended belly and hoped her child would live. Another searing contraction bent her over and then she threw up a viscous green liquid that stunk like rotten carrion.

"I need Sahn," she gasped, head hanging, long hair streaked with vomit. Sahn would know what caused this and how to fix it.

Usually, Sahn hunched over her shadow stick but not today. After searching unsuccessfully, Lucy joined Falda by what remained of yesterday's meal. Her friend's face was a pasty grey, eyes red and drooped as she slit the stems open and slurped down their slimy interior. Lucy did the same.

As she chewed, her gaze wandered to stick-that-kills leaning against the cliff. Raw weeping wounds swathed the inside of her hand from carrying it from the quarry. She had slathered them with tree sap, to protect the sores until they healed, but she wasn't worried. Blisters would never kill her. Man-who-preys would. Learning to throw his weapon as he did, that's what she must do.

Lucy's stomach churned, hunger fighting with nausea.

Never had she seen Man-who-preys leave a hunt without meat when he carried stick-that-kills where Lucy's Group often went hungry. She would practice with the hunting-stick after chores, even if she still felt sick.

A leaf cupped in her hand, she swiped up the last of the slimy roots, handing part to Falda and shoving the rest into her mouth.

"Eat," she motioned as her stomach rolled like waves in a lake. Falda's face tinged green but did as Lucy suggested. "Is this the babies, Falda?"

When her friend didn't answer, Lucy tried to stand but collapsed as cramps shot through her abdomen.

Is it time?

Her head pounding, she fumbled in her neck sack for an herb to dull the arrival of a new child, chewed it and swallowed. Then, she staggered to the edge of the camp and crumpled to the ground to wait. Sometimes it worked quickly, other times not.

One convulsion after another sent throbbing waves through her body. When her stomach wasn't tied in agonizing knots, she lethargically brushed away the mosquitoes that feasted on her arms. Sun moved a hand and another across the sky and still, Cat clawed her guts, intent on yanking them out through the hole in her belly.

"This isn't working." In fact, Lucy felt worse. "The blocks," she muttered and trudged to the side of the homebase where she stored them with her herbs.

Cousin Chimp taught her about these. She'd seen him vomiting one day, over and over and so violently he finally fell over. He lay still for such a long time, she threw a pebble at him, to wake him before a predator arrived. He sat up startled, wobbled to his feet, and meandered off on his awkward bandy legs. She shadowed him, worried he would lay down again, but he continued well beyond his troop's area to a clearing Lucy had never seen. A sniff found only the scent of Gazelle and Hipparion, nothing to indicate another Man-who-makes-tools' Group or a different band of Chimps.

Cousin Chimp seemed oblivious to everything except the effort it took to move. He stumbled down a short embankment to a parched plateau spotted with spindly shrubs and etched with desiccated grooves. Tilted blocks of white earth cut the landscape and the dust of something bitter blew through the air. The glare rebounding from the ground hurt Lucy's eyes and she squinted, peering through slits, until luckily Sun slipped behind a cloud and the painful brightness dissolved. Cousin Chimp continued forward, feet dragging, head down, and chin almost bouncing off his chest as he lurched toward something sparkly and white. There, he settled to the ground and licked. Nonstop. After some time, he returned along his backtrail without the wobble or the listlessness.

The next time Lucy felt nauseous, she followed the trail to the white blocks and licked them as she remembered Cousin Chimp doing. They tasted piquant, almost pleasant, sweet at times, tart at others. She slurped at the blocks until she realized her belly no longer ached and her nausea had left. Before returning to her Group, she broke off chunks to keep with her herbs.

Anticipating the same relief she experienced last time, she flopped to the ground and eagerly licked the rough white surface. The tangy flavor burst in her mouth.

"Falda," she called, her voice a whisper, and beckoned with a limp arm.

Together they lapped at the blocks but this time they failed though she licked and licked…and licked until her tongue became raw and red.

"Water... " Lucy motioned to Falda and tottered toward the lake.

Kelda yanked her arm. "Falda can't scavenge. You must help us." The female's voice dripped with thinly-veiled criticism but Sahn cut her off.

"Their babies make them sick. Leave them."

Lucy fluttered her hand and staggered to the pond where she buried herself in the silty floor. The bugs recognized an easy target and feasted in hordes on her arms and back. She didn't have the energy to stop them, breathing as other females-with-child before her did, but it only got worse.

"The dirt... Of course..." Lucy trudged to a corner of the camp, collapsed to her knees, and stuffed her mouth with gray, chunky earth.

She swallowed as much as she could and waited—hopeful and suffering. The stream gurgled and children giggled as they played. Somewhere, a mammoth bellowed its pleasure. The ground shook as giant-rhino galloped in the sheer joy of life on the savanna. The ever-present stench of sulfur surrounded them.

But the dirt did no good. Only one cure remained and for that, she must leave.

"Lucy!"

Ma-g'n. She tried to tell him she must find a cure for her stomach and would bring some for Falda but her arms wouldn't obey.

Skirting lake-where-herds-drink, she veered toward the hilly terrain where she hoped to find the treatment. It was all she could do to stumble forward, faltering at times, often leaning against a boulder or sapling for support. Without warning, her knees crumpled and she clutched her belly as it spasmed. The agony blocked out everything around her. If

Cat found her now, she would die. When the contractions subsided, she crawled along the pebbly ground, looking for the sour tasting-plant with a dark green stem and downy hairs across the blade. She sniffed or licked any plant that could be promising. If it tasted or smelled right, she chewed the stem or roots. In the end, they were always wrong.

Sweat stung her eyes and her legs cramped. The stench of vomit in her hair ripened and her body purged feces in a heavy yellow stream, but she lacked the energy to clean herself afterward. Every instinct told her to shelter for the night but too much depended upon her finding the herb. She drove herself onward, testing each plant, always disappointed.

Just as she gave up, she found it. With a quiet moan, she pounded the leaf into a noxious pulp and then choked down a fingerful. Keeping the whole mess down had more to do with the power of her will than the instincts of her body. After a few breaths, she repeated the process until she consumed every bit of the venomous material.

Her stomach churned and her mouth burned from the acidic taste but she didn't stop. Using the last of her strength, she immersed herself in the cool water of a nearby puddle and let her world dissolve into darkness.

Something awoke Lucy. She shook her head to clear it as her senses screamed. Panther and Hyaena prowled at night— did they awaken her? Alone, she was easy prey. Her gaze lurched from the savanna to a boulder bed to overgrown bramble bushes but nothing looked familiar. In the failing light, she reeled along her own tortuous backtrail but to her horror, it ended where she began.

How would she get home?

The sky faded from orange and yellow to black and grey and shadows engulfed the land in velvety darkness. Falda needed this plant so Lucy must get home. Slowly, she crawled up a tree, not caring that she forgot the vegetation that would cushion her head, and burrowed between narrow branches. Hyaena howled his presence and Owl hooted at some distant prey. The burr of grasshoppers as they sailed on the hot night air rang through the darkness. A family of bush pigs scurried out on a nighttime forage. She rested a hand on her belly and hoped she would survive.

The female should hear the crunch of his approach, the rustle when his spear prodded aside the twigs, and feel his gaze transfixed by the swell of her bosom against her folded arms. His breath turned into ragged gasps as he imagined burying himself in the abundant dark mane that reflected Night Sun's light. It became his choice whether she lived or died.

With a jerk, Xha realized this was the same female he'd pursued from her homeland—Lucy, he'd heard them call her. Despite the bruises on her body and the welts from bites, her beauty persisted—unlike the others. He drank in her lithe figure, the smooth hair that flowed like a waterfall over her back and chest, her slender but forceful body, quick and agile yet childlike. His heart pounded and his head spun.

Where was the rest of her Group, the ones who reeked of fear, believing themselves undetected as his hunters killed Hipparion? How could he miss the grass swaying where no breeze blew, the covey of guinea fowl roused from their rest? No animal moved so out of sync with Nature, only these. He could always find them, knew where they lived, but their meat tasted sour—eaten only as starvation food.

His hunters left for a new camp this morning and their path crossed this primitive band. He would have ignored them—it wasn't yet time to harvest more females or children—but one of the females wandered out alone. He shadowed her to see where she went and why she journeyed by herself. None of the kidnapped females had even a smidgeon of bravery. Rather than mount the most minimal defense, they trembled, many crying so hard they couldn't walk. To make matters worse, they didn't know how to strip a carcass or knap stones and cringed in Xha's presence. This enraged the warriors so that they beat the hysterical captives to death, turning their dead bodies into both food and bait.

But though they had no courage, the Man-who-makes-tools' females did possess traits Man-who-preys' females didn't. They could smell the rain before the dark clouds appeared and knew when it would be too hot to travel. Xha didn't understand how they did it but they were rarely wrong. More amazing, they were better trackers than his warriors. Xha included them on a hunt but once his males attacked live prey, they squealed and panted so loudly the prey took flight. The hunters again flew into a rage and slaughtered them, even as they cowered.

This female, Lucy, seemed to have not only those surprising traits but audacity, daring, and fortitude. She retraced her own steps and when that didn't get her home, found a safe place for the night. That sort of planning was unusual. He watched as she slept. At one point, she awakened just long enough to throw up a foul puke. When she again slept, he left, secure in the certainty he could have her when he wished.

Chapter Twenty-two

Lucy jerked awake, the thrum in her chest like a herd of Mammoth pounding across the plains. She couldn't see through the stygian darkness so willed herself to calm enough that she could hear over her own ragged breaths.

Nocturnal chirps and hisses. Panther screamed. Owl hooted and some animal scurried to shelter. No unusual noises, or motions but how much motion would she see from up here.

Still, the question remained, what woke her? In her dream, a male stood at the base of her tree, dark eyes staring up. She peeked down but saw only an iridescent snake slithering to his nighttime bed. Still, the slender male in her dream—the intensity in his eyes, the yearning in his long face—disturbed her. Before she could remember more, fatigue overcame worry and she drifted back to her dream of chasing Garv to the edge of the rift, laughing, until Garv morphed into a faceless being, hand gripping stick-that-kills...

The next time she awoke it was because a spider crawled across her face. She twitched and then stilled, letting her senses scan her surroundings. Where were the sounds of children at play or the grunts of adults at work?

With a start, she remembered her sickness, losing her way, building this nest, and the dream. Her belly rolled and she patted the round shape. How normal it had become to grow this baby. Calmed, she stretched, stiff from being curled around the tree all night, and poked an opening in the foliage to see where she was.

Fire Mountain still dominated the landscape, one flank covered with a profusion of verdant forest and the opposite side blackened by fire, the dry underbrush that should have offered protection gone. Scrubby undergrowth and boulder beds surrounded it, the foothills bordered by a narrow stream that dumped water into scattered ponds. Golden waves of poacea fluttered in the gentle breeze, and further away—a hand's width beside Sun—the Rift cracked the ground like a melon tossed from a cliff. The morning sparkled with dew and the perfume of water wafted over her. She recognized the tree she sat under when returning from the quarry and homebase popped into view at the edge of what she could see.

How did she get this far away?

The scents of Snarling-dog and Oryx drifted past her muzzle and her stomach rumbled.

"He will share."

When she dropped to the ground, she froze at the sight of prints. Something had run under her nest. A quick check of her surroundings found nothing dangerous so she bent to study the prints.

"Was that you below me, Oryx?" But these weren't hoof prints or the pads of Snarling-dog. These were shaped like hers though narrower and longer. To the side pressed an indent about the shape of a thumb.

"Man-who-preys," carrying his stick-that-kills. Her vision narrowed to a pinprick as reality assaulted her: "Why did he let me live?"

Her eyes misted and she fought the same helplessness she felt when Garv died and again with Ghael. Would she become like Krp?

No. Garv would be ashamed of her. She forced herself to stand straight, head up, feet apart, and dared Man-who-preys to show himself. Strength in herself was the only protection her child had right now.

When no one appeared, she put thoughts of Man-who-preys aside and headed after Snarling-dog-who-chased-Oryx. She needed food or she wouldn't make it back to homebase.

The unusual allies, Snarling-dog and Man-who-makes-tools, moved at a steady lope. They fell behind when Oryx sprinted and caught up when it rested. Lucy and Snarling-dog could run forever but Oryx had to rest to fill her lungs with air before again fleeing. Hunting with Snarling-dog was easy because danger never snuck up on him. His ears tweaked or nose twitched at the slightest sound or smell, often one she didn't notice, and the hackles on his neck stuck out as did Lucy's but his she could readily see. As long as Lucy kept an eye on him, she knew what he knew.

Lucy chased Oryx and Snarling-dog beyond the crest of the ridge, through a maze of boulders and brush, over ragged slabs of rock, and up the scrubby terrain of a scree slope where both vanished. When she crested the rise, she found heaps of watery dung and hoof prints but no Oryx. Snarling-dog continued the chase down the hill and out of sight but Lucy stopped. Oryx had escaped and she wouldn't waste energy on a failed pursuit.

As she caught her breath, she absorbed this new

landscape. In front of her unfolded a different part of the savanna, filled with lush forests, fast-moving rivers, endless golden grasses, and seared black rocks. In the distance was the Rift, its lofty banks in some places plunging and others eroded so ledges stuck out like steps. At the bottom stretched a distorted graben valley broader and deeper than any Lucy had seen.

There, a short way down the hill sprouted a meager stand of trees amidst a bed of boulders. On a dead limb to the side perched a motley collection of black and grey birds. They cawed and clacked, angry with her for some reason she didn't understand. She turned to go but paused when a figure stepped out of the shadows. It stood face-forward, the bully stance of Cousin Chimp but without his nervous energy.

It was Tree-man. These creatures moved upright as she did and were as agile despite stockier bodies. They scavenged and hunted more often in the forests than the savannas, more comfortable springing into the trees than running for safety.

Rarely did they confront Man-who-makes-tools but this particular Tree-man showed no fear. He stood, feet wide below heavy legs and bowed knees. His chest was shaped like Frog—wide at the bottom tapered to a narrow top—under shoulders that rippled with muscles. His arms were well-developed and gripped a rock so forcefully the knuckles shone white through the dark hair on his fingers.

The broad face returned her gaze, intense eyes a darker brown than Oryx and close together under prominent brow ridges, surrounded by the same dull fur that coated most of his body. The head seemed small for the beefy body. He guarded his movements, eyes never leaving Lucy, barely blinking. She would never intimidate this creature but she didn't need to.

He feared her.

Fright cramped his arm muscles, pulled his shoulders up and shortened his neck. His knees bent, preparing for flight even as he held his ground.

What kept him here? Lucy smelled acacia, poacea, the pungency of loam, and a whiff of smoke from Fire Mountain. She sniffed Oryx's distress and Snarling-dog's despair but nothing to force Tree-man to stay here, in front of her, when clearly fear consumed him.

Though they seemed to communicate among themselves much like her Group, Lucy had never talked to them but only because she hadn't had the opportunity.

"Hooy!" Lucy gently waved a traditional greeting and then offered it with more strength, more confidence. He cocked his head but returned nothing.

"Ooohh ooohh ooohh!" Lucy tried Cousin Chimp's pant-hoot welcome.

Still no response but Tree-man's ferocious image softened. He peeked over his shoulder. There, in the shadow of a boulder, huddled smaller versions of himself. A subadult—no, a female—stepped with grace and assurance in front of a young charge. She had the same sturdy brow and hirsute body as her pairmate but stood a full head shorter. Her breasts hung heavy with milk. She fed the infant slung over her hip the way Lucy would carry her child.

Tree-man motioned, "Run! _____ peril."

The older child darted into the background but the female remained beside her mate, strong, independent, and like the male, non-threatening.

Without warning, a thunderous explosion shook the earth. Over the female's head, the archipelago of brown-and-yellow volcanoes glistened against a sea of blue sky but one blazed orange and red as a column of fire and cinder shot up so high it almost touched Sun. Halfway down its flank, a fiery river coursed unabated toward Lucy's homebase. Another blast collapsed the entire side of the mountain.

The female turned to Tree-man and emitted a sound buried by another cacophonous rumble. Tree-man threw one last glance at Lucy before the pair evaporated into the jungle.

Instinct spurred Lucy to action. She must warn her Group.

Chapter Twenty-three

Megantereon ran side-by-side with Mammoth. Hare and Rodent dodged wild-beast and Snarling-dog. The urge to live outweighed the impulse to hunt. In the end, though, one after another, the terrified animals collapsed, exhausted, to be gobbled up by the flames, or they became confused by the impenetrable smoke and turned back into the inferno.

Fire didn't frighten Lucy. It cleared away the dead underbrush so new growth could spring to life and not only could she chew meat charred by fire easier, it lasted longer in the caches.

First, though, she must survive.

Blazing cinders burst around her. They seared her skin as she raced after a terrified Hipparion galloping toward one of the few remaining breaches in the wall of fire. Head high, it cut through the inferno, almost reaching the opening when a ball of flames exploded on its back. It screamed, slapping its tail across its back, swinging its head toward the searing wound, trying to bite the cinder. It neighed pitifully but no one responded. Finally, it crumpled to the ground, trembling, soon to be nothing more than a charred skeleton.

Lucy veered away, panic building inside of her. There

must be another passage but she couldn't see beyond a sizzling wall of flames taller than she stood.

Then, steps away, a new corridor opened. Through it, mingled with the acrid stench of burned flesh was the unmistakable fragrance of water. The opening was narrow so she twisted her body and flew through sideways. Scorching pain exploded on her neck as a cinder dropped into her hair. She slapped it away as she came out the opposite side, now flying across the tussock grass and into the lake, her feet sinking into the squishiness of the waterhole's bottom. She tumbled forward smack into a pig as it floundered in chest-deep water. Neither she nor the pig could swim but the choice between burning to death or drowning was easy. With flailing arms, she staggered onward, fell, swallowed a mouthful of water, and pushed to the surface, gasping in sweet life-giving air. The water cooled her scorched skin like baobab's shade on a torrid day.

Over and over, she sank, fought her way up just long enough to gulp in air before she sank again. She tried to think like a fish, arranging herself on her belly with legs extended rigidly behind her but she went under yet another time and groped her way back to the surface, coughing and sputtering in what she hoped would be air but usually contained mostly water.

She must go back, either that or die, but when she twisted toward the shoreline, a solid wall of animals greeted her, tumbling over each other in a frantic flight from the flames that licked right up to the waterline. They bawled, swimming over anything in their way. Lucy found a log and clung to it. At least, she stopped sinking.

A movement caught her eye—Crocodylus, gliding smoothly toward her, almost invisibly except that he swam against the tide of animals, hooded black eyes fixed on his next meal. His toothy maw snapped. A giraffe squealed and went under in a froth of pink bubbles. Before Lucy could gasp in terror, another Crocodylus snatched a pig and rolled the hapless creature into the depths where it would stay until suffocated.

Lucy panicked, trying to splash her log toward the opposite shore but got nowhere. A mammoth paddled her direction. Head up, tusks out of the water, the behemoth swimming with an ease and sureness Lucy envied but if she didn't move out of its way, it would trundle over her.

Another squeal and Cousin Chimp fell to Crocodylus. The only animal Crocodylus avoided was Mammoth. Skin too thick, tusks too long, it got a free pass.

Lucy had an idea.

She let Mammoth swim by her and then snagged one of its tusks and swung herself up on the animal's back. It bellowed, shook its head, but she clung to the clump of fur that sprouted between its ears and stretched her body down his rough hide, remaining as still as possible, legs straddling the behemoth and away from Crocodylus' maw.

After vain efforts to dislodge its unwanted rider, the Mammoth ignored her, maybe forgot she was there, and paddled on toward the lake's far side. Lucy gazed into the depths, amazed at the world below. Fish peered up at the intruder and then wound off in graceful serpentine movements. A wealth of unknown life meandered by, unreachable in their murky home.

When Mammoth finally trudged up the opposite bank, Lucy tumbled off its back, scrabbled away from the deadly tusks, and collapsed, snout out of the water. Waves rippled around her as Mammoth plodded away, into the bordering trees. Only then did Lucy take stock of her surroundings.

To her surprise, Tree-man with his family stood in the

reeds on the shoreline. He focused on her and she on him, each asking, '*How did you get here?*' He nodded as though acknowledging her cleverness, turned, and dissolved into the brush. The female, child in her arms, followed, tugging her other youngster after her. He refused, eyes glued to Lucy as though memorizing her features. Lucy felt the twitch of an emotion absent too long. She took a tentative step forward. Maybe that frightened him—he turned and raced after the female.

A chirp distracted her. A tiny bird perched on a nearby bush, head bobbing side to side, searching. Another time, it would be a tasty snack but today, it was a kindred creature separated from its family. After a final twitter, it flapped ash-cloaked wings and flew off. Lucy nodded to bird-in-search-of-family and left on her own search.

Chapter Twenty-four

By the time Lucy dragged home, night had come and gone. She chirred her tonal call even as a wave of bodies greeted her. She inhaled her Group, their odor mixed with water, the waste trough, and illness.

Who was ill?

"Lucy! Are you alright?" Ma-g'n kissed the singed parts of her body and patted her face and head.

Lucy clutched at Ma-g'n's arm. "The fire—?"

"It missed us. Come."

Ma-g'n shooed the children away from lake-by-home-base which made room for Lucy to sit while he prepared a leaf sponge to cool her.

"How dare you risk a child of the Group!" Kelda screeched as she shouldered her way toward Lucy. What hair Kelda still had bristled as she stomped her feet and banged her hands open-palmed on the ground.

"What if our males went to look for you? They could die!"

"Leave," Sahn ordered Kelda, and to Lucy's surprise, she did without another sound.

Lucy drooped. Kelda—again—was right. The Group

endured by the selflessness of its members. Lucy jeopardized everyone when she stayed away all night. Even Yoo knew better.

"You are burnt." Sahn teased her fingers through the singed hair on Lucy's back to expose raw fiery skin.

"I am healthy, Sahn."

The Group calmed as they realized Lucy and her child would recover. A rhythmic rumble rose from Sahn. Others took up the comforting sound as Sahn groomed Lucy, searching out and removing the lice behind her ears and at the nape of her neck, picking out debris and burrs, and smoothing the tight knots of hair. Ma-g'n worked on her back, with a scratch-pinch-scratch-pinch that soothed the burns.

Lucy relaxed, something she hadn't done since falling sick.

"Did you find the healing plant?"

Lucy jumped as Baad's voice woke her. It came out gruff but kind and his hands moved below his waist so no one heard his conversation.

"Yes," and offered the bedraggled bundle.

Something flitted across his face but he asked only, "Where?"

"I found it past the lake, away from where herds graze, up hill-that-shows-everything, and along path-that-leads-to-Rift."

Lucy spoke with grunts, chirps, and intricate hand motions to explain the expanse she crossed and where she located the plant, in enough detail that any Groupmember could find it should they need to in the future. She described the tracks under her nest and how Tree-man and his family warned her of the fire, embellishing nothing and hiding no details. Body language never lied and deception was meaningless in the Group.

When she stopped, Baad motioned toward the spot in homebase for those who were sick.

"H-here," he stuttered and fell silent.

Lucy rushed over, knowing she wouldn't like what she found. Falda, his pairmate and Lucy's friend, curled in a tight ball on a bed of bunch grass. Her pale skin was gaunt. Her mouth gaped, lips cracked and bloodless, her eyes scrunched closed against pain. She had become as old as Sahn and more dead than alive. Sahn sat at her side, one hand pressed against the younger female's brow, the other over her swollen belly.

Next to Falda lay a soggy pile of green noxious mucous like the squelchy interior of rotted stalks. Lucy touched it with her fingers. Damp. New. Sahn offered a wan smile.

"She collapsed shortly after you left. We can't rouse her and don't know what to do."

Sahn's hands moved peacefully but Lucy read the hopelessness on her face. A tear trickled down the elder's cheek and traced the grooves that etched her kind face. Her eyelids drooped, haggard with fatigue, the skin crumpled.

Lucy chided herself. *How did I miss Sahn's exhaustion?*

"I can do this, Sahn. You rest."

Lucy scooted in beside Falda and placed a hand on face, and gasped.

"Her face burns like a black rock under a searing Sun," Lucy whispered to herself. Falda who never laughed at Lucy's odd looks nor condemned her peculiar habits, Falda who wished to have their children grow together. Many didn't survive such body heat but Lucy would do everything she could to make sure Falda did.

She couldn't find moss so she snatched tufts of coarse grass. She pounded them to a pulp, soaked the mush in the river and with gentle fingers, patted it over Falda's fevered face and down her chest and abdomen. As the water chilled the female's skin, Lucy chewed the plant she'd found to the consistency of honey and dribbled it between Falda's grey lips one drop at a time. When she ran out, she started the process over.

Raza frowned.

Lucy rolled back on her haunches, exhausted. "Get me if she wakes," and left.

But she didn't rest. Instead, she took stick-that-kills and jogged to the meadow by homebase. From here, she could hear Sahn if she called but no one would bother her.

She balanced the long heavy pole above her shoulder and squeezed until she found the exact tightness that allowed mobility without slippage. She stepped one foot forward while raising the stick behind her, level to the ground as Man-who-preys did, cocked and released—and watched it plunge into the earth. She tried again and got a similar failure. She pictured how Ma-g'n had described their hold and adjusted her arm, pulling the elbow higher and her clenched hand closer to her ear. She flung the stick again and again, making minute changes each time until it finally dropped further forward of her last throw.

She stared, surprised. What was different? After a moment, she repositioned her hand as she remembered it had been, keeping her arm level to the ground, feet the width of her shoulders, and threw again. As before, this one landed further ahead of any other throw.

From that point, each effort improved on the last. Even when her palms bled, she didn't stop until she could reach the far side of the field.

Satisfied she now knew how to use stick-that-kills,

simply had to practice, there was one more task to complete. She walked across the clearing to a bordering forest, stood under one of the tallest trees, and tipped her head up. After shaking her arm to tamp down the ache, she selected a spot high above her head and imagined Man-who-preys sitting there, grinning, maybe flinging fruit and feces at her as the monkeys did. She replayed Ma-g'n's description of how Man-who-preys attacked the monkeys, thought back on her dream of the killer hunting Mammoth. His stance was wide, one arm stretched to the front as though pointing and the other—the one holding stick-that-kills—lagged behind, at shoulder height. After a breath and another, she hurled the enemy's stick upward.

It didn't even rise as high as the lowest limb. Blood from the blisters on the palm of her throwing hand made the handhold squishy so she switched to the other hand. It too had blisters but they no longer bled. She set up her hold, found the spot she wanted to hit, and flung the stick with all her might. This time, it bounced off the trunk and clattered to her feet.

Heaving the killing stick up into the tree was harder than she thought it would be. Somehow, the power she exerted to propel the stick across an open meadow failed to push it as far upward. It made no sense but she didn't care why, just kept practicing until it worked. Each time, stick-that-kills went higher until it finally bounced off a branch well above Lucy's head. She repeated that until she could hit what she aimed for with enough power to embed it in the tree limb. Then, both palms now bleeding, she trudged back to camp, leaned stick-that-kills against the wall, got the salve to soothe her hands, and rested next to Falda.

Raza joined her.

"Describe the tracks again." His authoritative gestures

matched the intensity of his face.

Lucy furrowed her brow. "It must be Man-who-preys—"

"No. He has never been to *this* homebase."

Lucy moved her hands quietly, not wanting to frighten anyone. "They were longer than mine but thinner," Lucy opened her palm and widened her fingers. "The toes and heel were connected by a narrow bridge. His stride was short when he arrived and long when he left."

Raza blanched, his jaw muscles bunched like a slab of earth.

Throughout the rest of the day, Lucy dripped juice into Falda's mouth and stroked her hair. Her friend never opened her eyes, the fevered face and cracked lips unchanged. As darkness blotted out Sun's light, the Group built a barrier to ward off predators drawn to the stench of imminent death.

Lucy laid next to Falda, not to rest but to soothe her when she moaned. Sometime during the night, the sickness that made her skin hot left and she drifted into a deep slumber.

Chapter Twenty-five

When Falda felt better, the Group traveled to the area destroyed by the firestorm to scavenge carrion and collect the tender new buds that poked through the burned thatch.

Lucy had other plans. She'd run out of charred wood and would have no problem finding it in this place. She found a perfect stump almost immediately, knelt down and cut away a chunk of a blackened wood. She bit into the piece and chewed, mixing it well with saliva, and then let it trickle down her throat where it could sooth the fire below. The bigger her belly, the more it convulsed and cramped. As she waited for the treatment to work, she loaded her arms with as many pieces of wood as she could hold. Soot soon cloaked her fingers and left dark lines across her face from when she swiped her hair from her eyes.

"Lucy. See what I found. Rodent!"

A wave of nausea filled Lucy's throat with bile but she managed a weak nod before throwing up a noxious fluid. Falda had no stomach sickness with her baby and didn't understand Lucy's cramps or nausea.

"What a wealth of food." Ma-g'n hurried toward Lucy, a half-eaten frog in one hand and a dik-dik slung over his shoulder, to which Lucy responded with another brutal retch. He froze in place, head tilted at an awkward angle, face drooped, fingers swirling the tissue of his battered ear until it resembled the twisted horns of Black-and-white-deer. After a moment, he offered, softly, "Ch-hee—would have liked you."

Ma-g'n never spoke of his child. The fact that he did so now chased Lucy's discomfort away, replaced by concern for her friend.

"He insisted I eat that, to help the nausea," and he pointed at the chunks of charred wood that filled her arms. "It worked, sometimes."

"I wish I could have met him."

His hands tried to move but locked into place, rigid and white. He had tried many times to tell Lucy about the wonder of his son Ch-hee, but before he could share even a handful of thoughts, his head would explode. What Lucy knew came from Sahn.

***

Ma-g'n took his son Ch-hee on long treks to teach him about the life that shared their habitat. Ch-hee never forgot a smell, absorbing everything as other children did games.

One day, Ma-g'n and Ch-hee tracked deer-that-fled-leopard. The air was pure, filled with cloudless sunlight and dew-laden bushes. He explained to his son the important clues to look for when tracking. Though his head throbbed—in his eyes today—spending time with Ch-hee made him forget everything else.

In fact, he became so engrossed, he missed the cessation of Cousin Chimp's chatter and failed to notice when the first Spotted-hyaena emerged from the edges of the meadow. Or the next. The initial hint that he and Ch-hee were in trouble sounded like a soft growl. To the side, heads down, hackles up, trotted a pack of Spotted-hyaena. They studied him with malevolent yellow eyes, tails stretched behind skinny bodies and hackles stiff in the menace of an imminent attack.

"Stay calm," Ma-g'n motioned and listened for his Groupmates. "They will leave when they hear the Group."

But the only sound came from Spotted-hyaena. Ma-g'n pushed his child back as he grabbed a scraggly bush and waved it through the air in front of the alpha. Snarls echoed from behind and Ch-hee whimpered. When Ma-g'n whirled, he gulped in horror. The animal's golden eyes glistened, fangs bared as panic rolled off Ma-g'n. The leader growled. Ma-g'n knew Spotted-hyaena was testing him, that he should step forward with raised arms, bark and snap, but he instinctively backed away, the youngster clutched to his chest.

I must attack so they don't. With a false bravado, Ma-g'n let out a ferocious howl and brandished his stick.

"Ma-g'n! Where are you?" Raza, his voice soft with distance.

"Raza!" Ma-g'n tried to sound strong and ended up desperate.

The alpha paused to assess the voice—but for just a moment. It was too far away and the creature in front of him too frightened. These animals entered Spotted-hyaena's territory. No one did that unless they were stronger or stupid.

He padded forward, knowing the rest followed. He hissed as he drooled saliva, still tinged with blood from the last meal. The tall one attempted a show of bravado when he snarled with his tiny mouth and snapped with his flat teeth, but the shorter one could barely stand his legs shook so violently. His brown-and-white eyes popped open and seemed to take over the small face. The putrid stench of panic poured from every part of his insignificant body.

As the pack tightened the circle, the leader analyzed his

adversary to find the weakest. Yellow eyes glinted with purpose as he turned to his choice.

"No!" Ma-g'n wrapped his arms around Ch-hee.

"Ma-g'n! Where are you?"

"Over—" but he never completed his plea before one Spotted-hyaena lunged, knocked Ma-g'n down, and yanked the child away. Several others hissed, preventing Ma-g'n from interceding as the pack tore Ch-hee's leg from his body and trotted mere steps before stopping to consume it.

"Ma-g'n! Get up!" Raza rushed to Ma-g'n's side and held him from racing to his child. "It is too late."

Eyes bulging with terror, Ch-hee screamed as another yanked his arm until it too gave way. He fainted. His silence invited the rest to finish him. Some chewed his remaining appendages while others tore into his chest.

"We must go," Raza motioned, gentleness balanced by urgency. "Spotted-hyaena will attack us next."

Ma-g'n didn't want to live without his child but Raza dragged him away.

***

Since that day, nightmares consumed Ma-g'n. Ch-hee pleaded for help as Ma-g'n stood by powerless to stop his death, sometimes at the hands of Spotted-hyaena, other times by Man-who-preys. Ma-g'n begged them to take him but always, they took Ch-hee.

A growl dragged Ma-g'n back to reality as Snarling-dog entered the clearing.

"We go." Lucy thrust Ma-g'n and Falda in front of her and they hurried away.

***

Spasms buckled Lucy's knees and drove her to the ground. Sahn guided Lucy to a spot piled high with fresh grass and the last of the flowers to soften the baby's entrance into the world. When it dropped, Lucy sliced the umbilical cord with her cutter, freeing the beautiful fuzzy male child of the tether. Then, Lucy licked away the blood and mucus that coated his body, cradled him in the crook of her arm, and guided his mouth toward her nipple. He would be called Lucy-one until he found his own call sign.

As Lucy-one suckled her breast, something she couldn't name welled up inside of her and with it an unbidden thought: She would do anything to protect her child.

She stroked the infant's downy fuzz, the smooth skin on his face and hands, and flipped him end over end to inspect every round new surface. Settling him face down on her lap, preparing to finish cleaning the fluids from his mouth, she froze. Emblazoned on his shoulder was a baobab-shaped mark.

Like Garv's.

Before Night Sun came and went, Falda's infant too arrived.

It took no time for both babies to find their call signs. With his non-stop gurgles, Lucy-one became Voi and Falda-one, who mimicked Voi's every move, became Voivoi. Night Sun disappeared and re-appeared many times as both babies learned to identify the smell and look of their mothers and Groupmembers, building the bonds required to thrive. Raza and Baad spent long days hunting as was expected, and the other females completed Lucy and Falda's work. Only Kelda complained though her whining silenced around the infants.

Lucy felt so content, she almost forgot about Man-who-preys.

Chapter Twenty-six

Sometime during the last cycle of Night Sun's regrowth, both Voi and Voivoi grew into children of the Group. They toddled throughout the homebase, splashed in lake-where-children-play, and visited the latrine ditch on their own, always together. That made them the Group's responsibility and allowed Lucy and Falda to resume their normal activities.

For Lucy, that meant she could travel with the males on the upcoming trip to the quarry. Raza had put it off as long as possible, hoping the tracks of Man-who-preys' within the Group's urine barrier would disappear, but they didn't and finally, the Group ran out of stones. The decision was made. Raza, Vorak, Ma-g'n, Kaavrm, and Ahnda would go, moving quickly with no wasted time.

As Sun's face slid over the horizon on the day of departure, Lucy packed her neck sack with succulents, corms, dried berries, a root the length of her arm, and leaves, snatched stick-that-kills from the wall where it always rested, and left with the males. Her arm swelled with power from the constant practice with Man-who-prey's killing stick. Her hands had toughened, blisters replaced with thick calluses. She could now hit anything she aimed at though she hadn't yet tried stick-that-kills on a hunt. In fact, she wouldn't. Lucy had other plans for it.

Each day as they traveled, Lucy searched for signs of Man-who-preys—footprints, the odd circular impression from stick-that-kills, his scat, even bent twigs that could only be left by an upright creature. She found nothing.

"They've migrated, Lucy. We're safe," though the tension in his body and the constant alertness in his face spoke a different message.

"Maybe," Lucy murmured though to her it was clear. When Panther and Long-tooth hunted, they were invisible.

Man-who-preys hunted.

They reached Fire Mountain without incident, loaded themselves with as many stones as they could carry, and set out on their backtrail. No one suggested resting overnight as they usually would after such a long arduous trek.

They had arrived at the foothills of Fire Mountain, not even far enough along the return journey to be tired from the heavy loads, when Lucy noticed an unnatural pile of obsidian, the same stone they carried, to the side of the trail but easily seen. She trotted over and bent, balancing on the balls of her feet since her hands were filled with rocks. The hair on the back of her neck tingled.

"Raza—over here!" She shouted his call sign and then motioned. There, tucked in among the slag lay a pile of the oddest-shaped obsidian rocks Lucy had ever seen. Each was bigger than her palm, wide and heavy at one end and tapered to a point at the other, and knapped on both sides making them thinner than anything the Group created.

Raza turned the stone over and over in his hand, confused. "I have visited many Groups of Man-who-makes-tools when trading for females. If they used this knapping technique, they would have shared it. This I have never before seen."

That left only one creature who could be responsible.

Raza squawked and the Group melted into the thistle bushes and boulders of the talus field. Lucy's ears pricked to the sound of Mammoth grazing, the huff of Snarling-dog at play, and the hoot from Cousin Chimp announcing that he found fruit. Somewhere a wild-beast rooted through the damp earth, grunting each discovery. If Man-who-preys lurked, he hid well.

"They never hide from us so why would they now? I think they're gone," Raza motioned.

"But why abandon these rocks?" Lucy motioned and then they both figured it out. "They're coming back for them."

***

Xha tracked the putrid stench of the Primitives as they left the quarry, stopping at the foot of Fire Mountain where the steep cliffs sloped into scrubby talus. Even a child would see their smear on the landscape. He watched as they poked at the carefully-knapped tools his hunters even now were returning to collect. If these Primitives took them, it would be their death sentence.

Though the kidnapped Primitive females had no idea how to make the carefully-crafted choppers his people used, he'd thought surely the males understood, but they didn't. The only one who showed any curiosity about this technique seemed to be the young female with the glistening hair.

It was surprising she traveled with them, the only female who did. A tightness gripped his chest. He must have this female. The sinuous motion of her body and the intelligence glowing from her eyes, like the sparks of a wildfire, promised

191

an unusual blend of menace and vulnerability. With her confidence and strength, she would breed strong children. If her whelp lived, he would take it, too. The females of these Primitives were more docile with their child's life at stake.

He turned away and then jerked back and squinted. He couldn't believe it—she held a hunter's spear? None of her kind carried one. Did she craft it herself? And how did she wield it with such grace and ease? A shiver ran through Xha. If he thought about it, he might call it respect but that was a concept he knew nothing about.

A grunted conference with his warriors and they made their decision.

Chapter Twenty-seven

The Group stopped for the night, exhausted by the pace Raza had set, barely cobbling together the bramble barrier before they passed out. Except for Lucy. Sleep alluded her as she tried to figure out how Man-who-preys made the tools she'd seen at Fire Mountain.

On the Group's final day of travel, Fire Mountain exploded. Sun dissolved behind a wall of smoke while the landscape turned from the multi-hued rich savanna colors to a monotonous monochrome grey. Accustomed to the leviathan's anger, the hunters continued, slogging through the thick carpet of residue, breathing with their hands over their mouths, barely able to follow each other's footprints before Fire Mountain's wrath buried them.

Lucy smiled. Nothing could find them now.

Which was how it happened.

Long-tooth had lived a successful life filled with battles, bitter cold, scorching temperatures, many mates, and hunger. Age slowed her, making it more difficult to feed herself and her cubs. Today, she brought down a lame wild-beast, a rare treat in her advanced years. Finished with what she wanted from the carcass, she lumbered off to a well-deserved rest, knowing the scavengers would flee when she returned for more. As she dozed, Fire Mountain shrouded her inert form in a gray cloak, only an indefinite bump warning of her presence.

"Food." Raza motioned toward a dead wild-beast being torn apart by a pack of Snarling-dogs. Overhead, Vulture cawed as though angry at the new scavenger. Raza poked a finger into a dung heap too big for Snarling-dog.

"Long-tooth Cat," he motioned to Ahnda, teaching. His hands went on to describe the cat's size and how long since she defecated based on its warmth and hardness.

"Why would she leave?" Ahnda asked but Raza didn't answer. Something moved not too far away, though he couldn't figure out what. Vorak, Ma-g'n, and Kaavrm were positioned to one side of the open field while Lucy had stationed herself by a berm where she could watch for the predator who owned the kill and warn the rest of them if it returned.

Raza, with Ahnda, moved into position, about midway between the groups, senses on high alert. He found a trunk where Long-tooth sharpened her claws. That didn't worry him. What set his chest banging was the scratches next to them.

Long-tooth travels with cubs.

Lucy hunkered down at the foot of the berm, listening and sniffing before climbing to the crest. Raza signaled something but a tree blocked her sightline.

That's when the aroma of Long-tooth's urine wafted under her nose, almost hidden by the sulfur of Fire

Mountain. She glanced over at Raza to see if he too smelled it. His face had paled, muscles tensed, and his eyes latched onto something in front of her. When she turned to see what captured his interest, bile burned her throat.

There, atop the berm she'd been prepared to climb, stood Long-tooth and her cubs.

Danger!
Arid weather hindered Long-tooth's sense of smell but today, the air was damp and thick. Her hackles stiffened as a stench she recognized invaded her domain. Proud and menacing with the confident bearing of an apex predator, she lifted her muzzle and cocked her head. Unmindful of the olfactory warnings that blared at their mother, the cubs cavorted through her brawny limbs, pawing and scratching at each other with undeveloped claws. High-pitched meows rolled from their mouths. Well-fed and playful, they exercised in preparation for an afternoon nap.

Long-tooth sniffed again, ears tweaked forward. Her great fangs curved well under her lower jaw and the serrated edges promised an excruciating death to any she angered. She wasn't hungry but would defend her cubs. Unaware of the drama unfolding, the babies sprang down the far side of the hill.

"Maybe Long-tooth will leave with her cubs," mumbled Ahnda.
Raza didn't think so. Most of the Group's hunters were downwind which meant Long-tooth would miss them but not Lucy. The slightest breeze would blow her scent right under Cat's muzzle. Raza willed Lucy to stand still.

Lucy held her breath. Her eyelids drooped to hide their

shine and she lay motionless until a spider crawled down her neck and she flinched.

There.

Long-tooth lapped at the humid air with her substantial tongue and identified the slow, upright beast. Its meat was tough with an acrid flavor that made her sneeze but she must protect her cubs. Snarling-dog would be happy for the food.

The cubs chose that moment to charge their mother in mischievous disarray. Without a thought, she lifted her front paw out of their way, expected them to roll through her legs and come to a halt. They were young and didn't want to be out of her sight.

Lucy gulped, horror-struck, as the cubs bounced past the she-cat and toppled down the hill like dry sagebrush. They got stuck on a boulder but their roughhousing dislodged them and they tumbled onward. One final drop and they came to rest against Lucy's knee. She froze, body still, knowing they couldn't miss her. They inhaled the smorgasbord of scents as Mother must have taught them to do. One swiped a paw as though a good-natured gesture and gouged a deep scratch that went from her eye to her lip.

Lucy wailed. The cubs yowled. Mother's purr turned into a rumble and Ma-g'n, Vorak, Ahnda, and Kaavrm fled for the trees.

But Raza stood, bellowed and waved his arms, demanding Long-tooth look his way. The big cat's bobbed tail froze as she swiveled yellow eyes between her cubs' howls and Raza's movement, deciding which was a greater threat to her children.

With a guttural growl, she sprinted toward Lucy.

Raza's distraction provided Lucy brief moments to bolt for the stand of acacia, the cutter she planned to use on the wild-beast still in one hand, stick-that-kills in the other. A frantic glance back told Lucy she wouldn't make it. Still she pounded on, huffing by the time she reached the lowest limb of the nearest tree. She dropped stick-that-kills to seize the branch and swung the other hand behind in a vain effort to push Long-tooth back while scrambling out of the way. To Lucy's surprise, instead of fangs ripping into her arm, Long-tooth whimpered and then nothing.

Shocked and bewildered, Long-tooth froze. These scrawny beasts who boldly walked upright didn't have claws. How did this one make her bleed? She pawed her face and licked the blood that dripped into a pool on the ground. Darkcub stroked her leg and Lightcub mewled. Neither understood the problem but Mother's actions worried them. Long-tooth tried for a fulsome growl to re-establish her superiority, but it came out weak and whiny. She trotted away, her cubs scampering after her oblivious to the close call.

Lucy shook, unsure how the small cutter damaged this immense beast no Groupmember faced more than once.

"What happened?" Raza and Ma-g'n gestured together.

Lucy had no answer, at least none that made sense. "I swiped the cutter backward. It cut Long-tooth's face as cub's claws sliced me." Lucy's body language showed an accidental swipe rather than a vicious attack like the mother would launch.

Long-tooth's chase scared off Vulture. That left the carrion unattended. Raza and Vorak pulled shreds of meat from the dead animal, both glancing often at Lucy. Kaavrm scowled, intent on getting what he considered his share of the carcass, and Ma-g'n seemed in a daze, at a loss to understand how Lucy could still be alive. He lowered his head in thought and then pulled the Pain-bark from his neck sack and chewed.

Before Lucy ate anything, she made a poultice from moss and held it to her cheek. Ma-g'n stood guard in case Long-tooth returned to reclaim her kill.

Chapter Twenty-eight

Raza twitched. He recognized the sound of a Mammoth in trouble. He silently beckoned Vorak and Gleb and hurried the direction it came from, glancing upward to see if Vulture and its family were gathering. The fact they weren't meant Mammoth still lived. Vulture only ate carrion.

Hunger gnawed his insides, a constant ache that never went away even when he slept. It had been too long since his last meal with flesh.

Vorak barked and Raza looked back without slowing. His partner grinned. "We will be first!"

The grass shimmered in the heat as Sun baked everything it could touch. Raza panted, sweat dripping from his face but didn't slow, not even when they left the area his Group claimed. Usually, he wouldn't hunt beyond the invisible barrier of their territory but this field, the abutting boulder bed, and the copse of trees that filled one side was unclaimed. Anyone could hunt here as long as they didn't interfere with others.

Part of the reason all recent hunts failed, maybe most of the reason, was Lucy hadn't been participating. In the past, she accepted that hunting put her child at risk, but her near-miss with Long-tooth frightened her enough she refused to go again until the child arrived. Raza hoped she'd change her mind. He relied on her quick-thinking and missed it today, and yesterday, and yesterday's yesterday. If she were here, she would have tracked Mammoth by now and they'd be hiding nearby, awaiting its death, ready to claim the scavenge.

Sun's rays moved from his face to his back, the fiery ball wandering a hand and another across the sky, never faster, never slower. Raza almost gave up, prepared to once again return to homebase without meat, when his nostrils flared. There, almost hidden by the detritus of the forest floor, lay a crimson drop, still damp.

Vorak hooted. "Injured-Mammoth's blood trail. I can almost taste the meat!"

Raza scooted forward, sniffed again and then listened for the enemy mighty enough to bring down Mammoth. The only sound was a faint wail—the cry of an injured Mammoth. He sprinted toward it, drooling with excitement, up a slight rise to the bluff of a low canyon. There at the bottom lay a Mammoth calf, panting shallow breaths, leg twisted at an unnatural angle. Her mother stood guard, trunk high, forelimb pawing the ground. The calf's eye, the one not submerged in the fast-moving stream that flowed through the canyon, begged for salvation. To one side, Snarling-dog darted forward and nipped at the baby, testing. Mother bawled and swiped at the scavenger with her mighty trunk and hurled a snoutful of muddy water his way. The baby tried to stand but mewed piteously as her leg crumpled.

"The herd tried to help." Raza pointed to a smooth gutter in the hillside created when hooves skidded downhill under an enormous weight. "There," he indicated gouges. "They dug in with their hind legs to lift her with their tusks but couldn't. The mother will not leave until her calf dies."

Gleb started to scramble down, but Raza snatched him by the scruff of his neck, right out of Snarling-dog's toothy maw. The canis had spied the intruders and darted up the cliff, hoping to attack before they discovered him. It almost worked. Raza pushed Gleb behind Vorak and began the slow process of slipping, sliding, and slithering down the cliff so they could hunker below and await Mammoth calf's death.

Their shadows had grown a hand, maybe another, when dark clouds spilled over the bluff, one after another until Sun no longer shone. The calf lowed at the first watery drops as though she knew this marked the end. The matriarch mewed, the bushy tip of her tail slapping flies from her rump, one eye on her baby as it tried and failed again to stand, the other eye on Snarling-dog. Soon, the clouds opened and rain fell in torrents. It overflowed Raza's protruding brows and he had to wipe it away to see. Gleb tipped his head and drank.

The baby mammoth gurgled, flailing her tubed nose in one desperate attempt after another to breathe as the puddle beneath her head spread and deepened. Snarling-dog shook from muzzle to tail, trying to rid itself of the heavy rain. Its eyes were ravenous and thin streams of drool dripped from both jowls. Its hunger may equal Raza's but it hated rain more. Finally, with one last vibrating growl deep in its chest, it slunk off, followed by the pack, undoubtedly planning to return with Sun the next day. Raza smiled. By then, he and Vorak would have stripped the body and left nothing but what they couldn't carry. The calf would feed his Group for many days.

The calf gave one final heave and then died. The matriarch bawled, flung her head in farewell, and plodded away. Raza grinned. This would normally draw hordes of scavengers—maybe other hominids—but the rain tamped down the odor. No one would know the carcass existed.

Rarely did Man-who-makes-tools arrive first to fresh meat. Usually, early scavengers did the hard work of penetrating the rugged hide to expose the tissues and internal organs. This time, Raza and Vorak must do it—and it took a long time. When the leg finally popped free, the males cut strips from it, passed some to Gleb, and then all stopped to eat.

Blood ran down Raza's chin and dripped to his chest as he stuffed a huge chunk in his mouth. Chewing, he wedged the bulbous end of the leg bone between his feet and slammed it with a cobble. A small chip burst loose which he discarded. Again he smashed the cobble downward, removing a long sliver, cactus spine-sharp and just as thin. After several more blows, the bone collapsed. Raza inserted the sliver into the exposed cavity, twirled deftly, and extracted the viscous marrow. He gave the stick to Vorak. When he bent sideways to tell Gleb he would get the next stickful, the youngster had passed out. Raza couldn't blame him. All day, he'd been doing an adult's work from his subadult body without complaint. It didn't matter. He'd take the next one and Gleb could have one when he awoke.

Raza was so intent on digging out the marrow, he missed the noise of feet sucking through mud, only noticing when the sound disappeared. Then he froze.

Someone is standing on the opposite side of the mammoth, Raza thought. *An upright, heavy male.* Another movement, this from the foliage off to the side. *More than one.*

Vorak heard nothing. Who would over the noise of slurping and chomping as he chewed through the fresh blood-filled tissues? Raza tightened his fist around his cutter and tensed as a Man-who-makes-tools male came into view, like Raza but different. His arms were loose at his side. His body, though huge, was gaunt. Where Raza's chest burst with muscle, the newcomer was raw-boned, almost skeletal. His frizzled hair grew long around hollow cheeks and a white streak creased the dull black. His mouth, with its cracked pale lips, gaped open but his eyes, when they met Raza's, sparkled with intelligence.

"Hraa," the stranger murmured, voice tentative, his angular face calm and devoid of menace. Raza cocked his head, unable to imagine why the male revealed himself to sturdy well-fed hunters.

"My name is Garv." His call-sign came out soft, without threat.

Vorak's head jerked up at the noise. "Aaaggh!" He shouted, dumping his meat to the ground as he leaped to his feet. He seized the closest weapon which ended up the bone sliver. The stranger named Garv stiffened but put up no defense.

"It's OK, Vorak," Raza vocalized, arm out and palm down, which awoke Gleb. The subadult jumped up, haunch high over his head, prepared to pound the intruder.

A gasp came from the foliage behind the stranger. Another male appeared, gaze moving from Gleb to Vorak and back. His skin bagged on a wasted frame. He wobbled from hunger, or fatigue, but something in his face told Raza that even exhausted, this male would defend his partner to the death. Garv pointed a raised hand to the new male without removing his eyes from Raza.

"This is Klvda," the call sign soft as he indicated the male. "I—we mean no harm!" He slouched forward and extended his hands, palms out. His light-brown skin contrasted with night-black fur. A gash the length of a hand and the thickness of a wrist festered on his thigh. He offered a slight smile and lowered his gaze, an indication of friendship among Man-who-makes-tools. Klvda kept an eye on Vorak.

Raza couldn't help but smile. *They trust each other as I do Vorak, and Lucy.* He measured the strangers for several long breaths. Something about their appearance, stature, and gestures nudged a memory.

Which was impossible. He had never met them. Man-who-makes-tools avoided others. Still, he couldn't shake the feeling. Garv watched him, seemed to read Raza's confusion. For some reason, Raza liked this male. More important, he thought he could trust him.

A shadow darkened the foliage. Vorak tensed as he stood. Even at full height, he came only to Garv's shoulders. The big stranger angled toward the shadow, still stoop-shouldered. A sibilant shush slipped through his lips.

"My Group. We tracked this Mammoth also." Garv nodded toward the calf.

When Raza said nothing, Garv beckoned and a small group of females and children stepped out of the vegetation. Their gate was shaky but they held their heads high and their eyes sparkled. There were fewer females than children, and the whole group would fit in a small piece of Baobab-by-homebase's shadow. Terror gushed from them, profuse and rank. The children clutched the females and wouldn't look at Raza. One screamed and fled, marking his trail with diarrheic scat. A female turned to Garv as though to ask, *'What now?'*

"We mean no harm to you," Garv repeated, again with the familiar open-hand gesture.

Raza considered the ragged cluster. He and Vorak were outnumbered but nothing about this assemblage struck him as treacherous. The adults stooped, legs trembling from the effort to support their meager weight. In their prime, they might have been formidable adversaries, but now Klvda seemed old and Garv worn out. Raza nodded toward Vorak and turned back to Garv.

"Sit, eat," Raza motioned, the gestures repeated by Vorak.

Garv sat across from Raza while the females and children squatted behind him. Klvda stood apart, observing, but his eyes watered and his hands shook from the mouthwatering aroma of meat.

Garv dipped his head to Raza, removed a slice of the torso, and gave it to one of the females who tore it into pieces for the children. After every female and child had food in their hands, Klvda and Garv ate. Raza was amazed at the serenity the stranger spread throughout his Group simply by his presence and actions.

Cautiously at first and then with hungry abandon, they all devoured the meat. Garv paused occasionally to observe Raza and Vorak as though evaluating what to say or do next. When everyone ate their fill, the children started poking each other and playing with the bones. Gleb edged toward tiny female, giggling at her antics. A chortle made Raza smile as the child who ran in terror a short time ago popped around Garv's bulk to grin at Gleb. Dark eyes sparkled over a pugnacious snout.

The baby mammoth was right to give up her life so this Group could live.

With hunger abated, Garv began his tale.

Chapter Twenty-nine

"We live—lived—beyond Fire Mountain. Our homebase bordered grassland that burst with berries, sprouts, nuts, corms, grubs, insects—so much food we never went hungry, even with the herds gone during the dry time. The waterhole filled all year long and the quarry could be reached within a day.

"We migrated far to find such a bounteous homebase, from a harsh world across the Rift where predators abounded and food was scarce." Raza stiffened but Garv didn't seem to notice. "We thought the benevolence of this area well-offset the danger of crossing the Rift until ..."

Garv's hands stuttered and he fell silent, his face drawn and strained. A young female with wide-set thick-lashed eyes and hair that swayed and glistened—like Lucy's—leaned over one of the children. Though her skin still retained the light color of youth, she was clearly the child's mother.

Klvda started to pick up the narrative but Garv motioned something Raza didn't understand and then continued.

"I need to tell the story of Pan, my child, and the night he and his brother didn't return home. Klvda wants to save me the hurt but I think you need to hear this from me." The female chewed her finger and the child buried his face in her lap.

"They were playing with Cousin Chimp as they often do. I didn't worry until Night Sun arrived but by then, I could do nothing. When Night Sun left and Sun returned, I went to find them." Garv touched the child whose head nestled against the female with the glistening hair.

Small's eyes were shut, thumb in his mouth. Tears seeped down Garv's face. Raza braced himself for what he knew would come next.

Garv's voice was hoarse. "I found Small, alone. He shook so badly, Sun moved a hand before he could choke out what happened. He and Pan were eating from a termite mound when Cousin Chimp screamed a warning and leaped into the trees. Before the children could escape, Man-who-preys captured them."

Raza jolted as though burned. The hand motion for the big head and long stick were unmistakable. Garv gave Raza a questioning look which Raza waved off, *First, finish, and then I'll explain.*

"One Small called 'Xha'..." this call sign came from deep in Garv's chest, "examined Pan and threw him to his partner. When he inspected Small, he flung him aside and left, Pan over his shoulder like I'd carry a carcass. When he and his partner were out of sight, Cousin Chimp shoved Small into the V of a tree trunk, and fled, squealing."

Raza shook his head. Never did his Group treat children with such violence, nor did Snarling-dog or Mammoth. All valued their young as their future. He shivered, wondering if that's how the Group's children had been treated so long ago.

Garv scratched his cheek and stared into the distance. "I promised Small I would bring his brother home. Man-who-preys had already killed so many of our males with their sticks that fly through the air," Garv lifted his arm and mimed throwing. "Only Klvda, my partner, could be spared to join me."

Misery pinched Garv's face, aging what should have been a youthful adult in his prime.

"We tracked Xha's footprints from the termite mound. He didn't hide his tracks or bury his scat, as though fearless. When we reached the homebase, it covered so much space I couldn't see from one side to the other," Garv stuttered, trying to explain the size, "with too many scents to distinguish one creature from another. They all blended into one horrid stench of blood, rot, sweat, and death."

Raza raised his palm to stop Garv. "Our Group includes as many males as have survived predator attacks during hunting and as many children and females as the males can feed and shelter."

Garv nodded. "We are the same but Man-who-preys' group filled an area as a small herd would. I've never seen a Man-who-makes-tools group that large.

"While we hid, a hunter arrived with the entire body of a small Okapi slung over his shoulder, all limbs unchewed, with one of Man-who-preys' sticks through its chest!"

Raza flashed to the deer Lucy had found. One glance told him Vorak did also. This was the same Man-who-preys they encountered. Xha must be the leader. No other animal he knew took carrion back to a homebase without lightening the load by eating first. Something niggled at his memory. In fact, he'd never seen Man-who-preys eat where they killed.

Klvda continued, voice subdued, breathing ragged. "Another Man-who-preys male arrived. He carried Qweg, a hunter from our Group, also with a stake through his chest. I thought he must be dead but he blinked. They threw him into a pile of other bodies and a female cut him open.''

He whisked tears from his eyes and picked at Mammoth's meat. "Underneath in this same pile was Pan's crushed body, his eyes sightless.''

Klvda fell silent as a shocked stillness enveloped everyone, interrupted only by a child's sniffles and a female's shss.

Garv motioned, "I went berserk. If Klvda had not held me back, I would have died there.''

Klvda grimaced as repulsion at Pan's death outweighed saving the life of his partner.

Raza gulped, unable to process what he'd just heard. They couldn't survive an attack from hunters such as these. No wonder Garv ran. Grasshoppers clicked on the dry air. Somewhere, a pig rooted in the arid earth. Cousin Chimp chattered as he prepared his nighttime nest. Garv roughed his fingers through his hair until he found the strength to continue.

"We raced back to our homebase only to find that death drenched everything like smoke from a wildfire. Blood as thick as mud coated the ground. Only those you see here survived.''

His hands spoke the word for 'dead', but not the usual motions for a life's end. Everyone accepted death from Cat or Fire Mountain as part of life, but Garv's movements included the 'violence' that Raza would forever associate with Man-who-preys.

"We fled, stopping for nothing. When the children tired, we carried them. When we exhausted our food, we ate what we could harvest while running. This mammoth is our first meat in… a while…''

Sometime during the tale, the children fell asleep. Garv met Raza's gaze. "They feel secure here, among you.''

Above them, thunder rumbled. What Raza must say would destroy the tentative security this courageous male garnered for his Group.

"They kill here, too

Chapter Thirty

By the time Raza finished the stories of his Group's experiences with Man-who-preys, Night Sun's pale disk and the twinkling lights it traveled with had made their way into the dark sky. Everyone found places to slumber—Raza, Vorak, and Gleb in ground nests and Garv's Group in the trees.

The combined Group left for Raza's homebase as soon as Sun peeked over the horizon. Despite his weakness, Garv shouldered both Mammoth haunches. Raza and Vorak each hoisted a foreleg and Klvda bore what he could, limping on an injured leg. Each female bounced a child on her hip. Gleb scouted ahead and invisibly.

Raza set a fast pace, the speed of stalking-Snarling-dog but slowed when Garv's hunger-weakened group fell behind. To offset the slowness, they traveled steadily without stopping to rest or drink. Garv gave Raza an odd look when Raza shared succulents from his neck sack.

"You use this?" He asked, pointing to the sack around Raza's neck.

"It's from Lucy, my pairmate."

Garv nodded but said nothing else.

Raza motioned across the flatland to a dense thicket of reed, cattails, and bunchgrasses. "A waterhole. We'll rest."

The females collapsed but watched the children with one eye and the beasts who shared the pond with the other. A rhinoceros, his enormous uplifted horn weathered and beaten with age, drank to one side. His benign exterior—an oversized body supported by short stocky legs—lulled others into a false sense of security but Raza knew from experience not to anger the beast. With skin too thick to penetrate and a brain unable to quit even a hopeless fight, he was a tenacious adversary.

When the rhinoceros finished, the Group took its place, squeezed between a family of Gazelle and an old scarred Mammoth. The water slid down Raza's parched throat, refreshing and cool. Done, he rested in the shade of a nearby tree while the children giggled and splashed in the shallow water, their problems forgotten.

Until a log that floated toward them blinked.

Raza bawled a warning as he sprinted toward Aqa, a child from Garv's Group, furthest into the pond and oblivious to the beast about to take her life. Raza's feet dug deep holes into the soft earth, chest pounding, but he was still too far away when the leathery snout popped open and spewed the rancid stink of decomposed flesh over everything. Aqa twitched at the stench, turning to see where it came from. No matter how hard Raza ran, how loud his howls of frustration, a child who had survived Man-who-preys now would die to feed Crocodylus.

And then, something streaked past him in a blur of churning legs and pumping arms. It was Gleb.

Raza yelled, "No!" Aqa could not be saved and Gleb

would die trying to do the impossible. He had never faced Crocodylus before. Raza pushed harder, desperate now to save both Aqa and Gleb, but it proved unnecessary. Gleb snatched the child fearlessly from Crocodylus' mouth and rolled away, the snap of jaws barely missing him. The vacant orbs stared in disbelief and the long body receded soundlessly from the shore. The other drinkers around the pond glanced at the commotion but did nothing, content Crocodylus ate elsewhere.

"Aqa thinks we play." Gleb motioned as he hugged the child, but his hands shook and his lip quivered.

Garv ran forward, panting, face pale, neck hair on end, eyes bright with emotion.

"I am thankful." He patted Gleb with a trembling hand, leaving Aqa to play with her new friend, and trudged away.

The male's head drooped and then his whole body shook. Again, Raza had felt what this stranger did. They had much in common.

Vorak interrupted the scene. "Snarling-dog has noticed our carrion."

Raza shouted, "Let's go," happy for the distraction. Everyone gathered their loads and hurried away. Aqa gripped Gleb's hand, face canted upward. Raza grinned. Children needed mentors.

***

From his spot atop Tallest-boulder, well above the sweltering grassland, Ma-g'n often caught the occasional breeze but today, during the hottest of the dry times, the heat was windless. The simple act of breathing felt like standing by a grass fire.

Most of the Group sat in the pond or the shade a tree, but here he stayed, worrying more with each breath. From this height, he could see across to the outcropping of rocks and the bluffs that marked the edge of the Group's territory. That provided plenty of notice if strangers approached the homebase. Today, though, he hoped to see the last group of hunters. The blistering sun had driven every savanna creature into its den, cave, nest, or wherever it could avoid Sun's heat. All of the hunting teams had returned long ago except for Raza, Vorak, and Gleb.

Ma-g'n squinted toward the horizon, as he'd done over and over, twisting a finger absently through the tangled strands of his ear. Where were they? Besides being too hot to hunt, the night birds had already begun their serenade. Cousin Chimp would soon tuck into tree nests, and Hyaena-dog would announce the start of his nightly hunt.

Surely the best hunters in the Group would return before that.

Finally, a blur appeared at the furthest edge of his vision. It bobbed up and down as though hurrying. It must be the hunters, ignoring everything they knew about safety in an effort to reach homebase before light dissolved into darkness. He chirruped their arrival, thought about sending some of the returned hunters out to help when the blur widened to what must be more than Raza, Vorak, and Gleb. One individual— he couldn't yet tell who—bent under the weight of carrion while supporting another so weak he staggered more than ran. They were followed by bedraggled males and weary females with children on their hips. Bringing up the rear, Ma-g'n recognized Gleb, his hand in that of a skipping child who bounced as she gazed up into the subadult's face, grinning as she clung to his arm.

By the time the large party passed Tallest-boulder, homebase overflowed with Groupmembers eager to greet the hunters, see the scavenge, and find out about the strangers. The Group didn't want new members, couldn't feed them.

Lucy was the last addition and before her, Ma-g'n himself. Raza knew that, as did Vorak, so why did they travel with these beaten-down creatures?

Ma-g'n's gaze returned to one of the males, as big as any Man-who-makes-tools' he'd ever seen. He would be intimidating if not for his wasted frame. Despite that, he slumped under the weight of a mammoth haunch on each shoulder. No one could carry that much yet he did. In him, Ma-g'n sensed power and confidence. It infused his body and leaked from his worn face. Something about his stance, the eagerness in his movements nibbled at memories, but he couldn't connect it to anything. Could he have seen him during his time with the chimps? Ma-g'n took a step forward, head canted, fingers twirling through his shredded ear, and felt a tingle. He pieced it together just as Raza called out.

"Garv!"

Ma-g'n glanced over his shoulder, toward the lake, wondering if Lucy heard.

Lucy swooshed Voi through Lake-by-home-base, back and forth and back again as he giggled and squirmed. A high-pitched whoop announced Raza's return. Lucy turned, assaulted by the smell of Raza, Vorak, Gleb, and other odors she automatically sorted through. They came from the strangers who arrived with Raza. Something about them put her on edge. Voi took advantage of the distraction to wriggle from her grasp but Lucy snatched him before he even got out of the cattail beds. A scent floated under her nostrils, an odor she associated with her old group. She tried to place it but excitement over the wealth of food Raza and Vorak brought, what must be an entire Mammoth, sidetracked her.

Lucy fingered cool water through her fur, a brief respite from the relentless heat, but she couldn't shake the uneasy feeling. Maybe because Raza never welcomed strangers and here he brought so many to the core of the homebase. She'd ask Sahn. Maybe they were here at her direction, like Lucy herself had been.

There she was, with Raza, eyes fixed on his face, feet spread beneath her squat short figure. So it had been planned.

"Sahn," she called. The elder turned and her face drained of color. Lucy hurried toward her afraid Sahn might collapse. "What's wrong?"

Lucy's hand tightened around her chopper and her muscles tensed as a male stepped in front of Sahn. How could he look familiar—

Her knees trembled. Her belly cramped and her hands shook. Blinking changed nothing. She watched powerlessly as Garv's focus moved from person to person. It stuttered at the sight of stick-that-kills leaning against the cliff and then continued. With a nod, he acknowledged his new groupmates one by one, until his eyes settled on Lucy. There, he stopped, face ashen.

"I thought you were dead."

Chapter Thirty-one

Lucy swatted at the cloud of buzzing mosquitos drawn by the sweat that leeched through her fur. Feq plummeted down the vertical wall of the Rift, chasing Garv, Lucy's intended pairmate. He never caught up but that didn't mean he wouldn't try. Lucy answered Garv's jaunty wave with one of her own. His ample mane bobbed behind his body, a white streak etched above his brow.

"Be careful, Garv!" The male's future belonged to her and their children. The bond was irreversible.

She shivered, wishing Garv hadn't discounted the dark clouds at the horizon, their shadows already descending the Rift walls, the wetness building around them even as Garv and Feq plunged deeper into the canyon.

The sky boomed and then, at the furthest end of the Rift, a wall of water appeared, roaring toward her.

"Garv! Feq! It's a flash flood!"

Feq turned and scrambled up but Garv was too far into the Rift to see what bore down on him.

In the time it took Garv to wonder at Feq's retreat, rain-that-floods dumped from the sky. Lucy's mouth moved but Garv heard only the water as it thundered through the canyon and caromed from side to side in its eagerness to drown the trapped male. *Within moments, his tentative grip slipped and he plunged into the stormy waters. The cold bit into his skin and he dropped to the gravelly bottom, bounced off the balls of his feet, and surfaced, gasping, and scrambled for a handhold. The raging water slammed him into a rock and dragged him under again as though he were a fly caught in a windstorm. He pushed upward only to sink again.*

His entire survival plan became holding his breath until he could reach the surface where he would gag and choke, flail wildly against the current, be battered by every boulder in the water's path, and go under before starting the process over again. Lucy's frantic figure bounded along the precipice, chasing him downstream until she ran out of room. She screamed as yet another wall of water smashed him against the canyon floor. He clawed upward and managed to choke in a taste of air.

Now Lucy was well behind him. Her mouth opened and her arms flapped, but the hammering tide continued to push him down the Rift. There—a tiny tree had been uprooted and bent into the violent water. With every bit of his remaining strength, he seized it and jerked to a stop—for an instant, until the roots pulled from the ground and the trunk with him attached lurched down the valley and around a switchback. He lost his hold and tumbled over and over, surging water foaming around him. At one point, he plunged over a cliff and into another rushing torrent. The force of the waterfall threw him to the bottom of the river bed. He pushed off feebly, arms flailing for the surface. He didn't think he would last much longer.

"So it ends here," he thought mildly as he stopped struggling and let the water crash around him, the vicious whitecaps thrusting him down and bouncing him along the jagged bottom until his numb brain gave up.

Feq clung to a narrow ridge, wet and cold, his insignificant physique almost invisible in the torrents.

"I'll get help!" Lucy motioned and ran for Old One.

"Feq and Garv. Feq again, but why Garv…" Old One muttered. Sunlight sparkled on the wet vegetation, the flash flood just a memory. Feq tried to climb Rift's face, but the wetness made his grip slippery and loose.

"Stay," Old One commanded with absentminded authority, and departed.

As shadows lengthened, Old One came into view on the valley floor. She walked slowly, collecting dead shrubs and twigs as she stepped. When she reached Feq, she piled it all into a tall heap and pointed from it to Feq. He shook his head and she began to walk away so he leaped from his narrow ledge into the springy scrub and—to Lucy's surprise—bobbed up. He scrambled to his feet and scampered after Old One.

But Garv was never seen again and grief swallowed Lucy's world.

Chapter Thirty-two

Boah, well-hidden within the periphery trees, peered across the scrubland. He scratched the lice behind his ear, swatted the gnats that swarmed his face and chest, and crouched contentedly to watch the loud hominids forage for food. He liked the female he met at the firestorm. Something he couldn't describe made him trust her, a feeling he'd never felt before and lacked the words or gestures to explain.

Earlier, the males from her Group walked right under Boah's tree, laden with a carcass and oblivious to the menace of passing through Cheetah's space. They survived only because Cheetah wasn't in her usual spot atop an abandoned termite mound. Since then, Cheetah had returned. He hoped the female's group would stay away.

Just as Boah decided he might as well return to Shee who would groom these itchy bugs from his fur, a gazelle, dappled coat rich in color, wandered into Cheetah's space. She nibbled sprouts, shaking her delicate head between bites. Downwind and hidden from view by the trees, Cheetah dozed, fur speckled with blood from a recent kill, paws dripping over the sides of the monstrous termite mound, a perfect position to observe everything around her. She probably wasn't hungry, sated by the earlier meal, but the aroma of Gazelle drifting across her nostrils awakened her. She turned just enough, eyes unblinking slits, but she didn't need to see it. Her nose found the scent trail and her tongue tasted it.

Boah grunted to himself as Cheetah slithered down the hill. He appreciated Cat's quiet approach as each paw moved soundlessly forward.

Gazelle has no idea her life is over.

Cheetah tracked Gazelle, remaining downwind and moving so smoothly the grass didn't even sway, imprinting in her mind the position of the soon-to-be-dead creature. When the herd had drifted too far away to provide security, Cheetah veered to the side and cut off Gazelle's escape.

Now she moved in, padding forward when the ungulate lowered her head to chew and pausing when she lifted it. Boah warned these beasts in the past but they ignored his coughs. Today, he settled on a comfortable limb, chewed on a large root, and watched. Experience told him there would be meat left over for him.

Like Gazelle, Cheetah blended into the early season wheat and forbs and the dark line that extended from her orbital ridge to her jaw matched the dead stalks around her. Cheetah stepped forward and then hesitated. She wouldn't start the chase unless confident she could bring Gazelle down quickly.

Gazelle raised her head, stood stiffly, neck arched, ears twitching. She twisted to see what her nose found. Her body quivered at Cheetah's scent, a gazelle's nightmare.

You are too late.

In a full sprint, Gazelle could outrun every animal alive. Except Cheetah.

Cheetah continued her slow walk toward the deer. A

reflexive hiss, one Boah heard only spoken by Cheetah, whispered her hunt.

Your herd won't save you.

A moment passed, a flick of her eyelid, a twitch of her ears and whisk of her tail and Gazelle fled. Cheetah went from plodding to full speed in a blink. Muscular leg muscles churned the sleek body toward her prey, beautiful in her pure economy of motion and strength.

Sprinting, long tail stretching from side to side to counterbalance her body weight, Cheetah overtook Gazelle and tripped her with a dewclaw. The tumble broke Gazelle's leg. Still, she tried to rise but the feline took Gazelle's throat in her mighty jaws, suffocating the animal, waiting for death to replace life. Whiskers twitching, Cheetah held. The gazelle squirmed, kicked, and stilled. Cheetah's eyes drooped as she panted.

Boah would wait.

Cheetah hauled the carcass to the shade and tore into it, emitting an occasional purr of contentment as she ate. Hunger slaked, she chirped *ihn-ihn* to call her youngsters. When she received no response, she left to collect the kittens.

Now is my turn.

Boah descended, waddled over to the dead gazelle, and yanked a leg loose and then a handful of ribs. A low rumble stopped him in place. He tipped his head and met Cheetah's feral gaze. Without looking away, he gauged whether he could reach the trees before Cheetah killed him.

Not without a distraction.

Cheetah slapped the ground with her paws and hissed as she prepared to destroy yet another bothersome prey. Boah howled and flung the haunch at the feline. It bounced off her delicate muzzle. She shook her head which gave Boah just enough time to escape to the lowest branch of a nearby tree.

Cheetah purred a final warning and reclaimed the purloined leg for her cubs.

Boah ate the ribs he'd managed to hang on to. If there were leftovers, he would take them to Hee and Shee. As he chewed, he watched the bipeds pause at Cheetah's call, sniff, and—satisfied that Cheetah hunted far away—return to foraging.

What odd weak creatures, with big heads and narrow bodies, unable to climb trees with dexterity or perambulate with any speed. How do they endure?

Chapter Thirty-three

Raza again asked Lucy to hunt with him. She wanted to, had planned to, but then Garv arrived. She couldn't stand the thought of so much time around the male she had never forgotten. She didn't know what to say or how to act so chose to avoid him, spending her time instead with Sahn learning to read the skies. Still, seeing Garv every night, conferring with Raza, took its toll. Her actions became distracted and muddled and sleep, what she got, was restless.

Raza finally insisted she talk to Garv. He knew their history and didn't care. His interest remained, as always, the safety of the Group and right now, Lucy made herself a vulnerability.

The opportunity presented itself when Garv's pairmate left with Falda to forage and Lucy stayed behind to prepare a poultice for a spider-bit Baad. She saturated a leaf in water and coated it with granules scraped from her white blocks. Then, she wrapped it crust side down over the bite, added a layer of damp leaves, and told Baad to sit still until she returned.

Against her will, she clumped across the clearing to where Garv sat alone. The memory of his broad strong chest against hers, the intoxication of his skin rubbing her skin, the sensation of their bodies together gnawed at her like rodent's fangs. Her chest heaved and her eye twitched, something that started when Garv died and stopped when she pairmated with Raza. Why had it returned?

Garv looked up from his knapping, gaze soft, head tipped as though expecting her. She rubbed her damp hands over her hair to dry them and pointed to the puckered scar that extended from Garv's hip to mid-thigh, remnants of the wound that once threatened his life.

"I-I wanted to check your leg ... It looks better." She taught his pairmate to fill the cut with a mixture of herbs and honey, wrap it with fronds, and reapply as needed.

Her resolve crumpled and a tear rolled down her cheek. "I thought you were gone. Forever."

He fingered the furrowed crevice over his eye, so deep Lucy could bury a twig in it.

"I tried... I couldn't get back after the flash flood. I don't even know how I reached shore." His head dipped and he studied the cutter in his lap, only partially knapped. "When I awoke, my head burned with buried cactus spikes. Every movement, pain drove me to the ground. I coated the gash with dung," to conceal the smell of blood from Snarling-dog and Panther, "and tried to retrace my steps," his hand motions added, *to you*. "But I was so dizzy and nauseous, I passed out, over and over until I no longer knew where I was much less where I needed to be. I couldn't think of anything to do other than crawl into a tree and wait until I recovered. The next thing I remember was Klvda stabbing at me with a stick to wake me. He pointed to the blood on the ground, making it clear any predator would find me, and motioned I follow him. We ended up at his homebase where they took care of me until I got my strength back.

"I owe him my life." Head hanging, he paused. The Garv Lucy knew never wanted to be in anyone's debt, especially not for his life, but once obligated, he would work until it was repaid. No wonder he had stayed with this new Group.

After a moment, he continued. "I asked Klvda about my Group—you—but he didn't know where you were. When he invited me into his Group, I accepted."

This time when he paused, he looked deeply into Lucy's eyes, trying to say something he didn't want to be put into words. After a moment, he blinked and shrugged. "When they decided to leave their homebase, to flee Man-who-preys by crossing the Rift, I gave up ever again seeing you."

She started to tell him how long she searched for him, how losing him tore her world apart, how she cared nothing for Ghael or Raza only him, but stopped when his pairmate arrived and squatted, face lowered, pounding a fistful of rhizomes.

"Lucy." Ma-g'n. "Voi needs you."

Lucy's head spun. She had so much more to tell Garv but today's time had passed. She took Voi from Ma-g'n's outstretched arms and held him so the baobab mark showed. When she glanced up to motion farewell, Garv stared at it, as did his pairmate. Lucy shoved some of Ma-g'n's Pain-bark into Garv's hand.

"This will help," and left, Voi on her hip, Ma-g'n leading. Voi twisted toward Garv and didn't turn back until the male disappeared from sight.

"What do I say, Ma-g'n?" Her hands spoke low on her body but she couldn't stop the tears that covered her face.

"Garv sees Raza cares for you and Voi. He will not interfere."

"It hurts, Ma-g'n. It still hurts."

***

The intoxicating odor that had filled the air the last time Night Sun was full, part thick heavy dung, part the fragrant flowers that bloomed after the rains, but primarily the blood and fluid of fragile newborns, had now gone, as had the herds. Now, the savanna smelled of decaying vegetation, dirt, and dust. The air had become almost too hot to breathe and the clouds nothing more than filmy white shadows. The tiny waterholes that spotted the savanna and the flatlands quickly withered and disappeared and then, when the streams that replenished the larger ponds dried to a trickle, so too did they. Lake-where-children-play became nothing more than a shallow pool of yellow-brown mud. The reed beds that bordered it, always a dependable source of food, shriveled and died which meant the dawn screams of birds no longer woke Lucy. With nowhere to clean themselves, the stink of the Group's unwashed bodies and the reek of their waste filled the homebase.

The herds would not return until the air cooled more each night than the night before and Sun stayed away longer than the day before. Lucy and everyone in the Group spent most of their time simply trying to survive.

"They found nothing," Kelda whined as the males stumbled in empty-handed.

Lucy spotted Raza at the front of a dispirited group. His eyes reproached her, *if you were with us, we would have meat.* She should take cool leaves to Raza but instead sat back on her haunches, sweltering, and wiped a hand across her wet brow as Sun mercilessly leeched what energy remained in her body from the weak diet of vegetables and roots.

"He is tired." Her motions indicated that 'tired' included 'frustrated', though emotion had no meaning to Lucy.

Sahn thwacked the ground, stabbed the hard soil with her digger, and sat back on her haunches with a sigh. "The earth is tired, too. These dry days are worse than before."

Lucy had lived here long enough to notice the changes to the land, too. The water was lower in the rivers, no longer even covering her ankles. This meant poor grazing which drove what remained of the herds further away.

Raza had been watching Sahn and now motioned, "We leave when Sun awakes."

No one wanted to migrate in the heat of the dry times but they had no choice. They must find food or starve.

Somewhere, Cheetah called her cubs. Lucy jerked her head toward Voi where he sat cheerfully with the other children, and relaxed.

He was safe.

Chapter Thirty-four

While Man-who-makes-tools prepared to migrate, desperate to find a homebase without shrinking herds and dried-up water holes, Xha's group flourished. They dominated everyone who crossed their path, took what they wanted and left nothing.

Xha, though, wanted Lucy. By the time he made the decision to kidnap her, and visited her homebase and the local waterholes, she had left, her passage erased from the rock-hard ground by time and the dusty wind.

Xha stared into the distance, seeing nothing, thinking. Lucy must eat. He knew where to look next.

The combined Group set out with Sun's return, pleasantly surprised by the cool morning. The children made a game of hopping from one clump of scrub to another. Shade was rare, mostly from scrawny thorn trees and those widely-spaced. Lucy watched for a baobab which would lead her to underground water. She found one and the Group rested while Lucy and others dug down deeper than her arm but finally reached water. They then soaked leaves in the sweet liquid, stuffed them in the neck sacks, and set off again.

Sun came and went and Night Sun shrank to nothing and began rebuilding itself and still they walked. When the smallest children tired of walking, the oldest carried them. The adults didn't complain even when the only food was dry moss and short tufts of tasteless grass flavored with the rare scorpion and the rarer snake. They simply followed in Raza's prints as he led them to each of the former homebases. When all stunk of Man-who-preys, no one argued as they moved on.

While the Group slept, exhausted from both walking and desperation, Sahn didn't. Instead, showing none of the worry she must feel, she traced Night Sun's movements, how it swelled and shrank, and the location of the tiny lights that shared the great orb's habitat. Never were they in the same place as the night before and never the same proximity to each other. She took note of the spin of the night sky and drew connections. Every morning, Raza adjusted the direction they would travel based on her observations.

One day, they arrived at a location many thought to be perfect. Melodic chirps floated through the sky. Flowers peppered the landscape, dense with butterflies the children happily chased. A waterhole shimmered, sparkling and cool. In the not-too-far distance loomed one of Fire Mountain's cousins which meant a quarry for the all-important hard rocks. Raza called a rest to the travel and Sahn set up her shadow stick.

The females and children spread out to forage from the abundant berries and fruits while the males explored. Over a rise, close enough to the Group's temporary homebase that it could be reached before Sun went to sleep, they found vast open fields of thick grass littered with skeletons of buffalo and mammoth; the dung of gazelle and Wild-beasts; and to the side of the clearing, the abandoned dens of Long-tooth and her kind, Snarling-dog, and his cousin Great-dog. Even those who thought nothing would make the female Sahn happy nodded approval. She had been right after all. This was the best of all the locations.

After Night Sun had shrunk, disappeared, and regrown, Raza approached Sahn while the rest of the travelers waited, tired and hopeful, no one doubting Sahn would approve of this glorious spot. Except Lucy. She had found trace of Man-who-preys. Though old, well-covered by debris and refuse, if they were voting, she'd cast one to leave.

Raza motioned to the Primary-female, "Here we have a pond, a quarry, and meat."

Sahn closed her eyes, swayed side to side with her hands pressed to the ground. After many breaths, she shook her head. That's all Raza needed.

"We leave when Sun returns."

"Why?" came an angry retort.

Lucy answered for Raza. "I found trace of Man-who-preys. We must escape his territory."

Someone snorted. "It's old," and added, "If we were alone, we would stay here." Another voice asked, "Why should we follow you?"

Raza didn't answer. Why would he? He spoke for himself, no one else. Many in Garv's group grumbled their agreement with the comments. They had no appetite for continuing. Worries about Man-who-preys had been left far behind and they lacked the trust in Sahn's guidance that Raza's Group depended upon like a protective dung coat.

Raza nodded. "I understand. Anyone who wishes can come with us," and then walked away to give each individual time to make their own decision.

The next day, with Sun still too new to burn off the early morning chill, Raza motioned his Group onto the forward trail and then paused just outside the temporary homebase to give those who would join him time to do so. Most of the original Group did though several elders blamed aching knees for why they must stay. Brum was the first surprise, though not to Raza. Brum realized the stay-behind group, with just Klvda and Garv, wouldn't have enough males to protect and feed the females and children. He had talked to Raza who shared information that clenched Brum's decision. He would help the stay-behind group get settled and return to Raza's Group when that was done. The scar on his battered face pulsed, his eyes fixed on Raza as he said goodbye to a male he trusted like no other.

Brum's son Gleb of course would stay, as an adult. He was as big and powerful as any male except Garv and had shown his skill in hunting. Brum would teach him everything he needed as quickly as possible. At Gleb's side stood tiny Aqa, clinging to his hand. She had become his shadow since he saved her life and now bounced with joy that he would stay. Kaavrm would stay also, claiming he would pairmate one of the females though no female joined him.

And then Lucy wilted. Yes, one more male would make a huge difference to the stay-behind Group but if Ma-g'n joined Garv's Group, it left her Group weaker. She approached him, intent on changing his mind but then changed hers. Each must make their own choice, for their own reasons. Lucy had planned to begin hunting again with Raza once they settled. She'd told Ma-g'n this. He certainly weighed this into his decision.

She pushed all of her Pain-bark into his hands. "Take this. You will find more," and with a sweep of her arm explained where. Her calmness couldn't hide her grief.

"I must stay, Lucy," and he pointed to Raza's Group. When Lucy turned, there stood Garv, shoulder almost touching Raza's, feet spread, eyes fixed on the faces he would leave forever. That included his hunt partner, pairmate, and remaining child. Lucy didn't understand his decision but breathed a quiet sigh of relief. Raza relied on Garv's wisdom, as did she.

Garv walked over to his pairmate, hands moving in intricate signals but she turned away, face troubled, body stooped. Garv crouched in front of Small and smiled into his child's frightened gaze. He patted and shushed him which seemed to help. As they left, Gleb lifted Small high into the air in a final salute to Garv until the bobbing figure dissolved into the browns and oranges of aged boulders and dried flowers.

The downsized Group, led now by Raza, Vorak, and Garv, moved ever onward. Raza avoided the faster but more obvious animal routes, choosing paths that hid their passage-- rough ground broken with trenches, craters, and scrub grasses through a landscape of sage and agave, over low hills with open scrub and sparse shade. Lucy scrambled up steep inclines overgrown with tasteless blackberries which she nevertheless picked clean, caring nothing for flavor, only for nourishment. Often using Stick-that-kills for balance, she slipped down eroded banks covered with weeds and scrubbrush, over one hillock after another, and around more boulders than she'd ever seen in her life. Once, she tripped over a rock into a crevasse filled with tangled roots and barely managed to claw her way out, even with stick-that-kills as leverage. Dust cloaked every leaf and blade, even her teeth and inside her nose. Cousin Chimp's pant-hoots or silence told her what she needed to know about predators.

Lucy, unlike Falda and Kelda, cheered that they had moved on. She didn't care about scratches and bruises or tired muscles as long as they escaped Man-who-preys. She didn't care even when prickle bush spines dug into her skin and palms. She extracted them without slowing, briskly wiping away sweat that dripped over her protruding brow and down her cheeks. She prepared for the worst by practicing with stick-that-kills every time they stopped to sleep.

Everyone worked as they traveled. Young Yoo gathered grasshoppers. The child Dar, excited to help, dug worms out from under tree bark or buried in deadfall and stuffed them in her small neck sack but to her dismay, it was always empty. Yoo laughed and showed her how to kill the wriggling creatures before they could escape. At times, the Group's only food was hard tree sap. Sucked, it tasted sweet and made them feel full.

When Sun's light gave way to darkness, the Group crowded together against a cliff or around the trunk of a tree, or a boulder if that's all they could find, and surrounded themselves with a barrier of thorn bushes. They slept facing out so someone would always see the approach of a predator.

"Lucy. Voivoi cut himself. Will this heal it?"

The youngers had chased each other's shadows, leaping from one dark blob to another and dodging crevices while they frolicked alongside the adults. No surprise Voivoi tumbled. The surprise was Voi hadn't also.

Falda held out a plant with small leaf tips and purple berries. Fleshy white roots clumped under the long stem. Lucy tossed it aside.

"I've told you before these are toxic." Lucy rubbed her eyes, too tired to care about the wounded look on her friend's face. She reached into her neck sack, pulled out a thick leaf and pulped it. She wiped the paste on Falda's fingers and motioned, "Dab this on his scratch."

Without another thought, she turned away, dark and

lonely without Ma-g'n to talk with. She hadn't realized how much she depended upon his friendship and his counsel. Some days, all she could do was trudge forward, search for enemies, stick-that-kills in her hand and Voi on her hip. She had no idea if they were leaving or entering Man-who-preys' homeland, moving away from or closer to the threat, and nothing she found gave her an answer. While she could move invisibly by herself, hiding her tracks on beds of rock and desiccated ground, the size of the Group made it impossible. If Man–who-preys wanted to follow them, he would have no problem doing so.

Fire Mountain must have seen her distress and assisted by belching a violent explosion that cloaked the ground with ash. Rain immediately followed which turned the ash into muddy sludge, concealing their prints from predators. When Sun broke through the dark clouds, as hot and relentless as ever, it baked the muck into a hard surface, burying the Group's passage where no creature would find it.

Lucy couldn't help but smile.

"Like this, Voi."

As rain poured down, Lucy collected water in a leaf rounded by the palm of her hand and then tipped it into her mouth. They found no waterholes this day or the prior day or the one before that. Lucy's throat was parched and her tongue felt like the fluffy inside of Cattail. The eldest and youngest suffered most and the shower proved a gift. They shrieked with joy as the sheets of water washed the salt and dirt from their fur and cooled their hot skin. It stung their faces but no one cared. Raza tried to quiet the excitement but gave up. No one would hear them anyway over the patter of drops on the desiccated ground, a sound like the slapping of hands on a hollowed-out trunk.

Voi watched Lucy and then shaped a small frond into his palm. When rain filled its natural bowl, he poured it into his mouth and waved his short arms in excitement.

She fingered water through his fur until it glistened with health.

"Now show Voivoi."

The elders showed the youngers, who showed friends. That was how they thrived.

Lucy loved rain. Not only did it wash her fur but it rinsed the Group's odor from the backtrail. Head tilted back, she let the drops pound against her face.

"Lucy—a tree frog!"

Ahnda joined her. Life had whittled away his roundness and replaced it with the lean build of a subadult. Though he still looked miserable without Gleb, he accepted the adult responsibilities required of him with so many males gone.

"Good catch, Ahnda," and she bit into the frog above its forelegs, removed the head and innards with a snap, spit them out, and shared the body with him. "You have grown up."

Ahnda straightened his back, raised his jaw, and courage rumbled from his body. He thumped his hand against his leg and hummed as he breathed in the richness of wet earth.

When all the travelers did was walk, search, walk, eat, forage, and walk, boredom became a perilous enemy. That's when the worst injuries and deadliest attacks occurred. Raza constantly examined the edging trees and the far-off horizon while Baad and Vorak searched beside and to the back. Ahnda and Garv scouted somewhere ahead. The only ones unaffected by this were the children who still giggled and dodged, catching shadows.

Raza froze. *That noise didn't belong.* He hissed and everyone melted to the ground like dying smoke. Only the slight bend of the fronds gave away their presence and then even that faded.

The forest stilled, a sure sign trouble lurked. Raza bored into the dark green of the trees. A snake slithered over his foot and Spider chased a beetle, their lives unaffected by the prowling Uprights. A Tree-man group ranged through the stout branches. Alarm flashed across the male's face and then his mouth twitched. What did he see? The intelligent eyes blinked and settled on Raza, willing him to remain still.

Something crunched, behind Raza the distance of a well-thrown stone. Slowly, Raza turned, arms tense, prepared for flight, searching for the animal that made the noise...

Chapter Thirty-five

Easy prey.

Long-tooth hugged the ground, well-hidden amidst the browns and yellows of the savanna. These odd beasts didn't scamper or scream when attacked like the Tree-men did and they always stood upright, visible from wherever Long-tooth lay.

Long-tooth eyed a tall male in the back of the pack. She would wait for his pride to move out of range and then with a feral roar, sink her canines into the slender neck at the exposed base of the skull.

Easy prey.

She crouched and waited. A breath, and several more. Long-tooth preferred Tree-man with his thicker if not softer meat but he escaped, now hunkered out of her reach.

She matched the creature's steps until she sensed the arrival of the kill moment. She rose like a mist, hackles up, and sprang, snarling her most fulsome growl, the one that terrorized her prey and made them freeze in the face of death. That gave her the extra moments she needed to attack.

But the creature didn't freeze. Instead, he leaped at her, roaring and brandishing a stout branch Long-tooth hadn't seen. Another from his pride, a female she thought too far away to help, flew toward Long-tooth as a sound exploded from her mouth. As her lethal claws and piercing canines stabbed forward, a vicious whack to her head stunned her.

Her jaws relaxed and she tumbled onto her side. Her vision grayed and her head spun. She shook, trying to regain her balance, and the stick struck again, shattering her deadly scimitar-shaped canine. She yelped and lights blinked in front of her. The stick flew up again but Long-tooth managed to dodge it and stumble away, wobbling as her 'prey' shrieked and howled.

Marshalling the last of her strength, she fled, trying to put as much space as possible between herself and these creatures before collapsing.

A sure meal turned into near-death. She would remember this.

Chapter Thirty-six

Lucy paused to rest atop yet another of the berms that towered over the endless grassland. She breathed deeply, favoring the foot that had been cut by a sharp rock hidden under debris. She'd swathed it in honey and wrapped it in a leaf but even with tendons, she couldn't keep the compress from wearing off. It wasn't just her. Everyone had some sort of injury. Nights, before Lucy went to sleep, she spent with her healing herbs taking care of one wound after another.

There in front of her, glistening under Sun's bright light, sparkled a pool. It was too small to attract many drinkers but sufficient for the Group's needs. Tussock grass surrounded it. Trees shaded one side and a depression to the rear formed a natural food cache. A family of wild-beasts moved along a shimmering stream where the Group would find the fine-grained rocks required to create tools. The proximity of Fire Mountain promised a nearby quarry.

Could this be the end of the non-stop walking?

Sahn walked calmly down the berm and across the plateau to a stubby cliff. Here, she flattened herself to the ground, aged face caressing the dirt, arms extended, hands moving gently palm down, fingers scratching. While she worked, Lucy jogged one direction around the area, Raza the other, both searching for signs of Man-who-preys—his scat, footprints, indentation of his stick, or his smell.

She trotted back to Raza's side and shook her head, as did he. When Sahn finally raised her eyes to Sun, a smile hovered over her lips.

Raza motioned, "We have found a new homebase."

The Group heaved a sigh, as much from fatigue as delight, and hurried about the business of setting up the camp. Sun already dipped below the horizon so preparations would be quick. The males made a cursory barrier with urine, one they'd fortify the next day. The females collected water-laden reeds while the children surrounded the sleeping area with thistle bushes, spiny side out and weighted down with rocks. Finished for the day, everyone tucked in to sleep in a pile of shared heat, tired but content.

Lucy, though, lay awake, listening to Garv's rhythmic snores and reassured by Raza's leg against hers. Barren branches sketched black shapes on the horizon. The groans and grunts of a hippo as it settled into the muck comforted her as did the whispers of night animals, the brush of coyote through the grass, the howl of Hyaena-dog, and the hoot of night-owl as it located prey. She stood and climbed outside the sleep barrier, walking into the expanding dark, cheered that much in Night Sun's sky remained the same.

When Sun returned with her light and warmth, Lucy went to find Sahn. The elder had already cleared an area to the side for her shadow-stick. There she sat, feet tucked under her body, denuding a slender twig. Lucy lowered herself and watched as the elder smoothed away every rough patch.

It relieved Lucy that Sahn found peace at New-homebase.

"Today, we begin to memorize each bush and fruit tree, who lives here, where to find termite mounds, and where the vegetables and herbs grow."

Sahn leaned toward Lucy. "You have other duties," and pointed overhead, telling Lucy when Sun reached that point, the males would leave to mark the territory.

Lucy packed her neck sack with edibles, picked up stick-that-kills, and trotted to the meadow by New-homebase. There, she practiced throwing until she could no longer raise her arm. Her dream came back—the swell of aggression as she plunged stick-that-kills into the hapless mammoth calf, the savage power and confidence that filled her body and spewed from her mouth. She lost herself in it as always and pushed herself beyond what she thought possible.

Panting, arm aching, body damp with sweat, she glanced upward. To her surprise, Sun had reached the point Sahn indicated would be when the males left. Lucy would join them, not to set the confines of their area but to explore it. Quickly, she slathered sap over the raw sores on her hands and hurried back to homebase. Raza, Vorak, and Garv were just leaving. Lucy patted Voi's head, scratched behind his ears the way he liked, and playfully brushed a hand over his face.

Kelda scowled as Lucy jogged toward the hunters. The loss of the males-who-stayed-behind made Lucy's tracking and hunting skills critical. The only one who objected anymore was Kelda and no one listened to her.

"I come, too," Ahnda piped in, sure of his place as the Group's newest adult.

"No." From Vorak. "You must watch over the females and children."

Ahnda nodded, accepting the decision.

Before they even lost sight of New-homebase, Garv and Vorak headed one direction while Lucy and Raza went the opposite. They'd meet on a distant hill Raza pointed out after marking the boundaries. As she and Raza worked, Lucy followed the progress of Garv and Vorak by Cousin Chimp's alerts to his troop that intruders were among them.

With Sun well past overhead, Lucy and Raza had almost reached the meeting point where together, they would eat what food had been found and then return to homebase. A chirp stalled them.

"A baby bird, in that tree," and Lucy pointed. Raza tipped his head up and picked out the tiny beak peeking out of a nest. The baby wouldn't have enough meat but one bird could mean a nest filled with eggs. That would be a treat. He leaped, wrapped his legs around the trunk, and then shunted his way up. Once he climbed high enough, he could see the nest, filled with eggs. He tested the limb and it bent.

He motioned to Lucy, "It won't hold my weight."

"Grab onto the trunk with one arm and stretch the other."

The mother bird must have planned for such an attack because the nest sat just outside his reach. He looked down at Lucy to see if she had any other suggestions. All he got was a shrug so he scuttled down.

By the time he and Lucy reached the hill, Garv and Vorak were already there. Raza started saying something but Lucy wasn't watching. She'd flattened herself to the ground, chin barely above the dirt, and started crawling toward a dark spot in the soil. She kept her shadow behind her, breath no more than shallow puffs, as she slid soundlessly across the dry surface. When she got within a hand of what turned out to be a rabbit's burrow, she paused, still and silent. Long furred ears poked from the hole. They twitched. Hearing nothing, they edged out enough that Lucy snagged them, yanked the hare from its tunnel, and snapped its neck.

She returned to the group and they divided the rabbit, finishing the meal with plants from their neck sacks. As they stood to begin the return to New-homebase, a snake flew past. Lucy snatched at it but missed as a stream of snakes hurled through the clearing and out the other side, into a bed of rocks and brush. She heard Raza hoot and Garv hop from one foot to the other, trying to keep from being bitten but the reptiles ignored them. Their goal seemed not to attack but flee an unknown predator.

"What's going on?" Lucy asked. Raza started to answer but silenced when Hyaena-dog howled a cry of alarm, answered by the *yip-yip* of its pups. Snarling-dog too bayed and paws pounded the direction taken by the snakes. Overhead, Vulture and his cousins almost blotted out the sun.

As she turned to Raza for an explanation, he shouted, "Down, Lucy!" Vorak was already flat on the ground.

In the blink of an eye, a rumble buried all other noise. Then the earth quivered as though the largest herd of mammoth ever seen thundered by. A deafening crack followed and then the earth split wide, devouring a gazelle midstride. A trunk shattered, cut in half by a fissure that broke open beneath it. A squeal abruptly ended as the earthen walls crashed shut, crushing whatever it swallowed.

Lucy clung to a deep-rooted bush knowing Raza, Vorak, and Garv were doing the same. She rolled around her anchor, the earth shaking her so violently she worried her shoulders would give out. The bush finally broke loose of its earthen bed and she grabbed another.

With a final shiver, the quaking stopped. Something far enough away not to be an immediate danger to the Group

bump-bumped, gave out a strangled screech, and then nothing.
Vorak wobbled to his feet and brushed chunks of dirt and
grit from his arms and hands. Raza shook from muzzle to
toes, dazed but uninjured. Lucy didn't see Garv. Maybe he
went to find the noise.

"Earth quaking. Do you have these where you lived?"

Lucy shook her head, her hands trembling too violently
to say more.

"You'll get used to them though this was worse than any
I've experienced."

Lucy pushed upright, limbs quivering. "Would those left
at new-homebase be OK—the children—Voi!"

Lucy sprinted toward their backtrail and almost collided
with Garv. He stood motionless, back to her. She skid to a
stop and peeked around his body to see what captured his
attention.

"We're trapped," he said as she asked, "Are we
trapped?"

A fissure spanned wider than the length of a tall tree, its
sides speckled with chinks and crannies and exposed layers of
orange and red soil and grey splintered bones. Stocky
rhizomes and bushy shrubs, uprooted from hardscrabble
beds by the earth quaking, clung for their lives to the vertical
walls, and blocky boulders stair-stepped down to a serpentine
river of frothing water.

Vorak pushed past her and then past Garv and crouched
at the brink of the chasm.

"I think this is where that death cry came from." He
tipped his head over the edge and smiled. "Wild-beast. Its
horn is wedged between the trunk of a fallen tree and the face
of the chasm. Its head is facing one direction, body the other.
No way it's alive. Snarling-dog can't reach it, down this cliff,
but Vulture can."

In fact, Vulture already circled, flapping its great wings, with more of its brothers arriving as they watched.

"I go," Vorak motioned to Lucy as he began his descent. "You keep Vulture away from me!"

Lucy fumbled around on the ground for a suitable rock but not fast enough. Vulture screamed as it sunk needle-sharp claws into Vorak's shoulder. Vorak bellowed, flailing at the massive bird of prey with one arm while hanging on to Wild-beast's horn with the other. Vulture couldn't lift the heavy male but hoped to dislodge him, freeing the carrion for itself and its brethren. Lucy flung the rock as hard as she could and it exploded against Vulture's body. The raptor shrieked, released Vorak, and tumbled downward. She must have caved in its chest. Vorak's wounds surely hurt but no one would know that by watching him. With a loud grunt, he tore the limb from the body, hurled it up over the bluff, and repeated the actions with the second haunch. That done, he scrambled up. She reached down to help but he didn't need any.

"You have a powerful arm," he motioned, oblivious to the blood pulsing from the deep punctures in his arm and shoulder, and then moved past and joined Raza in their feast. Eyes closed, Vorak licked the juices that dripped from the fresh meat. His tongue caught any missed specks of fat and sinew. He inhaled as he ate, the scent almost as tantalizing as the taste. No one enjoyed food more than Vorak.

"This," Vorak effused, pausing between bites, "is a great hunt!"

Raza cut off a chunk of dead-wild-beast and walked over to Garv where he stood off to the side. Garv ignored him, eyes fixed on something down the Rift valley. After one breath and another, the big male opened his fist and thrust forward a rock. Not just any rock, Raza recognized it as the distinctive cutter from Man-who-preys.

Raza's eyes dilated and the color drained from his face. "Where did you find that?"

Garv pointed at his feet. Darkness built in his eyes until that's all Raza could see.

***

Downwind, hidden in dense scrub, Xha watched Lucy and her Group devour the wild-beast he'd been chasing before the quaking earth interrupted him. He smiled. Food could be replaced. This female, she was rare.

Without a backward glance, he trotted off. Now that he knew the path she traveled, he had more important activities to complete.

Chapter Thirty-seven

Lucy crumpled. They had sprinted the backtrail to New-homebase, around boulders and the root bundles of uprooted trees, obstructions that should have been carefully and slowly skirted to prevent injury. But no one wanted to be cautious when they didn't know if the earth quaking had hit New-homebase.

Plus, something had frightened Raza and Garv, something they weren't sharing. Lucy figured she knew. What else could it be?

Once her breathing slowed, she looked for Raza, thinking he would be resting, but he stood ahead of her and to the side, motionless, head erect, shoulders back, eyes fixed on something that Lucy couldn't see. She carefully stepped forward until she could see what caught his attention. Her head drooped.

Blocking their path yawned a new rift, as cavernous as it was wide, its floor deeper than the Impassable-rift she'd crossed to get to Raza's homebase. Raza didn't have to tell her they must go around.

Her chest tightened and her eyes teared. If she could, she'd give up but didn't know how.

Sun slept by the time they found a crossing—precarious but workable—that spanned a narrow part of the chasm. Night Sun had already tiptoed through many of its lights when they reached New-homebase. Everyone in the Group greeted them. No one had gone to sleep, too worried about their safety. The carcass of Wild-beast was dumped in the cache, and the Group curled in a jumble of body parts to sleep. Usually, the snores of Groupmates or their kicks and jabs kept her awake but not tonight. Nothing bothered her. She awoke well after Sun to the sound of something being dragged. Lucy scrubbed at her face, stood, and slowly approached a disheveled heap of feathers.

"Ostrich?"

Vorak nodded and winced. The raw bloody puncture from Vulture was now swollen and filled with the gooey white pus that accompanied treacherous wounds and preceded death.

"I will fix this, Vorak."

As she dug through her sack, Falda yammered excitedly, eyes twitching to the far side of the pond where it merged into the stream. Kelda stood just behind.

"We tracked a desperate cry and found Ostrich in sand-that-kills."

Lucy stared at Falda, stunned. Since when did she—or Kelda—track prey?

"Sand-that-kills buried me to here," and Falda indicated her calf. At that depth, the bird simply needed to keep its head up to breathe until it regained its feet.

"Ostrich jerked and flapped until it was so exhausted, it collapsed and suffocated!"

Kelda's eyes sparkled with excitement and she moved toward Lucy. At first, she thought Kelda wanted to ask about Vorak's wound, but Kelda never even glanced at her pairmate. Did she seek approval for being a hunter? Or offer understanding because she'd ridiculed Lucy for doing the same? Lucy could imagine neither from Kelda.

Falda defeathered the bird, cracked the chest open, and shared the savory innards with everyone. Thanks to Ostrich-that-brought-its-own-death and wild-beast-that fell-in-fault-after-earth-shook, the Group ate well.

As quickly as she could, Lucy gathered what she needed for Vorak's wound and hurried over to where he sat, dabbing the angry red hole with a cool leaf.

"Let me do this for you, Vorak."

She poured honey into the puncture and sealed it with a root poultice all the while wondering what had changed in Kelda. She still argued with everyone but lately, she took a keener awareness in the male's work. The old Kelda would never have tracked Ostrich much less tried to scavenge its body from the death-sands.

"I must change this poultice every day, Vorak." He nodded and left to join Raza. Lucy tucked her healing materials away and hurried to catch up with the females and children. They headed to the meadow where they hoped to find dead-ostrich's eggs. Voi tottered after Falda, Voivoi to his side, both with the assurance of one who has never experienced death.

As Lucy entered the meadow, a young Tree-man crossed the opposite side. Stride long, something in his hand, he motioned to her but she didn't understand. Lucy flashed back to the fire and the Tree-man youngster, wondering if this was him.

Lucy sniffed and listened, exactly what she did every time she reached a new place, but found nothing. Then she joined the females digging in rhythm with the scrape-scrape of the okapi who rutted against a trunk and the crunch-

crunch of the small-antlered giraffe who ate with an unhurried grace. A porcupine, tasty but difficult to catch, waddled through the underbrush. At the edge of the clearing, a Canis family trotted in their awkward way as though life couldn't be better. The pups gamboled with each other as the parents hurried with ears erect. They huffed congratulations as Yoo downed a fat hare with a well-aimed missile, a grin stretching across their muzzles when Ahnda roused a ground-nesting bird and killed it with a rock.

Chapter Thirty-eight

Boah scanned for refuge as he fled. He'd harvested enough fruit to take some back to Hee and Shee but he would drop it if he must. Chimp screeched at Boah to run faster.

Boah enjoyed traveling with Chimp because the ape always found fruit and nuts. Hee's warning shout rang through the still air at the same moment Boah heard Long-tooth Cat's guttural purr. Cousin Chimp leaped up to a tree branch but Boah couldn't reach it. He fled. Ahead he spied a lower limb though even at a full sprint, Long-tooth would catch him. Still, he sped as fast as his bandy legs could carry him. Much to his surprise, he scaled the trunk and clambered high enough to be safe from Cat.

When he turned, Long-tooth wasn't there. She'd become distracted by the odd hominids, enraged they hunted within her territory. She faced them, tail straight behind, ears perked, ready to hunt.

"How do they survive," Boah mused, "…with their meager narrow faces, insubstantial mouths, and jaws that recede into their skulls? They are furless with flat snouts and they don't notice danger until it is too late, and they constantly fall on their round cushioned rear ends. It should get in the way of their running but oddly seems to help.

"Fear-grins flash across their faces as though they know—and accept—that risks surround them. But," Boah pondered, "...they direct that show of teeth to each other. Are they afraid of those they live with?

Boah munched on fruit as the odd animals continued to dig, blissfully unaware of Long-tooth. A child howled as he waved a dead bird. Long-tooth twitched toward it.

Boah wondered, "If they are alerting their band to Cat, why do they not flee?"

He also didn't understand why they were so loud. Their noise grated, telling every creature around where they were and how many. Why vocalize when hand signals and body gestures were quiet—and more efficient? It made no sense.

Boah was well-aware of the life and death struggle coming but cared little because it didn't involve Hee or Shee.

The females foraged tubers, bulbs, and worms and the children laughed and chased as Long-tooth slunk step-by-step, breath-by-breath, toward the group. Boah coughed, a clear signal any baby understood. A female heard him, glanced at her child, and then sniffed but smelled none of the potent feline odor that saturated the air downwind of her.

Finding nothing, she turned back to her digging.

Long-tooth crouched below the grassline and waited. She spent the majority of her day eating, resting, and preparing for the next meal. These hominids, though not as tasty as the chimps, were easier to stalk than the upright creatures with the deadly sticks.

Shadows shrunk as Sun climbed. Boah's chest heaved in and out, calm in his security. The strange females dug and huffed. The children pounded the ground, giggling as they imitated the females. Mosquitos buzzed as butterflies flitted from flower to flower.

Chimp fell silent.

Why do they ignore Cousin Chimp's silence? Boah shrugged.

Long-tooth crept within a run-and-a-leap of the group. Her eyes, golden like the color of dry grass, flicked through the assemblage. She settled on one of the smallest children. He sat as though fused to another youngster. Neither could defend themselves and no one was close enough to help when they would soon need it. They gurgled as the older children dug with limestone flakes and extracted juicy roots.

With a terrifying roar, Long-tooth leaped at the youngsters. One—startled—toppled over and rolled down an incline. The other, Long-tooth silenced as her yellow canines sank into the base of his head, snarling as it dragged the child away until it was out of sight. Too late, the adults howled strange sounds. They threw stones and dirt clods at Long-tooth with no effect. One female folded over and wailed a miserable plaintive cry.

Why does she now sound a warning?

The female he recognized as 'Woo-see' grabbed for the tumbled child. His arms flailed as he attempted to right himself, but he remained silent. She crushed him to her body as Boah's Mother would. Boah tipped his head, concentrating, and felt her relief.

Again, he wondered at these actions. Long-tooth was gone.

The jungle came alive once again as life echoed all around. The natural circle of life and death had played out one more time. As with the baby chimp, Boah experienced neither sadness nor guilt, just satisfaction he could now leave and find food for his Group.

Chapter Thirty-nine

The loss of Voivoi gutted Falda as the Rift ruptured the land, her buoyant optimism replaced by depression and her energy with lethargy. Lice nested with impunity in her fur and she refused Sahn's efforts to groom her. She pulled her hair out in fistfuls which left mottled flakey patches all over her body. She clawed at her arms causing the skin to bleed and then licked until the hair wore away leaving raw red tissue.

Kelda attached herself to Falda. When the distraught female slashed her arm open while chopping a tuber, Kelda wrapped it in moss and mud. Lucy offered a poultice but Kelda pushed her away, scolding her for letting Voivoi die. Lucy hugged herself in a vain effort to stop shaking.

Night Sun shrank and regrew and Falda only got worse. Her posture became stooped and she often forgot what she should be doing and where she was. Feral eyes tracked her, recognizing impending death, and still Falda couldn't accept Voivoi's fate as part of the same mystery that asked a fawn to forfeit her life so Long-tooth could live and Man-who-makes-tools could scavenge.

Voi continued to be gurgly and joyful. When Falda greeted him with tears, it bewildered him and he would assure

Falda he could find his friend if he searched just one more location. Then, he would toddle off, optimism undiminished by Falda's sadness.

As Night Sun returned to its full size, the welcome stench of dung not their own and the sweaty exhaustion of the returning animals perfumed the air. Every day, their lowing voices grew louder. With them would come the runoff from Fire Mountain and its brothers that would fill the ponds and nourish life.

Any hope that would bring a return to normalcy exploded when Gleb staggered into the homebase.

"Gleb!" Ahnda's hoot rang out.

Lucy jerked her head up in surprise, dropping the chopper she'd been knapping. The heat had rolled in this morning. She couldn't remember it ever being hotter.

"Gleb?" It couldn't be. "Gleb, here?"

When she finally located the ragged, filthy figure tripping into the clearing, she could see something was very wrong. If not for the facial features, she wouldn't recognize him as the strong and confident child, sure of his skills as an adult, who'd stayed with Baad and the left-behind Group. This creature couldn't protect himself much less others. He stumbled toward them, faltering with every step, face gray, shoulders badly sunburned below the mangy unkempt fur. His lips were cracked and bleeding.

"Water!" Ahnda motioned as he pulled Gleb into his arms.

Gaunt skin hung on what should have been a subadult's body. His eyes held none of the youthful intensity that always glowed from them like a fire. Scratches honeycombed his body, punctuated with yawning wounds and worm-infested gashes, some with red lines and others scabbed or healed. The stench of old sweat, mud, and excrement floated around him like a mist.

Gleb shoved Ahnda, his face a mask of terror. "You must leave! All must leave. Man-who-preys stalks us!" Gleb jolted wide-eyed toward his backtrail as though he expected an attack at any moment.

Ahnda placed his hands on his friend's cheeks and gently shook. "You are safe, Gleb. You are with us."

"We will never be safe again," Gleb whispered, his despair palpable.

Chapter Forty

Lucy carried Gleb's hot, limp body to the pond. There, she splashed water over his pallid face and dripped it between his cracked lips. Groupmembers delivered an assortment of berries and bulbs, but he wanted only leaf sponges which he sucked on silently as his panicky gaze jerked from one Groupmember to the next. When he found Lucy, he tried to crawl toward her.

"Raza... Baad—Garv... Where are they?"

"They hunt." Lucy added gestures for *away from harm.*

She groomed him with long smooth strokes to untangle his hair and remove the lice from his head and along the nape of his neck. Sahn joined her, cleaning with a pleasant *clack-clack* cadence as her teeth nipped against skin.

"Gleb, how did you find us?" Lucy moved her arms outward—*in this interminable wilderness.*

"Bent twigs... Scat... Man-who-preys found us—we must leave!"

Vorak knelt at Gleb's side. He wore his usual easy-going smile as he asked, "Where are the others?"

"Dead," Gleb blurted. His chest heaved like frog hopping through the rushes. No one had seen an entire

Group destroyed. No one but Lucy. Her head pounded so loudly, everyone must hear it.

It took a long time before Gleb calmed enough that Vorak could ask, "Tell us what happened, Gleb, so we can prepare."

Just when it seemed Gleb wouldn't answer, he began.

"Ma-g'n and I went hunting. We didn't know Man-who-preys was about to attack homebase. When we heard their howls, we hid. There were so many of them—I've never seen so large a Group! After they killed all the males with the killing sticks, they left, shoving the females in front of them, carrying the children like carrion."

His face twisted with anger and he bit his lip so hard blood trickled down his chin. "Ma-g'n held me back. I wanted to help."

His finger traced listlessly in the mud. "We entered the homebase. No one was left. We were afraid Man-who-preys-who-kills would return so we gathered what food we could find and went in search of your trail," motioning the size of their prints, the scat, bony litter from their meals, the cairns Lucy placed, and the brambled barriers left where they slept, "We were well on our way when Ma-g'n went back for the Pain-bark you gave him. I waited for him but he never returned so I finally continued alone."

Telling the story took the last of Gleb's energy and he fell asleep right there on the ground.

"You did this!" Kelda motioned, standing so close to Lucy the stench of a rotten tooth made the younger female gag. Behind her stood Vorak, head down, and Falda, eyes anxious.

"If you never came, our Group would have stayed together!" Her hair bobbed in rhythm with her hands and spittle sprayed from her mouth. "If not for Raza, Baad would have died bringing you here—you are evil!"

Lucy gaped as Vorak busied himself with a clod of dirt at his feet.

Falda tugged on Kelda's arm. "No, Kelda, Baad told me—" Kelda shrugged out of Falda's grasp and pinned Lucy with her glare.

"Falda's child died but yours lived!"

Confusion masked Falda's face. "Kelda, that's not her fault…", and fell silent as though she didn't know what else to say.

Tears sprang unbidden to Lucy's eyes. Falda didn't blame her for Voivoi's death.

Kelda continued. "You bring only death to us. You must leave!"

Lucy didn't hesitate. She was tired. "OK. I'll go."

With those simple words, her world crumbled. The carefully constructed plan, the promise to make a new life where she could raise her child in safety—and still, she made the same mistakes as before. The sparkly red crown of Fire Mountain and its cousins glowed against the darkening sky. A big gray pig with a silver mane led its family to the pond for a late-day drink, poking and snuffling as they went, but all Lucy could think about was how to escape.

"Kelda!" Sahn roared in a tone Lucy never heard from the elder. "If Lucy goes, I go. She is our future. As are you, and Falda and every member of the Group."

Kelda glowered at Vorak, but he said nothing, his discomfort as potent as Kelda's rage. For long breaths, no one spoke.

Sahn broke the silence. "When Raza returns, we search for Ma-g'n."

Chapter Forty-one

Lucy ran, burning lungs begging her to stop, brain screaming to keep going. She sucked in another ragged breath. Without the plant, Baad would die. Leaving alone would again anger every female in the Group but she didn't care anymore. She had already told them she would leave. Her last gift would be to bring the healing herb to Baad.

Yesterday, the day Gleb returned, the heat started early and worsened as the day progressed. Cousin Chimp languished in the canopy, too hot to play. Mammoth sprayed each other with trunkfuls of water. Snarling-dog stayed in his cool den and Canis slouched into the rare shade and panted. No birds called. The leaves of the baobab that marked the edge of their homebase stood wilted and still as though dead. Only the insects seemed unaffected.

The group again was hungry. They finished all the stored food days ago and could find almost nothing in the sun-hardened earth. When Sahn said she heard the herd's hooves and bawling voices, despite the heat, Raza, Garv, and Baad left with Sun's first light. What they found could save lives.

While they were gone, Lucy tried to dig for underground

plants but the earth burned her hands and blistered her feet. Instead, she sat in the shade, cushioned from the scorching ground by a pile of dried weeds to knap tools. When the stones got so hot they seared her fingers, she and the other females submerged themselves in the pond's cool water and did nothing. Every day, the heat deepened. Soon, the pond would be nothing more than a sludge-choked puddle but until then, the females basked in it and the children romped. They drove off any animals that wanted to drink because they didn't have enough to share.

Suddenly, Falda's voice rang out, cheerful and giddy. "Lucy! The breeze cools. Come. We will find nuts!"

A smile, absent since Voivoi's death, creased the female's face as she pranced and twirled. Lucy rushed to her side and dragged Falda into the cool water, coated her with mud and listened as the hollow beat inside her body thumped fast and faster. When viscous fluid erupted from her mouth, Lucy relaxed.

"She will get better."

Concern turned from Falda to the hunters. They were gone far too long.

Hyaena began his plaintive nocturnal howl by the time Raza materialized, tiny from a distance but running steadily toward homebase. Behind him, stooped and laboring under the weight of what could be a wild-pig, plodded Garv.

Where was Baad?

As Garv came into focus, she could see the fatigue and strain that masked his face yet he hurried. Why? The food would be welcome but not at the cost of his life. That's when the truth washed over her like water rushing down the face of a cliff.

When the males reached homebase, they greeted no one and everyone shuffled out of their way, giving Garv a clear path to the tiny pond. Garv dumped Baad into the water and submerged him up to his neck. His color matched the ash from Fire Mountain. Blood oozed from cracks etched into his bright red body. His chest was bruised and tender with the imprint of a hoof. His shoulder had a deep festering bite. Lucy coated every part of him with mud as she did Falda and then leaned back on her haunches and waited.

"What happened?" Sahn asked.

Raza touched Garv's arm and nodded toward the back of the huddled group. A glimmer of surprise crossed his face, but he said nothing. Then, he told their story.

"It was too hot for predators to be out—even Man-who-preys. We were just beyond Rift-where-wild-beast-died-after-earth-shook, planning to turn back, when we found Snarling-dog and his mate stalking an Hipparion colt and its wounded mother. We joined them. For some reason, the animals split up as did Snarling-dog and his mate. Baad followed the colt and Raza and I chased the mare, sure with her injury, Snarling-dog would bring her down. We agreed to meet back at a deserted cave we'd passed earlier.

"It didn't take long before Snarling-dog abandoned the hunt, toppling over in the shade of a bush, panting so fast he couldn't walk. We returned to the cave, thinking Baad would be there.

"We didn't worry until Vulture appeared overhead, joined soon by many of his cousins. They circled where Baad would have chased Hipparion."

Garv's body sagged as though under an enormous weight.

"We raced for the spot and found him, curled in a ball. He told us, before passing out, that the Mother Hipparion had rejoined her colt, trampled the female Snarling-dog, and then turned on him. She kicked him in the chest and bit his shoulder savagely. She prepared to kick him but something interrupted her and she bolted."

Garv turned to Lucy. "Your herbs—you can save him?"

His voice held such trust that Lucy could save Baad that Lucy knew she'd have to try. Her plan had been to leave with Voi when the heat broke but she would put that off until Baad healed.

"Yes," she motioned tentatively, knowing she had used the last of the healing plant Baad needed on Gleb and Falda. "I know where to get some."

Voi would be safe here, with Garv and Raza, until she returned. She jolted to her feet and sprinted away. No one tried to stop her, remind her not to travel alone, or offer to accompany her.

Sweat streamed down her back and matted her hair but she didn't care. She panted—more like a wheeze—from running too fast, too long but Baad's life depended upon her. Cousin Chimp hooted and Tree-man stared, both bewildered why she ran in such devastating heat when not chased. A spooked dik-dik fled in a flurry of hooves and poufy tail. When Lucy crested a hillock, it lay dead in a tangled heap. It ran faster than she but collapsed from the effort.

Lucy squatted in the shade of a baobab, ate her fill of dead-dik-dik, and set off again, leaving the rest for Snarling-dog.

She journeyed day and night and day again, pounding over hilltops and through jagged valleys, along the rift and across the land bridge she'd crossed with Vorak, Raza, and Garv. At one point, she found blood dripping down her face with no idea how it got there. She ignored it. It would soon stop bleeding on its own.

Born in a Treacherous Time by Jacqui Murray

Sun's light had again begun to fail when Lucy finally inhaled its scent. Ignoring the danger of traveling in the dark, she continued across a clearing, through low scrub, her way lit only by the pallid glow of Night Sun. Finally, she found what she thought was the right plant. She chewed the leaves into a sodden mulch which she pasted over the gash on her forehead. The rest, she stuffed into her neck sack. She would return to homebase with the light. Now she would sleep.

Just as she prepared to crawl into her nest, a bright ball the size of her fist cut through the sky. It had a fiery stiff tail and a pulsing radiance that lit the earth much as Sun did when it was awake. It roared as it charged across Night Sun's sky and attacked Fire Mountain. A shattering eruption drowned all other sounds. Flames spewed into the sky and licked the base of Night Sun. An orange and yellow glow blocked everything in Night Sun's domain.

Even Night Sun.

The tree next to her split with a cacophonous crack. All around her, fire and cinders rained down making the ground quiver like Canis when he shook water from his body. Lucy barely maintained her balance.

The quakes ended as quickly as they began but Lucy's ears rang so loudly, every sound was muted. She sneezed, over and over, trying to purge the acrid reek of sulfur mixed with burned flesh and singed fur. Clutches of birds took to the air as sounds Lucy could barely hear rumbled around her—the thunder of hooves, the crackle of wildfires, the raw bleat of death. A muddy fog spread up and out over everything.

If Night Sun hadn't been gone, it would have moved many hands overhead by the time the night quieted and Lucy stopped shaking and exhaustion overcame her.

Chapter Forty-two

Lucy awoke not to Sun's glorious warmth but to a diaphanous haze that shrouded everything. Last night's attack left a shroud of noxious smoke that burned Lucy's eyes and made it agonizing to breathe. She longed for the comforting twitter of birds, the snuffling of warthogs, or the swish of Cousin Chimp through the trees but heard only silence. After checking her neck sack for Baad's herb, she turned toward where she thought homebase lay.

She joined the stampede of life fleeing the area. Mammoth tried to escape the dust and smoke, accompanied by Giraffe and Wild-beast. A canis loped by, ears pressed back against his head and bushy tail bouncing. A smaller female and a pup shadowed him. The family melted into the fog.

She scrambled up a hill, sure she would find her direction, and froze. In place of her lavish forest and rolling savanna stood an ashy ectoderm of burning grassland broken here and there by blazing stands of withered trees. A chasm gaped as far as she could see in both directions.

A loud crack, a blow to her head and darkness encased her.

Chapter Forty-three

Something shook Yoo so viciously, he fell from his nest and smacked his head painfully. Woozy, he sat up and tried to figure out why his throat hurt.

"Garv!" he shouted, knowing the male who was always calm would explain, but he moved in a frenzy, faster than Yoo had ever seen him move, like Baad when Gleb brought a hive into the homebase and with it a swarm of livid bees.

"Yoo. We must go!!" Garv pulled him to his feet and prodded him toward a group clutched around Raza.

"Man-who-preys!" Gleb flailed his arms, trying to get Raza to listen. "They attack!"

Raza turned Gleb by his shoulders. "It is Fire Mountain, angry at us."

Yoo followed Gleb's eyes and gulped. Fire Mountain's face had burst into flames. Fire and thick black clouds shot skyward and cloaked the base of Night Sun in blood. Rocks rained from the mushroom-shaped cloud and crushed even the sturdiest trees as though frail scrub. Flaming rivers spilled down the flanks in bright strands. Yoo jerked at the sound of thunder as cliff-by-homebase melted into pond-where-children-play and a wall of water breeched the shoreline and flooded toward him.

Garv seized Yoo by one hand and Gleb by the other and they darted through pockets of blazing scrub, around the slivered remains of Sahn's shadow-stick, desperately dodging the waterfall of sparks that peppered everything. One singed Yoo's cheek making him yelp. He heard a voice calling his name but he couldn't get sound out of his mouth.

"Baad! We are here!" From Garv. Baad appeared out of the haze and crushed Yoo to his chest as Lucy squeezed Voi after Cat's attack.

Baad shakily motioned to Garv, "I am glad you are here, with us." His eyes glistened as his hands moved. Yoo agreed, but didn't understand why Baad chose this moment to share that sentiment.

"Garv. Why does the ground shake?" Yoo looked up at the stalwart male.

"I have seen many like this, Yoo. Don't worry."

Yoo didn't. If Garv and Baad were there, everything would be fine.

"What of Lucy?" Yoo signaled. "Is she back?"

Sahn pushed a hand at Yoo, *Wait*, and huffed, "I can't find Sweena or Dar."

Sahn tried to appear calm but Yoo couldn't miss her distress. Lucy, Sweena, and Dar were all gone. Yoo couldn't comprehend a world without that many Groupmembers.

Garv patted Yoo. "I will find them, Sahn. You take the youngsters," and he darted into the conflagration. Yoo thought he would never again see this male who always answered his question.

Garv knew as much as Lucy.

The smoke made it impossible for Garv to see—the children could be anywhere, hurt or hidden, too alarmed to come out. The fire hungrily consumed the brittle scrub that had been laid around the boundaries of the homebase to warn of intruders.

"Sweena! Dar!" He bellowed but his cries were lost in another raucous explosion. He hurried from one spot to another but found only fire and cinders until finally, there—a glimmer of movement in a boulder bed. He raced over and stooped. Looking back at him, buried far into the crevice were wide frightened eyes. He cocked his head and smiled, forcing his shoulders to relax and his hands to unclench. "We look for you. Come."

The children clung to each other. Their terrified gazes never left Garv as he lifted them into his arms.

"I have a better place to hide."

"Mir!" Kelda lurched to his side, clutched his arm. Her voice cracked. "I-I lost her!"

Garv smiled at Sweena and Dar. "Kelda knows where my special place is. She will take you."

Garv watched until Kelda and the youngsters reached the Group and then turned back into the flames. In no time, he found a red-faced Mir where the Group relieved themselves.

"A good idea, Mir, before we begin migrating." He squatted beside Mir and pretended to do his business. "I'll give you a ride."

Mir tucked pudgy arms around Garv's furry neck and they hurried over to the Group.

"You will become a memorable hunter, Mir. I can tell," and he clapped the child's shoulder.

When he ticked off the Groupmembers, Lucy and Vorak were still absent.

Where are you?

The Group ran, Raza leading the column and Baad at the rear. Behind them, the lake-where-children-play collapsed into a wide fissure that came out of nowhere. Ahnda jumped at another deafening crack but didn't look back, didn't want to see more of his world disappear. Another explosion thundered, so close he couldn't help but leap aside as the earth devoured vegetation, a fleeing hare, and a mouse family.

Ahnda shook with fear but kept running. When he glanced up, only a dull glimmer marked Sun's presence. What happened to the bright yellow ball? It should be awake, lighting the ground so they didn't step into fissures and cracks? Ahnda wanted to cry but had to keep running.

Yoo had never seen a day like today. Kee always told him to shelter when rain scalded his skin, as did Lucy, but if he did that, he'd be left behind. Besides, every Groupmate was being burned so he hurried onward, stretching his short legs as far as he could. He ached at the collapse of his ordered world but rolled his shoulders back knowing he must be strong for Mir and Dar. Ahnda gripped his hand and Yoo squeezed back, gaining strength from the almost-adult's reassuring squeeze.

"We will be fine," Ahnda assured Yoo.

How adult Ahnda is. I will grow to be like him.

No matter where Raza led them, Rift-that-kills stalked him. It consumed omnivorously—flora, fauna, the soil itself—first the slowest animals and then the mammoths, rhinoceroses, and pigs. Even the swift Hipparion and Oryx failed to outrun its appetite.

Garv emerged out of nowhere and nudged Raza. "I don't see Vorak. I'm going back to look." As quickly as he appeared, he melted into the chaos behind him.

Raza swatted Yoo on the rump to speed him up. The child tried to run but the ground beneath his feet disintegrated and he fell, now banging his body against a gulch that hadn't been there before.

"Ahnda!" The almost-adult gripped his hand, trying to drag him up the wall out of the chasm, refusing to let go. Yoo clung to Ahnda even when a rock knocked him in the head so hard he felt dizzy.

"Don't let go, Yoo—I will get you out of this!"

"Hang on!" Raza raced toward them as Ahnda strained to pull Yoo out of the Rift. The youngster's feet clawed for purchase, always ending up kicking at air. He'd never seen dirt simply disappear beneath his feet, or anyone's. Just when he thought he must give up, that if he didn't, Ahnda would die with him, Raza snatched his hand from Ahnda and flung him up and out of the fault. Yoo dropped hard on solid ground, bounced once, and then stood up. He patted a trembling Ahnda, as though to calm him down.

"I knew you and Raza would save me, Ahnda. I wasn't afraid,"

Yoo's confidence reassured Raza but the Rift remained hungry. Who would be next?

As though the monster heard him, a strangled cry rang out. Sahn had become trapped on the far side of another new fault, this one separating the Groupmembers from each other. Sahn lay prone on its edge, one hand stretched over the side gripping Mir. The child valiantly fought as Yoo had just done, to scrabble up a cliff even as the ground dissolved beneath her. Sahn would never give up, this Raza knew.

Her lips moved, sounds Mir would believe because they came from Sahn. Raza thought she might succeed, but then her grip failed. Mir slipped and grabbed onto a scraggly root, then kicked the earthen wall to eke out a foothold. Whatever she yelled made Sahn smile.

By now, the rift spanned a vast amount of land wider than Raza's height. He combed the area behind him for a bough that would reach the other side but everything around him burned. Sahn remained Mir's only hope. The elder strained her entire body downward, arm overextended.

"Grab my hand!"

Mir walked her toes up the cliff, her face etched with fierce determination, mouth a thin line of red that cut her jawline. A hand's width and another and their fingers touched—just as a blistering tendril shot up from the abyss and grazed Mir's skin. She screamed in agony and released her tentative hold on Sahn. A howl of anguish rang from both sides of the Rift but nothing from Mir. No cry for help. No anguish. One look at Raza communicated not pity for herself or sadness, but strength, peace that she had done all she could and that was good enough. Then, the flames consumed her.

Raza would have given up but Baad prodded him. "Sahn... Dar... They are still over there."

The fiery monster already anticipated its next victim. *Not from my Group.*

"Sahn. Toss Dar!"

Raza imagined Sahn's anguish. Mir trusted her and ended up food for a molten river. Sahn backed away from the edge, gaze latched onto Raza, clutching Dar as though she would never let go. She moved her head side to side with a fierceness Raza understood. He would try something else.

"Dar!" His frantic wave to the child went unnoticed as trees exploded behind her and fire lapped the ground at her feet. She lay, tucked against Sahn's chest, face passive, knowing with the surety of her short time on Earth that Sahn would protect her.

Garv materialized at Sahn's side. A tingle of hope rippled through Raza's body. The big male motioned something to Sahn that was obscured by the haze. Whatever he said worked and Sahn handed him the child. Raza wrapped his beefy arms around Dar and whispered until she settled.

Next, he caught Raza's eye, tipped his head forward, and sped along the chasm's crumbling edge. Raza matched his pace, heart racing, locked onto the flying figure who had become such an important part of the Group in such a short amount of time. His pupils contracted as he readied himself. Garv's lips formed a tight line. His muscles bunched and power surged as he marshalled every bit of energy for what he must do. With a howl, he flung Dar up and into the gap.

An intense calm overtook Raza and the world receded into the background until all he saw was the tiny form of Dar as it arched up and over the fiery chasm, her mouth open in a silent wail. Arms stretched to their limit, blood pumping in his ears, Raza snagged the child's leg and pulled her away from the abyss.

"We did it!"

He squeezed Dar against his chest, unwilling to let her go for fear the Rift would yet claim her, but there was one more important job to complete. Ahnda took Dar and Raza turned back to Sahn, still stranded across the fault.

"Sahn. Jump." Raza motioned with his entire body, hand movements firm and commanding, leaving no doubt in her mind that if she would jump, he would catch her.

She did.

From a full sprint, she leapt into the oblivion over the Rift just as the decaying ground disintegrated beneath her life-hardened feet. She stretched her old legs as far as they would go, threw her arms forward, bent her knees, and landed with an *Oomph* a hand's width on the side of life. Raza seized her wrists and hauled her away from the edge. The molten lava roared through the gully and lapped up the walls in a vain grab for her old feet.

It would have to feed elsewhere.

Sahn and Dar out of danger, Raza turned to Garv, stranded across the Rift with no way back, tall and proud, a satisfied smile as the world fell apart around him.

Raza must pick: Wait for Garv or follow the animals. If he left, he would never again find this spot amidst the devastation. If the cracked earth kept Man-who-preys across the Rift, what if Garv needed help?

"Vorak and Lucy are there, with Garv. They will find each other, Raza." This from Sahn. "And Ma-g'n."

Garv turned away as though he knew what the decision must be. Unless Raza could get his Group far from Rift-that-kills, they would all die. Almost without thinking, he moved to the front of the milling Groupmembers, all eyes on him, their trust in him complete. He would follow Hipparion and Mammoth, wild-beast and Snarling-dog, the snakes, spiders, and insects. If so many animals he respected took this path, it must be good.

Chapter Forty-four

Lucy shook her head, trying to order her thoughts, which sent an angry stab through her neck and made her head throb. Her nose twitched and her eyes stung as though assaulted by a dust storm. She wobbled to her feet and rubbed her eyes with grimy fists.

It didn't help.

The heavy soot filling the air made breathing painful. Every instinct screamed and nothing made sense. In place of her endless savanna lay a massive, bottomless ravine, so close if she stepped forward she would fall to her death. Steep walls plummeted to a fiery river of magma flowing with the charred bodies of those it caught.

She crab-walked backward, trying to escape before this new Rift devoured her as it did the rest of the world. She bumped into a tree and scrambled up the trunk and curled into a fetal ball. Several times throughout what must have been night, she coughed herself awake, finding the same lethal air and acrid stench. At one point, her skin seared like the red ant hill she once fell on so she tucked her arms under her body and pulled her knees against her chest. A crack exploded beside her, a whimper, and then nothing …

...She splashed in the iridescent water and searched for stones to knap. A scraggy canis stepped out of the reeds. His jaws were impossibly broad, framed in mud-caked fur, front paws the size of Lucy's belly, the curved claws leaving deep cuts in the shoreline.

"Are you lost?" The words came from his mouth, his yellow eyes kind.

She looked around to see who he meant, but she was alone. She advanced toward Canis, drawn by his liquid brown eyes. His shaggy tail dangled between mud-caked legs and swished as his jaw opened into a smile.

"Why do you think that?"

The friendly-canis-that-talks trundled off, peeking back over his retreating shoulder. "Leave or you'll die."

He vanished around a bend as Lucy wondered what to do.

Lucy awoke coughing and choking until tears spilled down her cheeks. The dense odor of mud, charred wood, damp ash, and burned meat doubled her over. When she regained control, she crumpled backward, eyes staring at nothing but cinder dust and gloom, and let her mind work.

She came up with a simple plan: Go home. Give Falda the plant she'd collected for Baad. Take Voi and stick-that-kills and return to Feq. Fire Mountain's anger and the explosion from the sky likely buried her markers but she would find him. She must.

That wouldn't be easy. What surrounded her was worse than she remembered the night before. Black scorched land stretched between decimated forests dotted with blazing fires and choking smoke. No signs of life, no bird chirps, and no insect greetings.

A huff sent tingles through her body and she canted her head down. There, close enough to touch, she found the

Canis from her dream, pinned under a toppled tree, a gash cutting his heaving chest. His tail flopped once and then lay still.

Lucy dropped to the ground and advanced with caution. Even supine, his muscles rippled as though prepared to flee, or attack. His jaw sprouted perilous canines and colossal grinding molars. His fur stuck out in tufts like prickle bushes. The exposed eye—dark and small like Snarling-dog—grabbed hers. The pink tongue hung from his mouth and bobbed in rhythm with his labored pant. The dirty tail gave another tired whomp.

"Why are you here, Canis? You left well ahead of me."

As though he understood, his black-lidded eye flicked to a dead female and her pup, both crushed by a fallen tree. Canis refused to leave them, his pack, not caring they would never again run with him through the fragrant grass. His loyalty benefited neither at this point but common sense played no part in his decision.

"You're injured." She hurled the heavy limb off his body and then petted the heaving chest and bleeding haunch, checking for breaks and swelling as Sahn would. Her gestures would be meaningless to the Canis but he let her touch his wound so must see her as a friend.

"I can heal this," and glanced around for moss. If it had ever been here, Fire Mountain's wrath destroyed it. Instead, she pulled stems and a root bundle from her neck sack, chewed, and pasted the gooey pulp over the gash. Next, she coated it with long-fibered leaves and then sealed it with mud. Her fingers worked with care, one eye always on Canis. His nose twitched and he sneezed, but otherwise lay still, body unflinching despite what she knew must hurt. That done, she groomed him as she would a Groupmate until the mud stiffened into a cast.

"Get up," she motioned, her hands gentle but firm. "You and I must leave."

He lurched to his feet, tottered over to his dead mate, and plopped down next to her, nuzzling his head into her neck while one paw rested on the pup, barely old enough to have known the rich life of its homeland. A sigh gurgled from his muzzle.

Lucy motioned, "I too lost a pairmate. I lived. You will, too."

He couldn't possibly understand her, so why did he look as though he did?

She shuffled to a nearby waterhole—more like a seasonal puddle than a lake—and slurped her fill, wiping an arm across her mouth when she finished and then trotted to the edge of Rift. She shouted, not because she expected an answer but her echo would help her gauge distance.

She heard nothing so turned to her left and shouted again but still nothing. One more turn, one more shout, and this time her voice came back.

"That way I will find my homebase."

The Canis watched as though listening. When she fell silent, he snorted a baleful sigh and limped toward her, favoring his good leg. Then, he sat gingerly and huffed again. His warm brown eyes overflowed with trust as though to say she would be his new pack.

"No. You must go to your kind," and she motioned outward, "and I to mine." Lucy gestured toward the fires and signaled the immediacy of their need to depart. Canis wagged his mud-caked tail, sweeping the ground behind him. Lucy tried again.

"Drink. This may be the last water you find." Even Canis' strong sense of smell would be no match for the sulfur spewed by Fire Mountain.

Canis bobbed his head in agreement. Shaking flies from his muzzle, he plodded through the scrub to the puddle and sucked the tepid water, now as much muck as liquid. He didn't seem to care. Pausing once, he glanced back at his family and took another long drink.

Lucy left. Though Sun had disappeared, the heat still slammed her. For a long time, she had fallen asleep every night wishing for the coolness of her trees. Now, she didn't care where she lived as long as it included Voi. Was he safe? If Garv was with him, yes.

She peeked over her shoulder, hoping Canis had finished drinking and gone in search of his pack, but instead, he had collapsed, good eye on her and head burrowed between muddy paws. She ignored him, continuing her march homeward, but every time she turned back, hoping he would be gone, he was watching her, every part of his body still except for the slow wag of his billowing tail.

"Canis," she motioned. "You must go. I am leaving. You will die if you stay."

A mewl slipped from his grinning snout.

With a downward tilt of her head, she admitted defeat. He would remain at his mate's side unless Lucy helped him. She jerked her head to say, *"Let's go."* In an instant, Canis trotted to her side. His body brushed her thigh and his steady pants added a rhythm to their steps.

"You want to join me? See if you can keep up."

Lucy set a brisk pace through the gray haze floating over them like smoke from a doused fire. If Sun traveled overhead, she couldn't see it. She listened for voices and heard only silence. She avoided the shattered chunks of uplifted earth and the still-burning plants. Ash shrouded the soil, dampened by mist into a muddy mess. Though Lucy smelled little beyond sulfur, Canis often found snake, rodent, wounded animals who couldn't flee, and birds too laden with cinders to fly. Once, Lucy snatched a dazed hare from his jaws, surprised he had not punctured the skin. She snapped its neck with a practiced twist and together they ate. Another time, he sniffed out an errant porcupine which he wisely disregarded.

Despite her order that Canis keep up, his injuries wouldn't allow him to do that so she slowed. Besides, she couldn't move quickly because everything around her was different. It would do no harm to accommodate him.

"Be careful. It is dangerous here."

Canis bounced.

"Walk quietly. Don't growl or yip. Stay by me so we can help each other," she motioned, explaining what it meant to be cautious. He responded with an abrupt bark or a mellow rumble, seeming to say he understood. Which he couldn't of course.

Together, they plodded along the endless plateau. The further they went the less hospitable the land. They regularly backtracked and detoured around large crevasses that prolonged the journey and stretched Lucy's already frayed temper. No matter which direction she turned, blackened charred earth greeted them. The thick smoke-filled air floated like vapor just above the brush making it impossible to move quickly. To distract herself, she spent much time explaining to the Canis how she so annoyed Kelda that she had been thrown out of her pack.

"I will get my child and leave. With you if you'd like. You are a better tracker than I, Canis, better than Snarling-dog and Cousin Chimp."

Night replaced day, though Lucy only knew this by the drop in temperature and the cricket chirps. As she worked the twigs into a comfortable nest, Canis circled the trunk, finally collapsing to his belly. His jaws opened in a friendly smile, his tongue dangled, and he panted his unbounded excitement for her company. Then, he snuggled up to the base of her tree, his shaggy tail rhythmically beating out his happiness.

She tucked her arms around her body, finding comfort in Canis' gleaming eyes, and slept contentedly as the sound of his breathing let her know he stood guard.

Chapter Forty-five

Another dismal day greeted Lucy. Canis shared a hare he found, charred to a softness that made it easy to chew. Their meal completed, Lucy dabbed mud on the Canis' wound where it had chipped away and rolled back onto her haunches to wait for it to harden before setting out.

After many breaths of companionable silence, she motioned, "Your family is gone. Mine may be, too, but we have each other."

She wrapped her arms around Canis' substantial neck and buried her face in his fur, oblivious to the dirt and twigs and dead insects embedded there. Her tears dampened his coat.

"I am Lucy, because of the sound I make. You are Ump, for the sound your tail makes."

Ump snorted, slapping his bushy tail against the ground, and then bounded forward.

"Wait!" Surprisingly, Ump stopped, at least long enough for Lucy to confirm his mud coating had dried and they could leave.

Lucy had only a general idea of where they should go, but trusted her innate sense of direction buttressed by odors, faint sounds, and the few meager visual clues available.

Everywhere they went, fissures striated the earth and volcanic ejecta pockmarked the soil. The only life not disturbed by Fire Mountain was the insects. They buzzed and swarmed, eager to feast on the warm living bodies, completely unaffected by the ashy air. She marveled at their resiliency but that paled next to their aggravation as she shooed them away over and over. Once, one snuck into her mouth and she swallowed it before she could spit it out. It tasted bitter with not even a mouthful of food. Ump's appetite, though, was less discerning. He stunned them with a swat of his enormous paws or snapped them into his massive jaws.

"It will take too many of those to satisfy you. Better find meatier scavenge."

Without the ability to see much around her, she found herself twitching at every sound and alerting to every scent. It exhausted her and she had one more reason to crave the blue sky and long vistas of old. Finally, they entered an area less burned than others where she picked out recognizable landmarks like hill-where-Man-who-preys-killed-Hipparion. When she tripped over a cairn she'd placed after the Group separated, she stopped midstride, distraught.

"Ump. I've gone the wrong way. We are headed away from my Group and back toward homebase-where-Ma-g'n-stayed-behind." Tears sprang to her eyes.

Ump panted, energetically wagging his tail, head cocked, eyes locked on hers.

"Yes, you're right. We are here and might as well continue. Maybe someone survived."

Usually, surroundings were familiar because she'd traveled there or heard descriptions. That meant she could move quickly and with confidence. Today, though, everything looked and smelled different, which slowed her considerably. That worked nicely for Ump and his injured side.

If not for Vulture's presence, she would have missed homebase-where-Ma-g'n-stayed-behind. The carrion eaters had already dug into the feast of bodies, squawking to their cousins, tearing long strips of bloody flesh from forms she barely recognized. Still, she crept forward hoping someone lived, Ump at her side, body tight to the ground, front paws scratching, both of them sniffing for anything other than death.

It didn't take long to find Man-who-preys' footprints, overlaid with debris. Ump sneezed and then shook his head, ears flapping noisily. Lucy tracked the predators as they attacked old-homebase and then left. "They advanced quickly and without warning," she motioned to Ump. "See the stutter-steps—that's where they threw stick-that-kills. They left more slowly, herding the survivors."

Kaavrm died fleeing, the killing stick through his back, but Klvda faced his attacker, stick-that-kills through his chest, fighting not fleeing. Not far away lay Garv's pairmate, eyes open and fixed, blood smearing a trail where she must have crawled after her kidnapped child. Did she wish Garv was there to defend her or happy he escaped? Despite what Gleb said, Lucy wanted to believe someone in the left-behind-Group survived but no one answered her chirred call.

When Lucy reached the clearing at the center of homebase, refuse that should have been stacked in neat areas cascaded over the ground. Pebbles lay in the shape of Sun but for what purpose? Dents were gouged into the earth.

Ump's ears pricked, hackles raised, and one leg doubled up in preparation to leap. Something was wrong. She petted his neck and let his warmth and power seep into her body.

A fragrance caught her attention, one even stronger than the diarrheic scat and cloying blood that cloaked the ground. It was Man-who-makes-tools' scent trail and it wafted at her from beyond these dead bodies. She followed it cautiously, body tingling, and crossed out the opposite side of the homebase to another of Fire Mountain's ragged crevices. The odor almost overpowered her, blood mixed with scat and urine and a smell she didn't want to recognize. She approached the edge, trembling despite the heat. She dropped to her knees and canted forward to peek over the lip, adjusting her hands as the earth crumbled beneath them. She hoped to find a Groupmate clinging to the ravine walls, wounded, too injured to climb and too frightened to call out.

But instead, she found another victim, Stick-that-kills through his chest, pinning him to the ground. He died on his stomach so she could see only the shredded ear that clung to the skull.

Ma-g'n.

He lied to Gleb. Ma-g'n didn't return for Pain-bark. He went to check for survivors. If not him, who would help? But Man-who-preys left warriors behind.

She reared back as though kicked and then howled. Ump's head popped up, ears alert, alarmed by the terror that poured from his packmate. He froze for a moment and then galloped to her side. His wet nose nuzzled her as he licked her arms and face.

"Ma-g'n, if only you had listened!" Heaving sobs punctuated her panted motions.

If I run from my problems, Lucy, how will I redeem myself?

Nothing would convince him that what happened to Ch-hee wasn't his fault. His own death ended his guilt and headaches, but what of his responsibilities to this Group? Lucy didn't understand how such a vibrant life could be gone, his last purpose to nourish the carrion birds and the worms.

Somewhere in a part of her she didn't know existed, an emotion bubbled up she'd never before felt, like the power that imbued her when she threw stick-that-kills but without the pleasure.

She wanted revenge.

Ump licked the muddy tears from her face and swished his tail side to anguished side. When that seemed to do no good, he patrolled the area where she lay, guarding his injured pack member. Dusk turned to night and Ump clamped his huge mouth around her limp arm, dragging her under a jutting earth ledge. He shook himself, circled several times, plopped to the ground, and rested his head on her abdomen. After venting a happy sigh, he started to snore.

A malodorous stench jerked Lucy back to consciousness. It took a moment to figure out what smelled so foul.

"Ump." He huffed blissfully into her face, seemingly pleased he'd managed to wake her. "Ma-g'n was my friend," she moaned.

Ump panted his understanding. Her upset was his upset.

"As you are."

He tracked her as she crawled into the nest built by a departed chimp. She shut her eyes, comforted by Ump's snorting until he circled her tree, put his head between his paws, and panting quietly, fell asleep.

Lucy's head throbbed. She forced her lids open but couldn't tell if it was night or day. The sky remained as dismal and dark as when she fell asleep. She tried to listen but everything sounded muted. Ump lay below, glittering eyes on her, body quivering and head bobbing. His tail batted out a salutation.

Climbing down, she squatted, knees under her chin and body angled forward for balance. She purged yesterday from her consciousness and absent-mindedly stroked Ump's neck as she considered her options. First she must find Raza. If Kelda told the truth, if he no longer wanted her, she would take Voi, stick-that-kills, and leave. With Ump.

Suddenly, the canis woofed and took off at a galumphing gallop.

"How does such a clumsy animal avoid being killed?"

Lucy chased, senses awake, but found no tracks, no scat, and no voices. When she caught up with the canis, he crouched, motionless, a rock's throw from a crushed wild-beast. His hackles stiffened and a low growl rolled from his chest.

Lucy motioned, "Wait."

Her hands differentiated between 'dead' and 'asleep'. The canis panted his agreement as drool dripped in viscous strands from his mouth. Lucy smiled. Like her, he knew that 'dead' didn't always mean dead. They hunkered against the sweltering ground, breathing in the alluring scent, melting into their surroundings, until she announced, "It's time."

Ump sprinted to the wild-beast and rubbed himself all over the dead animal before clamping his jaws around a haunch and pushing his paw against the chest. The leg popped loose and Ump plopped backwards, inelegantly righted himself, and trotted over to the shade to eat.

Lucy sliced around the other hip with her cutter and tried Ump's method of anchoring one foot to the body and then pulled with all her strength. The leg gave and she tumbled backward. Shrugging it to her shoulder, she headed for Ump. Bloody morsels dangled from his muzzle and his tail quivered in applause for her effort.

"We are alike," Lucy motioned as she ate.

Ump finished and rolled onto his back, legs dangling gracelessly. A snore rumbled from his prognathic snout. Ump might appear to be deeply asleep but his hindbrain never slept, always sniffing for danger. She could learn that from Ump.

A scent wafted past her, familiar but out of place. It came from beyond the wild-beast's carcass. She approached quietly, keeping the dead body between her and the unknown beast. Slowly, a figure came into focus. First, small eyes peered from a childlike hair-free face, wide-eyed with fear as it tracked her. Her shoulders relaxed and her mouth tugged into a smile.

"I know you," she gestured, palms up. "Tree-man child."

The face had changed since that day long ago. Now, the skin was drawn with hunger and sadness. Tension tightened his eyes and his fur hung dull and brittle rather than with the healthy sheen she remembered. His rapt attention darted from her to the dead wild-beast to Ump and back. Drool dripped from his mouth.

She peered behind him but he seemed alone.

"You're hungry. I understand. Getting lost makes me hungry, too." Lucy mimed grabbing a chunk of meat and stuffing it in her mouth. "Eat?"

Ump rolled to his belly, gaze on the Tree-man. The hairs on his neck and back bristled.

The youngster hiccupped.

"Come." Lucy motioned. Tree-man communicated with gestures so she thought the youngster would understand. Ump padded forward upright and stiff, head raised. Lucy touched his side and he lay down but kept his eyes on the newcomer.

The Tree-man child still eyed her suspiciously, feet rooted to the ground, so she tried again.

"Ump is a friend," and she scratched Ump's back: *He must be if he lets me do this.*

The canis gave a useless kick as his tongue lapped the air. When she stopped, he panted, thumped his tail, and pressed against her side.

Lucy almost laughed. How unusual it must look, her with a canis. She could still feel the child's fear but curiosity won out. With a gawky gait, he shuffled to Lucy's side and drank in the rich bouquet of meat and blood with his tongue. Hunger and fear bristled from every downy hair of his body.

"You are safe," and she motioned to envelop everyone.

The Tree-man youngster sat—more a collapse—but did no more than inhale the tantalizing aroma. Lucy extended a hand-sized piece to him. He leaned forward and snuffled. That proved more than he could resist and he dove in.

Together, they sat—Tree-man, Man-who-makes-tools, and Canis. Each quietly enjoyed their food in the company of strangers that for the moment, they would trust. In this simple act of sharing, Lucy could feel the youngster relax, if only a bit. She had no idea where his Father and Mother were but she sensed something traumatic had happened when Fire Mountain destroyed the land with its anger. She hoped that he—like her—was separated from his Group, nothing worse.

Without realizing, she made the decision to care for him until he could again find his Father and Mother. Chimp had done as much for Ma-g'n and saved the male's life. Tree-man had tried to warn her of the catastrophe coming when Fire Mountain first exploded.

She waited as the child slurped and chewed and Ump waited for Lucy to tell him what to do. At long last, the child rested his hands in his lap, cocked his head and met Lucy's gaze.

"Woosee," he murmured, the tone high-pitched, his

voice tentative but happy, as though he knew her.

After a moment, Lucy put her hand on her chest. "Lucy?"

He pawed her cheek with grubby fingers as she would pet Ump. She moved it around her face, hair, and chest. Then, using his hand, she stroked Ump's furry back and caressed his downy ears.

"Ump."

The child's body relaxed. The canine licked his lips, nose trembling, then sighed and curled head to tail. When Ump stopped moving, the child scooted next to Lucy.

"Lucy!" He duplicated the hand gestures for her call-sign perfectly but failed with the vocalization. "Ump!" He pointed gingerly at the canis, hand motions clarifying what his garbled words didn't.

She took his hand and placed it on his chest. "What is your call-sign?"

The hand motion for 'call-sign' confused him so she carefully moved his hand to her own chest. "Lucy," moved it to the canis and mouthed, "Ump", and then placed his fingers on the child's chest.

He bounced once and moaned, "Booooah. BoaaaHh," as he pounded his chest.

"Boah," Lucy repeated. "Boah-who-runs-from-fire-and-crosses-river. Where—?" `

She stopped just in time. What if they were dead and not just missing? Boah seemed oblivious to her distress. He leaped to his feet and cheerfully waddled toward the new rift. Did he smell Ma-g'n?

"I'm not going to follow, Boah." She couldn't bear the thought of again seeing Ma-g'n's mangled body but Boah continued.

"No, Boah. Stop." What if his family lay dead in the

same chasm as Ma-g'n, also killed by Man-who-preys? She hadn't looked any further than Ma-g'n, couldn't.

"Come back," she motioned but he squatted on the lip of the cliff, balancing his weight over the balls of his feet, and peered over. He ignored Ma-g'n, focusing instead on the wall just below him. He leaned over, stretched his arm down, and then flattened his body to the ground so he could reach further, grunting with exertion. After a moment, he pulled his hand up holding a squirming hare. Before he could scramble to his feet, it wriggled free. Ump took off after it.

Lucy sighed with relief. The look in his Mother's eyes when she hustled him toward the forest, how his Father stood tall, ready to protect him—their death would devastate him. She moved to Boah's side as Ump trotted toward them with the still-alive hare in his mouth. Lucy grabbed it, snapped the neck, and put it into her neck sack for later. No one was hungry. The wild-beast had fed them well.

With Sun dead, the only way to know day ended was when the heat diminished which had happened while they ate Wild-beast and chased Hare. Together, she and Boah crawled into her nest. Ump appraised the gray shadows that clung to everything around them and yawned. His gentle pant and occasional whump soothed Lucy's spirits until she lost consciousness, arms encircling Boah, his head nestled against her chest.

Chapter Forty-six

It took several breaths for Lucy to remember why Cousin Chimp didn't chatter and no birds cawed and who the creature a hand's width from her mouth was, with fingers searching her face.

"You are like Ump, Boah…"

He pushed his prognathic snout against her flatter face and inhaled. Lucy sat still as he picked through her hair, examined every louse, and either discarded or ate it. Ump frolicked somewhere, blissful yips announcing his exciting discoveries.

She squinted upward and saw only dust, haze, and darkness.

After she scattered the nest she and Boah had shared and descended from her perch, she pressed an ear to the ground. Nothing. Still, she checked the perimeter for tracks, scat, or damaged twigs though Ump would already have alerted her to threats.

They were alone, abandoned. As far as she could tell, no life existed outside of herself, Boah, and Ump. This was now her Group. They were small but efficient, and they made her happier than she remembered being since she mated with

Garv.

Boah appeared through the haze, hands clutching a branch popping with berries. Ump tagged along with a rodent between his jaws. He offered it to his packmates and when he got no takers, bit down hard to break its neck and ate.

Lucy paused occasionally as they traveled to scratch out seeds exposed by the fire. Boah watched with curiosity. Once he realized how available food became with this effort, he mimicked her actions and blissfully gorged as they walked.

But traveling all day proved hard on Boah. His pear-shaped body turned walking into a bobbing waddle. He could run faster than Cousin Chimp but not as far. If escape required both speed and space, he would die. What he did better than Lucy was scramble up trees and leap into the branches. As a result, she kept their route as close to the sparse trees as possible so he could escape if necessary. When life calmed down, she would have him teach her how he climbed so adeptly.

They had much to learn from each other.

Sleep-without-Night-sun came and went many times as Lucy forged onward with her new Group. The air choked her and Boah rubbed his eyes relentlessly. Even Ump tried to shelter in abandoned dens to wait for better weather. When Lucy and Boah continued without him, he had to race to catch up. Lucy about gave up finding her homebase when she came to the remains of the cliff that served as the entry point.

"Boah—Ump! We're here!" She stepped forward, calling for Sahn and Falda, then Raza or Garv, but no one greeted her. In fact, she heard none of the clamor of activity that always occurred at the homebase.

"I must be mixed up by the haze..."

She inhaled deeply but smelled nothing more than the

acrid stench of Fire Mountain's anger, still lingering in the humid air. She motioned Boah behind her and proceeded forward, past Boulder-where-Ma-g'n-greeted-hunters, and then stopped to listen before continuing. Ump pricked his ears, twitched his nose, and relaxed.

Lucy turned the corner.

In place of bustling open flat land flowing with life was a bleak vista strewn with great boulders and cracked slabs of earth, the brush replaced by prickly black stalks that crackled underfoot, Lake-bordering-homebase only a cavernous crater that percolated sludge and mud.

Fire Mountain had destroyed homebase and driven her Groupmates away, but where? At this point, she had no idea where to go or what to do. Returning to homebase had been her last hope and only plan.

"We will look around. Maybe they left clues," as she had marked the path to the new-homebase with cairns. "If we find nothing, we will wait here for Raza or Garv to find us. They need Baad's cure." Lucy raised her arms, fingers splayed, and rotated her palms skyward—motioning the need to remain.

Boah hooted agreement and Ump added his support with a vigorous woof.

Lucy scoured the surroundings but found no markers, no footprints, no trace she could follow, nothing but destruction. Surely they hadn't abandoned her.

But if they did, it answered her question.

More important right now was how she would feed her Group. The dead hare Boah caught was long gone. Since then, the search for food found only crisp crickets, dead rodents, and the occasional burnt snake, none of which appealed to Ump.

"Woo-see!" and Boah took off, weaving out of the

clearing in his clumsy side-to-side way. Lucy chased him past lone-baobab-no-longer-there, around cliff-that-can't-be-climbed-that-is-gone, and across what used to be verdant grassland filled with herds. She dodged chunks of uplifted soil taller than herself and jumped over cracks that hadn't been there before the earth shaking.

Finally, she figured out his target.

"Boah, stop." She pulled to a halt and barked after him. "It isn't there." No termite mound the height of Tallest-boulder could survive Fire Mountain's wrath. Like everything around, the insects Boah remembered would be dead or flown away.

When he didn't even slow, and with no better idea than sprinting pointlessly for a food source that didn't exist, she traipsed after him. Ump joined the excursion, yipping and frolicking as though playing a new game.

Out of sight for a moment, Boah yelped. Ump sprinted past Lucy, around a corner and yipped. By the time she caught up, Boah was already searching for a stick that would fit into the side vents of what remained the biggest termite mound Lucy had ever seen. Why and how Fire Mountain skipped it, Lucy couldn't guess. Still, surely, the insects had abandoned it.

"Tuuwwi!" Boah reproduced the hand movement for 'termite'. His eyes glittered.

"Yes—termites, Boah. You said that well!" Lucy exclaimed, as she would encourage Voi.

Boah finally found a stick, shaved off the nodes until smooth, and inserted it into one of the entrances. After a moment, he removed it—filled with wriggling termites. He extended it to Ump who sneezed and went in search of an appropriate meal.

"You, Boah, are brilliant," and Lucy found her own stick

and sat by another vent near Boah. As they ate, a porcupine wobbled over to the hill, swaying on its long-clawed hairless feet. She spent no time in their company so didn't know they enjoyed termites. All she knew was they were short-tempered and easily provoked, which never ended well for those around them.

"You too have been abandoned," Lucy motioned, cautious of its quills.

It faltered but continued forward until it embedded its narrow snout into the soil of the termite mound. There it chewed the gray dirt, swallowed, and consumed more, much as Lucy did when her stomach convulsed.

"Are you sick?"

Tiny ears flattened against a diminutive skull, it gulped down mouthful after mouthful of the sticky clay-like earth. After consuming more than Lucy could, it toddled over to a bed of stems and chewed them to a pulp. These it disgorged, rolled its face in, and then stood, head down as though waiting, the only movement a dip of its head with each shallow breath.

Boah and Lucy sucked down stickful after stickful of termites and still the porcupine remained motionless, like a prickly shrub, without even a twitch of its needles. Finally, it padded over to the edge of the clearing, pooped out worm-filled dung, and wandered away with stringy pieces of vegetation stuck around its face.

Next time, she needed to rid herself of the white worms, she would try Porcupine's method.

Boah finished eating and began to groom Lucy. The scratch of his long fingers felt different from Falda or Sahn but as comforting. When he completed the task, she groomed him.

The chill in the air meant it was bedtime and she lead

Boah to their previous night's nest.

"Aarg!" The frantic wave of Boah's arms made it clear he did not want to be here. His alarmed gaze darted from one tree to the next. A stench rose from his body that made Ump growl.

"Boah. Why build a different nest?"

To answer, he scampered from one side to the other, arms flying, eyes wild. That baffled Lucy. "Do you think sleeping in the same spot makes us easy prey? Snarling-dog returns to his den, and Cat too."

Boah cupped her face between his miniature hands, his eyes boring into hers with wisdom one so young couldn't possibly have. He petted her shoulder as though to forgive her stupidity and with a huff, dashed up the trunk and settled into the old nest. After a moment, Lucy joined him. Boah wrapped his arms around her and his face slackened, the comfort of her nearness stronger than the trauma. Ump padded the edges of their make-shift homebase until satisfied and then plopped down beneath them. With a rumble of contentment, he tumbled over and started snoring.

"Ump. Let's go."

Ump alerted to danger faster than Lucy. Since she couldn't go out with a Groupmate, Ump was an excellent—or better—choice.

Based on the warmer air, Lucy guessed day had arrived. Leaving Boah to sleep, she led Ump toward a talus field abutting the fringe of Fire Mountain. Ump panted, wagged frantically, and bounded away. By the time he returned with a rat, Lucy was loaded down with an armload of rocks. They weren't the best quality but would suffice for her needs. Together, she and Ump trotted back to the homebase where Boah greeted her with a screech and a tumble.

"Worried I left? You are pack, Boah. I will always be here for you."

Under Boah's watchful eye, Lucy segregated the rocks she'd collected into one pile that would make useful tools and another that would be for practice. Ump sat on his haunches and leaned heavily against her body.

"Watch my hands, Boah."

She struck hammerstone to core and flaked a stream of cutters. Then, she placed the core in one of Boah's hands and the hammerstone in the other.

"You do it." Lucy sat back, her intent unmistakable: *I'm not going to help.*

Oblivious to the delicate hold Lucy had used, he fisted the stones and crashed them together. A flake resulted but much too dull and thick to use. With her hands on his, Lucy helped him to try again. This time, he chipped off a slightly sharper but still inadequate flake. He dropped the rocks and bounced with excitement, picked them up, huffed, and repeated the process.

Lucy put her hands over his and demonstrated again how to hold the core and the hammerstone and strike nonstop to produce a stream of flakes.

"Now by yourself," and Lucy pushed back onto her haunches, hands in her lap.

He struck downward and then stopped, panting his excitement as he dropped the implements.

"Boah. Do it again and again." Lucy mimed how she held the stones and chipped a stream of flakes.

Boah tried but he just didn't get it. For one thing, although Lucy placed the hammerstone in his stronger hand for the rigorous task of striking, he often switched it to the other hand.

"Boah. Voi does this—not well, but he creates a

stream."

Lucy stopped herself. When she compared their hands, his fingers curved more and the thumb sat lower on the hand. Maybe this was the best he could do with this sort of hand.

Boah understand she disliked his actions and hung his head.

She patted his shoulder. "Try again."

It took almost until what Lucy now considered day to expire before Boah spit out a flake—followed by another and another.

"Boah!" Lucy's excitement spilled over into elaborate hand-gestures. Now, panting his pleasure, Boah made streams of flakes, each better than the last. When he completed a group, he snorted at Lucy and started again.

By the time the day's warmth had completely left them, Lucy was able to load a nice collection of choppers into his neck sack.

Their days passed happily, Sun shining a bit more brightly each day and everyone adjusting to each other and the new lifestyle. Lucy told Boah and Ump about her Group, confided her mistakes with Garv and Ghael, and shared the promises she made and failed to keep. Without hesitation, she told them Raza's Groupmates might force her to leave and Ump and Boah should consider that before joining with her. She wanted them to know everything about this person they seemed to hold in such esteem.

Both listened as though nothing could be more important than her instruction. Boah bounced and panted, and at just the right time, took her hand. Ump, too, seemed to realize the importance of this conversation and turned a furry, innocent face up to hers, communicating his confidence.

Each day, Boah became more skilled at mimicking signals such as *'follow'*, *'danger'*, *'food'* with great accuracy, but ideas like *'past'*, *'over that hill'*, *'before'* confused him, nor did he understand any concept beyond an action or place.

"That doesn't matter, Boah. You are like Voi." Lucy stared off, her thoughts sad. *"Voi… Are you alright?"*

The time finally arrived Lucy had to accept that no one was coming and she would have to find Voi herself.

"We go," she ordered one day as they descended from their night nest.

Boah waved his arms in agreement. Ump offered a happy shake of his tail.

"But which way?" Lucy motioned. Grime and smoke still hid the landmarks and Sun continued to be more of a dark sooty stain overhead than the source of heat and light. She sniffed but gained no clue.

"Let's start by finding food."

"Vulture," Boah signaled, as though everyone could hear unhearable sounds.

Ump whined acknowledgement.

"How…" but Lucy stopped. Sahn could hear the flap of wings and the voice of Vulture-who-no-one-else-heard. Always they found scavenge from her guidance. "Of course. You lead, Boah. We'll follow."

It didn't take long to find a Vulture-thick carcass with marrow-rich bones they could pick through for a meal.

Meal completed, they continued in Lucy's best-guess of the direction her Group would take. They slogged forward, sweat pouring down Lucy's chest and off her head. It felt like walking too close to a wildfire but didn't slow her down or persuade her to rest. All Man-who-makes-tools trekked vast expanses regardless of heat or cold, fatigue or soreness, in search of water and carrion, berries and fruits, and places to rest. She searched for signs of first her Group and then a migrating herd.

Too soon, Boah needed to be carried.

"You are heavy. You walk."

He trundled onward a short distance and then again, reached his long arms toward her: *Carry me.* After several passionate nonverbal pleas, Lucy settled him to her hip. He wriggled his way onto her back, arms around her neck, and gripped her body hair for support. If this was her new Group, she would adapt.

But she couldn't carry Ump so when he started lagging, she came up with an idea.

She flung an arm forward, motioning, "Ump. Sprint ahead and wait."

The canis did better with short sprints than long jogs. He pounced his front paws to the ground and dashed off. When she and Boah reached him, they found him resting, head between his paws. Seeing them arrive, he leapt up and, after a spirited tail thrash, set off again.

Ump became their advance guard.

Neither Ump nor Boah reacted to Lucy's growing concern as she found more and more oddly crushed scrubbrush, footprints with the odd bridge between ball and heel, and other evidence that Man-who-preys had been—or still was—here. He moved quickly. The condition of the tracks and the hardness of the droppings told her he had passed this way yesterday's yesterday or earlier.

Why did he remain in this devastated region?

Chapter Forty-seven

"Falda. Stop this." Sahn gently shook the defeated female to emphasize her demand.

"I can't," Falda motioned.

Flashfires threatened to trap them. The ground continued to swallow flora and fauna alike though not as often and not without warning. Still, chaos had become the new normal.

"We will be fine. You will see." Sahn raised her chin. Falda and Baad's illnesses slowed the Group but that mattered less than staying together. Much of the Group's strength was their size.

"Kelda said Lucy made Fire Mountain angry. I'm glad she left, Sahn." Falda nodded to herself, lips moving, and hands jerking out the conversation.

"Kelda is wrong about that."

The young female shook her head, not even listening. "Kelda is lucky to be dead."

Sahn answered just to engage Falda with the Group. "We don't know Kelda is dead," though she was trapped behind a wall of flames the last time Sahn saw her.

Falda answered moderately, "We will all die, Sahn. Raza,

Garv, Vorak—everyone—has vanished... We have no hope."

"You are wrong again. We have Baad. You have me. We will be fine."

Falda shook her head and shambled on. "I know nothing of how to exist with these horrors. I raise children. I forage. The males defend us, hunt for meat, and find the homebase. Why have they all left us?"

Sahn missed Lucy's quiet strength and thoughtful approach to problems. Falda had collapsed under the weight of the Group's difficulties. She could no longer scavenge much less keep track of Voi. She would take his hand but become distracted by pretty much anything, forgetting the child couldn't find his way without her. Sahn now walked with Voi.

"I screamed t-to him!" Falda stammered.

"Who do you mean? Baad?"

"He never looks at me. How do I make him angry?"

She turned toward Sahn with a start. "Sahn? Where is Kelda?" Falda brightened and displayed her old concern. "Baad—is he ahead?"

"They will be here soon," Sahn crooned. *Maybe it is better Falda forgets.*

Sahn drove the Group forward with a sureness of purpose she didn't feel, refusing to be defeated by the trauma around her. Voi matched her step, swinging his arms in rhythm with his marching feet, mimicking the tilt of her head and cant of her shoulders. He was the balm for her eviscerated life and gave her hope for the Group's future. For him, she would lead.

"Where is Lucy?" Falda interrupted Sahn's thoughts. "Voi needs her..."

Without waiting for Sahn's answer, Falda bounded after

a butterfly desperate to find a flower to pollinate.

"Maybe Baad can calm her…" and Sahn slowed until her brother caught up.

Anyone watching them would think Baad traveled at the back to secure the column but that wasn't why he stumbled awkwardly at the rear of the Group. In fact, he started in the front. First, the females and then the children passed him. When Falda slowed so Baad wouldn't fall behind, no one objected.

"Baad. Falda needs you."

Sahn touched his shoulder as she spoke. If he heard her, he gave no indication, shuffling one foot after another, eyes unfocused. No predator would miss these traits. His arms dangled and his mouth sagged open as though he lacked the energy to close it. Sahn shook her head. Baad still suffered from the sun sickness. Without her prodding, he would forget where they headed or who belonged to the Group he now led.

"I will get us there, Baad. You must recover. We need you."

Sahn would follow the animals. The rumble of their feet left a trail even one her age could track.

Voi mewed like an injured cub and stretched his pudgy arms up. The child sensed her anxiety and asked again—how many times now?—where Lucy and Raza and Garv were.

The first time, she told him they would be back soon but he pointed out when 'soon' expired without their appearance. The next time, she said they were hunting but he reminded her they never hunted without guidance from her shadow-stick and it wasn't set up. The last time, she said they were at the quarry. He shook his little head, gazed at her innocently, and patted her arm.

"I know what you need," and Sahn squeezed him in a

giant cuddle. Voi moaned a satisfied gurgle, laid his head against Sahn's shoulder, and breathed serenely.

Sweena took Falda's hand, confident this adult would care for her, unaware Falda was broken.

"That's right, Sweena. Stay with Falda," Sahn instructed, relieved when Sweena beamed, pleased that Sahn trusted her.

"I worry about Falda," Baad muttered, eyes on his pairmate's halting progress.

"She will be fine. Give her time."

Sahn coped with problems throughout her life. Worry never altered the outcome. In fact, it often made it worse. Her stalwart brother, the one everyone turned to in Hku's absence, crumbled when the females were stolen. Even pairmating didn't help. When Lucy risked her life to save his, it reinvigorated him. He determined to repay her by paying more attention to the needs of the Group. When she disappeared—trying to find the herb he needed—he gave up. Sahn couldn't convince him that blame for her absence did not lay with him.

Now, she needed his leadership to find their new home, guidance to locate the rest of the Group, and strength to defend against Man-who-preys. She couldn't do it alone.

"Come back, Baad."

She began a canorous hum in tempo with the throb of her chest. Baad took up the cadence and the children added their high-pitched tones, and everyone adjusted their steps to the rhythm.

As the days passed, the Group adopted a routine. Sahn marched in front. The females and children foraged in the middle and Baad 'guarded' the rear. Sahn followed tracks left by the fleeing herds. Because the stench of sulfur remained overbearing, this became the only dependable trace. In the past, when the Group had no old homebase to return to, they would follow the herds, knowing the animals superior sense of smell would find water and grass, the basics of Man-who-makes-tools' lives. In that sense, this migration—in spite of the murky sky and the quiet—was no different.

What differed was the Group's size. They didn't have enough members to intimidate predators.

"We must find the others."

Sahn jutted her chin higher and confidence rang out with her every step.

Raza snapped his head up. "I heard something..."

Everyone flinched, fearful the noise meant a predator. Raza glanced at his tiny Group. With himself the only adult male, he entrusted Gleb and Ahnda—ready or not—with the duties of full-grown males. Their first duty was to train Yoo as a scout, a job usually done by much older subadults. As bright as he was, he would have no problem with it.

Raza relaxed and shut out all the dark thoughts that tried to take over his brain. It would work. They would survive.

"Dar. Stay here," Kelda ordered as she guided the child over the treacherous ground.

"But, Mir—we must find her!" Dar begged.

Kelda slapped her head and the child said nothing more. In the absence of Sahn and Lucy, Kelda performed all the female jobs by herself. That included protecting the children, teaching them to migrate, and raising them to adults. Raza would thank her when he got a chance.

They continued onward. Until Sun could penetrate the haze, they had only a general idea of when day became night. Yoo stayed at Raza's side, mimicking the side-to-side movements of his head. The child that marched through their homebase with a twig over his shoulder had died with the

left-behind Group. In his place stood a miniature adult, eager
to take on an adult male's responsibilities. He collected
whatever unburned stalks he could find and grubs that
weathered the inferno by hiding under rocks. Once, he
stumbled over a hare, shrouded in grey ash and to him
nothing more than a bump on the ground, and killed it when
he snapped its neck.

"Your first kill!" Raza motioned with a cheerful grin as
he slung the downy body over Yoo's shoulder. "Food for the
Group. You have done well," Raza complimented.

Yoo beamed and walked straighter, with a confidence
that hadn't been there just steps before. He gripped the ashy
paw and glanced often at the dead animal.

It started first as a soft, almost pleasant rain that cooled
their skin and cleaned their hair-fur, but it grew quickly to a
driving storm, beating down so hard that puddles popped up
wherever a depression existed. Worse, it seared like prickled
cactus being poked into an open wound. Raza gave Yoo
broad leaves to hold over his head but they couldn't cover his
limbs.

"We must find shelter," Raza shouted to Gleb and
Ahnda above the thump of the rain. With the ash washed
from the air, he could see what he hadn't before and started
to sprint.

"There!"

Up ahead, a ledge that jutted from a cliff would shelter
them until the biting rain ended. As he approached, a darker
spot bloomed against the rocky background, like a stain on
the cliff or a depression in its face.

Or a cave.

"Wait until I see if it's safe!" It must be the den of
Snarling-dog, hopefully unoccupied. He flew through the

mouth and huffed to a stop, prepared to fend off the inhabitants. One sniff told him it was empty, had been for quite a while. He motioned the rest of the Group to enter. They all gathered in a tight group, eyes adjusting to the darkness, the water dripping into puddles at their feet. The cave was not even the size of the shade under baobab-by-homebase, but sufficient as a refuge because they were such a small Group. Parched bones and scat littered the cave floor and the stink of urine and rotted flesh permeated the air. The females and children hunched together against the cold walls, knees against their chests for warmth, eyes relieved that at least, they no longer hurt.

"I thank you for this cave," Kelda motioned, movements gentle as she described the difference between clean and fire rain. For one, Kelda tap-tapped with her fingertips and the other she pounded fists against her chest.

She leaned toward Raza and motioned, "The rain will wash away our tracks. Will the others—and Lucy—be able to find us?"

Raza stepped back, amazed at Kelda's concern. She blamed Lucy for causing Man-who-preys to stalk the Group and refused to accept her as a hunter. When Fire Mountain exploded and Lucy didn't return with Baad's healing herb, Kelda carped that Lucy fled, wanting only to save herself, abandoning those who had taken her in. With Lucy gone and no one to disagree, Raza expected Kelda to maintain that story but to his surprise, she seemed to put her differences with Raza's pairmate behind her.

"She is strong."

"Her hunting skill will save her, Raza. I recognize that now."

Between fatigue and a basic trust in the goodness of his Group, Raza never considered a deceptive side to Kelda's comments. He looked at her with a fresh attitude. In place of the chronic complainer now stood a different Kelda, one that put aside her misery and loss for the good of the Group. Where Falda buckled under stress, Kelda bent like a tree in a wind storm.

Unexpectedly, Kelda had become an asset.

"You are a good friend to Lucy. Vorak is a lucky male," and he promised himself to give Kelda a new start.

When the rain stopped, the Group crept out of the cave. For long breaths, they milled around in a disorderly cluster, unsure what to do. The water washed much of the ash from the ground yet still, nothing remained the same. The children whimpered and Kelda hugged them.

"Shss! Raza will know!"

She placed a hand on the youngest as Raza stood silently, back to them, hair and hands dripping. He felt the weight of each face that turned to him expectantly, trusting. His thoughts swirled, not sure of the answers but knowing there was no one else. After a breath and another, he lifted his snout and breathed in.

"This way." Raza motioned with a self-assurance belied by the circumstances, believable because it came from him.

Yoo and every other youngster bobbed agreement in awe that Raza knew the route.

"What a great male."

"I will grow to be like Raza. I too will find the way for my Group."

Raza straightened his back, lifted his snout to sniff his surroundings, and strode ahead at a brisk pace, as though sure a better future lay just beyond the horizon.

Day became twilight and then night, each barely distinguishable from the next. Raza sounded their entry-point call time and again. Never did he hear a response but he continued marching forward, as strong and sure as at any time in his life. Eventually—and fortunately—he found a euphorbia, blackened by fire from its roots to tip but for no good reason still stood. Here he gathered everyone to sleep.

Chapter Forty-eight

Again the ground shook. Raza fought for balance, cutter in one hand and stick-that-kills in the other. It was night and Raza traveled alone.

That couldn't be. If he had to travel at night, which he rarely did, Vorak would be with him. Night belonged to Leopard. Raza stepped back into the shadows, trying to remember how he got here.

That's right. Vorak disappeared. Garv went to look for him. That's why he was alone. Voi toddled into view across the clearing. Kelda stood nearby but turned her back on the child.

"Why are they out at night?"

Owl's hoot rang out, round eyes glistening in the darkness, announcing its hunt. Raza thought Kelda would grab Voi, but she seemed distracted. Leopard's distinctive *ihn-ihn* echoed across the meadow. Raza stiffened, hand clenched around stick-that-kills.

"Run, Voi!" He shouted, but it came out a whisper. He tried to go to the child but tripped. Pain shot through his knee. He ignored it, pushed up, leaning heavily against stick-that-kills. He could see Leopard's ears poking up above the grass, focus on Voi. She edged closer, purring a warning.

"Run!" Raza yelled again but Voi didn't hear.

Wings thudded in the night air, Owl's *hoo-hoo* deafening. Raza tried to rise but his re-injured knee collapsed. He gripped the killing stick, trying to push himself up, but his damaged finger dissolved and he fell forward with a crash.

Leopard glanced at him and then leapt.

Voi howled.

"Kelda—help Voi!" But his mouth made no sound and the female continued to dig vigorously for a root, back to Leopard, ignoring the impending death of the child she should protect.

"Raza." The voice shouted in his ear and the shaking started again. Raza flailed his arms but couldn't reach Voi.

"Raza!" It was louder this time.

He popped upright, eyes bursting open. Faces peered at him. "Vorak—Garv! Voi is in danger!" His voice cracked.

"It is us." Concern and fatigue tinged Vorak's voice. "We found you."

Raza struggled to sit up as he separated dream from reality. He scuttled over to Vorak and Garv, not believing they were real until their shoulders touched. Immediately, the load he'd carried since Fire Mountain's explosion and the Group's fracture melted away. Their presence meant any problem could be solved. Together they could beat back any challenge. Raza soaked up the welcome in their faces, absorbed their strength, and the world clicked a step toward normalcy.

Raza began. "Ahnda and Yoo are here—and Gleb. And Kelda." He grimaced at the memory of her part in his dream.

Vorak motioned, "Sahn?"

"She must be with Falda and Baad. And Voi."

"I am thankful Garv found you, Vorak." Raza couldn't hide the tremor in his hands. He could see the fatigue in both male's faces and bodies, and something else. He shrugged it off. They would tell him when they were ready, even bad news about Lucy.

With a sigh, he pushed that worry aside, to be dealt with later. Instead, for at least a short time, he would enjoy their company, pretend all was as it had been.

Finally, Vorak motioned, "I've never seen the land like this. Death covers everything. All life flees." His hands differentiated between 'flee in fear' and 'flee to find a new homebase'. "But Man-who-preys stays." His hands moved low on his body, communicating both apprehension and confusion.

"They are many," and Garv spread his arms to indicate more than the size of this Group even before fractured. "More than the Group that killed Pan." His child's call sign came out soft but his posture showed no weakness, only determination.

"Why does Man-who-preys remain?" Raza asked Garv and then Vorak but neither responded. It didn't matter anyway. He understood Garv wanted to confront them but Raza had seen the death and mayhem these killers left in their wake. Sharing the territory didn't work. Nor did confronting them. Every time either of those happened, Groupmembers died. They must flee to where Man-who-preys wasn't.

Raza slapped his hands on his chest. "We must find the others, but first you eat."

Kelda chopped at a palm heart, finally cracking open the white crunchy interior. Ahnda found a dead palm tree. Its outside leaves and bark had burned but the insides remained untouched. It would feed the Group for days.

"Falda, Lucy—Sahn. All gone. Voi—it is good Voi died. The child didn't fit in..." Kelda muttered to herself so Raza wouldn't hear. She could tell he wanted to trust her and she didn't want to destroy that. She didn't care that she must work much harder than ever before. Without Lucy, she had Raza and without Sahn, Kelda became Primary-female. No one argued with the Group's Primary-female.

"We are better off. I raise the children. Raza hunts. He should stop worrying," Kelda thought to herself as steps approached. She raised her head, eager to share her latest insights on their plight, but they stuck in her throat.

Hair ragged, body slumped, face drawn, and still strength emanated from his sun-lined face.

"Vorak..."

She gazed from Vorak to Garv to Raza. Did Raza know?

The adults squatted on their heels facing each other while the youngsters played close by. Ahnda joined the males and Yoo edged in, remembering his first kill. Raza motioned his agreement with a subtle nod. Garv stood by, silent and distracted.

Vorak told the assembled Group about the deep chasms that made passage impossible.

"I can find no path to where Lucy went for the healing herb."

Raza gulped. How would he continue without her? He quickly masked his distress and responded, "One who fought Cat-with-cubs cannot be destroyed by Fire Mountain. She may have crossed back before the Rift became impassable and now searches for us." Hope made his voice shake.

"Raza, I must tell you something. About Lucy." Vorak's motions were hurried as though what he needed to say must be done before he lost courage.

"Vorak—Raza is busy." Kelda tried to pull him away. "As Primary-female, it is my responsibility—"

A glare from Vorak silenced her.

Raza glanced from one to the other, confusion clouding his eyes. What did they know about Lucy they were afraid to tell him?

Vorak turned back to Raza. "Lucy may never come back," and Vorak told him everything, about Kelda's accusations, how no one sided with Raza's pairmate—not even Vorak, how she left soon after to find the healing herbs for Baad thinking she would be an outcast when she returned.

"I lost my temper. That's all." Kelda stepped toward Raza, slowly, hoping to soothe over her attack on his pairmate. If it were anyone other than Vorak telling the story, he might believe her but he trusted his hunt partner more than any Groupmate, including Sahn.

He seemed mystified at first and then miserable, shaking his head as his hands stuttered a question, "Lucy thinks we would take Kelda's side?"

Before Vorak could answer, Kelda blurted, "Look at what has happened since she joined us! Hku died—Voivoi died. Fire Mountain destroyed our home. Man-who-preys killed Garv's Group! Even she must see that evil follows her. Raza, she didn't even defend herself!" Kelda sputtered to a stop, and then spit out, "That child is not even yours!"

Garv suddenly appeared within a hand of Kelda, eyes like burning cinders, jaw clenched, knuckles white on knotted fists. "You are the reason my Group stayed behind. You are why they are all dead."

Kelda shuffled away, shaking, gulping with terror. Raza's gaze bounced from her to Garv. He was always the fierce male with the soft voice, the strong leader and competent hunter. He rarely confronted anyone and never took sides.

When angered, though, Raza now realized, Garv would be your worst enemy, like Fire Mountain if he billowed smoke and steam.

Raza mentally reviewed when Garv's group stayed behind. For the first time, Raza wondered why Garv had joined them.

"You came with us, Garv, left your pairmate and child, your hunt partner, but why? Out of loyalty because we rescued you?"

Garv didn't seem to hear Raza. Neck ridged, chest rippling with muscle, malice seeped from him that would frighten Snarling-dog, and he directed it at Kelda. He took a step forward, fists clenched, mouth in a snarl. Raza stopped him with a hand on one shoulder, Vorak on the other, both gently tugging him away from something he wouldn't be able to come back from.

"We are tired. We talk later."

Vorak, Raza and Garv left to patrol the perimeter.

"I am pleased you are back. The Group needs you," Raza motioned quietly to Garv, his voice uncharacteristically emotional.

Garv nodded but said nothing. Raza wanted to talk to him about Kelda and Lucy but didn't know where to begin. Garv and Lucy had a bond Raza could never hope to equal. He didn't care. Lucy would never mean to Raza what his first pairmate had. Putting that aside, the Group was safer and stronger with both of them. Raza didn't want that destroyed by Kelda's misguided actions but didn't think Garv would stay after hearing what she had done.

When everyone tucked in behind the thorn bush barrier, happy to have the males back, Raza lay awake, listening to the snores of his Groupmates, the night sounds of crickets and

Owl, knowing Garv was far too angry at Kelda to let this go. The Group might have to pick between them. If he sided with Garv, would Vorak leave with Kelda?

The quiet tread as someone circled homebase interrupted his musing. Raza froze, recognizing the distinctive *thump-thump*, and began to tremble. Would they always be hunted?

Behind him, another set of eyes blinked, fearless and steady and far wiser than their young age.

Chapter Forty-nine

The first thing Raza did when he awoke was seek out Gleb. He found him by the stream, body unyielding, face like stone, eyes dark holes ringed in red moving steadily across the land. He didn't react to Raza's approach, no greeting, no deference to his adult status. Since rejoining the Group, without being asked, Gleb made it his responsibility to guard the homebase's perimeter but with an intensity that saddened Raza. Gleb was a subadult. He should expect Vorak and Garv to protect him, should ask them his questions but he didn't.

"I heard them last night." Gleb motioned without turning, muscles tense, and head moving back and forth without pause. "I lost them in the talus field. They left this."

Raza wanted to admonish him for going out alone, under Night Sun, but it seemed foolish. Gleb had traveled by himself at night from homebase-where-group-split. He had become more of an adult than many.

Gleb rubbed his raw red eyes, the only visible evidence of the fatigue he must feel, and handed over a palm-sized black rock chipped on both sides and tapered to a sharp edge. Raza recognized the workmanship as no doubt Gleb did.

"I want to learn to use Man-who-preys' killing stick."

His hand motions were abrupt and uncompromising.

"Only Lucy knows how."

"Garv does too. I've seen him." He never looked at Raza except in passing, eyes always roving across the horizon.

"I'll talk to him," and Raza moved downstream where he could be alone to process again being hunted by Man-who-preys, Kelda's treachery, Garv's reaction, and maybe the most important, the loss of Lucy.

Until Vorak's confession, he never thought he'd really lose Lucy. Every part of his life was better because of her, from hunting to healing. He'd known from the beginning that Garv was the father of her child but it didn't matter. How right Sahn's decision to send him for her. What would he—the Group—do without her?

He missed Sahn. She always had answers.

To his surprise, he bore no anger for Vorak. His partner's strengths offset Raza's weaknesses. They were parts of a whole, neither complete without the other.

"Raza. We must talk." Vorak approached quietly with a respect usually reserved for Baad or Hku.

"Sit, my partner. We must solve this problem."

Raza had changed. The youthful, exuberant male Vorak grew up with had become wise. In ways Vorak couldn't comprehend, Lucy gave Raza a strength Vorak never got from a female.

"Raza—"

"Say nothing, Vorak. I understand. You and I are partners. I trust even your mistakes."

Vorak couldn't think of a response so they sat quietly, elbows resting on their knees, eyes flicking through their surroundings while the water washed the shores and flies buzzed.

"They came last night, Vorak. Gleb found *this* outside our camp." He pulled Man-who-preys' cutter out of his neck sack. "I want to go to Lucy's home, across Impassable-rift, where Man-who-preys isn't."

That would be perilous for any Group but theirs had too many females, elders, and children and not enough males. Could they do it? Still, what choice did they have?

It took Vorak a moment to respond but then his hand motions were calm, unhurried. "If we move slowly, cover our trail, yes, it could work." Then his eyes locked onto Raza's. "But how will Lucy find us?"

Raza stared off into the distance, knowing the right decision. His answered with a heavy sigh. "Man-who-preys is a greater peril."

The tantalizing aroma of dead scavenge wafted toward Sahn. Baad's injuries made it her responsibility as Primary-female to take care of the Group and that meant reaching the carcass before other scavengers, which meant hurrying. But 'hurry' was a relative concept for her aged, stiff body and her slow-moving Group. Baad now moved at the waddle of a sick porcupine. Falda moved quickly when not distracted by a blade of grass or a flower. Or anything else.

Another odor floated with the carrion scent, from a stand of fire-ravaged trees. This one she knew. Her eyes popped open, breath quickened, and she wailed.

Raza squatted over a dead she-cat, fresh and without signs of predation, ears straining to create a picture of what was happening around him. His rumbling hunger stilled at the sound of keening from a nearby boulder bed. He sprinted through the brush and around a massive rock.

There Sahn stood, shoulders back, body rigid, and

mouth open. With a whoop, he grabbed her as Ahnda scampered up the hill and Voi tottered babbling toward him.

"Voi—of course you are safe! You have been with Sahn!"

As he crushed Voi to his chest, he panned over to the rest of the found-Group. Falda stood rooted to the ground like the deer who realizes Cheetah stalks her. Baad barely noticed him.

No matter. That could all be fixed now they were again together.

***

Other ears perked at Raza's whoop. A deer raced for cover, a hare shot for its burrow, and Xha turned to seek the figures that went with the sound.

"The weak Primitives."

The herds had disappeared which left Xha's hunters famished. They even consumed the newly-stolen females, the ones they'd planned to mate with for new babies. If he didn't find food soon, the band would die. He'd located Man-who-makes-tools' new homebase a few days ago, hoping to steal their food—or the female they called Lucy—but they had vanished.

"Go." Xha motioned toward the sounds.

***

Garv should enjoy the warmth of the reunited Group, but without Lucy, the jovial banter sounded hollow. After a respectable time, Garv climbed behind the thorn bush barrier and closed his eyes. Soon, everyone joined him in contented slumber.

The temperature increase that marked Sun's return awakened the Group. Each day, Raza could see more of the battered land and less to be hopeful about. Sinkholes studded the ground, themselves connected by the yawning grooves

Fire Mountain's anger had etched into the earth. Food was scarce though rotting carcasses abounded. These almost always crawled with the white worms that made them poisonous to eat. At least, the insects were well-fed. Somewhere, a baleful call echoed Raza's feelings.

"Raza." Garv startled Raza from his thoughts. "I go to find Lucy."

In one arm, Garv held Lucy's stick-that-kills, and in the other, Voi. The youngster slept comfortably with Garv. Raza took in the calmness and determination of the male's face and shook his head.

"I must go. She is my pairmate. You lead the Group to a new homebase. When I find Lucy, we will join you."

"No, Raza. They trust you." Garv's gazed softened and he placed a leathery hand on Raza's shoulder. "I will find her for you."

His assurance invited no discussion. Raza ground his teeth, knowing Garv was right but uncomfortable with the conclusion. Finally, he bobbed his head. "Voi… " *You will keep him from Kelda.*

"Yes." Garv turned to go and then twisted back. "Tell Gleb when I return, I will teach him to use the killing stick."

Without further delay, Garv picked up his neck sack, already loaded with food and stone tools, and left. Raza stared at the departing figure. A shiver ran through his body, as though he would never again see this stalwart, steadfast male. He took a few breaths and turned back to the immediate problem of survival.

Chapter Fifty

"Sahn." Raza wanted to explain why Garv left, with Voi, but she raised a crooked hand as she labored to her feet. "Voi was in jeopardy here. We are too but for a different reason."

Raza clenched his jaw and joined the Group, steps crunching in the dead grass. If not for the traces that must be Man-who-preys, he would have suggested they stay until Vorak was well-rested. Instead, today, they would move on. He shivered, part from his unseen enemy and part from the cold of this harsh new world. Would Sun ever again share its warmth and light? His sparse fur, usually sufficient for any chill, now left him shaking, wishing he grew a thick pelt like Long-tooth.

"We have no food," Kelda complained. Falda, always now at Kelda's side, added a noncommittal wave and a small stiff nod. With Sahn back, Kelda reverted to her usual grumpy self, offset by an eternally optimistic and healed Falda, resuming the dysfunctional friendship they had before Lucy arrived, as though nothing had ever changed.

"Gleb, Ahnda—scout ahead."

"I join them," Yoo insisted to Raza.

"No, you will slow us." Gleb interjected before Ahnda answered.

Ahnda cast a sympathetic glance toward Yoo and trotted after Gleb, headed for a stand of trees that would provide a good view through the haze, or as good as any other. Yoo accepted the decision without question. Gleb's experience as the only Groupmember to survive a battle with Man-who-preys commanded admiration from peers and the youngers even though Gleb refused to talk about it. In fact, he shared nothing personal anymore, not even with Ahnda. He focused only on preparing the Group to kill before being killed. Nothing else reached that level of importance, not even hunting.

Raza moved forward, gate wide, pace strong, Vorak at his side.

"Gleb will be a different type of Primary-male than you or I, Vorak."

Vorak exhaled agreement and then dropped back to the middle of the column.

The children squealed with excitement as they discussed what life would be like in the far-away land of Lucy's birth but Raza couldn't shake the bad feeling that puckered the back of his neck. Wherever they went, Man-who-preys managed to arrive first.

Still, neither he nor Baad had seen them in Lucy's homeland, at least not for sure.

The Group forged onward, between the fault and the cliffs, the same general direction as Mammoth and Giraffe but in rougher terrain to conceal their tracks. At Raza's insistence, the travelers used only hand motions, no vocalizations. Raza never took his eyes off the surroundings, strained to hear everything happening around him, lapped at the scents he couldn't see but might taste, all to find danger before it found him.

At the right moment, and that was up to Sahn, they would veer off this trail and head to Impassable-rift. A new homebase where earth didn't quake, where Fire Mountain didn't erupt, and where Man-who-preys didn't dog their lives, that's what mattered now.

Still, memories of Lucy haunted Raza. Every hillock they crested, every copse of trees transgressed—every stream sighted—he hoped would reveal her. No matter how haggard and tired, how hungry and worn, she would be the most welcome sight of this journey.

"Raza?" Falda breathed heavily as she caught up with him at the front of the column, Baad puffing at her side. He'd become protective of her since recovering from the sun sickness. Raza thought Falda might be carrying a new child.

She motioned to the ash that covered their footprints. "How will Lucy find us?"

"Garv will find her and then find us," Raza answered with quiet motions and a gentle pat to her shoulder. "He knows where we head."

"What if he fails?"

Raza groaned to himself and then glanced sideways at Falda. Did she hear him? It served no purpose to show weakness.

"Shhh." Baad leveled his hand over the ground as he looked first at Raza and then Falda. "Lucy has fought Eagle. She is strong." Baad took Falda's arm and they dropped further back in the column.

"Raza," Sweena's high-pitched voice called from behind. A smile tugged at his lips as he turned.

"No! Do not bother him!" Kelda shoved the youngster into the group of children.

Raza felt a niggling contentment at the resumption of the natural order.

"We sleep here for the night," Raza motioned to Vorak. He pointed to a burned-out tree with desperate leafless branches but a thick trunk that would provide protection from predators, not that they'd come across any in a long time. "At least we will have water." It was a tiny stream but the best they'd seen in a long time.

"There's a hill." Vorak jutted his chin toward a high point on the horizon. "We may see the herds from the crest."

Raza hooted, calling Ahnda and Gleb back from scouting.

The females immediately began to gather corms and nuts and track down snakes, rats and any animals they could stun with a well-thrown pebble.

"Baad! Come with Vorak and me to hunt!"

Baad didn't see them, too busy motioning something to Falda, low on his body for privacy, so Vorak and Raza left.

Carcasses littered the ground but white worms and shiny green flies crawled through them. Raza learned long ago that picking out these pests did nothing to remove the sourness that made him sick. The temporary homebase became a grey blur on the landscape by the time they crested the hill they hoped would reveal their forward trail. Raza sagged.

No herds. Where were they?

But something did catch his attention. He blinked as his eyes adjusted and then squinted across the plateau, not sure what he should be seeing. It could be Ahnda and Gleb, returning, but it didn't move. Finally, antlers gave it away.

"An oryx!" Vorak exulted, and sprinted down the far side of the hill toward what they hoped would be the Group's meal.

When they reached Oryx, it was still warm. This close, they could smell the blood, the rich tissue, and even the bowels evacuated at the animal's death. The ash and smoke in the air must be why Snarling-dog and Vulture hadn't discovered it.

"This will feed us well," Vorak reveled.

Raza stopped Vorak from approaching as he feverishly checked the ground, not able to believe a predator didn't lie in wait, ready to pounce. He found only Oryx's footprints. It seemed the animal had simply dropped dead. When he assured himself there was no danger, Raza pulled out one of the strong vines he carried in his neck sack, remembering Lucy explaining its usefulness, and then wrapped the vine around the carcass so he and Vorak could drag it back to the temporary homebase.

The smell of fresh meat arrived first. The Group rushed over to meet the males, everyone talking at once about a meal that would include more than dried roots and hard berries. Raza and Vorak barely got the carcass to the clearing where they would eat before Groupmembers began to tear away chunks of flesh, drink the blood, and consume delicacies the eyes, tongue, and innards. The long bones with their rich marrow were saved for later.

Gleb and Ahnda didn't get back until much later, when only Raza and Vorak were still awake. Exhausted but pleased, they carried a pigeon and a small pig missing only its forelimbs.

"There is sign of Man-who-preys everywhere but we didn't see them. Their tracks are deep, as though they are chased—or chasing." Gleb turned to Raza. "We must pursue them. They have our Groupmates." He clenched his fists and added, "They have Aqa."

At the mention of the tiny child who called Gleb her

protector and savior from Crocodylus, Raza finally understood the depth of Gleb's anger. She had lived through the attack—or Gleb would have seen her body—and one as young as she could be trained to accept a new lifestyle, as Mag'n had. She would be a prize.

"She knows Man-who-preys killed Pan, from her old Group. I promised that would never happen to her."

Carefully, Raza asked, "Did you see prints like ours with theirs?" Raza motioned, quietly tearing a chunk from the pig.

Ahnda shook his head but Gleb remained still. His face burned with the bottomless anger that ravaged his thoughts. Raza wanted to tell him he understood, that decisions made in anger rarely worked well, but instead he said nothing. Gleb would figure it out. For whatever reason, Man-who-preys no longer took the children with them. Most likely, they were dead. Raza couldn't risk any of his small Group tracking what probably wasn't there. When Gleb grew up, especially if asked to lead the Group, he too would have to make decisions for the good of the Group.

As Ahnda and Gleb left to join the rest of their sleeping Groupmates, Raza stayed behind, thinking not about Gleb's loss but the strength that came with his anger. Man-who-preys' concepts of 'murder', 'kidnap', and 'a joyful kill' were foreign to Raza though he wondered if it might serve them well to adopt a more aggressive attitude. Like Gleb's.

Maybe when Lucy returned, she could teach all of them to use the killing stick

For the first time in a long time, Falda slept without dreams of fire and death. The happy shrieks of children awoke her and she stretched, reaching for Baad but found emptiness.   "He's at the stream."   Kelda sat by Falda, hands in her lap, gaze on the younger female. "Raza and

Vorak are scouting as are Ahnda and Gleb." Kelda wore her usual expression, as though she'd just eaten spoiled fruit.

Falda looked at Kelda with respect. "Without Sahn, everyone turned to you as Primary Female, Kelda. I did nothing to help Sahn."

"You are young, Falda."

"I was frightened. I couldn't think beyond my fear."

Kelda offered what for her, passed as a smile. "It will come. You'll see."

Kelda's empathy cheered Falda. With Lucy gone, who else could she talk to?

"Baad got up and down all night. He said his arm hurt. I think he fell over a rock. I'll check on him."

Kelda handed her a chunk from Oryx's haunch and Falda set out for the stream that flowed into the waterhole at the edge of the temporary homebase, the most likely place to find Baad. As she approached, something about his stillness and the way he sat worried her.

"Baad—I have food."

When he didn't answer his call sign, she handed him the meat. "Here. I can get more if you're hungry."

Baad ignored her, intent on licking a sore spot on his arm, so she left.

Chapter Fifty-one

Raza scrabbled for hand- and footholds on the near-vertical slope. Finally, he pulled himself over the lip and reached down for Vorak. Once over the ridge, both males collapsed, panting in ragged gasps and swatting at a bevy of flies drawn to their sweat.

"This was easier when we were young," Raza motioned between tortured breaths. Last night's meat had given him more energy but not as much as he used to have.

They'd been dodging mammoth-sized boulders scattered across the scarred terrain by Fire Mountain, heading for this hill. It turned out to be much further out than the ones they climbed yesterday and much taller. Raza hoped from its crest, they could find a bridge across the Rift.

He panted heavily, waiting for the thud inside his chest to slow. Once he could breathe without wheezing, he trotted to the far side. The fissure they'd been following extended farther than he could see in every direction. Pockets of fire glowed while volcanic fumaroles blew dark soot and gas into the air, but no bridge.

"I don't see the crossing Garv mentioned," Vorak motioned.

Worse, the only other way to traverse the gorge—climbing down one side and up the other—was blocked by a deep river that filled the bottom and stretched across further than any tree could reach.

"There's a taller hillock," Raza motioned. They scrambled down, through a debris field, over a boulder bed, skirted a dried lava bed, and clawed their way to the top of this, the latest tallest hill. Raza straightened to his full height, damaged knee crackling, buffeted by hot wind, Sun shining fitfully, hopeful as the world opened before him.

He slumped.

The fault swelled broader and deeper than ever. New cracks split the face, each a different color and consistency. A smudge of movement in the far distance caught Raza's attention. It could be Lucy or Garv. It could also be Man-who-preys.

Whichever, it gave them a place to start. They would see whose footprints led to the movement.

As he and Vorak jogged back to tell the Group they found a destination, Raza tripped and fell through a crack in the earth, landing on something soft and squishy. He shook himself and peered up into the bleak darkness above, trying to see what he'd fallen into.

"Where are you?" Vorak's muffled voice called.

Raza pushed to his feet and felt the ground sink with every step, as though he walked on death sands. But unlike death sands, he could easily lift his feet. He stretched his arms out and touched the sides, and then tried to work his way up one wall only to slip back. The dirt though was soft. With time, he could dig footholds and climb out but first, he needed to let Vorak know where he'd gone.

Translucent shafts of light shone through a roof made of what must be foliage. "Vorak! Here! Down below!" Raza called up but got no answer.

This must be one of the sinkholes that honeycombed the terrain. As his eyes adjusted to the darkness, he could make out bumps and curves in the shades of black. He moved his hand over the rough bottom until he reached a cold leathery hide with patches of hair and a sticky sap. He jerked back.

"A dead Mammoth!" Raza was about to shout again when his hand found a smoother hide, sleeker and less bulky. He traced along what must be the back to a long, muscular, furry tail.

"And a dead Leopard!" Mammoth must have fallen in. Leopard jumped in to feed on the carcass but died from the fall. Raza shuddered at how close he came to the same fate.

As he prepared to yell again for Vorak, something scurried over his foot. He jerked back and beady red eyes blinked at him. Before Rat could skitter away, Raza grinned, grabbed its tail and swung it to keep the gnashing teeth from his body.

Tilting his head up, he yelled, "Vorak! See what I've found!" And flung the rodent up through the gap he'd made falling through the coverage. Vorak hated rats more than snakes or scorpions or any other living creature.

"Rat!" Disgust filled his hunt partner's voice but Raza laughed again, the first time he'd done so since Fire Mountain exploded

"There's not only Rat down here, Vorak. I also found Mammoth and Leopard. Come. I can't scavenge all of this by myself!"

Vorak warbled to call the Group and then descended into the pit trailing a vine he'd found on one of the less-burnt trees. Together, he and Raza tore the carcasses into chunks and pitched them up and out the opening. Groupmembers then traipsed them back to the temporary-homebase. When they'd harvested everything they could, they shimmied up the vine and hurried back to enjoy their feast.

"Baad won't move, Sahn, even to eat. I don't know what to do," Falda sounded desperate.

Sahn's joints ached without Lucy's herbs and she wished she had joined the younger female the last time she harvested the Pain-bark. But she hadn't so sucked in her chest and shuffled toward her brother, hurrying faster with each step.

Every member of the Group trudged into homebase, heavily burdened by the carcasses Raza and Vorak found. Sahn couldn't stop drooling, her stomach rumbling with anticipation, but first she must check on Baad. She agreed with Falda, it was odd that he sat quietly, dully swatting the fleas that infested the reeds and licking his arm rather than following the scent of meat. Even if Falda weren't so worried that she skipped eating to stay with him, Sahn would be.

"He's hungry, Falda. That's all," she motioned, even though she knew hunger wouldn't cause him to sit still so long. She thought of reasons why he would, each worse than the other.

She hurried faster.

"I've been scratching his shoulders and neck but he just stares across the water and licks his arm." Falda's motions were bleak.

Sahn observed her brother, the odd bend of his arm and the gray shade of his skin. Something was very wrong. She touched his lower arm—

"Argh!" Baad yanked backward and Falda squealed. The bump Sahn had noticed earlier in the day, the one he told her didn't hurt, had swollen to the size of Ostrich's egg.

She pushed Falda back and took a position beside Baad. From here, the gaping wound was obvious. Sahn touched it more gently but Baad still blanched. The white bone that should be inside his skin had punched through.

"How do you ignore such pain, Baad? Why didn't you call for help?" Sahn didn't expect an answer.

She had seen many wrecked bones. Often the limb swelled and turned red. In the worst cases—such as this—the bone popped through the skin. Many didn't survive. Sahn's spirit sagged when she saw the angry red fingers already clawing up his arm. She thought back to conversations with Lucy about the best herbs for this sort of illness.

"The bone must first be pushed back where it belongs."

Falda broke into tears.

Using a bone sliver from a dead Mammoth, Sahn stabbed into the swollen red lump. Green and white pus pumped from the wound and pooled in Baad's lap. He never whimpered, never even winced. With the bump drained, she wriggled Baad's arm into a rough approximation of where it should be and tugged the ragged skin until it closed over the break.

"Dar," she shouted, "Bring honey! Yoo—stand right there."

Sahn wiped the honey over the laceration, letting it fill the inside. Then, she covered everything with moss and leaves, hurrying so nothing that would worsen the red fingers had time to get inside Baad's body.

She motioned Yoo into position next to Baad. "Rest his arm in your lap, Yoo. Don't let him move it."

Sahn gathered fibrous smooth-skinned leaves she'd seen at the edge of the creek and layered them over the honey-moss-leaf treatment. Then she burrowed into the muddy bank for the tacky clay needed to cover the break from wrist to elbow. She smoothed it to a uniform, flat surface, added another layer of moss and more dirt and leveled it again.

Through all of this, Baad displayed neither discomfort nor relief. After she finished, she sat back on her heels, knees against her chest, face sad.

"It is good we have extra food," Kelda muttered.

Sahn nodded absently. They must delay their departure until the cast hardened.

On the day after the day after Sahn set Baad's arm, Sahn declared the cast hard enough to travel. As they gathered food into their neck sacks, the sky exploded, turning the ground to a muddy, slippery mess. The storm didn't end until Night Sun came and went many times, long after the Mammoth and Leopard meat turned rancid and the white worms appeared.

It did give Garv and Lucy time to catch up, which they didn't, but Raza refused to dwell on those who were missing. Garv would find Lucy and together they would find the Group.

When a murky Sun finally peeked through the cleansed sky, they set out. Often, Fire Mountain and the earth's quakes destroyed Groupmembers but the Group persisted. Death was part of life.

Chapter Fifty-two

"This cannot be."

Fire Mountain glowed, its peak outlined in red and orange, smoke billowing down the slopes. "Have we returned to where we started?" Lucy motioned to Boah and Ump as they stood on the precipice of what looked to be the same Rift they left so long ago.

A good question.

Both Boah and Ump rested on their haunches and tipped their heads to the side. Any decision would be acceptable to them.

"We must get over there," and Lucy pointed across the chasm, where Voi needed her. "But I don't know how." The walls plummeted to a water-filled gorge.

Lucy knelt over the prints that covered the ground. "Those who arrived here chose different directions. I want to go where Man-who-preys didn't but I can't pick his tracks out."

Ump proved every day how well he followed scents. He'd even tracked her several times when they'd played the child's game of hide-and-find, trotting immediately to her hidden spot, nose to the almost-invisible footprints she left.

But any from Man-who-preys, if here at all, were well-mixed with so many others, she wondered if Ump could tell the difference. Still, it was worth trying.

"Ump, smell this trail," but Boah jumped in ahead and embedded his nose in the trail Lucy pointed out. After inhaling deeply, he waddled off as though following a scent trail and then flopped to the ground to dig for worms. Ump padded over to Lucy, pushed his muzzle into the mass of prints, snorted deeply, and then jerked his head up, ears tweaked. After one frozen breath, he took off at a dead run for about a blink, changed directions, batted at a fly, and disappeared around a hillock. She heard excited whines which excited Lucy, only to have Ump return, snout coated in ants.

"How did you take care of this before I found you?"

He plopped to his haunches and licked at the ants with his long tongue. Lucy picked them from his face and fur and when she finished, Ump lapped Lucy's face in pleasure.

Clearly, she would get no help from Ump. Lucy squatted on her heels and placed a hand on Ump and another on Boah. In their time together, they'd come to realize this meant she wanted their attention. Both turned to her, resting on their haunches.

"Given the option, my old Group would travel away from Man-who-preys." She made sure her voice sounded calm, strong, and in control with none of the worry that nibbled at her insides. "We go this way."

Lucy led her small Group through the mix of old burnt and new green grass. Boah stayed at her side while Ump frolicked somewhere ahead. The occasional 'Woof!' told Lucy about his exciting finds.

She approached another of the many treacherous chasms or maybe just another part of the same Rift that plagued her progress. Fatigue almost made her miss the scent. Her stomach fluttered and she glanced back at Boah who eagerly chomped through dried berries from a partially-burned bush. If she was quick, she could check the scent before Boah finished.

Crouching down, she peered over the edge. At the ravine's bottom, blackened by fire and locked in Long-tooth's jaws, lay the Tree-man who warned her of the fire. Boah's Father. Lucy scuttled back from the precipice but Boah had already inhaled the comforting perfume of his family.

"Boah. Stay away."

"Hee!" Boah pant-hooted and scampered toward a much-anticipated reunion. He galloped past Lucy and tumbled to a stop at the bluff of the Rift. His gaze went first to Lucy, as though to ask why she hadn't called him, and then over the lip where he found what remained of the proud male Lucy remembered.

"Aaarrr!" A terrified howl rang from Boah, noises she'd never heard him make before, didn't even know he could. "Awake! Up!" A guttural shriek poured from the child, filled with more misery than she thought any creature could feel. He gestured shakily, eyes darting from her to Hee, and then tried to descend the slope but couldn't find a path that wasn't a cliff. Lucy walked further down the Rift, hoping only Hee died, that his mate and child were still alive.

But that was not to be. Her stomach clenched and her breathing got short and shallow. Hee must have turned, beckoned his family to run faster. That's when Long-tooth seized him from behind just moments before the fire devoured both of them, followed quickly by his pairmate and baby, leaving nothing behind but their scent.

Lucy hurried to Boah but Ump reached him first, panting, tail wagging vigorously. Boah tumbled over, shaking violently. Lucy sobbed with him, the history of this Tree-man family, their struggles and victories, brutally destroyed. No one would ever remember Hee's successful flight from the hungry fires or his compassion for an unknown creature. He would thankfully never know that his final effort to save his family, even at the cost of his own life, failed.

"Noble Tree-man. I will help Boah as though part of my Group, as you helped me," Lucy whispered as she cried.

Boah licked Lucy's face, surprised by the wetness.

"They are tears. I am sad for you," she motioned.

Boah stiffened and flashed his fear grin. Her upset frightened him.

"I am not angry, Boah. This means I care for you," but Boah shook, covering his face with his hands, whimpering. When something upset his leader, he—as would any child in her Group—blamed himself. Lucy stifled her tears and groomed him, hoping to bring a small measure of peace to his tormented soul.

***

Far down the same Rift, using stick-that-kills to balance himself, Garv pressed his ear to the ground while watching the backtrail. A dust storm or a flock of birds that suddenly took to the air could indicate someone or something followed him. Food was plentiful and risks minimal—because most life had fled—but the nonstop search drained him. Soon, he would have to quit.

Voi toddled along, oblivious to the difficult decision Garv faced as well as the one his mother must make if she returned to the Group—if Kelda had the power to eject her from the Group.

The Lucy Garv knew wouldn't leave without Voi. For that reason, he kept going.

He jogged faster, determined to at least find her, tell her

what happened, and let her make a choice. Voi curled to his chest, tied with a vine and coated with a layer of mud to tamp down his fragrance. He remained silent, understanding that the sound of a child would attract unwanted attention.

Garv paused to listen without the noise of his feet. This time, an anguished cry drifted through the thin atmosphere. It sounded like Cousin Chimp or maybe a Tree-man but Raza had seen none of either. He assumed that Fire Mountain's anger drove them, like Raza, away from the Rift so who howled with such anguish?

Putting the cry out of his mind, he considered what to do. By now, Lucy surely found the medicine for Baad but probably couldn't find a way through the cracks and rifts in the earth's skin.

The plaintive call echoed again. Even Voi turned at the need that leeched from its hollow tones. Something about its pitch made Garv study the landscape.

"Is that a figure?" He climbed a berm for a better view. The call came from a stand of trees that abutted the Rift. Could it be Lucy? Had she fallen?

Another voice, this a howl of victory. Wolf tracked food and summoned his brothers. Garv grabbed Voi and jogged around a switchback where he could have an unobstructed view of the copse of trees he'd identified. He settled Voi into a small depression and then searched for prints. If he had heard Lucy's cry, she could only reach those trees by traveling this path. Eyes locked on the ground, he found old tracks of mammoth, wild-beast, deer, and sand fleas, and vast swaths of rodents.

Overlaying those were fresh tracks, left today or yesterday. One set must be Lucy for they matched his prints, except smaller. As he suspected, she followed the herds, thinking the Group would do the same and at some point she'd cross their path.

Odd that she traveled with someone who left shorter and wider prints, a mixture of hand and foot like Tree-man's. But that was impossible. Intertwined with both lay prints of what must be the largest Wolf Garv had ever seen. Could this be the beast who now called his brothers to eat? Though neither Lucy nor the Tree-man showed signs of distress—no limping or bleeding—maybe one of them was injured, or sick. Or the Great-wolf might stalk them simply because they were alone, without the defense of a Group.

He scratched his chest, trying to unravel what he saw. It surprised him how close Great-wolf passed to his potential prey.

A screech dragged him back to reality and then a blur of feathers and talons—Eagle in her death dive. Garv followed Eagle's path, wondering what prey it found, and froze. Voi had crawled out of the protective crevice and now tottered toward Garv, waving his arms, a grin spread across his cherubic face. The child weighed little enough that Eagle could carry him back to her nest for her eaglets to pick through the flesh. Garv's mind stilled, his focus matching Eagle's. He had only moments before the treacherous beak penetrated Voi's skull and the claws perforated his vulnerable underside but that's all he needed.

"No!" Garv roared as he exploded forward, driving his legs into the hard ground, swinging stick-that-kills in front of him. A perplexed look crossed the child's face, asking why this most important adult would yell at him. Tears spilled as he tripped and tumbled into one of the many fissures that splintered the ground. Garv cracked the killing stick against Eagle's fragile ribs. She squalled, hovered momentarily, and then retreated. Garv prepared to take another strike but the raptor left, no longer wanting this fight.

Garv pulled Voi from the crevice and wrapped him in his arms moments before the brawny male's legs buckled and he fell to the earth. Cuddled in Garv's embrace, Voi calmed sooner than Garv did.

Wolf howled again. He called more cousins to what must be a large feast.

"We must go."

With stick-that-kills in one hand and Voi in the other, Garv sprinted toward Lucy, hoping he would get there before it was too late.

Chapter Fifty-three

Lucy awoke, sensing something she had yet to identify. Boah slept on, unaware of a menace. They covered a lot of ground yesterday and he was so tired he didn't even bother to look for food, simply built the nest and dropped into sleep.

A growl rose below, soon joined by more. She peeked down at the slobbering jaws of a pack of wolves watching her through predatory eyes.

She gasped. *Where is Ump? Is he alive?*

She shook Boah's curled body. "Be still," and indicated the wolves.

Boah howled and scrambled upward, almost falling from the tree in his abject horror.

"Be gone!" Lucy ordered the wolves without effect. "Leave us!"

One wolf leaped, yellow eyes furious, jaws bristling with fangs. Powerful legs thrust its muzzle up almost to her feet. The dirty curved claws of enormous front paws dug deeply into the trunk. Lucy roared, hiding her panic behind bared teeth, but Boah stank of terror.

"Go!" she screamed, emphasizing it with a vicious swing of a bough. Wolf dodged and snapped refusing to be intimidated. She flung the branch but Wolf pivoted away. From the base of the tree, Ump howled.

"Ump—stay away!"

The canis' sociable temperament was no match for these predacious beasts, but he ignored her plea. He roared and slapped the ground as he assessed Wolf for weakness. He had none.

The wolves charged, pushing Ump back with ease and turning to the real banquet. If they couldn't drag her from the tree, they would simply wait until Lucy and Boah became so exhausted they fell from the tree into their maw. Lucy wrapped her arms around Boah and he buried his face in her shoulder.

Is this how we will die?

A monstrous growl sounded from the opposite edge of the clearing.

More arrive to enjoy the feast.

Lucy twisted as she held tighter to Boah. An immense bear charged, roaring his dominance as he thrashed a huge club at the wolves. He hissed, smacked the ground, and then lunged again. Ump, sensing an ally, sidled closer to the bear and growled at Wolf while the bear flung a missile that hit one of the wolves right above his eye. With a yelp, it scurried away.

The pack parted, revealing the largest Wolf Lucy had ever seen. Yellow fangs and blood-red lips dominated its face. Golden eyes fastened on the bear. Its prickled gray pelt stuck up like cactus spikes and its toes dug into the earth as he advanced. A low growl fell from its jaws and frothy saliva dripped as though to say, *"This is our food. Leave or we destroy you too."*

The bear stood firm. Ump, emboldened, remained beside him, eyes wide, ears flat, a snarl vibrating deep within his chest. Lucy stopped breathing.

The bear waved the substantial branch in front of his body and glared into the wolf's eyes. When he caught the beast's attention, he roared and slammed his club into the animal's body. There was a crack as its chest caved in. The momentum tossed it through the air and it crashed down with a yip. It tottered to its feet and limped into the bushes.

Without their leader, the wolves whined and pranced, unsure whether to attack or flee. The bear had no such doubts and charged the most aggressive remaining beast, swiping a claw across its face. Tissue separated showing bone and muscle, just missing the eye. Blood poured down its cheek and its jaw slackened. With a strangled yelp, tail between its legs, it fled with the rest of the pack close behind.

The bear's victory didn't mean Lucy's freedom because he now owned the prey. Maybe Ump could distract him, but the canis stood frozen, head down, tail tucked, mouth hanging open while the bear loomed over him, staring.

"Ump—go!"

She hugged Boah tighter, sure the next sound would be this monster tearing her apart. Ump howled as he crept backward until he bumped into her tree. Smart enough to know he'd lose an attack on bear-that-fought-off-wolves, he dodged up and back in a determined effort to stay between the bear and Lucy. Baying nonstop, he thwacked his front paws to the ground, pounced and withdrew as he threw his body side to side.

Ump refused to save himself so Lucy must find a solution that would save all of them. The bear faced Ump, head down, arms outstretched.

Grasped in his fist was stick-that-kills.

"Man-who-preys!" The cry exploded from her mouth. "He can't climb," she motioned with a confidence she didn't feel. "We are safe." Why tell him stick-that-kills could easily reach them? "Ump—go. We are fine!"

"Lucy?" The bear looked up.

"G-Garv?" She cried as Ump growled and Boah collapsed in terror, tumbling to the ground and landing a hands-width from Ump.

She drank in Garv's presence, strong and commanding as though he ruled the world. Ump bounded forward, eager to stay between Boah and the bear and Lucy. Hackles raised, jaws slobbering, great head hunched, he would be a formidable opponent. Oddly, his tail shook furiously. Garv's attention darted between Lucy and Ump and Boah and back to Ump.

"Ump. It's OK."

Her forceful voice calmed the canis. He cocked his head as though to assure himself he heard her. With a final yip, he plopped to the ground, panting self-congratulations. Garv shook his head in confusion and eyed Lucy as she descended and circled the canis' neck in a hug.

"You are a fine defender-of-pack-against-unknown-bear," she crowed.

Ump relaxed but Boah whimpered which made Garv roar and slump into a defensive crouch Lucy recognized as his attack position.

"No, Garv. These are my Group."

Lucy moved toward Boah as he wailed in panic.

Garv's brow puckered as he tried to make sense of her gestures for 'Boah' and 'Ump'. Boah's fear grin matched his submissive body posture. As soon as Garv stopped looking at him, he escaped, each step marked with diarrheic scat.

"They have no families. I promised I'd take care of them," Lucy motioned as though this was the most natural of statements. Ump spread his powerful jaws into a smile as his head bobbed up and down to the rhythm of his enthusiastic breathing.

"They are no threat to us."

This, Lucy directed toward Boah, invisible in the scrubby underbrush, unaware that the overpowering fecal stench told them where he hid.

"Boah. See Ump has relaxed. Wolf is gone. We are safe," but he refused to join her.

"Why are you by yourself?" Lucy turned to Garv, eyes questioning, and then she figured it out. "You have come to tell me—"

Her throat tightened so she couldn't speak and her eyes filled with tears. She was saved from saying more by a gurgle at the edge of the clearing. She turned toward it and then back to Garv, confused.

"Here." He trotted over and withdrew a round bundle from amongst the leaves.

"Voi..." Lucy managed no more than a whisper. Her heart pounded and she panted a shallow wheeze. "How... How did you bring him?"

Garv answered with a tired shrug. The child snuggled into Garv's hip, calm in the face of events around him, confident in this male who brought him so far.

Lucy's hands floated toward Voi as though on their own. The child slipped into her grasp, round and warm. He fit into the curve of her shoulder as though that was what he should do. She burst into tears and Garv folded his arms around them. While sobs shook her body, he held her, rocking back and forth. When Voi squirmed for air, Lucy gathered him into her lap. Ump padded over and flopped onto his side, head on his paws. Boah waddled forward but maintained a secure space between himself and Garv.

"Thank you for finding me."

A tired smile creased Garv's face as Boah shuffled forward another few steps. "Man-who-preys stalks the Group but Raza refuses to leave without you."

Lucy thought about that for a long time before she spoke. "I have the plant for Baad," and she patted her neck sack, "but I will only stay if they accept Ump and Boah. I am happy with my new Group, Garv, as happy as I've ever been," *except for my time with you.* Her hands were tired but sure.

Seeing Lucy's calmness with the stranger, Boah approached to within an arm's length of Garv, a comical fear-grin plastered across his face, bouncing until his legs buckled and he fell to the ground. Lucy moved closer to Garv with a grin. "You worry him."

Garv glanced between Lucy and Boah, then Ump and Lucy, and responded simply, "I can't wait to hear how all of this came about."

Lucy smiled. "Boah is much like Voi. Just… different. Ump—well, everyone should have an Ump in their Group. He is never deceptive," *like Kelda,* "hunts well and bravely, and always support me."

She could see the tension melt from Garv's neck. Even Boah did. He crawled a bit closer to the big male, still never removing his eyes from him.

"I will get leaf sponges," and Lucy moved away so smoothly Voi didn't wake up. By the time she got back, Garv lay on his side, eyes closed, snoring gently. Boah, too, slept.

The day had cooled by the time Garv shook himself awake, still surprised he'd found Lucy. Even after Kelda's vitriol and Falda's passivity, Lucy thought first about finding the plant for Baad. Garv soaked in her kindness, doubting he could ever get enough of it. She flourished in her life away from Kelda and the Group and glowed with a confidence he only suspected that day long ago when she became his pairmate. He watched her approach, Boah and Ump at her side, Voi on her hip, her skin flushed with the bite of the crisp water. She handed him a soggy leaf sponge which he sucked hungrily.

"Boah," she motioned toward the child. When she sat, he collapsed at her side. "Garv and Voi are now part of our pack," Lucy motioned. "We will all take care of each other."

She hugged Garv, motioned for Boah to do the same while she sat Voi on her lap. Boah wrapped his long arms around the entire group as Voi grinned. Out of sight, Ump barked with an urgency that pulled everyone to their feet into a dead run toward his voice. The shoulder-high thorns thickened as she neared the stream where they'd heard Ump's bark but she didn't slow, worried Ump was in trouble. When she reached him, his muzzle thrashed through the shallow water, jaws snapping and paws spread solidly beneath his body.

"Ump! What are you doing?"

Ump twitched his head up and threw a fish over his shoulder. It writhed and flailed until Garv stabbed it with Stick-that-kills. Then, everyone shared Ump's food, sucking the fish's flesh from bones and chewing the reeds growing along the edge of the stream.

As they ate, Garv explained about the eruptions, Mir's death and Dar's survival, the Group's separation and reuniting, Vorak's honesty in defending her, how much Raza missed her, and how his strength guided everyone. Lucy listened while she ate and then groomed Voi. Boah snuggled into Garv's lap, grabbing his hand and placing it on the fur behind his ear. Ump gawked into Garv's face throughout the story, enraptured. When Lucy finished grooming Voi, the child plopped his squatty body beside Ump and began grooming the canis' sides, legs, and tail—the only part of the gargantuan animal he could reach.

"Raza wanted to come for you but must take the Group to safety."

"Of course, he must do what best serves everyone."

"They will follow the herds away from Fire Mountain and the earth quaking. That's where we'll find them."

He didn't tell her Raza planned to recross Impassable-rift and find Lucy's brother. There was time enough to do that when they reunited.

Excitement flashed across Lucy's face. She must yearn to see Raza—Sahn—and others in the Group but she wasn't the same person as when she left. If Kelda didn't like her before, she'd despise her now.

Ump nuzzled into her lap, his snout finding the pleasant smell of Voi. The child grabbed a handful of Ump's coarse hair and buried his face in it. Boah pounded the ground and frog-jumped in his excitement.

Garv relaxed for the first time since Lucy had disappeared. Even though he doubted she'd find such contentment when she returned to the Group, he would do everything he could to make that possible. Ump stretched and yawned, took a turn and another and resettled. His muzzle dangled over the side of Lucy's leg, eyes trusting, his entire body at rest.

"Garv, is it odd that I would give my life to save Ump's. He and Boah are my responsibility. They are happy when I am. Is that enough?"

"That would be enough for me."

"When did I change?" she asked as they curled together. Garv wanted to tell her it happened when she joined Raza, that this Lucy here was the Lucy he pairmated with, planned to spend his life with, but he couldn't. She belonged to Raza, not him. He'd promised to bring her back.

"Wolf pack may return, Lucy. We must leave."

Chapter Fifty-four

Boah waddled toward Lucy, shredded tissue from a dead shrew dribbling down his chest. Around his neck hung one of Lucy's neck sacks stuffed with food and a cutter which an investigation by him proved to be sharp. When it cut his finger and blood beaded along the tip, he stared and then licked.

"Glll." His hand motions indicated if Lucy wore the odd sack, he would, even if it hurt.

Lucy whistled for Ump. He romped over, a rat in his mouth and poked his muzzle into Lucy's face to scrape the almost-dead rodent against her lips. She shook her head. *I've eaten.*

"Here." She touched her sack and Boah's and tied one around Ump's neck. "No," she ordered gently when he dipped his jaw down to the fragrant concoction. When he tried to bite it again, she pushed his head away and growled in the tone she used to warn him off.

Ump understood and with a final sniff, bounded off on their forward trail. Voi flew after him as fast as his toddle would carry him. Ump stopped, yapped and wagged briskly until the child caught up, and then sprinted off again. This they repeated until Voi grasped Ump's furry sides and hung on. The canis slowed, seeming to appreciate that Voi, like his pup, couldn't move as quickly as an adult.

Garv shrugged. "Ump will track better than I."

Garv and Lucy followed Ump, Boah holding Garv's hand, along the Rift valley. Lucy expected the furious river at the bottom would dry to a trickle by the time they found a downward path. Garv and Lucy took turns carrying stick-that-kills. Both felt safer with it in their hands.

When there weren't interesting scents to investigate, Ump trotted with them, bumping against Garv's leg, bushy tail wagging. Voi tired of running alongside Ump so straddled the canis' back and clung to his pelt. Garv watched, amazed how easily Voi, Boah, and Ump played together, clearly happy to be with this pack. Garv failed to hide a smile which brought another fear-grin to Boah's face.

Their daily routine never varied: Garv and Ump searched for tracks while Lucy, Boah, and Voi searched for food. Nights, they slept tucked into trees. Garv grew to appreciate Ump's defensive position below.

Daylight came and went over and over with no sign of the Rift ending. Each day became less hazy but Sun often hid behind its filmy shroud. Happily, the nights were warm enough that they no longer had to sleep in a shared bundle of warmth. Lucy couldn't decide if Ump's or Boah's fetid breath was worse but knew sleeping was more restful if they were at a distance.

After Night Sun whittled away and reappeared, she finally found the cairn that marked her backtrail but there was no transversal across the Rift. She stood quietly, studying the expanse, but nothing matched her memories. No quiet stream flowed. No shade trees. No Hipparion nibbled at stubby tufts or the long golden grasses that hid their progress. Just desolation. Worse, with walls so steep they couldn't be climbed, there seemed no way across.

"If I crossed here, the bridge I used is gone." She spoke softly, her words puzzled. How could it disappear?

Garv scratched his arm. "It must have been here when I followed your tracks." Confusion creased his face.

They continued along the Rift's lip, less hopeful with each step. Finally, they rested. Ump dropped beside Garv as if to say, "What took so long?" Voi and Boah sat by the canis and groomed his dirty fur.

"Even if we can't cross anymore, we should have found the Group by now. Raza and I agreed to meet there." Garv pointed to a position across the chasm and far down their backtrail. "Are we too late?"

"Ump can find them by following your scent, the same way he finds shrew and wild-beast."

She pressed Ump's nose into Garv's stomach and then his feet, sniffing deeply to demonstrate what the canis should do. He snorted in and wagged his tail at the new game. She trailed him along their backtrail, letting him make the connection that he was following Garv's scent and then pushed him forward, away from where they were.

With a '*Woof!*' he bounced off. Lucy grabbed Voi and gave chase, Garv at her side. Boah scrambled to his feet and raced after them.

Days turned to nights, Rift swelled wider and deeper, and still Ump loped forward, bearing confident as though any moment he would find the spot. He often yipped from ahead telling them his location and occasionally returned to visit. Lucy would snort in Garv's scent with him and he'd set off again.

As another day passed, Sun barely above the horizon,

Lucy heard Ump snarl.

"Ump!" Lucy sprinted toward his voice, thoughts heavy with worry. Finally, there he stood spread legged on the precipice, his powerful body leaning into the emptiness. His hair prickled and his muzzle aimed across the divide.

Like tiny ants on the tip of his snout, figures milled about.

"Ump found them!"

They must wonder at the canis that faced them, full-bodied and aggressive. Did they notice his flapping tail and perky ears? Did they hear the friendliness in his voice that Lucy had grown to recognize? She skidded to a stop beside him on the crest of a vertical wall that plumbed downward a hand's width in front of her feet. She clamored and waved while they jumped up and down like frogs, screeching as more figures appeared across the Rift.

"Sahn! Falda! Ahnda—and Baad!" Lucy called their names across the divide, her usual cautious demeanor giving way to exultation. She raised Voi high and swayed him side to side as muted shrieks reached her.

Voi fought against her and she plopped him down beside her. Ump plowed his front paws forward, charged but went nowhere, and wagged furiously. Boah cowered until Voi took his hand and together they bounced up and down like tumbleweed blown by the wind, barely cresting the nodding heads of the waist-high grass. Garv moved to Lucy's side to add his height.

"We must be quiet," Garv admonished.

Lucy remembered the traces of Man-who-preys that dogged their steps. Did they hear her, even now planning his attack?

"This way." Lucy waved long sweeping but silent movements down the Rift.

She imagined a nod from the figure that must be Raza and set off with renewed energy. They traveled for days and nights and still no bridge. The only good news was that Night Sun had resurfaced, wan and weak but with enough light to guide their steps. If Night Sun could survive, so too could Lucy and her new Group.

One day, the Rift expanded into a lake so vast it extended from where Sun awoke to where it slept. Ump plopped down, confused, Boah at his side, both unsure why Lucy stank like fear.

How can we get around this behemoth?

"Lucy..." Garv tried.

"We will find a way," Lucy responded softly without letting him finish. She filled her voice with enough assurance that Garv believed her.

"Boah, stay with Garv and Voi."

She left, Ump at her side, sniffing as though this would be the best game ever played. A stocky graying figure—it must be Baad—split off from the Group and trotted the same direction that Lucy did. Soon, both were out of sight and Garv settled to wait. Boah and Voi picked at the ground, chased after ants and scorpions, and snacked on earthworms.

Sun came and went, came and went again, and still Lucy didn't return. Garv began to worry.

Garv knapped a stone, trying to recreate the tool of Man-who-preys, as Voi and Boah harvested grubs and worms from the nearby trees. Sun rested only a hand above the horizon, a bright orange glow, when Ump romped into view. He cavorted as though the world overflowed with joy and excitement, his big plumy tail fanning an enthusiastic breeze. Garv leaped to his feet, excited to hear what happened, expecting Lucy would be steps behind.

But she wasn't. Ump reached Garv, licked a sloppy wet tongue across his cheeks, and still no Lucy. Just as Garv started toward the spot where Ump first appeared, Lucy broke free of the shadows, head drooping, no sign of her usual careful back and forth awareness of her surroundings. He waved but got only a slight bob in response. When he shouted, she looked around as though uncertain. Her chest heaved and she tilted side to side. Her skin had become slack, eyes dull.

Something was terribly wrong.

He sped toward her, not sure she would reach him on her own.

"Lucy—I'm here!" His chest throbbed, nausea hovering at the back of his throat.

She gave no indication of seeing him. Instead, she looked past, eyes glazed, each step slower than the last. The agony that radiated from her face made Garv catch his breath. Just as he reached her, she collapsed, body shaking.

"They slaughtered him."

"Who, Lucy?"

"Baad screamed—Man-who-preys stabbed him... Stick-that-kills... Shrieked in excitement. I... hid..."

With a stagger, she fell against him.

"Now they will go after the rest of the Group."

Across the Rift, the small figures milled around. The Group, though still large enough to intimidate predators, seemed small without Baad. They stood, strong of body, questioning Lucy's reappearance, wondering where Baad was.

"They must flee, quickly."

She drank in their appearance, burned their memory into her mind. After a long breath, she picked up stick-that-kills and moved to the edge of the precipice. She lifted her arm over her head, balanced the weapon as she'd practiced, raised it over her shoulder, and threw it with a strength she had never before possessed. Those on the other side couldn't fail to recognize stick-that-kills. Their faces curved upward along its arc as though willing its flight, silent as it descended and crashed to the floor of the Rift canyon. Lucy smiled at a subtle nod from Raza. He understood and turned back into the forest, as did every female. There—choppy angry movements—surely Kelda grumping about something. One female clutched Kelda. Dear Falda—she would be terrified without her pairmate to tell her all would be fine.

Now Vorak left, with his broad shoulders and tall body. Lucy unclenched her fists, happy that Raza could still rely on Vorak. Most of the children were too short to reach over the scrub that edged the Rift but that bobbing figure must be Yoo. Nothing in life defeated his optimism. Next went Gleb. No other child walked like an adult. They would need his strength.

At the last was Ahnda. The youngster had become a man since Lucy last saw him. He turned, searching her huddled Group. Ump was too short but Ahnda could surely make out Boah. He must wonder why she held his hand. Ahnda raised an arm in farewell, such a forlorn movement, but it spoke volumes about his feelings. Something made him twitch sideways—probably Kelda grousing at him to hurry—but he again waved and then sprinted into the forest.

They evaporated, knowing that never again would they be reunited with their Group.

Lucy turned away, shoulder touching Garv, absorbing the warmth and strength of his body. Sun dropped to the place where sky meets earth. How strange the world continued.

Boah and Garv led with Lucy behind. Voi placed his tiny hand in her limp one, trusting her. Ump nudged against her side as though knowing he needed his support.

Without warning, the night skies exploded in color—sparkling paths of light that streaked to earth and guided the way to their new life.

Epilogue

No one told Lucy and Garv that they began man's great African exodus toward the cooler and calmer climates of the Mediterranean, Europe, and Asia. Their willingness to journey marked man's flexibility, adaptability, and elasticity— hallmarks of an evolutionary fitness that would challenge Nature for control of the world. All Lucy knew was her future lay elsewhere.

She and her new Group turned away from their ancestral homes, toward the shining lights—a new life with its magnificent aromas of bush, soil and wind, its bird songs and buzzard cries, its hum of life. They left, spirits buoyed by companionship, chasing a distant dust cloud that surely ended in a herd.

All life needed to eat.

Want More?

Click if you'd like to be notified when the sequel to **Born in a Treacherous Time** is available:

Crossroads: The Journey Home

Read a sneak preview on the next page:

Chapter One

Her foot throbbed. Blood dripped from a deep gash in her leg. At some point, Xhosa had scraped her palms raw while sliding across gravel but didn't remember when, nor did it matter. Arms pumping, heart thundering, she flew forward. When her breath went from pants to wheezing gasps, she lunged to a stop, hands pressed against her damp legs, waiting for her chest to stop heaving. She should rest but that was nothing but a passing thought, discarded as quickly as it arrived. Her mission was greater than exhaustion or pain or personal comfort.

She started again, sprinting as though chased, aching fingers wrapped around her spear. The bellows of the imaginary enemy—Big Heads this time—filled the air like an acrid stench. She flung her spear over her shoulder, aiming from memory. A *thunk* and it hit the tree, a stand-in for the enemy. With a growl, she pivoted to defend her People.

Which would never happen. Females weren't warriors.

Feet spread, mouth set in a tight line, she launched

her last spear, skewering an imaginary assailant, and was off again, feet light, her abundance of ebony hair streaming behind her like smoke. A scorpion crunched beneath her hardened foot. Something moved in the corner of her vision and she hurled a throwing stone, smiling as a hare toppled over. Nightshade called her reactions those of Leopard.

But that didn't matter. Females didn't become hunters either.

With a lurch, she gulped in the parched air. The lush green grass had long since given way to brittle stalks and desiccated scrub. Sun's heat drove everything alive underground, underwater, or over the horizon. The males caught her attention across the field, each with a spear and warclub. Today's hunt would be the last until the rain—and the herds—returned.

"Why haven't they left?"

She kicked a rock and winced as pain shot through her foot. Head down, eyes shut against the memories. Even after all this time, the chilling screams still rang in her ears...

The People's warriors had been away hunting when the assault occurred. Xhosa's mother pushed her young daughter into a reed bed and stormed toward the invaders but too late to save the life of her young son. The killer, an Other, laughed at the enraged female armed only with a cutter. When she sliced his cheek open, the gash so deep his black teeth showed, his laughter became fury. He swung his club with such force her mother crumpled instantly, her head a shattered melon.

From the safety of the pond, Xhosa memorized the killer—nose hooked awkwardly from some earlier injury, eyes dark pools of cruelty. It was then, at least in spirit, she became a warrior. Nothing like this must ever happen again.

When her father, the People's Leader, arrived that night with his warriors, he was greeted by the devastating scene of blood-soaked ground covered by mangled bodies, already chewed by scavengers. A dry-eyed Xhosa told him how marauders had massacred every subadult, female, and child they could find, including her father's pairmate. Xhosa communicated this with the usual grunts, guttural sounds, hand signals, facial expressions, hisses, and chirps. The only vocalizations were call signs to identify the group members.

"If I knew how to fight, Father, Mother would be alive." Her voice held no anger, just determination.

The tribe she described had arrived a Moon ago, drawn by the area's rich fruit trees, large ponds, lush grazing, and bluffs with a view as far as could be traveled in a day. No other area offered such a wealth of resources. The People's scouts had seen these Others but allowed them to forage, not knowing their goal was to destroy the People.

Her father's body raged but his hands, when they moved, were calm. "We will avenge our losses, daughter."

The next morning, Xhosa's father ordered the hunters to stay behind, protect the People. He and the warriors snuck into the enemy camp before Sun awoke and slaughtered the females and children before anyone could launch a defense. The males were pinned to the ground with stakes driven through their thighs and hands. The People cut deep wounds into their bodies and left, the blood scent calling all scavengers.

When Xhosa asked if the one with the slashed cheek had died, her father motioned, "He escaped, alone. He will not survive."

Word spread of the savagery and no one ever again attacked the People, not their camp, their warriors, or their hunters.

While peace prevailed, Xhosa grew into a powerful but odd-looking female. Her hair was too shiny, hips too round, waist too narrow beneath breasts bigger than necessary to feed babies. Her legs were slender rather than sturdy and so long, they made her taller than every male. The fact that she could outrun even the hunters while heaving her spear and hitting whatever she aimed for didn't matter. Females weren't required to run that fast. Nightshade, though, didn't care about any of that. He claimed they would pairmate, as her father wished, when he became the People's Leader.

Until then, all of her time was spent practicing the warrior skills no one would allow her to use.

One day, she confronted her father. "I can wield a warclub one-handed and throw a spear hard enough to kill. If I were male, you would make me a warrior."

He smiled. "You are like a son to me, Daughter. I see your confidence and boldness. If I don't teach you, I fear I will lose you."

He looked away, the smile long gone from his lips. "Either you or Nightshade must lead when I can't."

Under her father's tutelage, she and Nightshade learned the nuances of sparring, battling, chasing, defending, and assaulting with the shared goal that never would the People succumb to an enemy. Every one of Xhosa's spear throws destroyed the one who killed her mother. Every swing of her warclub smashed his head as he had her mother's. Never again would she stand by, impotent, while her world collapsed. She perfected the skills of knapping cutters and sharpening spears, and became expert at finding animal trace in bent twigs, crushed grass, and by listening to their subtle calls. She could walk without leaving tracks and match nature's sounds well enough to be invisible.

A Moon ago, as Xhosa practiced her scouting, she came upon a lone warrior kneeling by a waterhole. His back was to her, skeletal and gaunt, his warclub chipped, but menace oozed from him like stench from dung. She melted into the redolent sedge grasses, feet sinking into the squishy mud, and observed.

His head hair was sprinkled with grey. A hooked nose canted precariously, poorly healed from a fracas he won but his nose lost. His curled lips revealed cracked and missing teeth. A cut on his upper arm festered with pus and maggots. Fever dimpled his forehead with sweat. He crouched to drink but no amount of water would appease that thirst.

What gave him away was the wide ragged scar left from the slash of her mother's cutter.

Xhosa trembled with rage, fearing he would see the reeds shake, biting her lip until it bled to stop from howling. It hardly seemed fair to slay a dying male but fairness was not part of her plan today.

Only revenge.

A check of her surroundings indicated he traveled alone. Not that it mattered. If she must trade her life for his, so be it.

But she didn't intend to die.

The exhausted warrior splashed muddy water on his grimy head, hands slow, shoulders round with fatigue, oblivious to his impending death. After a quiet breath, she stepped from the sedge, spear in one hand and a large rock in the other. Exposed, arms ready but hanging, she approached. If he turned, he would see her. She tested for dry twigs and brittle grass before committing each foot. It surprised her he ignored the silence of the insects. His wounds must distract him. By the time hair raised on his neck, it was too late. He pivoted as she swung, powered by fury over her mother's death, her father's agony, and her own loss. Her warclub smashed into his temple with a soggy thud. Recognition flared moments before life left.

"You die too quickly!" she screamed and hit him over and over, collapsing his skull and spewing gore over her body. "I wanted you to suffer as I did!"

Her body was numb as she kicked him into the pond, feeling not joy for his death, relief that her mother was avenged, or upset at the execution of an unarmed Other. She cleaned the gore from her warclub and left. No one would know she had been blooded but the truth filled her with power.

She was now a warrior.

When she returned to homebase, Nightshade waited. Something flashed through his eyes as though for the first time, he saw her as a warrior. His chiseled face, outlined by dense blue-black hair, lit up. The corners of his full lips twitched under the broad flat nose. The finger-thick white scar emblazoned against his smooth forehead, a symbol of his courage surviving Sabertooth's claws, pulsed. Female eyes watched him, wishing he would look at them as he did Xhosa but he barely noticed.

The next day, odd Others with long legs, skinny chests, and oversized heads arrived. The People's scouts confronted them but they simply watched the scouts, spears down, and then trotted away, backs to the scouts. That night, for the first time, Xhosa's father taught her and Nightshade the lessons of leading.

"Managing the lives of the People is more than winning battles. You must match individual skills to the People's requirements be it as a warrior, hunter, scout, forager, child minder, Primary Female, or another. All can do all jobs but one best suits each. The Leader must decide," her father motioned.

As they finished, she asked the question she'd been thinking about all night. "Father, where do they come from?"

"They are called Big Heads," which didn't answer Xhosa's question.

Nightshade motioned, "Do they want to trade females? Or children?"

Her father stared into the distance as though lost in some memory. His teeth ground together and his hands shook until he clamped them together.

He finally took a breath and motioned, "No, they don't want mates. They want conflict." He tilted his head forward. "Soon, we will be forced to stop them."

Nightshade clenched his spear and his eyes glittered at the prospect of battle. It had been a long time since the People fought.

But the Big Heads vanished. Many of the People were relieved but Xhosa couldn't shake the feeling that danger lurked only a long spear throw away. She found herself staring at the same spot her father had, thoughts blank, senses burning. At times, there was a movement or the glint of Sun off eyes, but mostly there was only the unnerving feeling of being watched. Each day felt one day closer to when the People's time would end.

"When it does, I will confess to killing the Other. Anyone blooded must be allowed to be a warrior."

She shook her head, dismissing these memories, focusing on her next throw. The spear rose as though lifted by wings, dipped, and then lodged deep in the ground, shaft shivering from the impact.

Her nostrils flared, imagining the tangy scent of fresh blood as she raced down the field to retrieve it, well beyond her previous throw.

"Not even Nightshade throws this far," she muttered to herself, slapping the biting insects that dared light on her work-hardened body and glaring at the males who wandered aimlessly across the field.

"Why haven't they left?"

Another curious glance confirmed that the group looked too small. She inhaled deeply and evaluated the scents.

"Someone is missing."

Why hadn't her father asked her to fill in?

Irritation seared her chest, clouding her thoughts. A vicious yank freed the spear and she took off at a sprint, wind whooshing through her cascade of hair. Without changing her pace, she threw, arm pointing after the spear, eyes seeing only its flight.

Feet pounded toward her. "Xhosa!" Her father's voice. "I've been calling you."

She lifted her head, chest heaving, lost in her hunt.

He motioned, "Come!"

What was he saying? "Come where?"

"Someone is ill."

It all snapped into place. "I'm ready."

She knotted her hair with a tendon and trotted toward Nightshade, newly the People's Lead Warrior. One deep breath and she found the scent of every male who had earned the right to be called hunter except Stone. He must be the one sick.

Nightshade nodded to her, animated as always before a hunt, and motioned. "Stay close to me."

Nightshade's approval meant no one questioned her part—as a female—in this hunt.

A deep breath stifled her grin. "I will not disappoint you, Nightshade."

And she wouldn't. Along with her superior spear skills and unbeatable speed, her eyes possessed a rare feature called farsight. Early in their training, Nightshade had pointed to what he saw as a smudge on the horizon. She not only told him it was a herd of Gazelle but identified one that limped which they then killed. From then on, he taught her hunting strategies while she found the prey.

Xhosa and Nightshade led the hunters for a hand of Sun's travel overhead and then Nightshade motioned the group to wait while he and Xhosa crested a hill. From the top, they could see a brown cloud stretching across the horizon.

Xhosa motioned, "This is a herd but there are no antlers and the animals are too small for Mammoth." A breath later, she added, "It's Hipparion."

Nightshade squinted, shrugged, and set off at a moderate lope. If she was wrong, the hunting party would waste the day but he knew she wasn't wrong. Her father joined him in the lead with Xhosa and the rest of the males following. Nightshade chose an established trail across the grasslands, up sage-covered hillocks, into depressions that would trip those who didn't pay attention, and past trees marked by rutting. At the end of the day, they camped downwind of the fragrant scent of meat and subtle Hipparion voices.

Sun fell asleep. Moon arrived and left, and finally, Sun awoke. Everyone slathered themselves with Hipparion dung and then warily flanked the herd. When they were close, animals on the edge picked up their scent and whinnied in fear, pushing and shoving to the center of the pack, knowing that those on the outside would be the first to die.

Xhosa pointed to the edge of the field but Nightshade had already seen Leopard, lying atop a termite mound, paws dripping over the sides, interested in them only to the extent they meant food. Xhosa imagined the People as Leopard would see them.

"We look benign, Leopard, with our flimsy claws, flat teeth, and thin hide, but we can kill from a distance, work together, and we never give up a chase that can be won. You, Leopard, can only kill when you are close enough to touch your prey—and you tire quickly.

"Who hunts better?"

Leopard answered by closing its eyes, rolling over, and purring.

The battle began and ended quickly, the hunters killing only what they could carry. They sliced the bodies into portable pieces and slept curled around each other in a copse of trees. When Sun awoke, they left for home, shoulders bowed under the meat's weight, leaving the guts for scavengers. Xhosa hefted the carcass of a young Wild Beast to her shoulders. The animal had crossed her path as she chased a Hipparion mare and her colt. One swing of her warclub, the Wild Beast squealed and died. It provided more meat than the colt and would be a welcome addition to the People's food supply.

Sun was almost directly overhead when her father diverted to a waterhole. The weary but happy group dropped the meat and joined a scarred black rhino, a family of mammoth, and a group of pigs to drink. Xhosa untied the sinews that held the Wild Beast to her shoulders and splashed awkwardly through waist-high cattails and dense bunchgrass. Broad-winged white-bellied birds screeched as they swooped in search of food and a cacophony of insects chirruped their displeasure at her intrusion. A stone's throw away, a hippo played, heaving its great bulk out of the water, mouth gaping, snorting and grunting, before sinking beneath the surface.

Within moments, the air exploded with engaging dung smells.

Her feet burrowed into the silt as she pulled the tendon from her hair allowing it to tumble down, covering her back, too thick to allow any cooling breeze to penetrate but like Cat's pelt, it kept insects from biting and warmed her in the rainy times.

Nightshade stood close by, legs apart, weight over the balls of his feet. One hand held his spear, the other his warclub. Even relaxing, he scanned the surroundings. When his gaze landed on her, there was hunger in his eyes.

Her breath caught. That was his look for females before mating but never for her. She flushed and splashed water on her head, enjoying the cool bite on her fevered skin, gaze drifting lazily across the pond. Sun warm on her shoulders, breeze soft against her body, scent of the People's meat behind her, the whisper of some animal moving in the cattails—she wanted to burst with the joy of life.

Like that, everything changed.

"Big Heads," she muttered and ticked them off on both hands. "Too many—more than our entire group."

Her father had predicted trouble.

She studied the Big Heads, their swollen top-heavy skulls, squashed faces, brow ridges rounded over beady eyes, knobby growths under small mouths for no purpose she could imagine. Their chests were small, legs long, and bodies lacked the brawn that burst from every one of the People's warriors, and their spears, unlike the People's, were tipped with a rough-hewn stone about the size of a leaf.

She strode to her father, head throbbing, throat rough and dry. He acknowledged her presence by moving a hand below his waist, palm down, fingers splayed, but his gaze remained fixed on the strangers, thoughts unreadable.

After a breath, she motioned, also low to her body,

"Why do they constantly grunt, chirp, growl, and yip?" No animal this noisy could survive.

Her father said nothing, calmly facing the strangers he considered enemies, arms stiff, spear down but body alert in a way he hadn't been a moment before. Xhosa wondered if this was what her instincts had been screaming.

Slowly, the Big Heads confronted her father's stalwart figure. One pushed his way through the group, muscles hard, piercing eyes filled with hate. Someone else shouted the call sign Thunder, making the male who must be Thunder snap a call sign—Wind—as though he'd eaten rotten meat.

"Those two must be the leaders," her father motioned. "And brothers."

Both were the same height with thick straight hair that hung past their shoulders. Thunder had a scar that cut his face, making him look resolute and intolerant. For the other, face smooth and young, the word 'hopeful' popped into Xhosa's thoughts. Why, Xhosa had no idea, but something told her Hopeful Wind wouldn't win this battle.

As if to prove her right, the Big Heads behind Thunder flexed their arms, waved their spears, and bounced to a rhythmic chant. Someone beckoned Wind but he walked away, head down.

A purr made Xhosa jerk. A hungry Leopard stalked the People's meat. Xhosa started toward it, to protect it, when a scream punctuated the air.

Xhosa snapped toward the sound. One of the People's warriors clawed at a spear lodged in his chest, blood seeping between his fingers.

"They threw that all the way across the pond— Father, how can they do that?" No one was that strong.

"Run!" Her father bellowed.

Over her shoulder, Xhosa heard the pounding of

retreating feet but she never considered it, not with the mass of bawling Big Head warriors plunging into the shallow pond, spears thrust forward, rage painting their faces.

"Why do they attack, Father? What did we do?"

He shoved her away. "Go! Get our People to safety! I will slow them!"

"No," she answered softly. "We stay together! *We*, Father. I stand with you!"

His eyes, always soft and welcoming, held hers for a moment as though to object but instead, offered the faintest of smiles and then confronted the onslaught.

Xhosa broadened her stance, picked the closest Big Head, and launched her spear. It flew true with such power it penetrated the male's throat and into the next warrior. Both fell, dead before they hit the water. When a Big Head spear landed at her feet, she seized it, warclub in her other hand, throwing stones in her neck sack.

"I am blooded!" She screamed. "I do not flee in fear!"

Her scalp tingled and her eyesight grew vivid as everything about her grew stronger, harder, and faster. One enemy after another fell to the skill of Xhosa and her father. Her chest swelled with pride. No one could beat them. These creatures would soon withdraw as did all the People's enemies.

She buried a spear in a young warrior's thigh. He screamed, tears streaming down his cheeks.

"You were never stabbed?" With a snort, she yanked the weapon from his leg, eliciting another anguished howl. He was not much older than she. Maybe he too fought his first battle.

She threw the bloody spear at another Big Head who collapsed, blood bubbling from his mouth. Out of spears, she hurled stones from her neck sack, dropping one warrior after another, her barrage so fast no one could duck.

But there were too many. One moment, her father brandished his deadly weapons. The next, the Big Head Thunder appeared, obsidian eyes blazing, white scar pulsing. He caught Xhosa's eye and sneered as if to say, *Watch what I do to your Leader.*

A bellow came from the Big Head Wind, "Thunder! Stop!"

But Thunder jeered. "You are weak, Wind!" And he drove the spear's stone tip into her father's chest, twisting it as he did.

Xhosa's hands flew to her mouth as fury burned through her. Her father, the one who believed in her above all others, pled, *Go.* With the spear thrusting grotesquely from his body, he slammed his warclub into another Big Head who made the mistake of considering her father a walking dead. A loud crack told Xhosa the warrior's chest had caved in. Xhosa started toward him but Nightshade grabbed her.

"You can't help him. We must get the People to safety!"

Body shaking with rage, she shook loose and squared off to Thunder. "I will destroy you! As I did the one who killed my mother!" She gripped her warclub, head high, body blazing with fury, never wavering.

His eyes widened in surprise. He hadn't known.

Her father hurled his last spear and impaled a charging Big Head as another clubbed him. He legs collapsed but he kicked ferociously, tripping one and another before they overwhelmed him, pummeling him with clubs until he no longer moved.

Nightshade forced her away. "We leave our meat. They will let us go," or scavengers would take the food.

To her horror, she chose life over her father and doing so, abandoned her belief in fairness.

Her father saw the Big Heads first and let them be. Xhosa would never make that mistake..

About the Author

Jacqui Murray lives in California with her spouse and the world's greatest dog. She has been teaching for 25 years, is the editor/author of over a hundred tech ed resources and an adjunct professor in technology-in-education.

You can find Jacqui Murray on her website:
https://jacquimurray.net

Twitter:
https://twitter.com/WordDreams

LinkedIn
https://www.linkedin.com/in/jacquimurray

BIBLIOGRAPHY

1.   Allen, E.A., The Prehistoric World: or, Vanished Races Central Publishing House 1885
2. Brown Jr., Tom, Tom Brown's Field Guide: Wilderness Survival Berkley Books 1983
3. Caird, Rod Apeman: The Story of Human Evolution MacMillan 1994
4. Calvin, William, and Bickerton, Derek Lingua ex Machina: Reconciling Darwin and Chomsky with the Human Brain MIT Press, 2000
5. Carss, Bob The SAS Guide to Tracking Lyons Press Guilford Conn. 2000
6. Cavalli-Sforza, Luigi Luca and Cavalli-Sforza, Francesco The Great Human Diasporas: The
7. History of Diversity and Evolution   Perseus Press 1995 Conant,
8. Dr. Levi Leonard The Number Concept: Its Origin and Development Macmillan and Co. Toronto 1931
9. Diamond, Jared The Third Chimpanzee   Harper Perennial 1992
10. Edey, Maitland Missing Link Time-Life Books 1972
11. Erickson, Jon Glacial Geology: How Ice Shapes the Land Facts on File Inc. 1996
12. Fleagle, John Primate Adaptation and Evolution Academic Press 1988
13. Fossey, Dian   Gorillas in the Mist   Houghton Mifflin 1984
14. Galdikas, Birute Reflections of Eden: My Years with the Orangutans of Borneo Little Brown and Co. 1995
15. Goodall, Jane In the Shadow of Man Houghton Mifflin

1971
16. Goodall, Jane The Jane Goodall Institute 2005
    http://www.janFriendshipegoodall.com/chimp_central/c
    himpanzees/behavior/communication.asp
17. Goodall, Jane Through a Window Houghton Mifflin 1990
18. Grimaldi, David, and Engel, Michael Evolution of the
    Insects Cambridge University Press 2005
19. Human Dawn: Timeframe Time-Life Books 1990
20. Johanson, Donald and Simon, Blake Edgar From Lucy
    to Language Simon and Schuster 1996
21. Johanson, Donald and O'Farell, Kevin Journey from the
    Dawn: Life with the World's First
22. Family Villard Books 1990
23. Johanson, Donald and Edey, Maitland Lucy: The
    Beginnings of Humankind Simon and Schuster 1981
24. Johanson, Donald and Shreve, James Lucy's Child: The
    Discovery of a Human Ancestor Avon 1989
25. Jones, Steve, Martin, Robert, and Pilbeam, David The
    Cambridge Encyclopedia of Human Evolution
    Cambridge University Press 1992
26. Leakey, Richard and Lewin, Roger Origins E.P. Dutton
    1977
27. Leakey, Richard The Origin of Humankind Basic Books
    1994
28. Leakey, Louis Stone Age Africa, Negro Universities
    Press 1936
29. Lewin, Roger In the Age of Mankind Smithsonian
    Books 1988
30.   McDougall, J.D. A Short History of the
    Planet Earth John Wiley and Sons 1996
31.   Morris, Desmond Naked Ape Dell Publishing
    1999
32.   Morris, Desmond The Human Zoo

Kodansha International 1969
33.   Rezendes, Paul Tracking and the Art of Seeing: How to Read Animal Tracks and Sign Quill: A Harper Resource Book 1999
34.   Savage-Rumbaugh, Susan, et al Kanzi: The Ape at the Brink of the Human Mind John Wiley and Sons 1996
35.   Spencer Larson, Clark et al Human Origins: The Fossil Record Waveland Press 1998
36.   Stringer, Chris, and McSahn, Robin African Exodus: The Origins of Modern Humanity Henry Holt and Co. NY 1996
37.   Strum, Shirley C. Almost Human: A Journey into the World of Baboons Random House 1987
38.   Tattersall, Ian Becoming Human: Evolution and Human Uniqueness   Harvest Books 1999
39.   Tattersall, Ian et al Encyclopedia of Human Evolution and Prehistory, Chicago: St James Press 1988
40.   Tattersall, Ian Fossil Trail: How We Know What We Think We Know About Human Evolution Oxford University Press 1997
41.   Tattersall, Ian The Human Odyssey: Four Million Years of Human Evolution Prentice Hall 1993
42.   Thomas, Elizabeth Marshall, The Old Way: A Story of the First People Sarah Crichton Books 2008
43.   Tudge Colin Time Before History Touchstone Books 1996
44.   Turner, Alan, and Anton, Mauricio The Big Cats and Their Fossil Relatives: An Illustrated
45. Guide to Their Evolution and Natural History Columbia University Press NY 1997
46.   Vogel, Shawna Naked Earth: The New Geophysics Dutton 1995

47.   Vygotsky, Lev <u>The Connection Between Thought and the Development of Language in Primitive Society</u> 1930
48.   Walker, Alan and Shipman, Pat <u>Wisdom of the Bones: In Search of Human Origins</u> Vintage Books 1996
49.   Waters, JD <u>Helpless as a Baby</u> http://www.jdwaters.net/HAAB%20Acro/contents.pdf 2001
50.   Wills, Christopher <u>Runaway Brain: The Evolution of Human Uniqueness</u> Basic Books 1993

READER'S WORKSHOP QUESTIONS

Setting

- What part did Nature and the land play in Lucy's ability to survive and thrive?
- How does the setting figure as a character in the story?

Themes

- Discuss Lucy's respect for all animals. Why do you think she felt this way?
- Why did Lucy and her kind survive Nature's challenges? Discuss how her brain offset the ineffectiveness of her physical attributes?
- We know *Homo habilis* died out, replaced by more-advanced humans, *Homo erectus*. What characteristics in Lucy's story help to explain why that happened?

Character Realism

- What traits did Lucy have that made her a survivor?
- Do you relate to Lucy's predicaments? Does it remind you someone you know struggling to raise a child, fit into a new group, or survive a toxic environment?

Character Choices

- As the earliest in man's genus, *Homo*, what moral/ethical choices did the characters in this book make? Discuss why the animals are referred to as 'who' rather than 'that'.
- Discuss Lucy's family dynamics. For example, how did the Group raise children? How do other primitive tribes handle families?
- What events triggered Lucy's evolution from passive Groupmember to adoption of the survival methods of Man-who-preys (Homo erectus)?

Construction

- Discuss how Lucy communicated—with body language, gestures, facial expressions, and the rare vocalization. How effective do you think it was? How is it relevant today? What present-day animals communicate with methods other than words?
- Discuss why Lucy's people used long names to describe places, such as 'lake-where-children-play. Discuss why other primitive tribes use these sorts of names rather than proper nouns.
- Discuss Lucy's lack of a number system and how she described quantities (such as 'group large enough to fit in Baobab's shadow'). Discuss how other primitive tribes have considerably limited number systems even today.
- How did early man make sense of the moon disappearing and reappearing over and over?

Reactions to the Book

- Did the book lead to a new understanding or awareness of how man evolved to be who we are today? Did it help you to understand some aspect of your life you might not have thought about?
- Did the book fulfill your expectations? Were you satisfied with the ending?

Other Questions

- What do you think will happen to the characters beyond the end of the book?
- Have you read similar books? With a similar theme or set in the same time period?

18321506R00224

Printed in Great Britain
by Amazon